THE LOVE AND LIES S

A LIE IN CHURCH

JULIET EVER

A LIE IN CHURCH
Cover Design: Angus Woodiwiss
Art: Ana Novaes
Editor: Jovana Shirley,
Unforeseen Editing, wwwunforeseenediting.com

To those still haunted by the past.
Your past doesn't define you.

AUTHOR'S NOTE

Content warning: This book contains topic which maybe triggering to some readers (substance abuse, talks about suicide, and sexual assault) Please don't read any further if any of these topics triggers you.

CHAPTER **ONE**
COMPLICATIONS

The quick clicking of heels resonating from a short distance woke me up. My eyes flickered at the sun peeking into my room from my window. Still dazed from sleep, I tried figuring out if it was morning or afternoon. The acute and distinct sound caught my full attention, and the loud footsteps were now approaching my room. My sluggish brain tried to process what was happening.

"Chloe, are you ready?" My sister's voice sent me flying from the bed to the door to stop her from entering my room.

Shit! Today is the wedding.

I looked around for the wall clock and checked the time. I still had forty-five minutes to get ready.

"Chloe?" my big sister called, trying to open the door, but I pushed with overwhelming might on the door and succeeded in locking it.

"Almost ready. I will be out in a minute!" I said breathlessly.

"Why did you lock the door?" she asked, knocking harshly.

"I don't want you to see how fabulous I look yet." I giggled nervously, feeling her roll her eyes from the other side of the door.

"Whatever. Hurry up. I can't be late for my best friend's wedding. I'll be downstairs."

I waited for her to leave before running to my closet to pick out the dress I'd bought last week for the wedding. I laid it on the bed and undressed quickly, almost tripping on my pajama shorts as I pulled them down my legs.

During my whole twenty years on earth, I had never taken such a quick shower. I slipped on my peach corset tulle dress that stopped above my knees. The off-the-shoulder sleeves were made with delicate lace. I loved the dress because it went with the light shade of my skin, enhancing my blue eyes.

"Chloe!" Ciara called.

The aftermath of her voice rang in my head. It made me feel like a child being scolded for playing in the mud.

"Coming!" I yelled back as I brushed my hair and prepared to style it to perfection.

"Chloe, come on. We're gonna be late," Ciara shouted from downstairs, her patience seeping out of her.

I didn't blame her. I'd feel worse if I were in her place.

We were going to a big wedding—a billion-dollar wedding sounded more appropriate since the two wealthiest families in Beverly Hills were getting married. Well, I considered myself poor since I was living off my parents' wealth.

It was Ciara's best friend's wedding, and I wanted to tag along mainly because of the cake and mouthwatering cuisine. Food was life— I'd always defend that quote.

I didn't know much about her best friend, but I knew they had been joined at the hip since senior year, and Ciara was going to be the maid of honor. I'd never wanted to go to the wedding. I had loads of schoolwork due on Wednesday, especially an eight-page essay, but when Ciara had kept talking about the wedding and how spectacular it was going to be, I'd become intrigued.

Now, she was waiting for me while I struggled with the chignon I'd decided to make. I'd had everything planned for today's event, but it was falling apart. My dark brown hair was long, making it hard to style it the way I wanted. The dress made me feel like an angel as I stared at myself in the mirror mounted on the white dresser, but I was not even close to being considered an angel. I blocked the memories away with a fake smile.

I kept my eyes on the mirror as I used each pin to hold my thick hair in place, but it was a complete disaster. I was in this situation because I'd forgotten the time for the wedding.

"Coming. I just need to put in the last pin," I lied.

I had two pins in between my lips as I struggled with the one in my hand to hold my hair. I had spent almost fifteen minutes on my hair. Who knew a chignon was this hard to do? I wouldn't be surprised if my big sister decided to ditch me—it was her best friend's wedding—but I wouldn't miss the cake for the world.

"Oh my God, Chloe, what the hell are you doing up there?" Ciara yelled.

She was my ride to the wedding and my invitation as well.

"Chloe!" Mom called.

"Honey, hurry up." I heard Dad's voice next.

"Almost done!" I yelled back after I succeeded in putting in the last pin.

Next time, I would use YouTube. I believed YouTube had all the answers to every difficult task in life. I smiled at myself in the mirror, impressed with my handiwork.

I grabbed my makeup kit and went to work. I was about to use the dark eyeliner when Ciara yelled my name again, making me smudge it against my cheek.

"Great," I growled, grabbing a wipe to clean the charcoal color streaking my face.

"I give up. I'm leaving. Sofia will kill me if I show up five minutes late," Ciara said.

If only Mom had allowed her to spend the night at Sofia's house. She couldn't even attend the bachelorette party because our mom believed it was a lame party for ill-mannered women.

"Wait, give me five seconds!" I screamed, grabbing my purse. I packed my lipstick, eyeliner, and jewelry inside. I picked up my strappy heels and rushed out of the room like my ass was on fire.

"Sorry, I was styling my hair," I rasped, running down the stairs barefoot, like someone escaping from a psychiatric ward.

Just when I was about to get off the last step, the worst happened. Everything in my purse fell out, and when I tried to pick them up, my hair loosened as the pins dropped. I stood upright and stared at my sister, who looked at me with murderous intent.

My parents looked frustrated too—Mom mostly. She was the type that expected you to never do anything wrong. She loved perfection, and right now, I was the opposite. They might die from a heart attack when they discovered the truth about their *perfect* daughter.

I could keep up the facade; I had done it for years.

"Sorry, I will just pick them up and—"

Ciara cut in, "You know what? I can't wait anymore, not even for you to breathe. Call your boyfriend. I'm sure he won't mind giving you a ride."

I hated when she was angry. There was this look she always gave me, like I was the worst person to ever exist on earth.

Her dark eyes blazed in anger as she stared at me. It was as if I could see the fire in them. She had our father's dark eyes while I'd inherited Mom's cold blue eyes. I envied her perfect height and oval face. She could be mistaken for a model. I, on the other hand, could be mistaken for a fourteen-year-old.

"But I don't have an invitation," I grumbled.

Ciara groaned and searched her fancy round golden purse and then threw the invitation card at me with an icy look. "Happy now? Thanks a lot, Chloe, for making me late to my best friend's wedding. Remind me not to pick you as my maid of honor, not even one of the bridesmaids."

Ouch!

"Ciara." Mom stepped forward in my defense.

"Sorry, Mom. Sorry, Dad. I have to be on my way."

She looked at me, the expression on her face so grim that I wanted to run to my room and forget about the wedding. She turned away and headed for the front door. I knew I had to face my parents next.

I turned to look at them with a sheepish grin plastered on my face. Mom folded her arms, and her fierce blue eyes focused on me like a camera. She was tall—taller than Dad and everyone in her family. I guessed Ciara had taken a quarter of that gene while I had taken Dad's short gene.

"Chloe," Mom started.

Her whole demeanor reminded me of my high school principal. That woman was Ursula's twin sister who'd escaped from the sea.

"You owe your sister an apology, and this should be the last time you try something like this. We didn't raise you to be so tardy."

"I get it, Mom. It won't happen again," I grunted.

"Good. Give Grey a call now. If you're twenty minutes late, then forget about attending the wedding."

"Mom," I grumbled.

"Twenty minutes, Chloe," she repeated.

"Dad." I gave him puppy eyes.

"You heard your mom."

Why doesn't anyone treat me like the last born in this family? I thought we got special treatment.

He always sided with his wife. How could I forget that? If there was anything I had learned about their relationship while growing up, it was that Mom had the upper hand.

"I didn't mean for any of this to happen."

"Remember, this family has a reputation. It will be best if you don't ruin that," Mom reminded me. She was probably thinking about her classy group of friends who only gathered once in a blue moon to sip expensive wine and envy each other's designer clothes.

It was always about the family's reputation. Every freaking mistake I made ruined the family's reputation.

"I won't." I forced a smile and went back upstairs to my room.

I'd been faking smiles my whole life, hiding the pain no one ever noticed—not even my parents. I only hoped I would never fail them or give them any reason to be ashamed of me *again*.

Wait until they find out about Dominiano.

Luckily for me, my boyfriend, Grey lived close by. I finished my makeup and put on my jewelry and heels. Mom called my name when Grey arrived. I hurried down the stairs with a big grin.

There he was in a slim-fit black suit that he'd matched with black Chucks, looking cool and handsome, as always. His curly hair looked perfect from here, tumbling to his forehead like bangs. His soft smile made his brown eyes sparkle with an irresistible charm as he held my gaze.

My parents stared at us as we reached out to hug like two lost lovers finding each other after years of endless searching. I tried to suppress the wide smile on my face as I moved closer to touch him, but Mom's voice interrupted us.

"You're running late."

Mom believed that only married couples should show affection in public. She'd told me it was a waste of time since we were not going to end up together in the future.

We had rules in my family, like we were not allowed to date until we were eighteen. We could move out of our parents' house to live on our own when we were done with college and had a decent job. Mom had told us she was brought up that way and it was the reason for her success and reputation as a surgeon.

I doubted that.

Dad had once told me she had a strict father who'd left a scar on her arm. It made sense why she always wore long-sleeved clothes.

I had broken the first rule. I'd started dating at fourteen. In fact, I'd dated four guys before I turned eighteen, and I was not planning on staying with my parents until I was done with college. Mom might have succeeded in talking me into attending a college only fifteen minutes from home, but graduate school would be my decision to make.

I loved my freedom, and I wasn't getting it here. I could only access my trust fund when I turned twenty-two. Two more torturous years to go. I planned to elope once I got access to it, maybe on a continent far from home.

I hooked my arm with Grey's and stared at my parents. Mom's eyes fixated on us, and it was an effort not to roll my eyes at how she monitored us like a hawk, waiting for the perfect moment to strike.

"Be on good behavior, Cassandra."

I hated my middle name, and Mom only used it when she wanted to express how serious she was. I always saw Mom as a dictator. Her reputation was like oxygen to her.

"I will. Bye."

"Bye, Mr. and Mrs. Simpson," Grey said, smiling firmly.

"Make sure you return home with your sister!" Mom yelled after us as we stepped outside and walked to the car.

"I have goose bumps when I'm around your parents," Grey whispered to me when we were out of earshot.

I giggled, facing him. He looked elegant and gorgeous. I ran my fingers through his soft curls and smiled at him. His mixed genes from his white father and Sudanese mother had done him good. His father was a movie producer, and his mom was a powerful attorney, but they lived in New York, and he'd moved here with his elder brother during his junior year in high school.

"You look hot. I'm so jealous," I said, frowning.

His brown eyes glimmered under the sunlight. I traced his chiseled jawline and cheekbone with my fingertips.

"You look ravishing. Why don't we skip the wedding?" he said, putting his arm around my waist, sliding it slowly to my hips.

He leaned closer to my face to kiss me. I slightly parted my lips to welcome his.

"Cassandra." I heard my mom's voice.

We both looked in her direction and found her staring at us from the doorway.

"We were just leaving."

We rushed to where his white Tesla was parked and got in.

"Wow." He laughed.

"You should be used to her by now."

"Trust me, I'm still trying."

We left for the wedding, laughing.

I guessed it would've been worse, going with Ciara while she was fuming with rage and holding an invisible dagger over my head.

CHAPTER **TWO**
THE LIE

We got to the wedding early enough, so we snuck in and sat quietly near the back. The last seat behind us was occupied by two old ladies who looked like twins; they wore similar clothes and had the same chin-length hairstyle. I gave them a soft smile after taking a seat next to Grey.

Interlocking my fingers with Grey's and resting my head on his strong shoulder, I admired the exquisite decorations, giving the church a fresh and magical aura. It was a big church, decorated with white roses, large garlands, and gold embellishments that reminded me of fairy-tale weddings. Each pew was adorned with silky white and teal ribbons.

The groom was already at the altar. His black tux fitted his tall frame and solid arms. I could only imagine the taut muscles beneath his clothing. He looked uncomfortable as he stared straight ahead at the door, not sparing anyone a glance. Maybe he was nervous.

The church was full. Dark teal and gold dominated the other colors in the building. I must admit, the color scheme was beautiful. Good thing I had a little bit of gold here and there on my dress.

"We are just in time," Grey whispered when the violinists started playing.

The sweet melody from the violins made everyone look alive as they sat up with wide smiles. A few people swayed to the smooth flow of the spectacular cadence, the rich sound uplifting their mood. I felt so excited; the anticipation gave me butterflies. The last time I had attended a wedding, I was six. I could only remember crying and asking the bride to give me her tiara.

Everyone looked back when the large church doors opened. I couldn't help but admire the wedding dress. It was a gorgeous, otherworldly spectacle. It was made with lace and silk, hugging her small build. The deep V-line on the dress almost reached her belly button, but I loved the extra details, like the sparkles that caught every eye. The big crown on her head looked like it was made with real gold, turquoise, sapphires, and diamonds. Her lace veil was so long that her maid of honor—my sister—had to stay five feet away to avoid stepping on it.

Sofia smiled as she took slow steps with an old man, who I assumed was her father. They marched down the aisle, decorated with white petals. She was Chinese American; she'd been here her whole life, but Ciara had told me she could speak Mandarin, and she was teaching her. Her dad was a multimillionaire and a member of the United States Senate.

My sister trailed behind, looking stunning in her gold haute couture dress and sleek, neat bun. I still felt awful about what had happened this morning.

"Ciara is killing it in that dress," Grey whispered with a whistle.

"Hey, she is my sister." I glared at him, jealousy getting the best of me.

"Sorry, I didn't mean anything—"

"Shh," one of the grandmas behind us cut him off.

"Sorry," I apologized to the lady, but she ignored me.

We sat in silence for the remainder of the procession. The bride joined her groom at the altar. Her dad beamed at everyone, walking to the seat his beautiful wife had reserved for him.

The groom didn't even turn to look at the bride's face, not even a glance.

"That's cold," I whispered to Grey.

"What?" he asked, barely paying attention.

"The groom didn't spare his bride a look."

"He is going to be seeing more of her."

"Have you noticed how still he is?" I whispered, staring at the groom, who hadn't smiled since his bride had joined him.

"He is probably nervous. I would be, too, if it were me. He is tying his soul to one woman."

I tried not to be offended by his last comment. We'd only been together for five months, and I didn't know if I should be bothered by his words.

"Is anything wrong with that?" I asked, raising my eyebrows at him.

"No, of course not." He sealed his words with a thin smile.

I studied his expression for a while before returning my gaze to the altar.

The ceremony started smoothly. Grey and I whispered to each other whenever we noticed anything interesting. Like the old man who almost hit his head on the seat while sleeping. And the lady who kept touching her makeup and blowing kisses to her mirror. Why was she even here?

It was time for the vows. Grey was already bored and kept himself busy with his phone. I found it disrespectful, but I guessed this wasn't his type of scene. I must have dragged him away from his annoying frat friends, but relationships involved sacrifices and compromise.

Sofia was pretty, her pale skin looking so smooth from here. Her stylist had done a good job with her dark hair. Her makeup was glamorous. I could see the different shades of eye shadow and glitter from here.

She said her vows with so much joy, but the groom kept staring at her with a blank expression. He looked like he wanted this to be over.

Is this an arranged marriage? I brushed my thought away and focused on the altar.

When it got to the groom's turn to say his vows, silence consumed him.

I nudged Grey and pointed at the altar with my chin. "He is tongue-tied," I whispered.

"Now, this is getting interesting." Grey sat up straight and put his phone away.

Sofia seemed scared; she called his name, but he looked void like nothing mattered to him. The priest repeated the vow, but the groom didn't answer.

I wondered how the groom's stoic expression managed to make him look like a model posing for a photo. I mentally slapped myself for the thought in my head.

Sofia smiled at the congregation, like she wanted to tell us everything was okay, no need to panic. She tried to suppress the fear surging through her as she stepped closer to her groom. Her hands shook, gripping one of his hand. She stared at his face. She appeared so tiny next to him. I watched with keen interest as she spoke to him softly but with clenched teeth.

A lady stood up and walked to the altar. I assumed it was the groom's mother from the resemblance. She whispered a few things to him and returned to her seat with a nervous grin.

The priest repeated the vow, but the groom was still mute. People began to murmur.

"Should I record this? It would hit a million views on YouTube," Grey asked, picking up his phone.

"Don't even think about it. She is Ciara's best friend and a human," I warned him.

He frowned at my comment and sat back in his seat.

Sofia was trying to get her groom to say something, but his expression said he'd rather be anywhere but here.

"I'm sorry, Sofia. I can't do this," the groom said aloud, making everyone go quiet.

"What are you talking about?" Sofia asked with a frightened voice.

"I don't want to hurt you, but we can't carry on with the wedding."

Everyone gasped. I didn't though, but laughter overwhelmed Grey.

"You find this funny?" I asked Grey, giving him an incredulous look.

"Yes, it's like a comedy show. I should have brought some popcorn."

I shook my head at his lack of empathy and stared at the couple.

"Why?" Sofia asked, already crying. "Why?! What did I do, Tristan?" she screamed.

"Do you think this is all part of the wedding? It could be an act. People always want to go extra these days," I asked Grey.

"No, I don't think so. The bridesmaids look shocked, and the dude sounds darn serious," Grey pointed out.

"You didn't do anything. I'm sorry … I just can't." He stepped back, removing the ring she'd just given him.

The congregation started murmuring again, this time louder.

"Tristan, what are you doing?" the beautiful lady I assumed was his mother shouted from her seat.

The girl beside her, looking sixteen, tried to calm her.

"I'm in love with someone else, and we have been seeing each other for six months now," the groom admitted.

Another gasp from the congregation.

Sofia crumpled onto the marble floor; Ciara tried to help her up, but she wouldn't let her.

"While you were dating my daughter?" Sofia's mom stood up with tears in her eyes. She looked so fragile.

Her husband held her back when she wanted to go to the altar. I wished he'd let her go, so she could slap the devil out of Tristan for ruining her daughter's life.

"I'm sorry, but I can't leave her, not when she is carrying my baby."

The church was in an uproar after the groom's confession.

Sofia was crying her eyes out, smudging her mascara and eyeliner. She could have taken precautions and used waterproof make-up. I mean, one was bound to cry on their wedding day. I wasn't implying that something like this always happened, but something always made the bride or groom tear up. I felt so sorry for her.

"Wow," I mumbled, staring at the asshole, who still looked relaxed, like he hadn't just caused havoc in front of God. At least he was confessing, right?

"Who is she? What does she have that I don't?!" Sofia screamed, hitting his long legs with the bouquet in her hand—poor flowers.

Tristan Sanchester, as written on the wedding invitation card, appeared emotionless as he watched her cry—as if he never wanted to get married in the first place.

He looked familiar, but I couldn't pinpoint where I had seen his face. It was probably on a magazine. With that face, definitely a magazine.

"She is everything I ever wanted; she is here." The groom smiled immediately after finishing his sentence.

He must really love her.

There was a sudden silence in the building, a silence that could detect the slightest sound. Sofia stopped and looked at the whole congregation. Everyone started looking around, even me. I was curious too. I mean, how could his lover attend the wedding? Had they planned this?

"I'm so glad you invited me to this wedding," Grey said, amused.

My sister seemed confused and shocked as she stared at her best friend, not sure of how to help her.

"Stand up, you slut! Show your ugly and shameless face!" Sofia yelled. "How dare you show up at my wedding!"

To be honest, Sofia looked crazy, but who wouldn't lose their sanity after hearing that from the man you were about to tie the knot with?

"Where is she?!" she screamed at his face.

Tristan looked at the congregation, and everyone followed the movement of his eyes. I did too.

Is his lover really here? Who can it be?

He left the altar and took steady steps down the aisle. The silence in the church made his footsteps loud. All eyes were on his every move, like he was a magnet for curious eyes.

"She is really here," Grey said close to my ear, almost freaking me out.

Tristan kept walking to the back, and I was starting to think he wanted to run out of the church. Or was his lover one of the grannies behind us?

Our eyes met, and he didn't look away. There was just this weird chill I felt when our eyes collided. I couldn't explain it, and it scared me. I quickly turned my gaze away from him before people thought I was the one.

"He is coming here, and he is looking at you," Grey whispered, and my eyes whipped toward Tristan.

He smiled at me as he got closer to where we were sitting.

"What is he doing?" I turned to Grey, but he was giving me a weird look, as if he was trying to figure out who I was. I opened my mouth to say something, but I wasn't sure what I wanted to say as I tried to fathom what was happening.

I hoped Grey wasn't suspecting anything about me being the groom's pregnant lover. How was that even possible? I didn't know him. I looked behind me to check for any person besides the two grandmas who were already staring at me with disgust.

I returned my gaze to Tristan, and he was standing next to me with a charming smile I wanted to scratch off his beautiful face. It couldn't possibly be me.

"Hi, my love," he said with his hand extended toward me.

"What the hell?"

CHAPTER **THREE**
GOOD LIAR

"What the hell?" I stared at his hand and his face. "Are you confused, or do you need glasses to see clearly?" I asked.

He smiled sweetly at me, like I'd just complimented him.

"I know you're mad at me for taking the wedding this far. I'm sorry," he said so softly that it sounded true.

I searched for the right thing to say, but words failed me. I was too shocked to utter a word to this stranger calling me his lover.

"Chloe?" I heard Grey's voice. Disbelief was evident on his face as his eyes narrowed and eyebrows lowered at Tristan's words.

"Grey, you know he is lying. I'm just seeing this douche bag for the first time."

"Oh, hi, Grey. Chloe told me a lot about you," Tristan said with a grin and extended his long hand for shaking. Grey kept him hanging, and Tristan gave up, dropping his hand with a suppressed chuckle.

"When? I don't even know you?!" I asked with a hot glare.

"What exactly did she tell you?" Grey asked with a hard look, his strong jawline clenched.

"We needed a cover for our relationship. Thanks for being there, man," Tristan said smoothly with that smile I was starting to hate.

How could he act so cool while ruining someone's life?

"What?" I stared at Tristan.

What is he playing at? Is this a prank show?

I looked around for any hidden cameras or mics but was met with a hundred pairs of eyes.

What is happening? I was speechless for a while; I thought my brain had shut down to take a rest, and I was left on my own.

"A cover?" Grey cocked his eyebrows in question at me.

I couldn't believe he was buying Tristan's expensive lies.

"Chloe Simpson!" Sofia's voice shut everyone up.

I turned to look at her as she marched toward us, holding the bottom of her wedding dress for easy movement. My eyes caught a glimpse of Ciara; she looked like she was having a hard time breathing. The color from her face drained.

I turned to look at Tristan, who was looking down at me like I was an interesting piece of art he'd just discovered. His scrutinizing stare held a deeper mystery. I was going to interrogate him and show everyone he was lying.

"Okay, if what you're saying is true, then where did we meet? When is my birthday? What is my favorite color? Food? Allergies? Spring or summer? Do I shave or—"

"You!" Sofia's loud voice cut me off, and she stole the spotlight—not like I was complaining. Her perfect hairstyle was already disheveled, and her makeup wasn't helping her situation. Black tears stained her cheeks, and the corners of her eyes were smudged with wet mascara. But

I couldn't blame her for looking like a zombie.

How did I even get involved in this mess? I only came for the cake!

"Sofia, I swear he is lying," I tried to explain.

"Chloe, there's nothing to be afraid of. We can't keep it a secret anymore." Tristan's soft voice came from beside me.

"Hide what? I don't know you!" I yelled at his face.

"Really? 'Cause I'm starting to think this is all true." I was surprised that had come from Grey.

"Grey, you've known me for a long time. Do you really believe this guy?"

"Yes."

What a straightforward answer.

I froze for a moment, hearing his reply; those three letters were like bullets shot into my heart. It hurt because it was as if I'd handed him the gun to protect me, but instead, he'd shot me right in the face with the same gun I'd trusted him with.

"It wouldn't be the first time you had an affair with a married man, Chloe. I thought you closed that chapter of your life," Grey said, looking disappointed.

My face went pale, and I could hear a few people murmuring.

How can he bring up the past in a situation like this?

I was kind of hoping this was part of the wedding, and Tristan and Sofia would laugh at my face, telling me it was all an act to entertain the congregation, but I didn't get why I had to be the main character.

Was I supposed to play along or remain clueless? I was so confused, and my senses were taking forever to analyze the situation. I turned to Grey, trying to pound some sense into him. How could he give in to Tristan's lies so easily?

"Grey ..."

"Maybe he is the reason we don't go past kissing. I always thought it was because of your parents, but now, I see the reason. I always knew you were hiding something," he said, stepping away from me like I carried a contagious disease.

"Are you for real? You're an idiot if you believe a word that left his mouth."

"Am I, Chloe? Given your history, we both know what you're capable of. I'm out of here." He glared at Tristan before walking away.

Wow, he was using my past mistakes against me.

"Are you breaking up with me?" I held back my tears. I needed to hear him say it.

"Were we ever in a relationship? I was just a diversion, remember?" The pain and resentment in his voice made my eyes burn, but I refused to cry.

"Grey …" I called, but he didn't wait to listen to whatever I had to say. He walked out of the church.

I bit down on my wobbling lip, holding back my tears. There was an awkward silence in the church. I could feel everyone's eyes on me, as if I were on the biggest stage in the world and everyone was waiting for me to give an outstanding performance.

"Well, that was easy. I figured it would be hard for you to tell him the truth," Tristan said behind me.

I turned around to face him. At that moment, I wanted nothing more but for him to drop dead. I clenched my fist, hoping he could feel the waves of anger radiating from my body. My blood was boiling.

What is this asshole up to, and why me?

Don't punch him, Chloe. Don't break his nose, Chloe. Don't knee his crotch, Chloe. Just stay calm and convince everyone he is lying.

"Why are you doing this?" I fought to keep my tears at bay as I spoke.

"You should calm down, babe; it's not good for the baby if you're angry," he said with a worried tone, his blue eyes looking at me like he adored me.

"What baby, Tristan?" I screamed.

"Babe, I understand you're scared everyone knows about us now," he said, trying to touch me, but I moved back, my face twitching with rage.

God, what a good actor, but why is he wasting his talent on me?

"Who would've thought the innocent-looking little sister of my best friend was this vile?" Sofia squeaked.

I turned to look at her and immediately wished I hadn't. "Sofia, I—"

She cut me off with killer eyes. "Is that why you avoided me every time I came to visit? Because you were sleeping with my boyfriend?"

Am I trapped in a horrific dream? That had to be the only explanation.

"No!" I snapped. Someone had to believe this was all a lie.

"I swear I'm seeing him for the first time. I had homework and projects from school when you—"

"Oh, please. Enough with the excuses. The truth is out already, so stop denying it. How could you be so wicked?"

I was speechless.

Why is everyone believing him? Do I look pregnant? Why would I even wanna get involved with this psychopath?

"I'm sorry, Sofia. I wish I'd told you earlier," Tristan said with a tone that could convince anyone this was all true and real.

My case was different. It was as if I were screaming but no one could hear me.

"You just ruined my life, Tristy." Sofia sniffled, heavy tears mixing with her mascara and streaming down her cheeks like black ink.

Tristy? I tried not to laugh, even with the situation at hand. It sounded like the name of a candy bar.

"You just disgraced me and my family in front of hundred people" she said, sobbing. Her shoulders sagged.

"I'm sorry," Tristan said.

"I hope you have a miscarriage and die in the process." She lashed out at me with a burning stare, storming out of the church while crying.

Well, that is harsh, and I hope you trip on your heels and smash your face on the ground to the point that no one recognizes you, I wanted to yell after her but stopped myself.

I understood her anger, but why should I be the only one blamed? My only crime was attending the wedding.

Sofia's parents stood up and walked toward us. Her mother was already in tears. I felt so guilty, like it was really my fault.

"Mrs. Nova …" I kept my mouth shut when her husband shot me a cold glare.

They walked out of the church quietly. I guessed it wasn't a wedding drama; it was real.

"Are you happy now?" I turned to Tristan with teary eyes, but I maintained a straight face.

"Yeah, I'm happy we finally got to tell everyone the truth, and we can be together now," he said with a soft smile that made his stupid blue eyes sparkle with mischief.

"Truth? You know this is all a lie! Wake up from whatever this is. I don't wanna be a part of it!" I yelled.

"Babe, we can't keep hiding," he said softly, placing his hands on my shoulders.

Even on my five-inch heels, I felt so short.

How To Get Away with Murder. I should have joined my best friend, Vina, to watch that series. I could really use some tips right now.

"Babe," he called, looking straight into my eyes.

He just ruined the meaning of *babe* for me. He was a pro at this. I must admit, the way he'd said the word sounded like he'd known me for a long time. His eyes focused on me, as if whatever love story he'd made up was true.

"I love you, and we are going to bring up our baby together in a happy home," he whispered, not breaking his gaze away from me.

My eggs are still untouched, dude. They have never seen a sperm.

"What are you gonna gain from this, huh?" I asked, pushing his hands away.

I knew everyone was watching us, amused by my dilemma. I thought of running out of the church, but what would people think about it? I needed to prove my innocence. Running away would only give the wrong message.

Something flickered in his eye. *I must prove to everyone he is lying one way or another. Maybe if I piss him off to his breaking point, he will reveal the truth.*

"You know what? All I need right now is a doctor."

I saw fear in his eyes, but it vanished in a second.

"I'm out of here." I turned to walk away, but he held me back.

"Babe—"

"Don't *babe* me!" I tried to pull my hand away.

Oh, good heavens, I didn't sign up for this.

"I get that you're upset."

"Oh, I am way past upset."

"Aren't you tired of hiding, Chloe?" He looked so serious, like he'd just switched personalities with someone else.

For a moment, I almost believed he knew me. I had been hiding, trying hard to fit into people's expectations.

"We kept hiding because of what people would say about us. Well, I'm sick of that."

I shook my head in amazement. He was damn good.

"You're insane!" I yelled and pulled my hand away with all the strength I could summon.

"I know how scared you are, but we can't keep it a secret anymore. I don't care what anyone thinks. I'm going to take care of you and our precious baby. We don't have to live in fear. We can be happy now," he said in a voice that sounded like he was about to break down.

I would have believed him if I wasn't the victim. He was *that* good. I never thought I'd come across an award-winning liar.

"I stopped the wedding for us, for you, for the baby. I know you're scared about what people will start saying, but I will always be by your side. We are in this together." He said it like he was saying his vows.

I was surprised when the congregation chorused, "Awww."

Come on, people. This is not the time to fall for his charm!

Tristan's lips wavered, and he stepped closer, knowing he had the congregation's support now. He took my hands. I tried pulling them away, but he held them tightly.

How many fights do I have to put up? Will everyone believe me if I take off my heel and pluck out his eyeballs?

"We'll get through this, Chloe, I promise," he said as if he meant every word, and I had to remind myself that this was all an act.

Why is he doing this? If he didn't feel like getting married anymore, he could have stopped the wedding and left. No need for more drama.

I turned my head to look at everyone in the church; they were all staring at me like they wanted me to admit everything was true. Some were smiling, and others gave me a look of contempt. My eyes stopped moving when they landed on my sister, noticing her hands were fisted by her sides. Our eyes locked, and I felt like I'd found my savior. My sister could prove him wrong. She'd known me her whole life; we shared every secret. She knew this was all a lie.

She started walking toward us in her white Louboutin T-strap pumps that clicked on the marble floor, and I smiled. At least I had someone to save me from whatever this psycho was up to.

I pulled away from him as she got closer, but she wasn't smiling. I suspected it was because of Tristan.

Kick his ass, Ciara! Tell him not to mess with your kid sister.

My shoulders relaxed with hope when she stopped in front of me, but what happened next, I didn't see it coming.

Ciara gave me a slap, the sound of it echoing in the church. I heard a few people gasp. I was shocked too. My cheek stung at the contact. It was the first time in months she'd ever hit me. I touched where she'd just slapped me and stared at her with wide eyes. She didn't look like she regretted it.

The last time she'd slapped me was because I had eaten her last piece of pizza that she was saving to eat later. It resulted in a fight, and I'd ended up with a sore arm.

My jaw was slightly down as I stared, wide-eyed, at my sister, who I looked up to.

Tristan's towering form moved in front of me, taking a protective stance, hiding me from my sister.

"That's enough. If you touch her again, I will charge you with assault." He sounded very angry.

I stared at his broad back as his tall frame shielded me from my sister's wrath. A tear rolled down my left cheek. At this point, there was no need to try to convince anyone of the truth. My sister, with whom I shared everything, believed the lies too.

CHAPTER **FOUR**
HOPELESS

"Stay out of this, Tristan. This is between my sister and me," Ciara said, sounding very upset. Her forehead creased in anger as she looked behind him, meeting my frightened eyes.

"She is my girlfriend, and I won't let you hit her again. I swear to you, if I see any mark on her face, I'm suing you."

I should applaud this guy. He sounded very angry, and Ciara appeared scared for a moment.

Why was I even hiding? I had to face her. Hiding was only going to make everyone think all this was true. I wiped the tear that had escaped from my left eye and walked forward.

"Babe …" Tristan grabbed my arm.

"Get your filthy hands off me!" I snapped, pulling my hand away. I met my sister's heavy gaze.

"Do you realize what you just did?" Ciara asked.

"Ciara, I don't know what he's talking about."

"Stop with the lies already!"

I flinched at the furious tone of her voice.

"You also believe he's telling the truth? You really think I'm pregnant?" I asked with tears gathering at the corners of my eyes.

"Obviously."

"You've known me since I was a kid. I've shared everything with you. We live in the same house. Does any of this make sense to you?!"

At this point, I couldn't hold the tears back even if I shouldn't be the one in crying. Rage boiled within me, my emotions wreaking havoc throughout my body. The intensity of what I was feeling burned me inside, and if I let it all out, it would cause a massive fire.

"Yes, and don't act like some kind of saint. You have done worse. I thought that part of your life was over," she said with glossy eyes.

"Ciara, this is all a lie! Can't you see that? I'm not that person anymore, and you know that."

Did he cast a spell on everyone?

"Stop already. Don't you have any shame left in you? You could have gone for anyone, Chloe! Why him? He is my best friend's fiancé."

"Was, and don't talk to her like that," Tristan corrected, stepping forward.

"Can you please not say anything?" I said, looking up at his face, his blond hair now a mess.

His expression softened as he met my eyes, making him look like a lost puppy, except a monster lurked within that softness he let on.

"I can't just stand here and watch her speak to you like that," he said with *fake* concern.

"What do you think Mom and Dad are going to say?" Ciara questioned me.

"I'm going to explain everything to them. At least they will listen to me," I said, feeling hopeful.

"You're a tramp," she said in disgust, walking away.

I dug my nails into my palms. I could burst into flames from the anger consuming me.

"Are you okay?" Tristan asked, leaning closer to my right ear.

Clenching my fists, I turned around and punched him in the nose. The congregation gasped.

"I. Hate. You," I said, grabbing my purse from my seat and using it to hit him.

I felt drained and frustrated. My only option right now was to show a pregnancy test to my family. I was tired of fighting everyone, trying to explain that this psycho was lying.

Touching his nose, Tristan stared at me like he hadn't expected that from me.

"I will fight for our love, no matter how much you resist it. We deserve to be happy," he said, stepping forward.

I wanted to give up. The rage flowing through my cells could turn me into the Hulk right now, which I would love so I'd be able to smash Tristan into a doormat.

I needed someone to believe me, someone to listen to me. I had never felt so invisible in my life. I took a deep breath and did the only thing I could think of. I screamed. The scream stretched on as my vocal cords tried to keep up. The whole church went silent, and for the first time, I saw regret mixed with fear written all over Tristan's face.

"I don't know anything about this man. I'm not pregnant. If someone can get me a pregnancy test right now to prove to everyone he is lying, I will wait," I cried, the tears running down my cheeks to my chin.

I wished someone would listen to me, but as I looked around the room, they were all quiet, just staring at me like I was the psychopath here.

I was desperate, so I took off one of my heels and brought it close to my stomach. "If I have to push the tip of this heel into my stomach to get you to trust me, I will," I said.

I could never do it, but I needed to push him to tell the truth. I already had enough scars to conceal.

I could see the fear on everyone's face, Tristan's included.

"Tell them the truth, or I will do it," I dared him.

"Please, think of the future of our baby," he said, stepping closer but I stepped back. "Chloe, put that shoe away, and we can talk this out," he said calmly, as if he were trying to tame a wild beast.

"You are not gonna get away with this. After I get out of here, I'm going to the pharmacy to get a pregnancy test, and I will sue your psychotic ass for defamation of character," I said with gritted teeth.

"Sure, but you need to be alive to do that," he said, taking another step closer.

Someone snatched the shoe from behind me. I turned around and saw an older lady. She looked concerned with her lips tensed.

"Babies are too precious and innocent. Leave the child out of this," she said softly and walked away after giving Tristan my shoe.

"Hello, everyone. Can I have your attention, please? I'm sincerely sorry for everything going on. Sorry you had to witness this. I'm deeply sorry. I hope you forgive us for wasting your valuable time."

I turned around to look at who was speaking and saw Tristan's mom standing behind the pulpit at the altar.

Her voice was so rich and eloquent as she addressed the crowd. "You can return to your various homes. Thank you for coming."

People stood up and started leaving the church, but their eyes remained glued on us. Some went over to speak to his mother, and others smiled at us as they left. Fake smiles that probably hid their true judgment.

"He is lying! I swear on my ancestors' graves, I am not pregnant. If you can all wait here while I get a pregnancy test and—"

"Please stop. We have done enough. No more hiding. We can be happy now," Tristan cut in, holding my cheeks. His long and rough fingers cupped my face, his large palms fitted the whole of my face.

"Wow, when are you going to quit?" I pushed his hands away.

Two girls, about my age, walked up to us with wide grins. They had matching hairstyles and the same golden cami satin dresses hugging their clear skin.

"I was expecting you to grab her hand and run out of the church," the one with the auburn hair said, giggling.

It took everything in me not to pull her hair and tell her none of this was funny.

"That was brave of you, Tristan, to fight for the woman you love," the other girl remarked, twirling the ends of her sandy-blonde hair.

"Anything for her," he added softly.

I felt his eyes on me. I guessed I hadn't punched him hard enough.

"You're so lucky, Chloe."

I rolled my eyes at her statement. There was no need explaining the truth to these empty heads that were gawking at him.

"Please don't be mad at him. He really loves you and wants the best for your baby. I wish you both a happy life."

I ignored them, and I stared into space with a clenched jaw. I wanted an explanation from him before leaving. Why me? Maybe there was more to this because it still felt surreal.

Soon, the church was empty. I turned to Tristan. I opened my mouth to say something, but I heard his mom's voice.

"Tristan," she called, sounding so calm, but there was a hint of anger in her voice.

I turned to look at her. She was walking toward us with the girl I had seen earlier, and an older woman followed. I assumed from the slight resemblance that she must be his grandmother.

His mom looked stunning in her golden gown, covered with a sheer knee-length jacket. He'd definitely gotten those blue eyes from her.

Tristan moved closer, put his arm around my waist, and then kissed my cheek. I could feel his unwanted breath brush against my jaw.

Eww. I tried to pull away.

I was sure this counted as sexual harassment. The charges I would place on him would send him to jail for years without bail. I tried to wriggle out of his hold, but he tightened his grip around my waist. I stepped on his foot until he let go.

"Please, play along," he begged.

"No! Tell your family the truth," I demanded.

I thought of what his mom would say to me. She stopped two feet away from us.

"Mom, I'm sorry," Tristan said.

"You should be. Do you know what you've done?" Her fancy eyeglasses with shiny crystals on the frame fitted her oval face. I could swear she had gotten a chin job from how pointed it was.

"Oh, don't be like that, Carmen. He followed his heart," his grandmother said with a wide smile.

"Mom." His mother groaned, looking at his grandmother.

"What? I knew right from the beginning that he didn't love that spoiled brat." His grandmother rolled her eyes with her chin raised in confidence.

"Mom, that's rude, and we are in church."

His grandmother waved it off without a care. The girl beside her suppressed her laughter.

"Isn't she beautiful, Grandma?" Tristan proclaimed, looking down at my face.

I didn't know why, but I was relieved that I had no pimples on my face. "She is a goddess. I knew you had good taste," she whispered, giggling.

"Thank God you changed your mind. Sofia would've kept stealing my lipstick with the excuse of borrowing it." Tristan's sister sighed.

"Keep your mouth shut, Nora. Adults are talking." Her mother shot her a glare. "And don't say that outside."

"But you told me on my birthday that I was an adult," Nora grumbled.

"How long have you been pregnant?" his grandmother asked me.

My throat went dry. "I'm not preg—"

"Six weeks," Tristan answered sharply.

"Your stomach is still as flat as the surface of a table," she said, staring at my stomach.

"That's because I'm not pregnant. Just take me to a doctor, so we can solve this once and for all," I said, but they didn't seem to believe me.

"It's okay, honey; we support your love for each other. You don't have to be afraid," his grandmother said softly, taking my hand and giving it a squeeze.

I opened my mouth to defend myself, but Tristan cut me off, "It's too early for her to show, Nana. Don't worry; you'll be the first we call once the baby bump is visible."

I stiffened when he placed his palm on my stomach, like there was really a baby in there.

What is he up to?

He was taking his act too far. He shouldn't be touching me. He had

39

no right. I smacked his hand away, and his grandmother laughed.

"Oh." His grandmother nodded with a grin.

"Can we focus on the issue at hand?" Mrs. Sanchester said. "Nora, take your grandmother to the car."

"Take good care of yourself and the baby. And, Tristan, make sure you bring her home sometime." His grandmother said as she walked away.

"Sure."

There was a long silence after they left. I wished I'd left the church earlier and not even bothered staying back to explain myself because in the end, it was of no use.

His mother was tapping her heel on the floor, looking agitated. I didn't even know what to say to her. I wasn't sure she would believe me. After seeing how his family was, I decided to just keep my lips sealed.

She finally raised her head and stood upright. I should tell her to take me to the hospital.

"You should have said something, Tristan. We would have canceled the wedding to prevent all this. I don't care about our family's reputation, but the Novas won't let this go that easily."

"I know," he said.

"You're coming with me tomorrow to see them, and when you're done here, go and apologize to Father Andrew for ruining everything."

"I promise I will."

She exhaled deeply, and her eyes rested on me.

"I don't know who this man is. I have no idea why he is doing this to me. You have to believe me, please."

"How old are you?" she asked instead.

"Twenty."

His mother nodded and walked away.

What's that all about? She hadn't even listened to me.

"Why did you do that?" I asked him, pushing at his chest with all my strength, the rage inside of me giving me superpowers because he stumbled back.

"Okay, I deserved that." He winced.

"What the hell was that? I need some explanation after the nonsense you just pulled."

"I'm sorry. Give me a few hours, and I will fix it," he said, regaining his composure.

"You are kidding, right?" My expression turned to stone.

"No."

I closed my eyes as I inhaled deeply and then breathed out. "Why? Why did you do that to me?"

"I can't tell you right now, but give me some time to fix this, and you will have your boyfriend back and an apology from your sister."

"That's all I get after you humiliated me? It won't fix the damage you've caused. Why did you do it?" I mumbled, raking my hair back.

"If you want money, just name the price."

"No, I don't want your shitty money. How could you do that to me and not give me a reason?" I said, staring at the altar like it could provide all the answers.

"I had to or else she would have been mad at me, and she didn't want me to get married. I didn't want to betray her," he said.

"Who is *she*? Is it your real mistress?" I asked, but he said nothing. "Tell me!"

"Thank you for being here today, Chloe," he said.

He'd just ruined my life like it was nothing, and that was all he had to say?

I had to see my parents; they were the only ones who would believe me and clear this mess.

"You need help. I hope you get that in jail because that is where you are going to be when I'm done with you," I said and walked away to the exit.

"Chloe, wait," he called, but I kept going, not looking back.

I groaned at the discomfort of walking with one heel. I went back and snatched my shoe from him, and then I walked out of the church.

I took a cab to the nearest store and got a pregnancy test. I looked out of place as I stood in front of the Cashier who stared at my dress.

"Trouble in paradise?" The Cashier asked.

I glared at him and paid for the pregnancy test. I grabbed it and stepped outside the store. I called for a cab and chewed on my fingernails the whole ride home. I gave the driver the money left in my purse when he stopped the car in my driveway.

Rushing out, I headed home, but I paused when I saw three suitcases on the porch—my suitcases. My parents stood next to the suitcases along with my glaring sister. Mom was crying, and Dad was trying to calm her down.

"Not you guys too." Hopelessness washed all over me as my mind meshed into a myriad of jumbled thoughts.

I exhaled deeply, forcing a smile.

"You got this, Chloe. You got this." I gave myself a pep talk as I approached them.

My mom detached herself from my dad's hold, staring at me as I got closer.

If looks could kill, Ciara would have killed me multiple times with her murderous stare. My palms felt sweaty as I stopped one foot away from my suitcases, trying not to think about the reason they were outside.

"Dad, Mom, it's not true," I said slowly, as if it would make them understand me better.

"Told you she would deny it," Ciara said immediately after I finished my sentence.

"I thought it was over. You promised me you'd never be that girl again," Mom sobbed.

"I have changed. I'm telling the truth. I'm not pregnant, and I can prove it to you. I have a pregnancy test right here." I showed them the small packet.

My parents stared at the packet; they almost looked convinced as their shoulders relaxed, but I could tell my actions in the past were blurring their trust in me.

"If you will just let me in and ..." I tried to go into the house, but Ciara shoved me back. *What did I ever do to her to receive such coldness?*

"I will take a pregnancy test right now and show you I'm not ..." I struggled to open the packet with shaky hands, but my tears had left me weak. "Please let me prove it to you," I begged.

"Fine, I want to believe you, Cassandra, but if this turns out to be true, I don't know what to think anymore," Mom said, making way for me to enter the house.

I rushed into the house, everyone trailing behind me. Ciara followed me upstairs and waited outside the bathroom door as I took the test. A part of me was scared for some reason. I bit nervously on my lips as I waited for the result to show. I sighed in relief when I saw the negative sign.

I opened the door with happy tears and a big grin as I showed my sister. She took it from me and examined it.

"I told you I'm not pregnant," I said, smiling excessively.

Ciara said nothing. I got no reaction from her.

"It's right there—negative," I pointed.

"Did you wash your hands after taking the test?" she asked.

I was confused. "No."

"I will show Mom. Clean up," she said, looking inside the bathroom with her face twisted in disgust.

I looked behind me and saw the mess I'd made. My shoes and purse were on the floor, and tissues littered the counter. I had been in a hurry and panicking, so I'd tossed everything on ground.

"I will be down in a minute," I said and shut the door.

I cleaned up quickly and washed my hands. I couldn't wait for my parents to apologize for doubting me. I wanted them to know I was a better person now. I picked up my purse and left the bathroom. I rushed and met my family downstairs.

"I told you I wasn't pregnant." I grinned.

I focused on my parents, waiting for them to welcome me back into the house, but they were silent, like they hadn't heard a word I'd said. I expected a smile and maybe an apology, but Mom was in deep tears. Dad looked heartbroken with his face numb and body limp.

"What?" I asked, slowing down.

Mom shook her head and cried harder. Dad tried to calm her down. I looked over at my sister, and she avoided my eyes.

"Get your things and leave," Mom said.

"What? Why?"

"You know why," Mom said, looking furious.

"I don't get it. The proof is right there. I'm not pregnant."

"How delusional are you? The result says you're pregnant!" she yelled and threw the pregnancy test at me.

I froze, speechless and disoriented.

CHAPTER **FIVE**
RUINED

I picked up the pregnancy test with shaky hands and read it. I stopped breathing as I stared at the two pink lines. I could feel my body shaking. There had to be a mistake, or the device was faulty.

How is this possible?

"It was one line, I promise. I don't know how … Ciara, you saw it. Tell them," I stuttered, looking to my sister for help.

She said nothing.

"I will try it again. Give me some time."

"I can't put up with you anymore. You will always trash this family's name. Get your stuff and leave," Mom said.

"The test is wrong," I cried. "You have to believe me. I don't know him. I just saw him for the first time."

I searched their faces for any indication that they believed me, but when Dad shook his head in disappointment and Mom cried more, I knew I had to try harder.

"Mom …"

"Stop, please," she said, staring at me with puffy eyes and tears wetting her cheeks. "You ruined this family like it's nothing. Why him, Cassandra?"

I opened my mouth to explain, but she continued, "You were using Grey all along. Who are you?" She looked at me like I was possessed and beyond recognition.

"It's me, Mom. It's me, Chloe," I said, trying to touch her but she pulled away from me.

She frantically shook her head, like she didn't want to believe a word from my mouth.

"Dad?" I turned to him to say something, but he remained silent, like he always did, turning a blind eye when I needed him.

He always agreed with Mom. Even if she chose to poison us, he'd pick her side. Sometimes, I wondered if we even mattered to him. He hardly ever stood up to her, even when she yelled and criticized him. He was like a ghost around her with no sense of self.

"Dad, please hear me out."

He turned away and walked to the backyard. My heart sank as tears brimmed my eyes. He shut the door without looking back.

"Dad!" I screamed.

"You were hell-bent on attending the wedding because you couldn't stand the thought of him getting married to Sofia." Ciara jabbed my heart, not helping my situation.

"No. I told you why I wanted to go to the wedding."

"You lied!" she yelled.

Who is this person, and what has she done to my sister?

"Grey was a good guy. Even though I never admitted it, he was much better for you than that man," Mom said.

I didn't know what to say to her. If no one was ready to believe me, then why was I trying?

"Are you ready to become a mother, Cassandra? Do you know what people are going to say about you? About this family?" Mom asked.

I whimpered, not knowing the right words to say.

"I'm not pregnant. You have to believe me," I pleaded.

"You know, I always had a feeling you were hiding something, but this isn't close to what I thought it'd be," Mom cut in with her teeth clenched. Her veins bubbled out of her forehead.

"Your sister told us what you did. I can't believe you did all that behind our backs. You fooled us. You never changed, and you will never change. What you did behind our backs is enough to convince me you're not the daughter I raised."

"What?" I looked at Ciara for an explanation.

"Are you going to deny what you did after you returned from the camp?" Mom asked.

I looked away from Mom. I didn't know what mattered anymore—proving I was not pregnant or convincing my parents I was still the same daughter they loved.

"Oh mom, she snuck out every night to see her fourth boyfriend the son of a druglord, who tried to rape her." Ciara smiled wryly at me when she was done talking. The expression on her face was almost unsettling, like a snake about to bite.

My heartbeat stopped, and my tears froze. I turned my head slowly to look at my sister, who used to keep my most perilous secrets secure. All I could see was red. If someone had told me the person I was staring at was my sister, I would've laughed and called them crazy. Ciara was like my twin sister even if she was five years older. She was my best friend, and we had grown up, doing everything together. We'd developed our language and always confided in each other. Now, I could not recognize the person staring at me with cold eyes. I'd thought she'd always have my back.

My sister had crossed her heart not to tell anyone, especially my parents. That night was something I never wanted to recall. I'd had nightmares for months after that horrifying incident. But she'd just spilled it like I hadn't cried my eyes out that night, to the point that I had gotten a fever.

I heard my mom gasp, my body numbing as her intense eyes burned me with ice. The truth was out—the truth that had diverted my mom's attention to my past instead of the situation at hand.

"Is it true? Did that really happen?"

I swallowed, nodding.

She went pale, covering her mouth to suppress her sobbing.

"Mom …" I tried to touch her, but she stepped back, as if physical contact from me would kill her.

"I'm sorry." I sniffled, lips quivering.

"Before you leave, just know we've cut you off. You don't need us in your life anymore. I don't even know who you are. Leave and never come back," Mom said, staring at me like she didn't recognize me.

"I do need you, Mom," I said with a shaky voice.

"I don't think so. If it were up to me, I would take your last name away. You don't deserve to be called a *Simpson*," she said sternly. "I don't care if you're pregnant; neither do I care if you are having an affair with an older man. You went against every rule, just for your pleasure and stupidity! You were already out of my life the first time you even thought about it. Seriously, Cassandra, drugs and sex? I taught you better," my mom said, bawling her eyes out like she was the victim.

"I have given you everything I could, and it's never been enough for you. Leave right now. I can't even look at you," she said and turned away.

"I'm not leaving." I shook my head.

Mom turned to look at Ciara, ignoring my protest.

"Get her out of this house. Your suitcases are already outside. I hope he makes you happy." She sniffled and headed for the stairs.

I ran to hold her back, but Ciara got in the way.

"Mom, please." I tried pushing past my sister, who was stopping me. "Mom!" I screamed.

Ciara pulled me to the door until I was outside the house. She shut the door behind her and refused to let me in. I stiffened. I wasn't ready to accept the fact that my parents just kicked me out. I pulled away from my sister's hold, gazing at her villainous demeanor. A two-headed witch with multiple personalities.

What did I do to her?

"Why now? You promised!"

"Why?" she asked, stepping forward slowly. "Remember I told you I was dating Sofia's cousin." I knew where this was going. "He dumped me over the phone immediately after he got the news. According to him, he couldn't date someone related to the person who made his family a thing for mockery."

"You didn't have to go this far!" I snapped.

I didn't care if she was five years older than me. If she hadn't said that, I would have gotten a chance to convince Mom.

"He was going to propose, Chloe!" she screamed. "Sofia told me he was going to propose!" she sobbed.

I knew marriage had been her last ticket of escape to be away from my mom's controlling grasp.

"But then he heard what had happened at the wedding. You just had to steal my happiness like you always do," she said with pure disdain, like she wouldn't mind killing me on the spot.

"You really believe I'm pregnant? You saw the test. There was one line. I don't know how it suddenly turned to two," I asked softly.

"I don't know what to believe anymore. You were never who you said you were from the beginning, pretending to be the perfect daughter in front of Mom and Dad when behind their backs, you're wild and crazy."

"You're supposed to have my back and help me through this. Not add more fuel to the fire!" I yelled.

"You did that yourself. I only opened their eyes to the truth. It wasn't going to stay hidden forever, Chloe," she retorted.

"They didn't have to find out this way," I whimpered.

"Well, now, they know. You're welcome," she said, as if I were supposed to thank her for spilling my secrets.

"Don't do this, Ciara. I'm your little sister, the one who holds on to you tight during thunderstorms and steals your food when you're not looking," I reminded her.

My words got to her because she looked away, trying to shake the memories off.

"Ciara?"

"I have my own life to worry about. I lost my best friend today and now a sister. I was also about to become someone's fiancée." She forced the tears down.

"I'm still your sister," I mumbled. Weakness consumed me, like her words had sucked out my remaining oxygen supply.

"I hope you're happy."

She turned to leave, but I held her back.

"Don't leave me too. Please talk to them."

"You chose this path right when you turned fourteen."

"I changed when I met Grey. You know that."

"I don't know you!" she said, pulling her hand away.

"Ciara, wait." She ignored me entered the house, slamming the door.

And she was gone.

I ran to the door and knocked.

"Mom! Dad! Ciara! Please let me in." I pounded my fists on the door with tears flowing down my cheeks. "It's not true."

No one came.

"I'm still your daughter. You can't just kick me out," I whimpered, my face all wet and my nose runny.

"Please," I begged, resting my back on the door.

I flung the pregnancy test away, enraged and devastated. Leaning on the door, I slid slowly to the ground and broke down. The only people I'd thought would have my back wouldn't even hear me out. I waited, hoping someone would open the door and let me back into the house, but nothing happened.

An hour passed, and I was still waiting. My neighbors pulled into their driveway, staring at me as they exited their car. I expected them to walk up to me and ask questions and maybe help, but they walked straight into their house. They weren't just my neighbors. I was their babysitter—favorite babysitter, according to Mrs. Darnley.

I picked up my phone from my purse and called my sister, but it went straight to voice mail. I was about to call my mom when a sleek black SUV stopped in front of my house.

A man who looked to be in his mid-forties stepped out. His bald head glistened under the blazing sun. He was short. I guessed he was five feet tall. His round stomach made his tux look tight, like if he stretched both arms, the buttons wouldn't hold anymore. His thin legs reminded me of a cartoon character from *Despicable Me*. He adjusted his tux and walked toward my house. I cocked a brow at him as he got closer. He didn't climb the steps. He gave me a firm smile and stood straight, like he was being controlled. I noticed the white gloves on his hands.

"Hi, I'm Morris." His accent was hard to place.

"Can I help you?" I asked, not wiping my tears away or composing myself, like my mom would want right now.

"I'm here for Miss Chloe Simpson."

I stared at him closely. "Are you a journalist?" I asked.

"No," he answered with the same neutral expression.

"Then, what do you want?"

"Mr. Sanchester sent me to get you."

"Tristan?"

"Yes, Miss Simpson."

"Why?"

"I was asked to keep an eye on you to make sure you're okay, but you don't look good. I informed Mr. Sanchester of your situation, so he sent me to come and pick you up."

He sent someone to spy on me?

I chuckled humorlessly at first and stared at him, waiting for the truth. "Wait, you're serious?"

"Yes, ma'am," he replied with his fingers intertwined and placed in front of him.

Should I trust him? What if he's a hit man, sent by the Novas to kill me?

I stared at him for a while. He had none of the qualities of a hit man from what I had observed. I closed my eyes and rested my head on the door.

It seemed my parents didn't plan on letting me back into the house. They wouldn't take me back even if they knew the truth. It didn't matter if Tristan had lied or not. I had already broken their trust.

I had nowhere to go, no relatives that I knew of who would let me stay with them. Mom had control of my account because she was the one who'd opened it for me, and she'd made me quit my last job because she didn't like me coming home late. So, I had nothing.

My head hurt from crying and shouting. I felt hungry and thirsty. That was the least of my problems right now. I needed Tristan Sanchester's location, so I could murder him, and he'd just made it easy for me.

I stood up with a sigh. "Take me to that asshole," I said, clenching my fist.

I turned around, and my heart skipped a beat as I noticed my suitcases were missing. Morris was waiting for me with the door open, gesturing for me to enter. *Gosh, he is weird.*

I walked to the car, taking the backseat. I stared at my house as we pulled out of my driveway. I wiped my tears away and tried to toughen up. I saw my sister staring at me from her room. I raised my middle finger, pointing at her frigid face.

My phone rang as my house disappeared from my view. I reached for it quickly, wishing it were my dad calling me to come back home, but I felt disappointed when I saw it was my best friend, Belvina.

"Hey, Vina," I said weakly.

"Are you really pregnant by Tristan Sanchester?"

"No!"

I heard her exhale in relief.

"*Gracias a Dios.* But is it true? The whole love thing?"

"Of course not."

"I was telling my parents he was lying, but they won't even listen to me. Are you okay?"

"No, my parents kicked me out."

53

She gasped. "*Ay Dios mio.* No way! They believed that devil? I was kinda convinced at the beginning. Wow, he is good." I could tell she was eating from the way she spoke. From the sound, I concluded it was her favorite Paqui tortilla chips.

"It's not that. Ciara told them everything," I told her. My eyes stung as I replayed my sister's betrayal. It hurt so much more than any heartbreak I'd experienced.

"That two-faced *puta*. So, what are you going to do?"

"I'm going to his place, so if you hear on the news about the murder of Tristan Sanchester, don't be shocked. Just make sure you come to my trial and visit me every day in jail." I saw Morris look back at me with a horrified expression.

"I understand your rage, Chlo, but listen to me. Take a deep breath, exhale, and go get that motherfucker! I'm here if you need backup."

I smiled for the first time since the shit that had gone down in the church.

"Do you know why he did it?"

"He won't tell me." To be honest, a part of me felt relieved and happy that someone believed it was a lie.

"Have you thought of taking a pregnancy test? Maybe go live on the internet and show everyone the result," she suggested.

"I did, but something weird happened. I'm so confused and frustrated right now. I'm not sure if I'm in my body." I was tearing up again. My head was tearing apart.

"*Lo siento, cariño.* What happened?"

I told her about the pregnancy test, and she went silent for a while. I was scared she might believe the whole lie too. There was no way I was carrying a baby. How was that even possible? Was I? The pregnancy test had come out positive, and I didn't know how.

"What in the Virgin Mary?" she gasped. "*Còmo*? Have you started drinking again?" she asked.

"No. You know I would never lie to you."

"*Se*. I know. You should have bought, like, five different pregnancy tests to test the accuracy."

"I will figure something out after I'm done with Tristan Sanchester," I said, mentally assuring myself I could get out of this mess.

"I know I still live with my parents, but if you need anything, please let me know. You could sneak into my room and stay with me without my parents knowing."

"No, it's fine."

"I love you, Chloe. Please don't go on YouTube. The comments there will lead you to suicide."

"It's on YouTube?" My heart stopped beating.

"Yep, two million views already."

I groaned, moving my already-messy hair back.

"We'll make that shithole pay for what he did. We'll fix this," she said loud enough for Morris to hear.

"Thanks, Vina. I feel better now. It means the world to me that someone believes me."

"Always. I will believe you, even when I'm old and suffering from Alzheimer's. No one's going to change that. I was so worried about you after I saw the news. I will call you later. My mom is back from the store, and I'm supposed to be making lasagna," she said quickly.

"Okay," I sighed in a low tone.

The rest of the ride was silent, and I almost fell asleep. I didn't know when we arrived until Morris came to open the door for me. I got out, looking at the luxurious three-story glass house, trying not to gape at the building as we went inside.

Everything inside looked expensive and well-furnished. I could see my reflection on the sparkling floor. There was a patio between the dining area and a large door leading outside, an exquisite interior that one could stare at for hours. I was in a bad mood, so I didn't bother looking around. I took a seat and stared at the large screen TV. I still felt so much rage. It was a wave of intense anger that channeled all my emotions and darkness, desperately in need of release.

This is not the package I asked for when I wished to move out. There is a difference, Fairy Godmother.

I felt so broken. All it had taken was a lie for my life to take another turn. For everything in my past I'd desperately kept hidden to come to light.

Why did Grey judge me on what happened in my past? He knows very well I'm done with that part of my life. Is it possible I got too drunk and forgot any details about meeting Tristan Sanchester? I have been sober for three years, and I have stayed celibate. There is no way I slept with him without having any memory of it.

I took off my shoes and leaned back on the seat. My legs felt numb, and breathing became exhausting. I felt detached from my body as I stared into space.

Am I really pregnant? I need to go to the hospital.

"Your suitcases are in your room. Would you like something to drink?" Morris appeared at my side.

"I'm not here to stay. Where is he?"

"He's out with a friend."

So, he was hanging out with his friend while I suffered from his lies.

"Morris," I called, sitting up on the plush leather couch.

"Yes, Miss Simpson?"

"Please call me Chloe."

"I don't think I can do that, miss."

I didn't have time to argue.

"What does your boss treasure most in this house?"

"The paintings on each wall. They're very expensive, and they mean a lot to him. And his achievements, like awards from around the world." He sounded proud of his boss as he spoke while I just smiled in my head.

"Could you bring them all here?" I could keep myself entertained before he returned.

"Sorry?"

"I want all the paintings and awards. Now, please."

He hesitated but walked away quickly after I stabbed my menacing eyes into his.

"You messed with the things I treasured most, and I will mess with yours." I knew I couldn't compare both, but I needed to cool off. Smashing those paintings and awards seemed like a good solution.

I stood up when he was done gathering everything. I stretched my arms and flexed my neck, preparing my muscles for the activity. I smashed each painting to pieces, screaming my rage out. I crashed the awards on the glass table, breaking it in the process. I broke more things as I recalled what had happened in the church and at home. I grabbed one of the glass shards from the center table I'd broken and waited for Tristan.

The place was a mess when I was done, and I was panting heavily from the work. I slumped on the couch and looked at Morris. He seemed horrified with his jaw dropped and eyes rounded. He reached for his phone and made a call.

That's right, Morris. Make the damn call.

CHAPTER **SIX**
BROKEN

I stared blankly at what I had done, and to be honest, I wasn't satisfied. I heard running footsteps.

"Well, that was quick." I grinned when Tristan appeared.

His honey-blond hair was tousled at the top, and a few strands fell over his forehead. He was still in his wedding suit, but the jacket was gone. His white button-up was still creased sharply and tucked into his pants. A fair guy with a lovely shade of black hair stood behind him; that must be the friend he had been out with.

He was slightly taller than Tristan and lean with just the right amount of muscle. His dark hair contrasted with his warm gray eyes. He reminded me of a male model I'd once had a crush on. He had a face I'd seen on a magazine cover with a casual outfit on and way too many rings on his fingers. But they suited him so well.

"Shit! She is really pissed," his friend said, folding his arms with an amused smile.

Tristan looked like he'd just seen a ghost. His lips parted slowly and then closed back, like he didn't know what to say. Running his hand down his face, he growled slightly. His eyes darted to my direction.

"What did you do?"

Was he blind?

"Oh, my bad. I'm just having a pregnancy tantrum right now. I'm carrying your child, remember?" My eyes held his in an intense stare.

He sighed and turned away from me, mumbling incoherent words to himself as he stared up at the ceiling.

"I asked for a few hours. I will fix this," he said, facing me. His eyes kept darting to the damaged paintings, and his fist clenched.

"Well, I was fuming in rage when I got here, and I needed to cool off. I came across these ugly paintings and the awards." I faked a smile.

"Ugly?" He cocked a neat eyebrow at me, staring like I was too dumb to differentiate between beans and pebbles.

"Do you know how valuable each of those paintings were?" His forehead creased, and his nostrils flared as he stared down at me.

I stood up and took slow steps toward him. I stepped on something, but I kept moving. "Valuable?" I laughed. I was on the verge of exploding.

I felt something pierce my foot, but I ignored it, moving closer.

"Are you comparing my life to that piece of crap?" I didn't want to feel intimidated by his height, so I maintained a safe distance between us.

His face grew stern at my words, distinct veins appearing on his neck. I was satisfied, yet still, it wasn't enough.

"You were the one who went overboard, Tristan. You took your lie too far!" Wow, all this yelling was making my head hurt.

"I will fix this, Chloe. Just give me some time," he grunted, fingers massaging his brows as he hissed again.

"You destroyed my life, and you're getting mad over some lame paintings and awards?"

His jaw hardened at my words. Man, it curved sharp.

"I want my life back. You have to fix this!"

He was quiet, but he stared at me like his mind was spinning with different ways to murder me.

Too bad, honey. I thought of that first.

"I don't care about your reasons. I am not interested. I want my family back. I want my boyfriend back! You have to tell them the truth." My voice escalated until I screamed. I was trying desperately not to do anything rash because just staring at him filled my head with murderous intent. I have never felt so much hate for someone.

"I can't. Not now," he said calmly, regaining his composure.

"Then, you leave me no choice." I didn't care about his height anymore. I stepped closer.

My grip on the glass shard tightened, bringing it closer to his chest. His friend took a step closer, and I shot him a glare. Tristan signaled for him to stay back.

"Why did you do it? Why me?" I asked, looking up at his face that looked unfazed by my action.

"I will tell you, I promise. Now, put the glass down."

"You don't get to decide that!" I said, placing the tip of the glass on his hard chest. "Tell me. I have nothing to lose, Tristan, so I don't give two shits about pushing this glass into your rotten heart," I demanded.

"I can't," he said.

"You can't?" I laughed hysterically.

This whole thing was driving me crazy. They all looked wary as they watched me, probably wondering if they should call for an ambulance to ship me to a psychiatric hospital.

I put the glass down, knowing I didn't have it in me to take someone else's life. All I could think about was making him feel the same pain I was feeling right now, but as much as it hurt, I couldn't do it. His friend signaled for Morris to take the piece of glass away.

"You had no right to do that. You don't get to ruin someone's life like that. You have no right to say whatever you want about my life!" I poked his chest with each sentence; it was so hard that I was scared it would fracture my finger.

"Better sleep with two eyes open because I will kill you in your sleep," I threatened.

He looked down at me with those alluring blue eyes I wished God had given to someone worth it.

"Okay." His voice reverberated with reverence.

Is this dude for real?

"Do you have any idea the damage you caused? You just stole everything from me, and you have the guts to act like you had the right to do that."

He stared at me like I was boring him with my words. Shaking his head, he looked back at his friend, lost in amusement.

"I'm talking to you, asshole!" I shoved his chest, but he didn't move.

I saw his hand clench, but his blank expression left me clueless. I ignored the sharp, sizzling pain pricking at my feet.

"Morris, show Miss Simpson to her room," Tristan said with a sigh.

"If you take another step next to me, I will snap your neck," I warned. Morris stopped. "I'm not staying here, but I'm definitely not leaving without you telling my family the truth."

I knew it wouldn't change anything, but I wanted them to know I was a better person now. I rushed to get my phone. There was a slight pain beneath my foot.

"You're bleeding." I heard a deep voice from behind. I was damn sure it didn't belong to Tristan or Morris.

I looked back at his friend, and he pointed at my bloody footprint. I rolled my eyes, returning to my search. I picked up my phone and returned to Tristan, whose eyes were on the destroyed paintings and awards.

I could tell he was angry, but he wasn't showing much of it. His lips twisted in a scowl as he exhaled.

"Here is my dad's number." I extended my phone to him, but he was still staring at the mess I'd made.

"How did you get all the paintings and awards?"

I moved the phone closer to his face in response. He grabbed it, and just when a smile was about to form on my face, he threw the phone across the room.

"Bro, what the fuck?" his friend said, walking to where Tristan had tossed the phone. He picked the pieces up with a slight frown stretching across his face. "You broke her phone, asshole," he said to Tristan, who didn't seem to care.

"Okay, good thing I have their number up here." I pointed to my head.

I saw his phone peeking out of his front pocket. He grabbed my hand when I reached for it.

"You can break whatever you want, however you want. I need time, and I already promised to tell you," he said calmly.

I pulled my hand away and stepped back, glaring at him. He stared back at me with a neutral expression. Tucking both hands in his pockets, he gestured for Morris to take me to my room.

"I need a glass of water. I will be right back," I said before Morris could get to me. I gave Tristan one last look before turning away to look for the kitchen.

"I will get—"

"I will do it myself," I snapped at Morris—poor butler.

"She's cute," his friend said as I headed for the kitchen.

I knew I was just a little girl in their eyes, but I would give them hell and show them they'd messed with the wrong girl.

The kitchen was always neighbors with the dining room, so it wasn't hard to find it. It was a wide kitchen with white and black furnishings and lustrous utensils. I tried not to admire the big kitchen as I opened the cabinets. I was greeted with fine china plates.

There you are.

I started dropping each on the floor, breaking them. Dropping more, I opened the next cabinet. He'd said I could break whatever I wanted. Well, he would watch me destroy this beautiful house of his.

Morris was the first to run into the kitchen, followed by Tristan's friend.

"Hey," Tristan's friend called, coming closer, but I threw more breakable things on the floor, pretending not to hear him.

"Chloe, stop."

I was going to make them regret every decision they had made in their miserable lives.

"That bastard thinks he can mess with my life."

I kept stepping on each piece as I walked. My feet had deep cuts already, but I wasn't concerned about that right now.

"Chloe."

He was starting to annoy me. I stopped myself from throwing the plates in my hand at him. I searched the next cabinet. I knew how expensive they were, and even if it meant nothing to him, at some point, he would get frustrated.

The next cabinet greeted me with beautiful sets of teacups and saucers. They looked unique and had vintage designs. Blue roses twirled round the cup, the rim covered in gold, and pure white contrasted with the blue flowers. I could stare at them forever; they were beautiful. Too bad I was too pissed to care.

"Don't even think about it," Tristan's voice made me pause.

I picked up the set of cups, facing him.

"Chloe, put those cups down, please," his friend pleaded.

What was so special about the cups anyway? They all looked concerned, as if I were about to jump down a cliff and end my life.

"Go ahead and break anything else but not those cups."

I sensed something in his voice, his eyes begging me to stop.

Why hadn't Morris mentioned the cups? If breaking these cups was going to hurt him, then I'd gladly destroy them.

"My life is more precious than these cups," I said, letting go, faking a gasp.

"Oops!" I said dramatically

CHAPTER **SEVEN**
CONSEQUENCES

There was a long silence in the kitchen after the cups dropped. The shards of glass caught every eye and evoked different emotions—fear, anger, and shock. It was like the calm before the storm, but I wasn't scared, nor was I satisfied. They stared at the pieces like I'd just broken the rarest piece of art.

Tristan's eyes moved slowly from the cups until they landed on me. I smiled smugly at him. He looked like he wanted to say something but was holding back. The veins on his neck and wrist scared me as his jaw hardened in anger.

"Why don't you go out for some air? I will talk to her," his friend said, trying to soften his voice and shielding me from his intense gaze.

His friend was slightly taller than him. I wondered who was older.

Tristan gave me a murderous stare. He pulled away from his friend and walked out of the kitchen. I stared at his friend, who seemed relieved for some reason. I was kind of confused—not like anything today made sense. I stayed mute as his friend turned to look at me. His scrutinizing gaze didn't intimidate me one bit.

"I get that you're upset, Chloe. Anyone would feel that way, but all we ask for is a little time."

"Do you know how absurd you all sound? I can walk out of here and get a pregnancy test to prove to everyone he is lying. I only need him to tell my family the truth."

Technically, the plan was to come here and murder him.

"Why did he toy with my life like that? I wanna know! Am I not allowed to at least know why he picked me and ruined everything for me?"

"Soon, I promise," he said softly, giving me a warm smile.

"Ouch!" I winced at the sharp pain squeezing my feet.

"I'm fine." I held my hand up, stopping him as he moved to help me.

"Morris, where is my room?" I tried to hide the pain in my voice.

"You're seriously injured, Chloe. Let me take you to the hospital to have it checked, or it will get infected."

"No, I'm fine," I refused.

"I insist," he said, stepping closer. "I'm not about to let you die on my watch. Can I?" he asked, gesturing to my bloody feet.

I hesitated for a few seconds before nodding my head. He squatted close to my legs to have a look.

"That looks bad. I'm taking you to the hospital," he said, standing up.

"My parents cut me off. I can't afford it," I said a little harsher than I intended.

"I will take care of the bill," Tristan offered, walking into the kitchen.

He looked collected now, and it pissed me off that my actions were not getting to him.

"No, thank you," I said, trying to fight off the pain.

"You will get an infection if you don't get this checked," Tristan said.

"And you're losing a lot of blood," his friend added.

They both stared at me, waiting for a reply, while I just stood there, glaring at them.

"So, what are you gonna do if I refuse? Force me?" I questioned. "I don't care if I bleed to death. I'd rather not live to see another miserable day."

They exchanged a look, communicating through their eyes. Tristan approached me and took me in his arms before I could protest.

"Get a towel and meet me outside, Adrian," he said, looking over his shoulder at his friend.

"If I die, just know you will never have peace. I'm going to go all horror movie on you," I said.

"You're not dying," Tristan hissed.

"Scared you won't survive one day of being haunted?" I said, and he shook his head at me.

Morris opened the back door to the black Lamborghini parked outside, and Tristan gently placed me on the seat, like I would break if he put more pressure.

His friend Adrian rushed to the car with a blue towel in his hand. They whispered to each other for a while, looking back at me like I was a lost kid they'd just found stealing from them.

"I'm right here; you don't have to gossip about me," I said.

"Don't worry, Morris; I will drive," Adrian said, walking to the front seat.

Tristan sat beside me on the backseat with the towel. I folded my arms and sat back, ignoring his presence.

"Give me your leg," Tristan said.

"I'm not allowing you to touch me again."

"I need to wrap this around your feet to reduce the bleeding," he said, clearly aggravated.

I rolled my eyes, placing my foot on his lap.

I tried to pull my leg away at the contact.

"Easy. Stay still," he said, holding my leg back, his rough palm circling my knee in a firm grip.

"Would you like some music?" Adrian asked from behind the wheel.

"Yes, please," I said, turning my face away from my bloody foot.

My feet were numb from the pain by the time we pulled into the hospital. Three nurses brought a stretcher to carry me. Adrian and Tristan insisted on going with me into the hospital room, but the nurses refused.

An old doctor came to examine me. Even with his glasses, he kept squinting his eyes, and I was worried for myself. He tried to have a conversation as he ran some tests and asked a few questions about my last tetanus shot. I only flashed him a smile, pretending to be interested in what he was saying. He made me miss my dad.

I thought of what was happening at home right now. *Do they miss me? Are they thinking about me? Am I really pregnant? How did the test turn positive?* I felt like I was living someone else's life.

I was pushed around in a wheelchair and brought to the doctor's office after they washed my legs and performed an X-ray.

"Good news: no infection, and the glass didn't touch your bones."

I smiled at the news.

"We're going to stitch it up and give you a prescription, but you have to take a wheelchair home with you."

"What?"

"You need the wheelchair for movement," the doctor explained, laughing at my reaction.

"Is it that bad? Will I be able to walk again?" I panicked.

"Relax, Chloe. It's only for a few days." He smiled.

"How many days are we talking about here?" I furrowed my eyebrows.

"A week, and you'll be back on your feet."

I exhaled in relief. "How do I bathe?"

"Um … ask a relative for help."

Great! I was the only female in the house. I would figure something out.

I screamed during the stitching even though I'd been given something to numb the pain. I refused to see my feet, scared to see how it looked.

"Have a nice day, Chloe."

"Thank you."

I lay on the bed with different thoughts in my head. Adrian walked in with the wheelchair. He beamed softly, indenting his deep dimples. I gave him an annoyed look and allowed him to help me into the wheelchair.

I didn't see Tristan when we came out. We drove back to his place without him. Adrian tried conversing, but I ignored him. I was quiet the whole ride, tangled in my thoughts and wondering how the hell I'd ended up like this.

Adrian took me upstairs when we arrived. Morris trailed behind him with the wheelchair. Honestly, I preferred to be carried around than being pushed around in a wheelchair.

"Would you like anything?" he asked, gently placing me on the queen-size bed.

A time machine to go back and not attend the wedding or any wedding ever again, I wanted to say.

"To be left alone," I said, lying on the bed. I sighed as he closed the door.

Where did that asshole gone? What am I still doing here?

My plan at the hospital was to get a pregnancy test and mail the result to my family. I couldn't blame them for their decision. I wanted to show I wasn't who Ciara had painted me to be. I had grown from that girl from years ago. I still needed my family even if they weren't the best version of what one would call a family.

I didn't know what to do anymore. I was exhausted, and my head was hurting so bad. I wished Vina were here to give me a hug and hype me up for trashing Tristan's place.

I wiped the tears rolling down my cheeks and stared at my room; it looked like a luxurious hotel suite. The smell of lavender in the air was comforting. The bed was wide, and the tall glass wall had a picturesque view from where I lay. There was a blue velvet couch at the end of the room and a walk-in closet next to the bathroom. A dressing table stood across the room with a tall mirror resting on the wall. A small desk was next to the nightstand. The walls were bare, except the large screen TV mounted on the wall opposite the bed.

I couldn't stay here, but again, I had nowhere to go, and my broke ass wouldn't be able to accommodate me for one night in a hotel. I wasn't prepared to live on my own, to handle the bills and adult responsibilities. This was not how I'd planned to leave home. I still had a lot to learn.

I buried my face in the pillow and cried. I screamed into the puffy pillow, punching it like it could ease my pain. I cried deeply, to the point that I started gasping for air. I heard a knock on the door, but I ignored it. I kept sobbing until I went to sleep.

THE LOUD KNOCK from the background woke me up with a frown. I was ready to yell at Ciara to get lost when I took in my surroundings, and everything came flashing back, like a movie. I asked the person knocking to come in. Tristan walked in with a small gift bag. I groaned and rolled my eyes.

"What do you want?" I questioned, already irritated by his presence.

"Did you sleep well?"

"I did until you ruined it," I said.

"How are you feeling?" he asked, gesturing to my feet.

"Like you care." I sighed while sitting up.

"You're my responsibility now."

I scoffed at his statement.

"Sorry I broke your phone. I got you a new one." He pointed to the nightstand.

I picked up the gift bag from the corner. It had my old SIM card too. I brought out the new phone and examined it.

"Thank you," I said, feigning excitement.

I threw the new phone across the room, and I studied his expression. He sighed softly, mumbling something before looking up to meet my angry eyes. I stared at him, wishing I could read his mind. I badly wanted to understand the situation.

"You don't like it?"

"A phone is the least of my problems right now, Tristan."

"I know," he said, taking a seat on the bed. "I guess you can't really judge a book by its cover. This was not what I was expecting when I approached you."

"Took you twenty-eight years of your life to learn that?" I sneered.

He was silent as he stared at my bandaged feet like it was a unique design he was seeing for the first time.

"I'm really sorry. I know my apologies are useless, but I want you to know you will have your family back soon."

"You know there were many women in that church who would've happily played your dumb game," I pointed out, feeling infuriated again.

He smiled, and I painstakingly tried not to hit his face with my wounded foot.

"Why?" I asked for the millionth time. I needed answers.

"I couldn't do it, and she didn't want me to."

I was still clueless at his answer.

"Who?" I asked, and he said nothing. "What are you up to, Tristan?"

He stayed silent, not giving me anything.

"You know, I can just rush to the hospital, take a legit pregnancy test, and get your ass to court. I will demand your whole wealth if I get the chance."

Who was I kidding? I didn't even have the money for a lawyer.

"If you want money, I will give it to you, but I really need this to work."

"What to work?" I pressed.

He went mute and kept his eyes on my bandaged feet.

"You just destroyed my life. The least you can do right now is tell me why I'm involved in this shit."

"I will. I need some time."

"How much time are we talking about here?"

"A month."

"A what?" I gasped. "You want me to stay away from my family for a month? What if Grey finds another girl?"

"Then, he never loved you," he said coolly.

"No, I can't wait for a month. You want me to put my life on hold for you? I'm trying to keep my sanity, so you won't end up dead."

"Three weeks then."

"No."

He looked away from my right foot, frustration stretching his facial muscles.

"I have a life to live. You've enjoyed your twenties; let me enjoy mine."

He breathed deeply, staring at me. "Two weeks."

Two weeks for me to figure out my life. I could stay here. At least I had a roof over my head and a butler to feed me. I would leave once he told the truth and get a job and an affordable apartment to support myself. I could move into a dorm room on campus, but I didn't want a roommate.

"Two weeks? I can work with that."

"But within these two weeks, you have to promise not to destroy anything in this house."

"Sorry, I'm not good at keeping promises."

"Chloe," he sighed.

"I will try, but you'll end up disappointed."

"Does it hurt?" he asked, running the tips of his fingers over my bandaged feet.

"What do you think?" I kicked his hand away.

"I brought your prescription."

"How thoughtful of you," I said.

"I'm sorry it had to be you and sorry it turned out this way." He gave me a bottle of water and the small pills.

"What were you expecting to happen? For a baby bump to suddenly appear and for me to proclaim my love for you?" I mumbled and took a sip.

He stood up, heading for the door. He picked up the phone I had thrown away on his way out.

"Don't worry; I will give it to charity," I said quickly.

He shook his head before throwing the new phone on the bed.

"Tristan," I called, sitting upright.

"Yeah?"

"Two weeks. If you don't fix this after two weeks, I will bring this beautiful house of yours down, and I will haunt you day and night while you rot in jail," I threatened.

"Okay," he said, walking out of the room.

"Jerk," I mumbled, looking at my surroundings properly.

The view outside the ground-to-ceiling glass was spectacular. The pool glowed in the dark under the moon, and there was a beautiful garden a few feet from the pool. If only I could move. At least not everything was built in glass. There was a shiny wooden block joining some parts of the building for aesthetics, I assumed.

There was a knock on the door.

"Come in."

Morris walked in with his fingers folded together, and as usual, his white gloves were still on.

"Good evening, Miss Simpson. How are you feeling?"

I still couldn't place his accent.

"Please call me Chloe."

"I'm sorry, I can't, Miss Simpson."

"Whatever. Do you need something?" I groaned in frustration.

"Mr. Sanchester sent me to get you for dinner."

"I'm not hungry."

My stomach decided to betray me by grumbling. I forced a smile and nodded. He moved closer to carry me.

"No, I'm good."

There was no way I was allowing the old guy to carry me. I was worried about his age and health. He looked fragile, and I was not going to take the risk.

"Tell Tristan I want him to carry me to the dining room, not you."

"I assure you, I won't drop you."

"Thank you, but no."

"I insist, miss."

"No."

After giving me a long stare, he gave up and left.

It took a few minutes before Tristan appeared. He scowled and moved to the bed. I opened my arms with a wide smile, finding joy in tormenting him. He scooped me up bridal-style and left the room.

"How old are you again?" he asked as we descended the stairs.

I wrapped my arms around his neck, scared he might drop me.

"Six," I replied, and he grunted.

He looked down at my face, and I smirked at him. He shook his head and mumbled something under his breath. I stared at his bobbing Adam's apple, and then my eyes trailed to his face. He didn't deserve such beauty.

"Stop with the look."

"What look?" I asked, still staring.

"You're creeping me out," he said as I moved my face closer.

"Can I feel your stubble? I have never touched stubble."

"No," he said with his nose wrinkled in disgust, but I did it anyway to piss him off. He groaned in annoyance as I ran my palm up and down his rough stubble.

"So, this is what it feels like?" I whispered.

"You've had your fill." He moved his face away from my touch.

"You're still here?" I asked his annoying friend, who was waiting at

75

the dining table.

Thank God Tristan put me down gently. I'd felt like he might let go.

"Ouch. I thought you'd be happy to see me." Adrian faked a pained face.

I rolled my eyes, staring at the food in front of me.

"Are we celebrating the wreckage you caused in my life?" I eyed the expensive wine more than the mouthwatering food.

Adrian chuckled, and I noticed a dimple. Tristan arrived with three wineglasses.

"Pass me a napkin," Tristan requested.

"Say please," I said, and he sighed.

"Adrian, would you mind passing me a napkin?" he asked his friend.

"Sure, man. Here you go." He gave it to him while I scoffed and rolled my eyes.

I didn't know I was starving until I tasted the diced steak with mushrooms.

"Morris, this is delicious," I said, smiling at him.

He was standing two feet away, like he was waiting to receive orders.

"I cooked it myself. Not him," Tristan said, sounding annoyed.

"Really?" I stared at the food and then at him. I gagged.

"I was about to tell him the salt is too much and the steak is overcooked," I said, reaching for my glass of wine.

Adrian tried to suppress his laughter.

Tristan was about to say something, but his ringtone stopped him. His facial muscles tightened as he looked at me, and his lips formed a thin line. He turned away from me, picking up the phone.

"It's my mom," he said to Adrian, leaving the dining room to answer the call.

"How bad is the wound on a scale of one to five?"

"Hundred."

"Do you know those paintings you destroyed could have made you the richest person in the world if all the money was summed up?"

"Who cares?" I reached for the wine and refilled my glass.

"And those cups you broke were—"

"I don't wanna hear it. Are you trying to make me feel like the bad guy here?"

"Sorry," he mumbled with an apologetic smile.

Tristan returned, and we ate in silence. Morris cleared the dining room when we were done. I couldn't believe I was dining with the person who had made me homeless, but I guessed it was better than starving and sleeping on the street.

"Adrian will take you to your room," Tristan said, standing up. He seemed to be in a sour mood since he'd returned to the dining area.

"No, I want you to carry me, not him," I voiced.

Adrian's lips curved upward in amusement as he sipped the remaining wine.

"Do you want to crawl to your room or let him take you?"

"None of the above. You said it yourself; I'm your responsibility," I retorted.

"Fine."

I didn't like the sound of that. He moved fast to where I was and threw me over his shoulder like I was a piece of cloth.

"This position is uncomfortable," I groaned, his shoulder bones pressing into my stomach. "Tristan, put me down!"

The pain increased as he climbed the stairs. His lean ass was staring at my face. I thought of pinching it but stopped myself.

"You're hurting me. I'm going to throw up if you don't stop."

He said nothing.

"You're choking the baby," I said, but the only reaction I got from him was a small growl.

"I will fart on your face if you don't stop." I wished I hadn't said that. I was glad he didn't say anything.

I endured the pain and tried to breathe. I was relieved when we got to my room. He threw me on the bed, leaving the room before I could say anything.

"That was a bumpy ride." I massaged the sore spot on my stomach, lying in bed for a while.

I crawled to the bathroom and washed my face in the bathtub. It was impossible to have a bath. I felt crippled as I pushed myself up my bed. I thought of my family and Grey.

How did this happen? Why did I ditch my homework for a wedding?

I went to bed quicker than I'd expected, my tired eyes giving up.

CHAPTER **EIGHT**
MISERABLE

I stayed in bed the next day, ignoring every person who knocked on the door to check on me. I wallowed in my misery as I hugged the pillow.

Belvina wasn't answering my calls, my sister had blocked my calls, and my parents had ignored all my calls too. Grey's line kept going to voice mail. I'd left, like, five voice mails, asking him to call me back and allow me to explain.

Morris brought lunch to my room and dinner too. He was so sweet to me, and I was starting to warm up to him. He told me he was from Venezuela, which explained the accent.

"Where's Tristan?" I asked when he came for the dishes.

"He is busy with work in his study."

"Tell him I need his help."

"You're sure I can't help you?"

"Yes, Morris."

Tristan showed up later. Black jogger pants showed off his slim and long legs. His sweatshirt hugged his taut torso, filling every space that I could make out his abs.

"What's the problem now?" He sounded tired, but who cared?

"I need to brush my teeth."

He looked at me like I was stupid. "Seriously, Chloe?"

"I can't move or stand."

"What do you want me to do?"

"Carry me on your back while I brush."

"Are you kidding me right now?" He gave me an incredulous stare.

"No."

"You'd better make this quick. I have work."

"Well, you put me in this condition, so deal with it," I hissed.

He came closer, and I hopped on his back with a sly smile tugging at my lips. I wrapped my arms around his neck as we walked to the bathroom. I felt like I was four again—when many people had enjoyed giving me piggyback rides. I looked down at his blond hair; it was a confusing color with different tones, like gold mixed with honey. He pulled me up on his back as we stood in front of the large mirror.

"Could you please put the toothpaste on the toothbrush?" *Why did I say please?*

He glared at me through the mirror before doing it. I wrapped my legs tightly around his waist to avoid falling as he let go of my legs to put the toothpaste on my toothbrush.

His shampoo filled my nostrils as I placed my head on his neck; he smelled like sandalwood mixed with his aftershave. I was tempted to sniff his neck. He smelled so good. He gave me the toothbrush and stared at me through the mirror. He cut some paper towel and gave it to me. I placed the paper towel on his shoulder and started brushing with one hand while the other stayed around his neck.

"Try not to get that on me," he said with disgust.

"This is so ridiculous," he said, and I rolled my eyes, ignoring his complaints.

He leaned closer to the sink for me to throw my mess away. I laughed at how stupid the whole process looked in the mirror while he appeared like he was contemplating flinging me around the room and walking away.

"I'm done."

"What now?"

"Drop me on the counter. I will rinse my mouth from there."

"Really, Chloe? Why didn't you sit there to brush?" he asked, getting pissed.

"I never thought about it." I shrugged coolly and rinsed my face and my mouth, but I was grinning in my head.

He didn't wait for me to dry my face; he carried me back to the room.

He stood in front of me with his hands tucked in his front pockets. I could tell he didn't like this one bit.

"Anything else?" he asked.

"Can you fill the bathtub for me? I like it warm," I said with a grin.

He nodded and left the room. I thought of how to get into the bathtub without his help, but it seemed impossible since I couldn't walk.

I wished I had Vina here to help me take a bath. I could allow him to put me in the tub with my clothes on, but I would have difficulties taking them off since I had been advised not to put my feet in water.

"Done," Tristan said, walking back into the room.

"Um … so this is what we're gonna do. You're going to keep your eyes closed as you help me into the bathtub."

"How do you expect me to see where I'm going?"

"I don't know." I shrugged.

"Why don't I call my mom to come and help?" he suggested.

I was uncomfortable with the idea, but it wasn't like I had a choice.

"Okay." I nodded.

"Do you need anything else before I leave to call her?"

"Can you pass me my pajamas? It's in the black suitcase." I wasn't sure. I suspected Ciara had packed my things. The bitch couldn't wait to see me leave.

I needed to unpack these suitcases, but I couldn't stand on my feet yet. *Do I even need to unpack if I'm leaving soon?*

He walked to the black suitcase. I watched him unzip it, and my eyes grew wide when I saw my underwear and bras scattered at the top. I turned my face away and pretended to be looking for something on my nightstand.

Really, Ciara?

"It's not in the black suitcase." I heard him say. He sounded like he wasn't bothered.

"Oh, okay. Thank you for your services. I will take it from here," I said, not looking at him.

"What are you looking for?" he asked.

"My crystal earrings."

"You're wearing them."

I paused and nodded.

"Good night," I said with a firm smile.

He was still squatting in front of the suitcase, and it was still wide open. *Did he touch them?*

"I will check the other suitcases."

"No," I said quickly. Who knew what he might see?

"It's not my first time seeing a lady's underwear, Chloe."

I tried to act confused.

"This." He held up my small black bra and lace underwear.

The nerve of this guy.

"Oh, that. You can close the suitcase when you're done drooling over my undies." I tried to joke, but he acted like he hadn't heard anything.

"Can you please close the suitcase and leave?"

He did, but he walked to the other suitcases and searched for my pajamas. He threw them at me and left the room.

I grabbed one pillow. Covering my face, I screamed.

Tristan's mom arrived a few minutes later in her designer fur jacket and yellow dress. She smiled at me as she entered the room.

"I will take it from here, honey," she said to Tristan who stood at the doorway and waved him off.

"How are you, dear?"

"Miserable," I replied, not returning the smile lighting up her pretty face.

"I know, and I'm sorry you feel that way. I wish things hadn't turned out this way. Sorry about your family."

"Save me the apologies. It won't fix the damage your son has done."

"Love is not easy, dear," she said as she helped me take off my clothes.

"This isn't about love. I don't even know him!" I exclaimed, feeling the rush of anger.

She said nothing. I was sick of trying to explain myself to everyone.

She brought me a towel and pushed the wheelchair closer. She helped me get into the wheelchair and wheeled me to the bathroom.

She kept talking about Tristan as she helped me wash my body. I found myself crying as she washed my hair and hummed in a soft tone. Why was I missing my mom and wishing she were here for me instead? I was used to her lack of motherly affection, but I needed her to hold me and tell me she still loved me.

"Oh, dear, don't cry," Mrs. Sanchester whispered, stroking my hair and putting one arm around me in a hug.

I welcomed the hug. I desperately needed it.

"It's okay, dear. Things will get better, I promise," she whispered, and I tried to believe her.

BELVINA CALLED THE next day during breakfast. Tristan had left early for work, so Morris was at my service. I answered the call with a mouthful of omelet.

"Hey, Vina."

"Sorry I missed your call. How is it going with Tristan? Is he going to tell the truth?"

"Not yet, but soon. And I'm in a wheelchair."

"A wheelchair? Did he break your legs? *Ay Dios mio.* Should I call your parents or report it to the cops?"

I chuckled, choking on my food.

"Was that a joke?" she inquired.

"No, I'm really in a wheelchair, but it's nothing serious."

"How come?"

I gave her every detail of what had happened, even the suitcase incident.

"Go, girl!" she said in a singsong voice. I imagined her throwing one hand in the air. "So, you're, like, crippled?"

"Temporarily, yes."

"Make him pay, Chlo. Give him hell!" She hyped me up. "Did he really touch your underwear?"

"Uh-huh," I replied, and she laughed.

"Did he see the padded bra too?" she asked with a dramatic gasp.

"I stopped using that last year."

"Oh, what about the Hello Kitty cotton underwear?"

"Can we please not talk about this?"

"Fine. Have you tried taking the pregnancy test again?"

"I threw it away. I need to get a new one, but my parents cut me off."

"I will buy three online and send them to you. Text me the address."

"You don't have to, Vee. I could just go to a clinic."

"We need to be sure you're not pregnant and how the hell the test came out positive."

"Okay, I will text you the address later. Thank you."

"Are you coming back to school?"

"Why wouldn't I?"

"Can you handle the stares and murmurs?"

"Yes, it's college. I don't think anyone will give a shit," I said dryly.

"Right, but I'm still worried since the news was all over the internet."

"I can handle it, Vee. So, tell me, what did I miss?" I asked eagerly.

"Can I call you back after my shift is over? Kelsey is already glaring at me," she sighed.

"Sure."

"Okay, bye."

"Bye," I said and hung up.

I groaned as I remembered my projects that were due on Wednesday. I spent the rest of the day on my projects. Thank God Ciara had packed them. How considerate of her.

I got tired and dozed off when I was done working on two essays for my English and Communication classes. It didn't take long before I heard a knock on my door.

I grumbled, trying to open my eyes. I succeeded and saw Adrian at the doorway to my room. He was leaning on the doorframe, smiling at me with his arms folded. *What a nice view. Am I in heaven?*

He wore black pants and a burgundy shirt that looked good on his fair skin. He had on large rings and gold chain necklace. His dark hair looked greasy.

I sat up with ease and brushed my hair back with my hand. "Are you lost?"

"No," he answered with a laugh. "I came to check on you."

"Oh, you've heard about the crippled girl."

"Yeah, does it hurt?" he asked with a smile.

"A little."

"Dinner is waiting. I will carry you."

"No, I want Tristan to do it."

"What are you afraid of? I won't drop you, I promise." He laughed.

"Nothing. This is Tristan's fault, so let him carry me."

"He is not well. You have no choice unless you want me to call Morris."

I'd told Morris this morning to stop bringing food to my room since the last one had dropped on the floor, and I'd had to watch him clean up the mess while I was unable to help.

"Fine," I sighed.

He walked to the bed with two long strides and scooped me up in his arms.

I regretted wearing a dress because his rough hand gripped my bare thighs, making it hard for me to concentrate on anything else. I decided to start a conversation to get my mind off the feel of him touching my bare skin.

"Do you live with Tristan?"

"No, but I hang out here a lot."

"Figured. Do you work for him?"

"We are business partners."

"So, you both own the company?"

"Yes."

I felt relief when we got off the stairs and headed for the dining room. Tristan was sitting at the dining table with all his focus on the tablet in front of him.

"You look well," I said as Adrian gently put me down on a seat.

"Actually, he is not sick," Adrian confessed. "He refused to do it, and since you don't like Morris carrying you, I decided to help."

I clenched my fists and my jaw, glaring at him.

"I'm tired, Chloe," Tristan grunted. I could tell from the dark circles beneath his eyes.

"I don't care. You're the reason I'm in this state, not him!"

"I will continue tomorrow. Let Adrian carry you." He dismissed me without looking at me.

"No," I disagreed.

He groaned and moved his tablet away, and then he looked at me. "Should I go on my knees and beg you?"

Was he really gonna do that? I mean, I wouldn't mind the gesture, but I was better than that.

I stared at Adrian. He was leaning back in his seat, watching with an amused grin as he took a bite from a strawberry.

"Okay, only tonight," I sighed, and Tristan breathed out in relief.

"You should have said yes. I really wanted to see him on his knees, begging." Adrian frowned, and Tristan glared at him.

"Do you guys drink wine at every dinner?" I asked as Morris filled our glasses.

"Yeah, it goes well with the food," Adrian said as he dished out the hot pasta.

I went for the Salisbury steak, sausage, and veggies.

Dinner was fun. Adrian made me laugh so much that I choked on my drink, but Tristan was too busy with work on his tablet.

Adrian carried me back to my room, but this time around, his hand didn't touch my bare skin.

"I need to brush my teeth," I said as he was about to put me down on the bed.

He took me to the bathroom, placing me on the counter next to the sink. He leaned on the counter, staring at me as I brushed.

"How did you feel when Tristan picked you?" he asked.

I spat out the paste in my mouth to answer him. "I thought he'd lost his mind or maybe it was wedding drama to amuse the congregation," I said and went back to brushing my teeth.

He laughed briefly and looked around the bathroom.

"I didn't see you at the wedding," I said.

"I was traveling. I returned that day and heard about everything."

"Did you know it was gonna happen?"

"Kinda."

I waited for him to say more, but he stayed quiet. *He knew Tristan was going to ruin his own wedding?*

I rinsed my mouth and leaned down to the tap to wash my face. Adrian moved closer, holding my hair back.

"Thanks," I said, washing my face.

"Nice birthmark."

"It's not a birthmark, but thanks." I didn't want to talk about it. "Please pass me the face towel."

I dried my face, and he took me back to my room. He slowly put me on the bed and stood in front of me.

"What's up with Tristan? Anything you wanna share?" I asked.

"It's not easy for him right now, but he'll tell you soon."

"Yeah, he has eleven days." I had the date marked on my phone's calendar and also an alarm set for that day.

"I'm sorry about your family," he said softly, taking the space next to me on the bed.

"Whatever," I mumbled, staring at my feet.

"I know there is so much you want to ask, but if you want to talk, I'm here." he said and nudged me playfully.

I smiled and stayed quiet.

"I still find it unbelievable that your family kicked you out. If they cared even a little bit, they would be next to you even if the whole lie were true. I can't imagine what you're going through. The people you needed the most in a situation like that abandoned you and …" He paused. "Chloe?" he called, touching my chin and raising my face. "Shit, I didn't mean to make you cry," he sighed and brushed the tears away with one swipe of his thumb.

"It's not you," I whispered and looked down at my hands again. "It still hurts every time I think of it. How they shut the door on me like I was a stranger to them. It's the worst feeling ever—to feel unwanted, unloved, and be treated like you are not enough. My sister didn't even try to …" I paused, choking on my tears.

The memories whipped like acid on a gash. I sobbed, putting my face down. I didn't care Adrian was next to me or how vulnerable I appeared.

"Can I hold you?" he asked, and I nodded.

His long arm wrapped around my shoulders, and I snuggled closer, resting my head on his solid chest as I cried.

"I'm sorry," he whispered. "I wish things hadn't turned out this way," he said.

I felt his warm lips on my forehead and the soft brush of his fingers on my arm. It took a while before the tears stopped.

"I should leave you to get ready for bed," he said, pulling away.

I fought the urge to drag him back. Everything about him was just comforting—from his voice to his smile and kind gestures.

"Yes." I nodded, wiping the leftover tears away.

"Please, don't cry again. Even if you make the cutest sounds, I still hate seeing tears on your face. You're enough, Chloe. Don't ever doubt that. Good night." He smiled and walked out of the room while I sat there, thinking about his last words.

"Good night, Adrian," I managed to let the words out after he'd left.

CHAPTER **NINE**
BRUISES

I could still feel the smile on my face after Adrian walked out of my room. It was too soon to be getting comfortable with anyone, especially someone related to the asshole who had stolen my life away from me. Adrian was sweet and had been so nice to me since I'd gotten here, but I didn't want to read too much into it.

I'd allowed him to see me cry like a baby and opened up to him about how broken I felt about my family throwing me out, and honestly, I felt lighter, as if a weight had been lifted off my chest. I guessed I never asked myself why my family had given up on me so easily.

I missed Grey. I wanted to hate him and stay mad at him for believing everything that had gone down in the church, but I wanted us to talk. He still refused to answer my calls or my texts.

I looked around, searching frantically for my phone to call Vina. I wanted to talk to her about Adrian. Maybe she would knock some sense into me and tell me not to warm up to him because he couldn't be trusted.

"Where is the stupid phone?!" I screamed in frustration.

I found it under the duvet and quickly dialed her number.

"Pick up the phone, Vina." I dialed again, but she didn't answer the call.

I grunted, burying my face in my palms. I groaned again, not sure what I was really afraid of.

A light knock on my door made me jump.

"Chloe, are you awake?" I heard Tristan's voice.

I reached to turn off the lamp, but the door opened. I pulled my hand away and stared at him.

"Why are you staring at me like that?" he asked, cocking his naturally carved eyebrows. He folded his arms and leaned on the doorframe, waiting for an answer.

"What do you want?" I asked, not looking at him. I hated his presence. Every time I saw him or heard his voice, I felt enraged, and I just wanted to ram my fist through his face.

He shook his head at my question and walked into the room.

"I didn't invite you in," I said, shooting him a glare.

"Why aren't you dressed for bed?" he asked, ignoring my anger.

"I was busy."

"Doing what?"

"Playing sudoku."

He chuckled, shaking his head.

To be honest, I despised that game. I could never understand it. My mom used to force my sister and me to play it; she'd said it was good for the brain.

"Do you need help with anything?" he asked, stopping a few feet away from the bed.

I admired his white sweatpants, wishing I could have them. I looked away and met his deep blue eyes.

"I thought you were tired?" I said, leaning back on the headboard.

"Yeah, but you're in my care so—"

"I'm good," I cut in.

"Okay, good night."

"I wish I could say it back, but right now, I'm just wishing you would roll off the bed and slam your face on the floor while sleeping."

He laughed softly, shaking his head at my comment. "Good night, Chloe," he said, smiling.

I hated myself for making him laugh and putting a smile on his face. Was I a bad person for wishing he never found happiness or anything to make him smile? I just wanted him to be miserable like I was—maybe worse.

I breathed out in relief as he turned to leave. He suddenly stopped, turning around. I gave him a questioning look.

"Are you sure you don't want me to help you with anything?"

"Yes," I said, waiting desperately for him to leave.

"If you need anything, let me know or tell Morris."

"Wait," I said quickly before he could walk out of the room. "I wanna go out for a walk."

"It's almost midnight."

"I feel incarcerated here. I wanna go out," I said, and he stared at me for a while, saying nothing. I needed some air and wanted to be away from this room. Maybe I could persuade him into telling me the truth about why he'd stop his wedding.

"Okay."

He walked to the bed and carried me in his arms downstairs. He placed me on the couch and went upstairs to get the wheelchair. He wheeled me outside the house.

We walked down the sidewalk in silence, the tall trees lining the pathway. The cars driving by left a burning smell of gasoline mixed with dust in the air. The moon and stars cast their light down on the earth, caressing my skin with their soft glow. The sound of the wind rustling the leaves and the insects chirring in the trees echoed around us.

"I'm sorry things turned out this way, Chloe," Tristan said after a while.

"If you are, why do you keep allowing the gossip to grow?"

"I never wanted this," he said, his tone coming out a little harsh.

"You won't tell me anything, so how am I supposed to understand what is happening?" I almost yelled. "I lost everything because of you, so do not expect me to sympathize with you on whatever you have going on. I want everything to return to how it used to be," I said, enraged.

I didn't care if I returned to my imperfect family or a mother who treasured her reputation more than her kids or the ignorant father who agreed to everything his wife said.

"I'm working on it," he said, and I scoffed.

"That's all you keep saying. At least tell me why you destroyed your wedding. How are things between you and Sofia? I'm sure she's desperate to slit your throat. I wouldn't mind giving her a hand."

The wheelchair came to a stop.

"Why are we stopping?" I looked back at him, and he was fuming with a clenched jaw.

"What?" I asked.

"Drop the jokes."

"I'm saying nothing but the truth. Sorry you're triggered." I tried not to smile.

"I need to get you inside. It's chilly outside," he said, turning the wheelchair around.

"I'm not complaining," I said, but he kept going.

We went back into the house, and he carried me to my room.

"I need to check your feet to be sure the stitches didn't open," he said after putting me on the bed.

"I'm fine," I said, not looking at him.

"I told you, you're my responsibility," he said, crouching in front of me.

"It's late, and I need to sleep," I said and tried to lie down, but he held my legs.

"There is a bloodstain on the bandage. Let me take a look," he said. "Please," he added when I tried to pull my legs away.

I sat up and allowed him to check the stitches. He left the room to get a first aid kit.

Tristan returned and unwrapped the bandage. I stared at the wall the whole time. The silence in the room was deafening. I didn't even know what he was thinking right now.

"I understand you're upset. I regret what I did, and I wish it were easy to fix the mess I made, but you need to stop with the jokes."

"Would you like to trade spots? Maybe you'd understand what it feels like to lose everything," I said, gripping the sheets.

"I know what it feels like to lose everything," he mumbled quickly.

"Sure," I scoffed.

He packed the first aid kit and left the room.

I sighed and lay in bed. I picked up my phone and decided to text Belvina. I sent, like, twenty texts with crying emojis.

My RINGTONE WOKE me up early the next morning. I searched for my phone with my hand half-asleep and found it close to my pillow. I was able to locate the answer button with my eyes closed.

"Hello?" I mumbled.

"You met Adrian Parker!" Vina's voice knocked the sleep out of me.

I groaned, opening my eyes. They lingered on the horizon. I had never been this grateful for a glass wall. The soft glow of the sun peeking from the east and illuminating the sky, blending perfectly with the deep orange and gentle purple color of dawn, was magnificent. I couldn't resist staring at it. It took me a minute to realize Vina was on the phone.

"Huh?" I mumbled and sat up, leaning on the headboard. "Wait, how did you know his last name?" I asked.

"I have known him since I hit puberty," she said in a *duh* kind of way. I rolled my eyes as if she could see me.

"Remember the hot guy on those magazine covers, who I had a mega crush on?"

"Yeah … wait, it's this Adrian?"

"Yes."

I didn't know how to feel about that. She'd had a crush on him. She'd even stalked him on social media. I remembered how she'd always kept herself busy with sport and business magazines, just reading about him and staring at his pictures. She'd had posters of him on her wall and made him a scrapbook.

"You'll be happy to know he is twenty-six. He was a popular swimmer before going into business school, and he dated—"

"I'm not interested."

"Oh, come on. He is hot and very attractive."

"You can have him."

"I'm so jealous you get to be in the same room with him." She groaned. "At least you have someone that hot to keep your mind off that *cabrón.*"

"I'm not looking for a rebound, jeez. I called you, so you could convince me not to trust him and that he is no good, like you always do when those creeps try to hit on me."

"That's blasphemy," she gasped.

I rolled my eyes and scoffed.

"Vina," I groaned.

"Sorry, but what are you so afraid of if he is as nice as you say?"

"I don't know. He seems like a friendly person, but I'm scared it is just a facade to cover up Tristan's ass."

"Is that all?"

"Grey," I confessed.

"Look, let Grey believe whatever he wants, but you need to move on. What he did was very stupid. You don't wanna return to someone who is quick to believe what people say about you."

"I just wanna talk to him."

"Your choice. Do whatever your heart wants," she said before mumbling something in Spanish, which sounded like an insult.

"So, what about Adrian?" I asked.

"Keep up the friendship. He might snitch on Tristan. Don't get too comfortable though."

"I swear you have the answer to everything," I praised her.

There was a knock on the door immediately after I finished my sentence.

"It's open!" I screamed.

I was expecting Morris to open the door, but it was Adrian. He gave me that charming smile and asked if he could come in.

"He's here," I whispered into the phone.

"Adrian Parker is in front of you?!" Vina screamed loud enough for him to hear.

Adrian cocked a brow at me. I forced a smile and put the phone down, ending the call.

"Hi," I said, sitting upright.

He wore a navy-blue two-piece suit with sharp creases, his hair was perfectly styled at the front, and he looked like a modern-day prince. As usual, he had on his rings and chain necklace that contrasted with his suit and dress shirt.

"Were you just talking about me?" he asked jokingly.

"No," I denied. My phoned chimed with numerous texts from Vina. I pushed the phone under my pillow with a tight smile.

He walked in. His eyes moved to my feet. "How is it?"

"Getting better, I guess," I sighed.

"Did you have a good sleep?"

"Yeah, you?"

"Splendid."

Good for him. It had taken me forever before I could get any sleep.

"Thanks for last night; it was nice to have someone to talk to."

"It's fine," he said with a soft smile, indenting his dimples.

"Why are you here? Aren't you supposed to be at work?" I asked.

"Tristan said he's too tired to drive, and since Morris has to be here for you, I'm his only choice."

"Or his lazy ass could get an Uber," I said.

"Nice idea. I'll tell him."

"I love your suit," I admitted, unable to hide the truth.

He had a unique style, and I would pay to see his wardrobe.

"Really? Now, I'm never taking it off," he said.

"Oh, please." I laughed.

"I will take you down. Tristan is still not well."

"Liar, but this is the last time you're helping him." I didn't even want to be close to Tristan after our conversation last night.

"Yes, ma'am," he said with a bow.

"I might ruin your beautiful suit." I frowned.

"It's okay. I always carry an extra set with me."

"Oh."

He gathered me in his arms like I weighed nothing, and we left the room.

"Your cologne is addictive. Is it weird for a female to use men's perfume?" I asked.

"Thanks, and no, I find it sexy. It's like wearing his shirt."

"Right. I guess you don't mind bringing me your cologne."

"Chloe Simpson, are you flirting with me?"

"You wish." I hit his shoulder, and he laughed.

"Fine, I will bring it to you. Is there anything else you need from me?"

"Yes, your dimples."

He laughed as we got off the last step. Morris was setting breakfast on the dining table when we arrived. The table was loaded with different breakfast items, so it was hard to decide what to eat. There were pancakes, waffles, French toast, bagels, Greek yogurt, bacon, sausage, vegetable salad, scrambled eggs, fruit salad, and Morris kept bringing more to the table, like we were about to have a feast.

"Good morning, Miss Simpson."

"Morning, Morris," I said chirpily.

"How are you feeling?"

"I'm good."

He gave me a smile and left for the kitchen.

"Mmm, waffles," I moaned.

I heard footsteps behind me, and I knew it was Tristan.

"Thanks for coming, man." Tristan's deep voice made my head turn around; he didn't spare me a look. He took the seat in front of me.

"Aren't you going to ask me how I'm doing? I'm in pain, you know," I said to Tristan.

"How are you, Chloe? Did you sleep well?" he asked monotonously.

"No, my body aches because my feet wouldn't allow me to sleep properly because you wrapped it too tight," I said.

"Morris will take you to the spa after breakfast," he said and started eating.

"I'm bored," I said. I saw his grip tighten around the fork.

"Go shopping or watch a movie."

"I don't want that."

"Then, what do you want?" he asked.

"Breakfast." I smirked and started to eat. I took a glance at Adrian and found him smiling.

"I bought you something," Adrian said, dropping a gift box in front of me.

I took it hesitantly. Wasn't it too early to be getting each other gifts? I untied the red ribbon and picked up the peach box inside. It had *Affirmations* written on the top. I opened the box and picked up the first card—self-love.

"Thank you." I smiled and put the gift aside. *Is the gift because of my breakdown last night?*

"I also got you this because I know you're dying to punch his face," he said, giving me a small pillow with Tristan's face.

"I customized it just for you." He winked.

Tristan pretended not to notice anything. I laughed as I took it from Adrian. "I hope it survives and lasts the day," I said, and Adrian laughed.

I looked back at Tristan. He wore a black wool suit with a silk black tie on top of his white long-sleeved dress shirt. His hair was neatly combed to the back. It looked good on him.

I noticed some exposed bruises around his right wrist. There was also a little cut close to the back of his palm. I wondered what had happened.

When he caught me staring, he pulled his sleeve down, covering it. I looked up, and our eyes locked. He gave me a weird stare at first and then concealed it with a smile. He looked away, facing Adrian, and they started talking about a board meeting.

I watched him for a long time before taking my eyes off him. I was starting to have a bad feeling about staying here.

CHAPTER **TEN**
UNEXPECTED

I spent my afternoon in my room, doing my last project. Morris came every thirty minutes to check on me.

After following up with a doctor, we went back to the hospital and had my stitches removed. My feet felt better. No pain, and only a few scabs were left behind. We took a walk down the hallway to exercise my legs. I felt like a baby taking her first steps; it was a weird feeling at first, but then I got used to it and began to walk on my own with no help. I was relieved I could finally return to school. I had missed a lot.

I got my things ready for the next day and watched monkeys doing adorable stuff on a geographical channel. Adrian didn't show up that day, so I was stuck with Tristan, who made me a little uneasy after the bruises I had seen a few days back.

I wanted to know what was going on in his head. There was just something about him. He seemed to be in a world no one was part of. He had been avoiding me since he'd caught me staring at his wrist during breakfast. He was only available when I needed him to carry me around.

I had gone days without even seeing him in the house. It was like I was living with a ghost. And when I got the chance to see him, he looked annoyed by my presence and wouldn't even speak to me. Sometimes, he stayed in his room the whole day and left for work before I woke up. He didn't like being around me. The feeling was mutual anyway. It just made me curious about his reasons. Only a few days left, and I'd be out of there.

I had always wanted to live on my own, but now, I was terrified as I thought of what my life would be like when I left here and got my own place.

"*I choose to release the past and look toward the good that awaits me,*" I whispered to myself as I read the affirmation card. I took a deep breath and stared outside the glass wall, savoring the sun's scorching rays.

I was deceiving myself with those words. I really didn't know what to expect after I left here.

THE PREGNANCY TESTS arrived on Tuesday. Vina had ordered them late. I called her on FaceTime as I opened the package. She was at her workplace but stepped outside to answer the call.

"You bought five?" I asked as I brought out the packets.

"Yeah, all from different companies."

I shook my head and laughed at her. I followed the directions and took all five tests. I set a timer and waited anxiously for the result. Vina told me about her encounter with an annoying customer and how she almost got fired for talking back and cursing him in Spanish.

My heart skipped when the timer beeped. I approached the counter where all five tests were lying.

"What do they say? Let me see," Vina asked.

"One line means negative, right?"

"Yes."

"It's all negative." I sighed in relief and showed her. For a moment, I'd thought they would come out positive. Wasn't that the weirdest feeling ever? To be scared of being pregnant when you hadn't seen a dick in three years?

"How long did you wait for the last one to read?"

"Three minutes."

"And it turned positive later?"

"Yeah, I don't know how. It was negative when I gave it to Ciara, but when I came down, it was suddenly positive."

"That's weird."

"Should I take a picture and send it to my parents?" I asked, feeling a little bit hopeful.

"They might think it's fake. Tristan is the only one who can clear this mess right now."

I sighed and sat on the floor. "Do you think they will believe him?"

"He started it, so why not?"

"I want them to know I have really changed. It sucks when people judge you based on your past mistakes and won't believe you are no longer the person they think you are," I mumbled.

"I believe you, Chlo."

"Thank you." I smiled.

"Gotta go before I give my boss another reason to fire me."

"Okay, I will talk to you later."

I ended the call and sat down there for a while, just thinking about my family and how my past had come back to haunt me.

I STARED AT Tristan's wrist during dinner, and the bruises were gone, but the cut was still visible. My eyes trailed up his exposed arms from his muscle shirt.

"How did it go at the doctor?" he asked, drawing my attention away from his wrist.

I was surprised he'd asked. He'd probably done it to distract me. I was certain he didn't care. Once he was done with whatever he wanted to do with me, he wouldn't bat an eye before kicking me out.

"It went well."

He nodded and kept staring at me. He looked away when Morris came to serve him some salad.

What is his secret? Why destroy your wedding? I asked myself, still staring at him.

Tristan was a handsome being, too hunky for my liking. I hated that he was good-looking. My eyes couldn't help but stare sometimes. I would picture him as Shrek from now on.

"If you don't feel like eating, then leave," he said, looking pissed.

"Are you talking to me?" I asked, looking around me.

He said something beneath his breath and continued eating.

"Are you by any chance having an affair? Is that why you stopped the wedding? And when you didn't find your mistress in the church, you picked me?" I asked, leaning closer on the table. "Are you still seeing her? Does she know about me? I demand an apology from her right now," I said, hitting the table to get his attention.

"Oh God," he grunted, biting on his inner lower lip and dropping his spoon.

He grabbed a napkin and dabbed at his lips as if there were a stain. He took a sip from his water and leaned back on the seat with an aggravated sigh. He gave me a hard glare and stood up.

"I will have my breakfast in my room tomorrow morning," he told Morris and headed for the stairs.

"Thanks for the chicken!" I yelled after him as I took it from his plate. "And tell your lover I'm waiting for her apology!" I added.

I smiled coyly at Morris, who was trying not to laugh.

I can't wait to get out of here.

To be honest, I was nervous about going back to school. Morris gave me a warm smile when he pulled onto Hills Avenue and parked the car in front of the college building. The blue color of the University of Beverly Hills logo brought memories of orientation week. I recalled when Belvina and I'd gotten lost on the large campus and ended up in the boys' locker room. We had gone red when we ran into five naked guys under the shower. We'd laughed about it for days and avoided the football team when school started.

Belvina and I were still freshmen; this was our second semester at UBH.

"What time do you finish?" Morris asked as I picked up my tote bag.

"Five thirty. I have two lectures today."

"Okay, have a nice day, Miss Simpson."

"You too, Morris." I got down from the car and headed for the entrance.

No one spared me a glance. I was relieved but paranoid.

At least not everyone was interested in some stupid gossip. I knew what had happened in the church was all over social media, and maybe

I was stupid to return to school while the subject was still trending. But I had missed out on important lectures and tests. I couldn't let what people think of me stop me from completing my education. Vina had advised me to drop the class this semester, but my whole effort on my previous tests and homework would have been useless.

"Hey!" Belvina screamed, waving at me.

I smiled as I ran to her and then gave her a rib-breaking hug.

I'd missed her so much. She was the only sensible person who believed me.

She hugged me back tightly, and it lasted longer than I'd expected.

"You smell so good. I don't want to let go," she grunted.

"I missed you too," I said, pulling away while she frowned.

Her large curls were wrapped in a small silk scarf that matched her tube top. The skirt stopped above her knees, showing off her small legs.

"Is it just me, or is your skin glowing?" Vina asked, smiling at me.

"Oh, please, my skin has always been like this."

We walked into our lecture hall and took our seats. The hall was almost full.

"How is Adrian?" she whispered, nudging me with her shoulder like she was dancing.

"Get lost." I pushed her back, and she chuckled.

"Is she still allowed to come to school after what she did?" I heard someone whisper behind me.

I knew that voice; it belonged to Claire Bluewater. Our parents were kind of close, but Claire and I were the opposite.

"I can't believe she's pregnant," her friend Erin added.

"Of all people, her sister's best friend? How shallow," Claire said, close to my ear.

No one in the class cared, but Claire and Erin planned to ruin my day. I tried not to let their words get to me. They were just trying to get a reaction.

"Good thing her parents kicked her out," Erin said, and they laughed.

I clenched my fists and snapped my head around. They both went quiet and stared back at me … waiting.

"Do you mind? I'm trying to study here," I said, smiling.

They whispered something into each other's ears and laughed.

I stood up, ready to beat the living daylights out of them, but our professor walked in.

"Try and calm down. Don't let them get to you," Belvina whispered, squeezing my arm in assurance.

No one seemed bothered about anything going on, but I still felt like everyone in the room was judging me and whispering. My stomach ached, and I wanted to throw up.

"Morning, class." Professor Clark waved. He smiled at us as he went behind his desk.

"Morning, Professor Clark," a few people greeted.

"How is everyone doing?" he asked as he turned on the projector.

Some replied while others remained quiet.

He always reminded me of Courage the Cowardly Dog. Something about the way he spoke.

"Watch and see. She might have a thing for Professor Clark," Erin whispered to Claire, loud enough for me to hear.

"Yeah, I mean, he's hot," Claire said close to my ear again.

Belvina held me back when I wanted to turn around.

There was no way I could attend this class. Erin and Claire were driving me crazy. If Vina wasn't holding me back, I would've turned around and rearranged their faces with my fists.

"I will use your notes later," I told Belvina, standing up.

She nodded, sending a killer look behind her. Claire and Erin smiled in return.

I could feel every eye on me as I walked down the aisle to Mr. Clark, who was engrossed in the computer in front of him.

"I'm not feeling too well," I said to Mr. Clark.

He waved his hand in dismissal without looking at me. I tried to calm down as I walked down the large, slightly crowded hallway.

Someone yanked my arm from behind and pulled me to a hidden corner. I was pushed to the wall so hard that my back hurt. Great, it was Ralph, Sofia's little brother, who shared a class with me. He had once been obsessed with me and tried to make me date him, but I'd turned him down.

"You slut!" he snarled.

What a misogynist.

"Ralph, let go."

"You ruined my family. You think you're gonna get away with that?"

I wasn't sure if this was just about Sofia. This was his opportunity to hurt me for turning him down a couple of times in the past.

"Is that why you refused to date me? Because you're into older guys?"

There you go.

"Ralph, let go!" I tried to push him off, but he pressed me harder to the wall.

"You disgust me." He spat on my face.

I wanted to knee him in the crotch, but he saw it coming and dodged it.

"Nice try." He pressed my body to the wall. "I just want to squeeze that thing growing inside of you." He poked my stomach with one finger. It was a brutal poke that felt like he was stabbing me. It hurt.

"Do you know what my sister is going through? She won't stop crying, and when she's in a bad mood, she won't stop shopping. Because of you, my family got humiliated." His nails dug into my skin with a clawing grip.

"Ralph, stop." I wished I could free my arms and leave a fist mark on his ugly face.

"I don't care." He pressed me harder to the wall.

"Let her go, Ralph," Grey shouted from the corner.

"You still wanna be on her side after what she did to you?"

Grey stepped closer and pushed him away from me. I adjusted my top and stared at both of them with tears at the corners of my eyes.

"Don't be a fool, Ashton. She used you," Ralph said.

"Leave her alone and don't touch her again," Grey warned. "Leave," he told Ralph.

Ralph glared at me and left.

"Be careful," Grey said to me and walked away without looking back at me.

"Grey, wait," I called, but he didn't stop.

I thought of going to file a report against him but changed my mind. I stared at Grey as he walked down the hallway and disappeared into a room. He was the last person I'd expected to come to my rescue.

I held my tears and made my way to the exit. Morris was surprised when I called him. He didn't ask me anything during the ride to Tristan's place, and I appreciated that.

I cried throughout the ride. Morris kept glancing at me through the rearview mirror. He gave me a white handkerchief. We walked in silence into the house, and I could tell Morris wanted to ask me something from the way he kept opening his mouth and closing it.

"Can I have a bottle of vodka and a knife?" I asked.

"A knife?" His eyebrows rose.

"Yes." He hesitated for a while before going to the wine cellar.

I waited impatiently at the dining room. I was frustrated I couldn't live a normal life again and scared of what people now said behind my back.

Morris brought everything I'd asked for, but he looked reluctant as he gave it to me.

"Don't worry about me," I said with a weak smile.

Tristan needed to feel my rage, the pain, and everything that had come with his lies, but how much damage did I have to do to make him feel those emotions? He deserved worse.

"Where is Tristan's room?" I asked, gripping the knife tightly.

He was quiet, not willing to tell me. I furrowed my eyebrows at him, urging him to answer.

"The room to your left."

"Thanks." I sniffed, heading for the stairs.

CHAPTER **ELEVEN**
ALCOHOL

I walked into Tristan's pitch-black room. I searched for the light switch and turned it on. His room lacked color. The gray painted walls looked dull to me. I'd read on the internet that the color of your room matched your mood. It was spacious and had a good view of the yard from the floor-to-ceiling glass wall. I could hear the birds chirping outside. I imagined they were rooting for me.

I searched for his closet and found it next to the bathroom. It was a huge walk-in closet that could fit a hundred people. I walked in with a malicious grin on my face. They said actions spoke louder than words.

I brought out my phone—the one I'd told Tristan I would give to charity, but I'd kept it for myself. I guessed he had seen me using it and refused to fix my old phone. I blasted "IDGAF" by Dua Lipa and stretched my arms. His clothes were neatly arranged, ranging from different colors, brands, and styles.

I ran the tip of the knife through the walls as I walked around the large room, as if I were marking my territory. This was going to take a long time. I held the knife in my hand and thought of where to start—his suits.

I sang along to the lyrics as I ran the knife through his crisp shirt. I danced and took shots from the bottle of vodka as I let out my anger on his clothes. I cursed when a few drops of the alcohol spilled on my shirt.

I ripped his clothes with the knife. Not all of them because I got tired. I slumped on the floor in the walk-in closet and sobbed. I could still feel Ralph's hands on me. I could still hear Erin and Claire's voices in my head.

After a while, I wiped my tears away and stood up. If there were an easy way to rip out Tristan's heart, I would have done it. I could use this knife and slice his heart into tiny pieces, spice it, cook it, and give it to his family as a gift.

I stripped and grabbed one neatly folded sweatshirt. I tossed my stained shirt to the floor and put on the sweatshirt. I was tempted to inhale his intoxicating scent. The red sweatshirt was comfy. I walked out of the closet with the bottle of vodka. I sat down on the floor and leaned on the wall.

I opened the drink and took big gulps. Grabbing my phone, I browsed YouTube. The video was still trending, and it seemed to be the latest gossip. I braced myself and went through the comments. I needed to drown my sorrows. There were over ten thousand comments.

I had been called a whore, a big disappointment to my family, a greedy bitch, and some insults I hadn't even known existed. I was surprised to see some people hyping me up and telling me to go get the money and ignore the haters.

I took more gulps and laughed at some of the comments. They were so stupid. Had these people had any breast milk when they were little?

"Chloe!" I heard Adrian scream my name as the door rattled open.

I was scared the glass walls would break. Tristan rushed in with Adrian behind him.

"Thank God," Tristan said, relief lacing his worried voice.

They were both panting with their hands placed on their chests.

I guessed Morris had told them. I glared at them and took another swig. Adrian ran his palm down his face and walked past Tristan, who was leaning on the wall and staring at the ceiling.

I sipped more of the vodka, and I was starting to feel the effect in my body. I stood up with the knife and my eyes on Tristan.

"This is all your fault!" I screamed, running toward him with the knife but Adrian held me back.

"Let me go, Adrian!" I struggled in his arms.

"Chloe, calm down."

"Don't tell me what to do. He ruined everything for me. Just let me kill him. Please."

"You're drunk. You don't know what you're doing," Adrian said, tightening his arms around me as I struggled to break free.

"I don't care! I want him dead!" I yelled, clenching my facial muscles, but Tristan just stared at me blankly and stayed still.

"I hate you and your whole existence!" I said, yet Tristan still looked unfazed. I stopped struggling as the alcohol had my brain all tied up.

"Are you okay?" Adrian checked my body.

I forgot I was only wearing Tristan's sweatshirt, and from the way I had been struggling earlier, I was pretty sure they'd both seen the color of my underwear.

"Yeah," I slurred, still glaring at Tristan.

"You're sure you didn't hurt yourself?" Adrian asked, still looking for any sign of injury. "Give me the knife." He collected it from my hand.

I was starting to feel dizzy.

Tristan walked into his closet and returned with one ripped shirt to show Adrian. I giggled and picked up the bottle to take a gulp, but Adrian snatched it.

"That's enough."

I wanted to argue, but I slowly blacked out.

I WOKE UP with a stubborn headache and a groan. Adrian and Tristan were sitting on the couch in front of me, staring at me with a look my parents would give me when I did something bad.

I sat up, trying to recall what had happened. I rubbed my temple to ease the pain.

"How are you feeling?" Adrian asked.

I pulled the blanket to my waist and moved my long hair back, so I could see clearly.

"My head hurts." I hugged my legs and stared at them with my head resting on my knees.

Their suit jackets were nowhere to be seen. Tristan's sleeves were folded at the elbows while Adrian's first three buttons were undone.

"I will get you some aspirin," Adrian offered and left.

Tristan sat back with his arms folded, giving me a scrutinizing stare with narrowed eyes that were focused on me. Images of me ripping his clothes and running toward him with a knife replayed in my head.

"What happened at school?" He looked calm.

I didn't know if he was mad about his clothes, but if he was, then he was doing a good job of hiding it.

I thought of what had happened in the hallway. It still sent a chill through my body. I imagined if Grey had never shown up to stop that psychopath.

"Chloe," Tristan called, sounding concerned. "What happened?" he asked, but now, his voice was laced with solace.

"What do you think happened? Did you think everything was going to be fine? I could feel everyone judging me like I was a mistake. To sum it all up, some moron harassed me in the hallway," I screamed, tears tumbling down my tiresome cheeks as my headache tore me apart.

"Give me the name of that moron."

"It's Sofia's younger brother."

"Ralph," he acknowledged. "I'm pressing charges against him. Don't worry about him."

"Everything is so easy for you, isn't it?"

His jaw clenched at my words, and he avoided my eyes.

"If it were, you wouldn't be here," he said softly under his breath.

I sensed sadness.

Adrian entered the room with a glass of water and two pills.

"Thanks." I smiled.

Tristan and Adrian talked in a hushed tone while I took the pills. Adrian turned to look at me after they were done conversing in a low tone.

"So, are you going back?" Adrian asked.

"No. I thought I could handle it, but it's too much," I admitted.

"How about signing up for online classes? I will take care of the payment," Tristan suggested.

"I will have to check if late registrations are still open for online classes." I sighed. I couldn't bring myself to drop all my classes though. I was afraid I might not graduate early. It would be my first time taking online classes. I didn't know what to expect.

"I will look it up and see what I can do," I said.

"I will help you with that tomorrow if you want."

I smiled weakly at Adrian. He was too sweet.

"I'm really sorry, Chloe," Tristan said and left the room.

The expression on his face had been hard to read, but I knew he felt bad about what had happened.

"Did he hurt you?" Adrian asked.

"A little." I rolled up the hand of the sweatshirt and showed him the mark Ralph had left with his fingers.

"Tristan is going to kill him."

"I don't know what he would've done to me if Grey hadn't stopped him."

"Your ex?"

"Yeah, I was shocked too. But he didn't even look at me. I can't believe he still thinks all this is true," I said with a frown.

"At least he still cares."

"I guess so," I mumbled.

"Try and get some rest. I will see you tomorrow." He moved to the bed and placed a kiss on my forehead.

"Bye."

He left the room, and I stared into space, lost in my thoughts.

ADRIAN SHOWED UP the next day when I was having breakfast at the dining room. He wore a white T-shirt above his gray sweatpants. He only had two of his large rings on today and one thin gold chain around his neck.

He approached me with a small smile. I wanted to poke his dimples so bad.

"You're early," I said.

"I couldn't wait to see you," he said, walking behind me and hugging my back.

I inhaled his cologne and fought the smile tugging at my lips.

"How are you?" he asked close to my ear before pulling away.

"Bored." I frowned.

He brushed his full hair back and took a seat in front of me. He waited for me to finish eating before I went upstairs to get my laptop. We sat on the large sofa with my laptop on my lap while Adrian took the space next to me.

I was lucky to find a few spots in three classes. I had to email the instructors. I signed up for Sociology, Math, and Art. I didn't know how they offered Math online. I only hoped I could catch up with the lectures.

"Your classes start next week," Adrian said when we finished.

"Thanks for helping."

Not like it was anything difficult, but I needed his company.

"It was nothing," he said, waving it off with his hand.

"I will get some snacks. What drink would you like?"

"Water. I'm not a fan of sugar," he replied.

I rolled my eyes at his answer.

I went to the kitchen. Morris was out, and Tristan had not left his room today. Morris had taken his breakfast upstairs, and Adrian didn't seem worried, so I assumed he was okay.

Adrian was laughing uncontrollably when I returned with the snacks. I screamed when I realized what he was watching. I threw the snacks on the couch and grabbed my laptop. I had never felt more embarrassed in my life.

It was the first twerk video I'd made when I was sixteen. It was awful, horrible, and an eyesore. I still didn't know why I'd kept it. My butt didn't even shake. I resembled a mother hen in labor.

"Oh my God, was that really you?"

"No." I gave him a dirty look, clutching the laptop to my chest.

"Can I watch it again?"

"No. And that was an intrusion of my privacy."

"Sorry," he apologized, laughter slipping out of his lips.

"Stop laughing," I groaned.

He nodded, putting on a straight face. It didn't take five seconds before he started laughing again.

"I hate you." I threw the snacks at him.

We spent the afternoon together, watching a movie on my laptop. He left when it started to get dark.

Morris was already back and was fixing dinner. I texted Vina as I waited at the dining table. She had been worried sick about me yesterday, enough that she wanted to come over. She sent a hundred laughing emojis when I told her Adrian had seen my disastrous twerk video.

"Miss Simpson?"

"Yes, Morris?"

"Do you mind going up to call Mr. Sanchester while I set the table?"

"Don't worry about it. I will call him right away." I smiled.

"Thank you."

I skipped up the stairs to his room. I knocked on the door, but no one answered.

"Tristan?"

No answer.

"Are you in there? Can I come in?"

He didn't answer.

I opened the door and peeped inside; the room was dim. Only the light from the bathroom brightened the room a bit. I heard a grunt, then a bang, another grunt, and more banging.

"Tristan?" I moved slowly toward the direction of the bathroom. My heart was beating so hard.

I froze at the sight in front of me. Terrified wasn't close to what I felt at that moment.

CHAPTER **TWELVE**

COLD

I had my jaw down as I stared at Tristan aggressively punching the mirror in front of him. The cracks on the mirror increased as he punched more. I had never seen him this angry.

He grunted as he sent another punch that shattered the mirror into pieces. I gasped at the sound, but I covered my mouth with my palms, stopping anything from escaping my lips.

My eyes drifted to his bloody knuckles. I could see the cuts, and I knew some pieces of glass were stuck inside, so how was he enduring the pain?

I waited for him to stop since the mirror was broken, but he kept punching the wall. I didn't know if I should walk in and do something, but what if he decided to punch me? He was blinded by rage right now, and it was terrifying.

He paused and growled. He looked like he was in pain. Not physical pain, but something else. I could see the guilt on his face as he tried to hold himself together. He pushed the broken pieces to the ground and cursed. He ran his fingers through his hair in distress. Mumbling something, he gripped the edge of the counter tightly. Looking down at his knuckles, he hissed in pain.

I made up my mind to leave quietly. I took slow and quiet steps to the bedroom, trying to hold my breath, scared he might hear it and punch the life out of me.

I sighed in relief when I made it outside. Who was I living with? I rushed to my room, but I kept looking over my shoulder to see if Tristan was behind me. I was still freaking out from what I'd just seen.

I locked the door immediately after I was inside. I called Vina, and she picked up on the third ring. I shared everything with her. I trusted her with every cell in my body, and right now, it was important to tell her everything in case I mysteriously died here.

"Hey," she said tiredly.

"Were you sleeping?"

"Yeah, I was about to say yes to Shawn Mendes."

I rolled my eyes like she could see me. Her obsession with Shawn Mendes was exasperating.

"Did something happen?" she asked with a yawn.

"Yes, Vina."

"Did you kiss Adrian?"

"No, it's Tristan."

"You kissed Tristan! *Cállate.*" She gasped.

"I didn't kiss him. I saw him punching the mirror in his bathroom."

"So? I punch my mirror sometimes, too, when I hate my reflection."

"Do you punch it to the point that it shatters and your knuckles bleed?"

"No. I love my nails."

"That was what I saw. He kept punching the mirror until it shattered into pieces, and he didn't stop. He went on punching the wall." I waited for her to say something, but she was quiet, so I continued, "There was so much aggression. It was terrifying to watch, believe me. It was like he was mad at his reflection or the mirror. I don't know. It's hard to explain."

"Why would he be mad at something so beautiful? Did you try to stop him?"

"Were you even listening to what I said? He looked like he was ready to punch whoever got in his way."

"So, you just left?"

"What else was I supposed to do? Scream?"

"I think you're overreacting."

"Overreacting? I just saw someone using a mirror as his punching bag!"

"So, you think he is insane?"

"Yes. Did anything I just say sound normal to you?"

"Did he see you?"

"I hope not. I tried not to make any sound as I left."

"I'm sure it's nothing serious. People do crazy things once in a while. Remember when you tried to drown your neighbor's dog?"

It had been an accident, but no one was gonna believe that anyway. My neighbor twisted the story. I had only been a kid and what had happened was not my fault.

"You don't get it, do you?" I sighed, falling to my back on the bed.

"I do. What do you want me to say? Hide in your room? Call 911?"

"Forget it. I will call you tomorrow."

"I can only tell you to pretend you didn't see anything since he didn't see you."

"So, I should not talk to him about it?"

"No, just act like you saw nothing."

"Okay."

"Good night. Love you!"

"Love you too," I said.

I hung up and stared at my door. My stomach grumbled. I was hungry, but I wasn't ready to face Tristan yet. I sat up and thought of how to handle the situation. Should I skip dinner or ask Morris to bring it to my room? My stomach grumbled more. I groaned and stood up. Maybe he wouldn't show up for dinner; he'd be too busy cleaning up.

I left the room. I took a glance at his door before going down the stairs.

I stopped in my tracks when I saw Tristan at the dining room, eating, while Morris poured him some white wine. Images of him punching the mirror appeared in my head. I got myself together and walked to the dining table.

All I had to do was act like I had seen nothing. I took a seat with a fake smile on my face. He didn't look away from his food. He acted like I was invisible.

Morris served my food and poured me some wine. I stared at Tristan's knuckles that were now wrapped with a bandage.

I looked away from his hands and stared at his face. He stared back at me with a neutral expression. He turned his face away from me and took a sip from his wine.

"What happened to your hands?" I asked, pointing at his knuckles with my fork.

He gave me an icy stare as he chewed his food. I waited an eternity between each second as he gnawed. Finally, I watched him swallow, expecting him to say something, but he went back to scooping some macaroni and putting it in his mouth, ignoring me completely.

Did he know I had been in his room? Maybe Morris had told him

I went to call him for dinner.

I started eating, but the silence was killing me. I took a glance at Tristan and found him staring at me, but his expression was ambiguous. I had never seen him drowned in such stark ferocity. I met his curious blue eyes and waited for him to say something, but he didn't utter a word. Tristan was like a complicated puzzle—and I hated puzzles.

If he had something to ask, he should just spit it out. Insecurity wrapped me by the neck, clawing at my consciousness, when people stared at me for longer than ten seconds. I looked away and ate my food with caution since he was watching me. His stare was drilling holes into my skin. I could feel it.

"Why are you so nosy?" he asked.

I felt like my blood was about to freeze.

"Huh?" I mumbled, looking at him. I raised my eyebrows, pretending to be confused. My body thawed slowly as I embraced his words.

He grabbed his glass, finished his wine, and stood up. I stared at him as he walked away, leaving me a bit confused.

"That prick," I mumbled, returning to my food. I could eat comfortably now.

"Morris," I called once I was sure Tristan was far from earshot.

"Yes, Miss Simpson?"

"Did you tell Tristan I went to his room to call him for dinner?"

"No, miss."

"Thank you." I was relieved, but why had he called me nosy? I was sure he hadn't seen me.

I picked up my phone and called Adrian on FaceTime. I really needed to see his smile and hear his jokes—something to get my mind off the image of Tristan punching his mirror. I used one of the cups to support my phone. He picked up the call on the third ring.

I choked on my drink when I saw Adrian standing in front of me with only a towel around his waist. Water dripped from his hair and rolled down his outlined six-pack abs and broad chest. His skin looked so smooth and spotless, like a porcelain doll. A tattoo was inked on the left side of his chest.

He smiled at me as he dried his hair with a white towel. If I wasn't choking, I would've been drooling.

"I'm fine," I told Morris, who was rushing to help me. I drank the whole wine and exhaled.

"Are you okay now?" Adrian asked.

I looked at the screen of my phone and tried not to let my eyes wander.

"Yeah," I replied, and he smirked. Why would he answer the call if he was just coming out of the shower? Not like I was complaining. I loved the view.

"I will call you later when you're done dressing," I said breathlessly as my eyes caught his V-line. I tried not to imagine his towel falling off.

"Hang on," he said when I was about to end the call.

He left, and I used the opportunity to check out his room. It was beautiful and very spacious. The white walls didn't have any pictures or paintings, and the room decor was simple. He returned, wearing black sweatpants and a red muscle top that showed off his solid arms. Adrian wasn't all that muscular, but I could tell he was athletic from his lean build.

"All good?" he asked as he brushed his fingers through his wet hair.

"Much better." I would never get that hot image out of my head.

"What are you eating?"

"Macaroni and sweet sauce. Morris is just too good," I said, smiling at Morris, who smiled back.

"I just ordered Chinese food. I have been craving it since this morning."

"I just lost my appetite because of you." I frowned, and he laughed.

"You want some Chinese food too? I could bring some for you or place an order to the house."

"No, I don't wanna hurt Morris. Maybe another day," I said, winking at Morris, who laughed.

"Where is Tristan?" Adrian asked.

"He is acting like my sister when she is on her period."

"What happened?" he asked, laughing.

I told him everything including the mirror incident. He needed to know. Maybe he could come and speak to him.

"Shit!" I heard him mumble.

He looked away and whispered another curse.

"He is doing it again," he said under his breath, his face tense.

"Doing what again?"

"Nothing. I will call you back." He cut the call before I could open my mouth to say something.

I stared at my phone screen, feeling frustrated. I finished my food and left. I tiptoed to Tristan's door on my way to my room and pressed my ear to the hardwood door to listen to what was happening inside. I ran to my room when I heard footsteps approaching the door.

I locked my door and laughed at myself. I undressed and took my bath. I waited for Adrian's call, but an hour passed without a response. I decided to exercise for a while. I stared at the night sky horizon as I stretched my legs.

My mind drifted to Tristan. I had never been this curious about anyone—well, except Marshmello when no one had known what he looked like. I wanted to know what was going on with Tristan and why

Adrian had had that scared look on his face.

He'd said something about doing it again. Was today not the first time? What the hell was going on?

I took a glance at the wall clock; it was almost midnight. Why was I still waiting for his call? My throat felt dry, and I had no water in my room, so I left for the kitchen. I held my phone in my hand, just in case he decided to call.

I was on my way down the stairs when I heard Adrian and Tristan arguing.

I moved back on my tiptoes and stopped at a spot where I wouldn't be seen. I leaned on the railing to hear what they were fighting about.

"You think this is easy?!" Tristan yelled.

"I know it's not, but you can't do this in front of her, damn it! You need to stop."

"I don't know what to do, okay? I never wanted this."

"She is here. Somehow, it's going to work."

"It has to work; I want it to work, but I wish there were another way."

"I know. She only has …"

My ringtone shut him up. I stared, wide-eyed, at my phone. Why was Vina calling me so late? I knew I was already busted.

I shut my eyes and wished I could disappear. I cursed mentally and looked down at my phone.

I rejected the call and tried to pretend I was coming downstairs, but luck wasn't on my side. I missed a step, falling on the stairs, making a loud noise.

"Chloe?"

CHAPTER **THIRTEEN**
D-DAY

"Chloe?"

I swallowed the dryness in my throat before looking at Adrian, who stood at the foot of the stairs. My heart squeezed like I was about to be hanged. Tristan came rushing and stood beside him. He looked angry. He gave me a prolonged look with his jaw slightly hardened and his eyebrows creased together in an annoyed expression.

He shook his head and walked up the stairs. I thought he was coming to help me, but all I received was a grueling glare as he walked past me. I refrained myself from grabbing his leg and pulling him down. What a scene that would be.

I looked at Adrian's worrisome face as Tristan slammed the door, which left my ears ringing.

"I was on my way to the kitchen for a bottle of water. Clumsy me missed a step," I said, laughing humorlessly at myself. "When did you get here? I didn't expect anyone to be up at this time." I continued with my act. Someone should hand me an Oscar.

Adrian had a smile on his face. A knowing smile that told me he knew I had been eavesdropping on their conversation. At least he didn't look pissed, like Tristan.

"Can you stand?" he asked, resting half of his weight on the railing.

"I will try." I tried to stand, but my ankle wouldn't let me.

"That's a no then." He walked up to me.

My feet fluttered as his hands wrapped behind my knees. He picked me up and took me downstairs. He gently put me down on the sofa, squatting in front of me.

"Which ankle hurts?" he asked, looking up at me.

"This one." I moved my left leg to show him.

He wrapped his callous fingers around my ankle and gave it a squeeze. I yelped in pain and tried to pull my ankle away, but he held me tightly.

"Relax," he said, smiling. He massaged the spot softly. "How much did you hear?"

"I was only there for five seconds before my phone blew my cover."

He laughed softly. "So, you didn't understand anything we were saying?"

"No, I was trying to put the words together, but it made me more confused. I think I got a headache from all my effort." I sighed.

"I know," he said with a warm smile and stared at me as if he had more to say.

"Are you still hoping to get back with your ex?" he asked.

"No, I have decided to close that chapter and move on. My best friend was right. He tossed me out of his life like I was a stranger to him. It didn't take me long to realize how dumb I was, hoping to talk things out with him," I said, staring at my short fingers.

"I'm really sorry for everything," he said in a soft tone.

I glanced at him and looked away, not sure of what to say.

"Why is he mean toward me? I didn't ask for any of this," I said, getting angry.

"Um … Tristan …" He looked away, as if he was contemplating telling me. "He is in a tough situation right now, but it doesn't justify his actions. You were not meant to see that. It must have terrified you, but he is trying to get better." He turned to look at me when he was done talking.

I raised my eyebrows, waiting for more explanation.

"He has a lot going on. I will advise you to stay away for a while, but keep me posted if anything happens."

"A lot going on? Like mentally?"

He laughed softly and stood up without a comment. What were they not telling me?

"I should be on my way home now," he said, looking down at his wristwatch.

"It's almost one in the morning. You should go to bed," he continued.

"I can go to bed whenever I want," I said, annoyed.

He stared at me for a while without a word, and it made me uneasy. I raised my eyebrow at him.

"You mean a lot to him, Chloe. Wait for him. He will tell you," he said softly, taking a step closer and brushing a stray hair back. "Please be patient with him. I know he can be an ass," Adrian whispered, tracing my cheekbone with his thumb.

I leaned closer to his touch, which sent goose bumps down my arms. The spot burned and made it hard for me to breathe.

My throat went dry from the lack of distance between us. Was he feeling what I was feeling? He was supposed to be a crush, but it didn't feel that way anymore. I looked into his gray eyes that stared back at me, searching. His eyes drifted slowly to my lips. I could feel the heat radiating off him. My lips parted slowly on their own, and I fought every nerve in my body telling me to close the space between us and initiate the kiss.

He pulled his hand away and took a step back. He tucked his hands into his front pockets, like they needed protection from something or someone.

I was disappointed, but I tried not to show it. I couldn't trust him even if he'd been nothing but nice to me, and I couldn't deny I was attracted to him. I was single, so no need to feel guilty. I was free to kiss other people. I wasn't obligated to anyone anymore.

"Give Tristan some space. Sleep tight, Chloe," he said and turned away.

"Bye," I said as I watched walk out. I stood there for a few minutes, just staring at the door and mentally cursing at myself.

I turned around to walk back to my room. I hissed at the pain around my ankle.

"Need help?" I heard from a corner. It nearly gave me a heart attack.

Tristan walked to where I was with his arms folded, his lips curled inward, and brows lowered.

I looked up and was met with his stupid blue eyes that seemed to have their own soft halo-like glow. He looked down at my legs and then back to my face, waiting for a reply.

"So, now, you wanna help?" I scoffed and looked away.

I tried to pass through the other way, but he blocked me.

"What did you hear?" he asked in a calm tone that didn't match the expression on his face.

"Nothing helpful with why I'm here."

"Don't lie to me, Chloe," he said, voice fluffed with fatigue.

"Does it matter? You're not gonna tell me the truth anyway."

"I promised to tell you; we had a deal. So, wait until the time comes and quit being nosy."

"Nosy?" I said with a short laugh.

"Good night," he said, walking away.

I balled my hand into a fist and glared at his frame. I thought of what Adrian had said and decided to stay in my lane.

TRISTAN IGNORED ME for the next three days. I didn't mind, but I felt I wasn't making his life miserable after everything he'd put me through, and it became frustrating. At first, I'd thought I could take it, but that was a lie. Lately, I had been punching and stomping on the pillow with his face that Adrian had given me. I lost count of how many times I'd cursed at it.

I didn't get why he was so mad at me. I hadn't chosen to be here or to be part of whatever he had going on, so why should I suffer his wrath?

This morning, I tried to say something to him, but he gave me a look that made my lips seal automatically. It was infuriating and was starting to drive me crazy. During breakfast, I dropped my cutlery, making a loud sound to get his attention. He looked at me, and I stared back at him, not smiling.

"I know Adrian says to give you space, but ignoring me completely like I'm invisible is ..."

He stood up and grabbed his tablet and phone like I wasn't talking.

"I'm leaving," he told Morris and stormed off.

Morris hurried behind him with his briefcase.

I exhaled and stood up. I had to prepare for my online classes. So far, it had been going well. Even better than my classes at the college. I was only having difficulty with my math, but it was no surprise since I sucked at anything that had to do with calculations. The short time given by our professor for the quizzes was just inhumane. How on earth was I going to answer sixty questions in forty-five minutes?

It was almost four in the afternoon, and I was struggling to allow the content in the book I was reading to sink into my brain. I sighed and left the room, shuffling my feet to go to the kitchen and pester Morris.

I stopped in front of Tristan's room. I looked around before grabbing the door handle. He wouldn't be home until six, and I was hoping to find something, anything to give me an insight on why I was here or maybe find out what he was hiding.

I slowly opened the door to avoid Morris getting suspicious. The room was dim and depressing, as usual. I closed the door and looked around, wondering where to start snooping. I walked to his nightstand and opened the drawers. I found stacks of journals and business magazines with him on the front cover. The journals were all blank. I walked to the other nightstand. I found a photo album, and I was about to pick it up when I heard footsteps. I thought it would be Morris, but I heard Tristan's voice.

"Shit, shit, *shit!*" I looked around for where to hide.

I closed the drawer and ran to the couch at the corner. I hid behind it as the door opened, and footsteps echoed in the room, matching the thumping in my chest.

"… have it ready before I arrive tomorrow. I need all the information you can get on her …"

I heard his footsteps getting closer, and soon, he was sitting on the couch. I pressed myself to the floor, as if it could help me disappear. I stiffened when he threw his head back, brushing his long fingers through his hair as he spoke on the phone. Just a tilt to the right, and he would see me. I held my breath, praying he wouldn't look my way.

My tensed muscles relaxed when he stood up from the couch after ending his call. I pushed myself up and peeked. He had his back to me as he unbuttoned his shirt. I looked toward the door. I wouldn't make it out without him seeing me. I sat back and waited for him to enter the shower.

There was a knock on the door, and then it opened.

"Sorry, sir. I wanted to ask if you've seen Miss Simpson. I made some pretzels for her, but she is not in her room, and I can't find her anywhere."

"Are you sure?"

"Yes, sir."

"Oh God, this girl. What is she up to now?" Tristan grunted. "Keep looking. I'm coming."

The door closed, and I heard feet shuffling. I peeked again and found him pacing the foot of the bed, his hands behind his neck.

"I seriously didn't ask for any of this, but I need her," he sighed and walked out of the room.

I stayed there for a few seconds, stunned and confused. I stood up and walked to the door. I opened it gently and peeked. The coast was clear. I sighed in relief and stepped out. I walked quickly to my room but paused when I heard Tristan's voice coming from my room.

"No, her phone is here. Looks like she was here a few minutes ago. I don't know, Adrian!"

I shook my head and entered the room. I wasn't expecting him to be standing in my room with all his buttons undone and his taut torso on display.

"She is here," he sighed into the phone and hung up.

"What's up?" I smiled.

He glared at me for a few seconds and walked out without saying anything to me. He made me so crazy that I wanted to rip him apart.

I skipped dinner, not wanting to feel angrier with Tristan's attitude toward me. Morris came to call me to eat, but I pretended to be asleep.

I spoke to Adrian the next day when he came to the house. He looked pissed after listening to my complaint about Tristan's attitude toward me. He left for Tristan's room with clenched fists.

I couldn't help but smile. Call me a homewrecker. I didn't care.

I didn't deserve to be treated this way. After everything I had been through because of him, I deserved the world. Tristan was supposed to be pampering me and offering me anything I wanted on a golden platter.

I sat back in my seat, not sure of what to do. What was Adrian going to do? He hadn't even said anything after I was done talking. I rocked in my seat, staring at the stairs and at Tristan's door, where Adrian's tall form had disappeared.

I didn't know if his room was soundproof because I waited for many minutes but heard nothing. My heart jumped when the door banged open. Adrian walked out, looking angrier than when he'd left to see him.

"Get everything you need. You'll be staying at my place until Tristan regains his senses," Adrian said, taking my hand.

"She is going nowhere with you!" Tristan's voice boomed from upstairs.

"You want me to leave her here, so you can keep treating her like she's not important in your life?"

"Leave her alone, Adrian," Tristan said, coming down the stairs with his long strides.

Adrian moved me to his back, blocking me from Tristan's reach.

"If you really want this to work, you won't treat her like crap."

Want what? Are they referring to me? I was so lost.

"I'm trying," Tristan sighed.

"You call this trying?"

Tristan was mute. I wanted to see the look on his face, but Adrian's towering physique made it difficult, even when raised on my toes, I could see nothing.

"Chloe," Tristan called. He sounded tired, not angry anymore.

I inched forward, but Adrian held out his arm, stopping me. Tristan's jaw clenched.

"You need her, Tristan. Stop treating her like shit."

Tristan mumbled incoherent words and ran his fingers through his hair. He walked to the nearest sofa and sat down.

I watched him as he buried his face in his palms. I thought he was going to break down, but nothing happened. Now, I was worried and very confused.

"Go to your room. I will meet you in a minute," Adrian said, facing me.

I hesitated as I looked at Tristan, who still had his face buried between his palms.

"Please go. I will come up later," Adrian said, forcing a smile.

"Fine." I frowned. I glanced at Tristan before leaving.

I stayed in my room for what seemed like an hour before Adrian showed up. He looked relieved as he walked to the bed. To be honest, I didn't want to leave. They were still strangers to me. I couldn't just move in with Adrian when I had only known him for two week.

He lay down next to me on the bed, and we both stared at the white ceiling. I was itching to move closer to him, to touch his hands and feel the warmth from his body.

"Am I still going with you?" I asked, turning to look at him.

"No, Tristan needs you here. You can come over some other time," he said, facing me.

He didn't look twenty-six. He was beautiful in every aspect. I found myself moving my hand and brushing the hair covering his right eye.

He smiled. Those damn dimples were going to be the death of me.

"Your eyes are really pretty. The clearest blue I have ever seen," he whispered, and my cheeks heated.

"Thanks," I mumbled.

"What if your family doesn't take you back?" he asked, changing the tense atmosphere between us.

"I will get an apartment and try to build a life for myself. Maybe move to Paris. I have always wanted to live in Paris," I said, smiling at the thought of it.

"I will miss you. You're the light everyone needs once in a while," he said, taking my hand.

I knew the day for Tristan to tell me the truth was drawing closer, and I'd be out of here. I should have stopped myself from getting attached, but it was impossible with Adrian. He stared at me with a softness I had never experienced.

"I want you to know you can stay here as long as you want if you're having a hard time, getting a place. Tristan is cool with it."

"Is he?" I scoffed, and he laughed.

"I will never forget when you ran after Tristan with a knife. I laugh every time I think about it. I wish I caught it on camera," he said, his laugh so satisfying and adorable.

"Will Tristan be okay?" I asked.

He moved his gaze away from the ceiling to look at me. His eyes roamed my face before fixating on my eyes.

"He will be fine. He will get through this," he whispered softly.

"Why am I here?" I wanted to know why Tristan needed me. Did he need my kidney?

"Only a few hours left for you to find out." He winked.

"Why can't you tell me?" I held back my urge to yell.

"'Cause it's not my place to tell you."

I groaned in frustration and looked away.

"I will be leaving."

I didn't spare him a look as he stood up from the bed. I closed my eyes as he moved to my side of the bed.

"I'm sorry," he whispered. I felt his warm lips on my forehead.

I opened my eyes when I heard the door close.

TODAY WAS THE day Tristan was supposed to tell me the truth. I hadn't seen him all morning. I was nervous, and I didn't know why.

I called Adrian, but he wasn't answering any of my calls. I knew Tristan hadn't left the house today, so he definitely should have been in his room. I decided I would wait for him to come to me first. I was ready to know the reason I was here.

I didn't have classes today. I watched a movie, but I kept looking at the wall clock.

Does he even know it's today? Should I go to him? What if he is still angry?

All these questions boggled my brain, almost giving me a migraine.

I stood up and left my room. I walked to the door to his room and raised my hand to knock but stopped. I paced in front of his room, thinking of how to tell him today was the day. I moved closer to the door again and brought my fist closer to the door, but I paused. Maybe I was being too pushy, but it was me who held the upper hand.

I sighed and walked back to my room. I called Adrian again, but he didn't answer his phone. I screamed into the pillow and decided to take a nap. When I woke up, it was past seven in the evening. I tried Adrian again, but he didn't answer.

I met Morris downstairs as he was finishing up dinner.

"Have you seen Tristan?" I asked, leaning on the countertop.

"Mr. Sanchester said he doesn't want to be disturbed."

I sighed and took a seat.

"Are you okay, Miss Simpson?" Morris asked, looking concerned.

"Yeah." I forced a smile.

It was hard to eat when a part of me was worried sick about Adrian and Tristan. I tried to convince myself there was nothing to be anxious about, but the weird feeling in my gut said otherwise. Every cell in my stomach was clawing at me. I was dying to know. I dropped my spoon and decided to go and check if Tristan was okay.

I ran up the stairs like I knew something bad was about to happen.

"Please be okay; please be okay," I mumbled, wrapping my fingers around the cold metal door handle. I turned it and pushed the door open.

The room was dim, but I could make out some furniture in the room. I didn't see Tristan though.

"Tristan?" I took slow steps into the room.

I tripped on something—or rather, someone. I looked down, and my heart stopped beating. I screamed, paralyzed in shock for what laid before me.

CHAPTER **FOURTEEN**

HOSPITAL

I wished I had gone to him sooner. I would have saved him.

A doctor and two nurses were still in his room. It had been an hour now. I bit on my nails as I thought of what was going on in there. *Is he still alive?*

Morris came to stand in front of me. He held out a cup of coffee and a doughnut for me to take.

"Please eat something."

"No, I'm not hungry," I said and looked down at my legs, which were still trembling. I tapped my feet on the neat floor to ease the eerie feeling that engulfed me like a blanket.

My eyes were sore from crying due to the conversation on the phone with 911.

When I found Tristan's unconscious body on the floor, I freaked out. I

knelt beside his unmoving body and called his name, but he didn't answer. I touched his hands, and they felt so cold. My heart pounded against my chest like a hammer. I thought he was dead. I screamed Morris's name, but he took forever to come up.

My hands were shaking as I dialed 911. Tears gathered in my eyes, and fear consumed me like a flame. I had never seen a dead person, so I didn't know if he was still alive or dead. I tried CPR, but my hands kept trembling nonstop, and I wasn't sure if I was doing it the right way. The room seemed to shrink, and I couldn't breathe. Everything became hazy until I heard a voice.

"Nine-one-one. What's your emergency?" a feminine voice came from the other line.

"I ... I just came to check on my friend and found him on the floor. He isn't moving. I think he's dead," I cried.

"Ma'am, breathe. I'm here to help."

I nodded frantically as if she could see me. I took a deep breath and tried to relax.

"I need you to do something for me, okay?"

"Yeah," I said, sniffling.

"Check if he is still breathing. Try and feel his pulse. Can you do that?"

"Okay." I placed my head on his chest and listened quietly.

His heartbeat was faint, but I was relieved he was still breathing. I placed two fingers on his neck, and I exhaled when I felt it. A euphoric wave of relief washed over me, yet I was trapped between human morality and vengeful irony. This was the man who ruined my life, yet I was the one who was trying to save him.

"Yes, he is still breathing, but it ... it doesn't sound good."

"I need you to keep checking his pulse while I send our team to you. Can I have your address?"

I didn't know the address, but Morris arrived right in time.

Then, we waited.

The paramedics arrived and took Tristan on a stretcher while putting an oxygen mask on his face. We followed behind in a different car. Morris assured me that everything was going to be fine as I cried like a baby.

I was an emotional mess when it came to losing someone. I didn't do well with deaths even if we were not related in any way. I was a wreck every time I was close to losing someone I knew.

AND NOW, HERE I was, saying a silent prayer in my heart for him. I wished I had approached him sooner. Who knew how long he had been on the cold floor, helpless and unconscious?

I brushed my brown locks back and squeezed my knees with my hands. Adrian was still not answering my calls or my texts. I hoped he was okay.

"Where is Tristan?"

I turned to look at the source of the voice. Mrs. Sanchester's fast strides approached me. The click-clack sound of her transparent slippers irritated my ears. Nora and Nana trailed behind her.

"Is my baby okay?" She had tears in her eyes, appearing so fragile like a single touch could break her. She looked so young and gorgeous in her red designer dress and silky hair. Everything about her screamed expensive, even her face. She stared at Morris, waiting for him to say something.

"We haven't heard anything from the doctor. She is still in the room with him," he told her in a soothing voice.

"Is Tristan okay?" Nora asked, sitting next to me.

I was surprised she'd spoken to me; I wasn't sure the Sanchesters liked me. I turned to look at her with a small smile. She was so pretty.

"He will be." That was all I told her.

His grandmother had a rosary in her hand as she listened to my answer.

"I told you to check on him every hour, so this wouldn't happen again," I heard Mrs. Sanchester say to Morris.

They were talking in a low tone, but luckily for me, I was very close to them.

"He forbade me from coming into his room," Morris explained.

"Is he still seeing his therapist?"

Therapist? Tristan had a therapist?

"No," Morris replied.

"Oh God," she groaned, placing her palm on her forehead, as if it would make her feel better.

It seemed this wasn't the first time something like this had happened. The door to his room finally opened, and we all turned to look at the tall doctor who stepped out with two nurses behind her.

"How's my baby? Please tell me he's okay," Mrs. Sanchester asked.

"He's okay, but he won't be accepting visitors until tomorrow," the doctor said with a soft smile. "Can I speak to you for a minute in my office?" the doctor asked Mrs. Sanchester.

"Sure."

I watched them as they walked away. Tristan was okay. I could finally breathe again.

Whatever the doctor was going to tell his mom, I wasn't that curious. I'd found pain medication on the floor in his bathroom. The small bottle for the medication had been empty, so how many had he taken? Why would he even want to hurt himself?

It was obvious something was going on with Tristan. Something they all knew, except me.

My phone rang, making every eye turn in my direction. I answered the call quickly when I saw Adrian's name on my screen.

"Chloe, are you okay? How is Tristan?"

"We are still at the hospital, but the doctor said he is okay."

"Text me the address. I'm on my way."

"Okay." I sent him the address immediately after ending the call.

Adrian arrived a few minutes later. He walked toward me with his long strides. I stood up and gave him a small smile. He looked really tired even the smile lighting up his face couldn't hide it. I could see the shadows underneath his eyes as he approached me.

"Chloe," he called with relief, pulling me into a warm hug.

I wrapped my arms around him, inhaling his exotic scent. It seemed to squeeze me into a sauna of sizzling bliss.

"Are you okay?" he asked, rubbing my back.

"Yeah," I said against his hard chest.

I realized this was a little awkward in front of Nora and her grandma. They believed I was pregnant with Tristan's child, and I was his girlfriend, and here I was, getting all comfortable in his best friend's arms.

I pulled away and tucked some stray hair behind my ear.

"Thanks for coming," I said with a dry throat.

"Sorry I missed all your calls. I left my phone at home, and there was too much work at the office for me to leave and get the phone," he explained. "How is he?" Adrian asked, taking a glance at the door to Tristan's room.

"He is fine now, but we can't see him."

He turned to look at Nora. "How are you, sweet pea?" he asked, smiling.

"I'm fine."

I saw a blush. I didn't blame her. Adrian was too good-looking and charming.

"Nana, how are you?" He squatted in front of her and took her hand.

"I want to see my grandson."

"He is fine, Nana. You will see him when he wakes up."

She nodded, and he stood up and faced me.

"Did you cry?" He stared at my face closely.

"I was scared," I told him, rolling my eyes.

"Adrian," Mrs. Sanchester called from behind, her cheeks wet with tears.

"Mrs. Sanchester." He turned to her and hugged her.

"He's doing it again," she sobbed.

"He'll be fine." He tried to soothe her.

She pulled away, dabbing her tears away with a handkerchief. "Did you know he stopped seeing Dr. Matt?"

"He told me he was okay and didn't need therapy anymore," Adrian told her.

"For how long now?"

"A year."

"You should've informed me."

"I'm sorry. He didn't want you to know."

I looked away quickly when she turned her eyes to me.

"Chloe."

I stared at her when she called my name. She walked closer, putting her arms around me.

"How are you holding up, honey?" she asked, pulling away.

"I'm … I'm okay," I stuttered.

She smiled at me, holding my hands. "Thanks for getting to Tristan when he needed you. I should take you to the doctor to check the baby after what you just went through, the shock and everything. We need to be sure you're both okay," she said, looking down at my flat stomach.

"I … no, that's not necessary. I'm fine."

This was my chance to prove to them that Tristan had lied, but I turned it down. This wasn't the right time for them to find out the truth. Tristan was still on the hospital bed. I couldn't add more fuel to the fire by telling them there was no baby and everything was a lie.

"Your health and the baby's are very important," she insisted.

"Seriously, I'm fine." I tried to convince her.

"Don't be stubborn and go with her already," Nana said from where she was sitting.

"Why don't you all head home? It's late, and you all look tired. I will make sure Chloe sees a doctor." Adrian finally came to my rescue.

"Please do that," Mrs. Sanchester said.

"I will take her to a doctor, I promise," Adrian said.

"Okay. Take care of yourself, honey." She hugged me again before letting go.

Nana came to hug me too, beaming at my stomach before pulling away.

"Bye, Chloe." Nora waved.

"Bye, Nora." I watched them as they disappeared down the large hallway until they entered the elevator.

I exhaled in relief when the elevator doors closed. Adrian chuckled beside me.

"That wasn't funny," I said, glaring at him.

"You should go home and get some sleep," he suggested.

"You need that more than I do."

The company business was taking a toll on him, especially with Tristan's issues.

"I will drop you off. I have to be at work before seven. There's a big deal I have to seal tomorrow," he said, glancing at his wristwatch.

"I'm not leaving yet." I wasn't ready to return to the big house while Tristan stayed here by himself.

"Why?"

"Morris will take me home when I'm ready." That was all I told him.

"Okay, but make sure you rest. Have you eaten?"

"Yes," I lied. I wanted him to go home, rest, and stop worrying about me.

"I will see you tomorrow." He placed a quick kiss on my forehead and headed for the elevator that had just opened.

I sat down and ran my palms down my thighs.

Morris sat at the other seat across from me. He was reading a sports magazine.

I looked around and stood up. I walked to the door and held the cold handle. Will the hospital kick me out if I went against their order? I only wanted to take a peek and go home. I opened the door and moved my head in to look at him.

He had an IV connected to the back of his palm and another tube in his nose. I checked behind me before walking in and shutting the door quietly.

I walked to the bed and stared at him sleeping. He looked so peaceful and adorable. I brushed his hair back with my hand. I wished I knew what he had going on. As much as I didn't want to be involved in whatever it was, I was still concerned.

"You will overcome this, I promise," I whispered. It had taken me a long time to overcome the darkness, though I didn't know what his story was.

I moved a seat closer and sat down. I planned to stay for ten minutes and leave, but I drifted off to sleep immediately after my head touched the bed.

"Chloe."

I woke up to someone tapping me lightly on the shoulder. I grumbled before opening my eyes. They met a pair of dull blue eyes.

"Tristan?" I sat up and looked around. I remembered walking in here to check on him, but I'd dozed off when I placed my head on the bed.

"Are you comfortable?" he asked hoarsely, still staring at me.

"Sorry. I didn't mean to fall asleep." I checked the room for a wall clock. I found one above the door; it was past three in the morning.

"You can sleep here." He pointed to the spot next to him. He moved to create more room when I stared at the space like it wasn't enough for me.

"No, I'm okay."

"It's fine. There's enough space for both of us." He sounded weak, and the nasal cannula in his nose moved every time he spoke.

"I don't think it's allowed, and I don't wanna make you uncomfortable with all the stuff connected to your body."

"I'm the one paying the hospital bill, and I'm very comfortable." I was getting worried about the way his voice sounded.

I shouldn't even be here, or welcome the idea of sharing a bed with a sick person, but I needed him to shut up since the more he spoke, the weaker he sounded.

"Okay," I agreed.

I took off my bunny slippers and gently climbed up the bed, scared I might hurt him. My body relaxed the moment it contacted the bed. I felt so exhausted and sleepy.

We had to share one pillow, but I didn't use the blanket covering him. The hospital gown he wore had only ropes at the back, and I knew he was naked underneath. His free hand moved to my shoulders, so he could lie down comfortably. I stiffened and looked up at his face. His eyes were closed.

"Is this allowed?" I whispered, feeling uneasy about sharing a hospital bed.

"Go to sleep, Chloe," he grunted.

My body obeyed. For the first time in days, I finally felt comfortable, shutting my eyes. In a bed not my own, far from home, and most certainly not alone. I fell into a deep sleep. I forgot where I was or who I was sleeping next to as I snuggled closer, feeling Tristan's chin resting on my head.

CHAPTER **FIFTEEN**
HEARTBREAK

I woke up when I felt something rough on my face. I opened my eyes and discovered it was Tristan's stubble. How had we ended up cuddling on the bed? I removed my hand around his torso and my leg that had somehow ended up on him, praying he wouldn't wake up as I pulled away. I quietly moved one leg over his body, trying to get down from the bed.

The door opened when I was about to get off the bed. The doctor's jaw slightly hung loose as she stared at me. It looked like I was straddling Tristan's torso; this was definitely the wrong position to be caught in. I opened my mouth to explain, but Mrs. Sanchester and Nana arrived. They stared at me, wondering what I was doing. I was so mortified; I didn't even know what to say.

"What are you doing?" I heard Tristan's rough voice.

"Um, I was about to get off the bed."

"Then, what are you waiting for?" he asked, looking toward the door. He turned back to me, and his eyebrows rose questioningly.

"Nothing," I scowled and got off gently.

"I told you no one was allowed in here. Do I need to remind you, this is a hospital?"

I was too embarrassed to look at her. I should have gone home after peeking, and I felt like a kid being scolded for stealing.

"I'm not complaining," Tristan said, adjusting himself to look at her.

"With all due respect, this is a hospital," the doctor said.

"Have you ever been in love, honey? She was too worried to leave him on his own. Let it be," Nana said sweetly and found her way in. She smiled at me and walked to her grandson.

The doctor fixed a smile and walked in. Mrs. Sanchester gave me a playful grin and entered the room.

"How are you feeling?" Nana asked, taking Tristan's hand.

"I'm fine." His voice said otherwise.

"You promised you wouldn't do it again."

Tristan didn't say anything. He just looked away.

"Mom," Mrs. Sanchester called with a glint of warning in her voice.

I assumed she didn't want her to talk about whatever was bothering him.

"Don't forget you have a baby on the way, a baby who will look up to you," Nana said softly, giving him a kiss on the head.

"I'm glad you're okay, honey," Mrs. Sanchester said, holding his hand.

Tristan gave her a small smile and looked across the room at me. I held his mysterious gaze for a while before he turned away and faced his mom.

The doctor checked the IV connected and asked him a few questions about his health. "A nurse will be here in the next thirty minutes to take you for your test. I will take my leave now," she said and left the room.

"I will be right back," I told them, heading to the bathroom to freshen up.

I stared at my face in the mirror and checked my pale eyes. There was a big shower in the bathroom. I could rinse my body quickly and return to the room. Luckily for me, there were two towels in the bathroom and an extra soap and toothbrush.

I put some toothpaste on my finger and rinsed my mouth. I didn't trust that toothbrush staring at me.

I removed my shirt. I stared at my back from the mirror. I rarely wore clothes that left my back open. I didn't want anyone to see the ugly mark on my back that reminded me of my past every time I looked at it.

Ciara didn't know about it, and I was glad she didn't. She would have happily told my mom when she was spilling all my secrets. No one, except Vina and Grey, had seen it, and I didn't want anyone else to see it. I kept staring at it, wishing it would disappear.

Suddenly, the door opened. I jumped and turned around quickly to hide my back. Tristan cocked a brow at me as he entered the bathroom.

I was too concerned about my back to care about my exposed chest. He took weak steps to the toilet, ignoring my presence. I quickly used my top to cover my chest. He didn't look like he cared, but I was scared he had seen the scar. I waited for him to ask about it, but he began to pee. I closed my eyes, trying to block the sound. I opened them when I heard the toilet flush. He walked to where I was and washed his hands. He didn't say anything to me as he left the bathroom.

I breathed out in relief. Maybe he hadn't seen the mark on my back—I mean, I had been quick to turn away.

I really hoped he hadn't. I wore my shirt and rinsed my face before leaving the bathroom, not bothering with the shower.

Adrian was in the room when I returned. He gave me a big smile and came to hug me.

"Morris told me you didn't leave," he said, scowling.

"I dozed off," I told him.

"I brought breakfast." He pointed at the takeout on the table.

Mrs. Sanchester was already feeding Tristan. I tried not to laugh at the way she was giving him the food like a baby. Tristan looked mortified. He tried to collect the food from her, but she wouldn't let him.

"I will drop you off on my way to work. You don't have a choice. You need to rest."

I drank the iced coffee after I was done eating the doughnuts and bagels.

"Thanks," I told him with a satisfied grin.

I glanced at Tristan, and our eyes met instantly. I looked away quickly and gulped down a bottle of water.

The look on his face was unreadable. Why did I keep feeling like he'd seen more than he let on?

TRISTAN WAS DISCHARGED a week later, but he wasn't allowed to return to work. According to Adrian, he had overdosed on pain and antidepressant pills. There were moments I wanted to ask him about his promise to tell my family the truth, but I decided to give him a few days to recover from what had happened. I made it my job to check on him once in a while. I wasn't going to let him die without telling me the truth. He spent all his time in the study and the kitchen. I had noticed how much he enjoyed cooking.

If Tristan had seen what was on my back, then he didn't care. He had not asked me about it—not like we talked about anything or conversed like normal people.

Adrian came over on Saturday. He spent half of the day with Tristan, briefing him on everything going on in the company, while I was on the phone with Vina, who wanted me to sneak into the garden, where Adrian and Tristan were engrossed in a deep conversation, so she could stare at Adrian from our video call.

The things you do for your best friend.

I decided to go downstairs for dinner after my stomach grumbled. Morris usually came up to call me when dinner was all set, but it was almost eight p.m., and I had not seen him. The dining room was empty as I walked in. Had I missed dinner?

I heard a clattering sound from the kitchen.

"Morris?" I called, walking into the kitchen.

"He is off today. It's his granddaughter's birthday," Tristan said.

I paused at the doorway to the kitchen and watched him as he chopped some vegetables like a skilled chef. I couldn't even hold a knife.

"Hungry?" he asked, taking a glance at me.

I was starving, and there was no denying he was a good cook.

"Who says no to food?" I said, walking to the marble island.

I took one slice of a cucumber from a glass bowl, watching him as he mixed the salad.

"Did you go to culinary school?" I asked.

"No, self-taught. My dream was to own a restaurant, but I had to take over my father's company," he said, bringing out a frying pan.

I felt my mouth watering at the sizzling sound of cheese and black cod. The spices filled my nostrils. I leaned on the counter and watched him until he was done. It was fascinating, watching how he set everything neatly and gently on a plate like it was delicate.

He placed the plate in front of me and gave me a fork. "Would you like anything to drink?"

"No," I said.

He nodded and turned to walk away. He paused and leaned on the counter for support. Closing his eyes, he took a deep breath. He looked weak from all the work. I knew he wasn't fully recovered yet. Too bad he'd chosen a girl who couldn't cook.

"Are you okay?" I asked.

I stood up and walked to him. He was still holding the edge of the counter for support. He gave me a firm nod and tried to stand on his own. I grabbed his arm to provide some support.

"Jeez, you're burning up," I said, immediately after touching his skin.

"It's fine. I missed my morning medication."

"I think you have a fever," I said, pushing myself up on my tiptoes to touch his forehead.

"I will be fine," he said, trying to pull away but I held him back.

"I have an idea. My mom always used it for me and my sister when we got a fever," I said.

"What?" he asked, looking down at me.

"Let's go." I held his arm and helped him out of the kitchen to his room.

"So?" he asked when we entered his room.

"You have a bathtub, right?" I asked, and he nodded.

I walked to his bathroom and filled it with lukewarm water. I called him in when the bathtub was filled to my satisfaction.

"It's not too cold, right?" he asked.

I smirked in response.

"It will help, trust me," I said, laughing at the expression on his face.

He took off his shirt, and I looked away as he undid his pants. I glanced at his taut torso from the tall mirror mounted on the wall.

"No, leave them on," I said sharply when he tried to take off his boxers.

He smiled and left his boxers on. I knelt in front of the bathtub.

"Shit!" he cursed at the temperature of the water.

I dipped one hand inside and moved closer to him. I placed my hand on his forehead, and he shivered at the coolness of my hand. I told him to lie down inside, but he refused. He was so adamant about it.

I sighed, standing up. I took off my long woolen jacket and stepped inside the bathtub in my thin-strapped dress.

"I guess we have to do this my way then," I said, reaching for the shower head.

I turned it on and sprinkled the lukewarm water on him. He gripped my arms as I sprayed it on his face. I tried not to laugh at how scared he was of the coolness of the water.

I checked his temperature as I sprayed more warm water on him. It was getting better. I brushed his wet hair back.

My dress stuck to my body like glue as I tried not to shiver. My skin bubbled with goose bumps, pinning me with the wrath of icicles. Tristan let go of my arms and looked up at my face.

"Better?" I asked, turning off the shower sprinkler.

"Yes," he said with a soft smile that made his eyes light up, the deep blue almost bewitching.

I looked away, pulling away from between his legs.

"Just stay for one more minute, and then you can come out," I said, standing up.

I stepped out of the bathtub, shivering. My body danced to the frigid air slicing at my thighs and shoulders. I really wanted someone to just cuddle with me.

I grabbed a big towel, catching Tristan staring at me from the mirror. He looked away, moving his gaze to the ceiling as he his head fell back. I looked down at my wet dress, discovering that it was now see-through. My black underwear was visible, and my pad-free bra made it impossible to hide my aroused nipples. My heart hummed for reasons I didn't understand.

"I need a hot bath. You can come out now. Sorry about the wet floor," I said, leaving the room.

ADRIAN SHOWED UP on Monday to work on something with Tristan. I had an exam in the morning that made me peachy the whole day. I almost finished a whole bowl of ice cream due to the wild anxiety that swarmed in me like busy bees.

Adrian decided to watch a movie with me when he was done with Tristan. We both agreed on a romcom. I had my head on his lap while he tried to braid my hair, which made my scalp hurt.

"I have to go. I'm running late," he said when we were almost done with the movie.

"Where are you going? The movie is almost over," I asked, sitting up.

He stood up, finishing his drink.

"I have a date at seven thirty."

My heart sank. It felt like a bucket of cold water had just been thrown on my face. My feet lost the willpower to move, my breath ceased, but my eyes … they immediately wanted to hide away in horror.

"A date?" I tried playing it casual.

"Yeah. Have any advice? I haven't gone on a date since I was twenty-four." Excitement etched his voice.

I wondered why. Any girl would want to date him.

"Who is she?" I asked, jealousy stinging my insides.

"A friend I have been seeing for a year now."

"Hmm," I hummed, biting on my lower lip.

"Any advice?" he asked again with his hands tucked in the pockets of his red hoodie.

"Just be you," I said, faking a smile.

"Thanks." He gave me a kiss on the cheek and left.

I leaned on the sofa for support. Adrian had just left me for a date. He was going on a date.

I guessed he didn't feel the same way about me. But the way he'd looked at me ... it was just a date, right? It might end up disastrous. I knew we were never going to work out, but I'd expected it to last a little longer.

My shoulders sagged. I took a glance at the movie we had been watching and frowned. I should have told him to stay. Why hadn't I told him to stay?

I turned off the TV and walked to the wine cellar. Some alcohol would do me good right now. I was frustrated about my exam score, and now, Adrian was no longer a free man. I returned to the living room and sat on the floor. I poured myself some tequila and played my favorite song on my phone.

I wasn't sure of the amount of alcohol I had taken before someone came to sit next to me on the floor. I turned to look at Tristan with hazy eyes, his scent surrounding me. I poured myself some more tequila and sang along to P!nk's song. I was waiting for him to say something, but he was quiet. I wasn't in a good enough state to engage in a conversation anyway. I leaned back and placed my head on the seat behind me. The alcohol was working.

"Do you always drink like this?" I heard him ask, and I felt his eyes on me.

I obeyed my subconscious. I knew at this point, I was vulnerable, and he might decide to ask about what he had seen on my back, if he'd seen it.

We were both quiet for a while, and I was starting to enjoy it until he spoke again.

"I'm ready to tell you why I said all that in the church."

CHAPTER **SIXTEEN**
UNDECIDED

Was I ready? Whether I liked it or not, some part of me had moved on. At this point, it felt like one of those secrets that I was better off without knowing. But who was I kidding? I wanted to know. I had to know.

I turned to look at him, but my head was acting funny. I closed my eyes and tried to listen to what he was about to say. I was not sober, and it didn't seem like a good time, but I wanted to know why I was here. My head was starting to spin, the more I drank.

"Well, it's about time," I slurred, trying to focus on one image of Tristan.

He reached for the bottle and took a big gulp, and then he leaned back on the seat. I was drifting to sleep slowly, but Tristan was already talking. I wasn't hearing anything. I stopped fighting it and closed my eyes and welcomed the darkness.

I HATED HANGOVERS. My stomach and my head made me stay in bed. I wasn't sure how I had gotten to my room. I winced, gripping the sheets. I needed some painkillers, or this agonizing pain would make me go crazy.

There was a knock on my door. I groaned before answering. Morris walked in with a small tray and a smile.

"Good morning, Miss Simpson. I hope you slept well. I made you some hangover soup."

"Hangover soup?" I sat up and collected it. I examined the pale-colored soup and tried not to throw up. I thanked him and braced myself to take a spoon. "Please get me some painkillers."

He nodded and left. It was my first time seeing a hangover soup, and it actually tasted good. After taking the soup and the pills, I went back to sleep.

When I woke up, it was past one. I took a long and soothing shower and dressed up in a red floral dress. I packed my hair up in a ponytail and left the room. Morris was making lunch, and Tristan was nowhere to be seen.

"Where is Tristan?" I asked Morris.

"Why are you looking for me?" I jumped from the sudden question from behind.

Tristan opened the fridge and grabbed a bottle of water. He was wearing swim shorts, and a gray towel hung on his left shoulder. His wet hair was swept back. I watched his Adam's apple bob as he drank the water.

I tried not to let my eyes wander around his prominent, abs and ridges on his taut torso. Man, it was getting hot in here. My eyes didn't miss the drop that slid down his lower lip until it reached the floor. I was still wondering how something so trivial he did without adding any effort looked so good. I pretended to check my short nails when he turned to look at me.

"I was taking a swim. I never told you I needed a babysitter," he said and left the kitchen.

"I just wanted to say thank you for taking me to my room when I was *wasted*!" I yelled after him.

I sighed and took a seat at the kitchen island. I couldn't remember much from last night. I knew he had been there, and I had been mad at my exam score and Adrian's sudden date night. He'd wanted to tell me the truth about what had happened at the wedding, and I'd somehow blacked out. *Idiot*.

"Do you need help with anything?" I asked Morris.

"No, Miss Simpson, but thanks for asking."

"Come on. You look like you have so much to do. Let me help. I have nothing to do."

It took him a couple of seconds to agree.

"You can stir the sauce for me."

"Awesome!" I rushed to the electric cooker.

"How did you know I had a hangover?" I asked.

"I saw you last night, sleeping on the floor in the living room. I tried to wake you, but you were too drunk to raise a hand. I picked you up and took you to your room."

I stopped stirring the sauce and looked at him. "You were the one who took me to my room?"

"Yes, Miss Simpson. You were all alone on the floor."

"Oh," I mumbled, erupting in embarrassment. I tried to hide my glowing cheeks. "Thank you, Morris."

He gave me a warm smile. I returned it and continued stirring the sauce.

I WENT TO the garden after having lunch alone in the dining room. Tristan had gone MIA again.

It was the weekend. I decorated my room with the flowers I'd gotten from the garden and did some homework before staying with Belvina on the phone for almost four hours, talking about random things.

I made Morris eat dinner with me and asked about his family. He had three kids and five grandchildren. His wife had passed away, and it broke my heart to hear about her death. She had been killed in a hit-and-run, and the cops had been unable to locate the person responsible.

I went upstairs to my room after helping Morris do the dishes. I showered and wore my shorts and a white hoodie. I watched a sad movie on my laptop because I couldn't go to sleep. After I finished the movie, I went on YouTube and found some prerecorded sounds to sing to. I didn't want to wake anyone with my awful two a.m. karaoke, so I pulled the duvet over my head, hoping it'd block out the sound as I sang the lyrics to "I Want It That Way" by Backstreet Boys.

My mind drifted to my family after I turned off the lights to go to sleep. I missed them.

The knock on the door made my heart jump. I hadn't expected anyone to be up so late.

"Chloe?" I heard Tristan's voice, and my shoulders relaxed.

Should I pretend to be asleep? Maybe it was urgent.

"Yes?"

"Can I come in?" His voice sounded like he had a cold.

"Okay," I said and left the lights off.

He opened the door after a few seconds. I stared at his silhouette at the door. He stayed outside, not coming in.

"Can I sleep here?"

"Why? What happened to your room?" I asked, and he said nothing.

"You wanna switch rooms?" I asked.

"No, I don't want to be alone with the thoughts in my head."

"Is everything okay?" I asked, switching on the light.

His eyes looked bloodshot, and his hair was a mess.

"Yes. I will just go," he said and turned away.

"Tristan," I called, but he closed the door and left.

I sighed and thought about what he'd just said. I stood up and grabbed my phone. I walked to his room and knocked on the door, opening it without waiting for a reply. The room was pitch-black, and I could hear movement on the bed.

"Tristan," I called.

"I'm here," he said from the bed.

I followed the direction of his voice and climbed into the bed. I felt the heat from his body as I lay next to him. My shoulders tensed at the slight contact of his body. I was able to make out the form of his body in the dark.

"You can talk to me about it," I whispered and got no reply for almost a minute.

"Thank you," he said.

Maybe I should ask him about his promise to reveal the truth and give me back my life, but now, I wasn't sure I had a life to return to. What difference would it make if he told everyone the truth? My family had already shown me they'd never support me in my worst moments.

Maybe I was getting too comfortable here, and I hated myself for that. I closed my eyes and tried to force myself to sleep.

"Can I hold you?" he asked after a while. He must have been having a hard time, falling asleep.

"Okay," I said.

I felt him snuggling closer, and soon, his arms were around me. I touched his arm to provide some comfort and let him know he wasn't alone. He pulled me closer, as if the distance between our bodies had not disappeared. I ran my fingers up his arm, trying to get him to sleep. I discovered he was shirtless as my fingers trailed higher to his shoulder.

Fuck.

"If you're uncomfortable, tell me," he said close to my ear.

"I'm fine," I said, trying my hardest not to get lost in the warmth from his body. I tried.

"You smell nice," he whispered close to my neck, his lips brushing against my skin.

"Thank you." I smiled and closed my eyes. I was comforting him—that was all this was.

I WOKE UP late. I left Tristan's room immediately after I found him still sleeping. I went to shower and changed into a white sundress. I put my hair up in a loose ponytail and applied my lip gloss. I met Morris in the kitchen, cooking, as if we had a celebration.

"Why are you cooking all this?" I asked, stealing one spiced steak he'd cut into strips.

"We are having guests."

"Guests?" I grinned and licked my finger, scooping in the sauce, and my tongue danced in delight.

"Mr. Sanchester informed me this morning," Morris told me.

I thought of who might be coming. *Do I have to play the girlfriend role?* It had been so exhausting the last time.

It didn't take long for us to finish in the kitchen. I helped to set the food at the table in the garden, where Tristan wanted it. It looked fancy as I stared at it from the porch.

"Well done, Morris," I said after he was done arranging the seats.

"You too, Miss Simpson." He smiled.

"Oh, it was nothing." I waved it off.

The doorbell caught our attention.

"I'll get it," I said quickly.

"It's my job, Miss Simpson; please allow me."

I hated when he spoke like that. I rolled my eyes in defeat while he laughed.

Tristan walked down the stairs in black jogger shorts and a blue T-shirt that hugged his flexing biceps. His blond hair had a few strands falling across his right temple. The color of his hair was still confusing, as if it changed color. It looked bronze today.

I was too busy staring at him to notice our guests. I turned around and saw Adrian in dark jeans and a white Henley. He left two buttons undone to show off his gold chains and toned chest. The lady on his arm spoiled my smile, drilling a hole in my chest.

Her ebony hair reached her waist, and she wore a green dress that showed off her perfect curves.

Tristan and Adrian shook hands while I stood four feet away, staring.

"Chloe?" Adrian's voice stole my gaze away.

"Hi, Adrian." I tried my best not to show the pain in my voice. The fake smile on my face hurt my cheeks.

"Chloe, meet Karen, my girlfriend."

Girlfriend?

"Hi, Karen." I beamed.

She was so pretty.

"Don't be like that. Come here." She withdrew from his arm and came to hug me. "Adrian told me a lot about you. Your eyes are so pretty," she said, looking at my face closely.

"Thanks." I grinned.

She was so sweet too.

"The food is probably getting cold. Shall we?" Tristan said, leading the way.

I walked behind Karen and Adrian, who had his arm around her waist. Jealousy ate me up, and my eyes drilled holes at where he touched her.

He pulled out a seat for her. I took the seat in front of them, and Tristan sat beside me. Morris started dishing out the food while my eyes were on Karen. She was beautiful, and her personality matched Adrian's—the smile and sweet gesture they both embodied made them perfect for each other.

Adrian and Tristan talked about work and sports while Karen tried to make conversation with me. She laughed at her own jokes while I stared at her with a fake grin. I wasn't good at faking my laugh.

She turned to Adrian and fed him a grilled shrimp; he fed her some strip steak with his fork. Tristan was too busy with his phone and food to care about anything. I sipped my wine, trying to drown the growing anger but it wasn't working. I poured myself more wine and drank the whole contents.

"Are you okay?" Karen asked, staring at my empty wineglass.

"Yeah." I smiled.

"Wow, your alcohol tolerance must be good."

"You have no idea," Tristan mumbled, still on his phone.

"I forgot something in the kitchen. I'll be right back." I stood up and left the garden.

I went to the yard and took a seat by the pool. I lay back on the long seat and took a deep breath. The cool breeze calmed me. I almost forgot about the lunch.

"Is this what you forgot in the kitchen?"

I jolted from the voice. Adrian gazed at my face with his brows creased in question.

I sat up, anger flowing like fireworks. He sipped the drink in his hand and took the other seat next to me.

"This is so comfy." He leaned back on the sun lounger, propping one knee up while the other lay flat on the seat.

"Why are you here?" he asked, glancing at me.

"Just felt like staring at the pool." I stood up to leave.

"Chloe," he called, stopping me.

"Yeah?" I turned to look at him.

He finished his drink and gently put the glass on the floor. He sat up with his scrutinizing stare pointed at me. I never thought I'd ever want to feel enraged at Adrian. He had been my breath of fresh air ever since the incident, but now, even he felt so distant. He had been like a comfort I needed in all the chaos. The only person who didn't make me feel so alone, but now, I wondered if it was all an act to keep me distracted from what his best friend had done.

"Come here." He pointed to the spot next to him, patting it.

My eyes moved from his gaze to the pool, as I wished the pain would float away.

"Please," he begged softly.

He grabbed my hand and pulled me to sit next to him. He kept staring at my face as I sat there.

"Your ears are cute. I have never seen you with your hair up."

I didn't say anything.

"Why aren't you saying anything or looking at me?" he asked, sounding sad.

"What do you want me to say? Congrats?" I asked, staring at him.

Control yourself, girl. Save your dignity.

"You look damn cute when you're angry," he said with low laughter. I shot him a glare.

"What's up with you?"

Are boys always this clueless?

"You didn't have to follow me here, Adrian!" I snapped, standing up.

"I was worried, okay? You were acting weird."

"Stop worrying about me. And don't call me cute!"

"What are you talking about?"

He stood up, and I stepped back.

"Nothing. You should go back to Karen. We both know Tristan sucks at making conversation."

"Is it Karen?" he asked, but I didn't say anything. "It doesn't change anything between us, Chloe. She's my girlfriend, and you are ... you are a great friend."

There, he'd said it—the phrase I had been dreading.

I gave him one last look and stormed off with one question bouncing in my head. *What the hell did I just do?*

"Chloe, wait," he said, but I didn't stop.

Oh my God, I wanna lock myself in a coffin right now.

Tristan stood at the door, staring at me as I walked toward him. I wondered how long he had been standing there. He stepped aside for me to pass.

I ran into Karen on my way to the staircase, and she asked, "Have you seen Adrian?"

I pointed to the pool and made my way to the stairs.

"Is she okay?" I heard her ask.

"She's drunk," Tristan told her.

I walked into my room and slumped on my bed. "What did you just do, Chloe?"

CHAPTER **SEVENTEEN**
FOREIGN

When I woke up, it was dark outside. I face-palmed myself when I recalled what I had done. I wouldn't be leaving my room anytime soon. I'd totally embarrassed myself.

I shouldn't have snapped; I should have pretended I was happy for him. I groaned and buried my face in the pillow. A cocktail of emotions pulled strings from all sides, but guilt galloped all over me. I had to avoid him until I came up with an excuse. I could tell him I was drunk. The door suddenly opened. I pretended to be asleep.

"I know you're awake."

I was relieved it was Tristan, but I didn't move.

"Are you feeling better?"

I gave up and turned to look at him. "I'm fine."

"Adrian told me you were feeling sick because you drank too much wine, which is weird because I have seen you finish a whole bottle with barely a buzz."

"Yeah, my body didn't like the wine."

"Call Morris if you need anything." He turned to leave.

"Tristan," I called, sitting up.

He stopped, turning around with a scowl etched in his forehead.

"Can you tell me what happened last night? I know I was drunk, and you were there, but the rest of my memory is hazy."

He folded his arms and leaned on the doorframe, smiling.

"What?" I asked, panicking.

He shrugged and walked away, leaving me confused.

Did we talk about something else?

My phone rang, breaking me from my train of thought. Vina's name blessed my blurry eyes.

"Hey, girl!" she screamed in a singsong tone.

I started crying with no tears.

"Chloe? What's wrong? Did Tristan do something to you? Should I call 911?"

"No, I made a mess, Vina. I did something stupid."

I heard her sigh in relief. "You burned down Tristan's house?"

"No, it's worse."

"What did you do, Chloe Simpson? Wait, did you murder Tristan? Just tell me the truth. I will come over and help you clean up and get rid of the body. Then, we'll run away to an unknown place in the world, leaving no trace behind."

I checked my phone screen to be sure I was still speaking to my best friend.

"Belvina Gallardo, are you okay?"

"Sorry. I just finished this horror movie, and it's messing with my head. What happened?"

I grunted before telling her my dilemma.

"No way," she gasped when I was done. "You had every right to behave that way, Chlo. I might have done worse if it were me. He led you on and now brings his girlfriend, the asshole. *Pedazo de mierda sin valor.* I will unfollow him right now on social media."

"I feel so stupid." I sighed.

"What are you going to do now?"

"Go invisible when I see him."

"Oh, you didn't tell me you had superpowers."

"Seriously, Vina, tell me what to do," I cried.

"To be honest with you, I think you should sort this out yourself."

"Any advice?"

"He already knows you like him. You can't change that. Wait and see what he will do. If he doesn't make … I'm telling you what to do, aren't I?"

"Uh-huh, go on."

"No, figure this out yourself. Good night. Love you." She ended the call before I could beg her.

It'd been two days since the incident with Adrian. I hadn't seen Adrian since my outburst, and Tristan had been keeping his distance from me. I hadn't gotten the chance to talk to him about our deal, and I was hesitating. Maybe I didn't want my old life back. Maybe Tristan's actions had opened my eyes to the truth about my family and Grey. Something must have happened to my brain for me to consider that.

I stayed in my room with three bags of potato chips, engrossed in research for my paper. I told Morris to only come to my room when it was time for dinner.

At 7:37 p.m., he was knocking on my door. I told him I'd be down in a minute, and he left. I cleared my bed and wore my big bunny slippers. I walked down the stairs, rubbing my eyes. I froze when I heard Adrian's laughter, and my heart raced. Feet glued to the ground, I forgot how to move for a moment.

I stepped back slowly, trying not to make any sound.

"Did you forget something, Miss Simpson?" Morris asked the moment he saw me.

I wanted the ground to open and swallow me.

"No," I said with a laugh but couldn't help glaring at him for ruining my escape.

I summoned every ounce of courage I had and went to the dining room. Karen wasn't with him. I sat next to Tristan, not uttering a word or making eye contact. I watched Morris dish out our food like it was the most interesting thing ever. I could feel someone's eyes on me, and it wasn't Tristan's.

From my peripheral vision, I saw Adrian standing up. I stopped breathing as he walked over to me.

"Can I talk to you outside? It's only going to take a few minutes."

I nodded, not trusting myself enough to say a word.

"I will be waiting for you in the garden," he whispered and withdrew, carrying his warmth with him.

I glanced at Tristan. He was already eating and didn't look bothered. I stood up, leaving for the garden. I tried to calm my breath as I got closer. I saw Adrian's broad and tall physique touching the garden gnome. I'd thought it was small compared to me, but it was an ant next to Adrian.

I walked to where he was, standing next to him. There was a long silence between us. He smiled at me like an angel, like he had done no wrong. I rubbed my left elbow, staring at the gnome too. He faced me, and I did the same. I bit my inner cheek as I waited for him to say something.

"I'm sorry. I'm really sorry if I gave you the wrong signal."

I was disappointed and heartbroken. "It's fine. I was drunk and said nonsense." I laughed off the pain.

"I wouldn't have brought her here if I had known. I can't imagine how you felt. I'm truly sorry." His gray eyes glimmered under the moon.

Was it possible to feel such disappointment adorned with grace?

"Adrian, I'm over it." No, I wasn't. I felt rejected.

Adrian was a ray of sunshine to everyone. He cared about the people around him. He spoke sweetly to everyone, he gave everyone that special smile, and he hugged them all the same. I'd misunderstood everything.

"Any guy would be the luckiest in the world to have you. I feel lucky right now. I mean, Chloe Simpson has a crush on me. I'm flattered," he said, and we both laughed.

His words poured on my aching heart like honey on a poisonous apple. No matter how much he sugarcoated it, I was still hurt.

"Stop," I groaned, unable to look at him.

"In my next life, I want us to meet in a different way. Things won't be so complicated," he said, looking up at the stars.

Be strong. Don't get emotional.

"Forgive me for hurting you, Chloe," he said after a long silence.

"It's okay," I whispered.

"Believe me, dating Karen doesn't change anything between us. You still own a special place in my heart. You're an amazing person—smart, funny—"

"Please stop," I cut in with a strangled voice, holding back tears.

I could see the moon in his eyes, and some part of me wanted to see the whole world in him too. I was my own world, and the sooner I acknowledged that, the faster I'd be able to move on—not just from

Adrian, but also from everyone else who held my heart hostage.

"Sorry," he said. "I'm starving. Can we go back inside?" he asked, a frown creasing his forehead.

"I hate you," I said, following him.

"Liar," he whispered.

Why was he so good at this? It was impossible to hate him.

Tristan was gone when we got to the dining table. His side of the table was clean. Morris took our food for heating.

Adrian lightly conversed with me. After a while, we were laughing and talking like nothing had happened between us. Like water under a bridge. Now, if only I could explain that to my invisible tears.

Maybe we were better off as friends. I didn't want to ruin that. He was still worth having around.

ADRIAN AND I were cool now. Friday afternoon, I was informed Adrian would be treating us to dinner in a classic restaurant.

I went online shopping for a dress and a pair of heels with Tristan's card. Morris brought it to my room when it arrived. I couldn't remember the last time I'd visited a classy restaurant or gone out. My mom didn't like Ciara and me staying out late with friends, and it still saddened me that if I hadn't gone the route I wanted, I would have missed out on the teenage thrills and fun. I knew I had gone too far, and it'd gotten me into a big mess, but I had moved on from it even if I had a big scar on my back, reminding me of my foolishness.

I had a good feeling about tonight's dinner. I knew Karen would be there, but I didn't care. I would try to be friends with her. She was a sweet soul.

At seven twenty p.m., I was running around, trying to put on my earring. Tristan had sent Morris, like, three times to come up and call me.

I had everything under control until I decided to do a neat bun. I sucked at styling my hair, but in the end, I got it. All this planning reminded me of the incident. I still wanted to know why Tristan destroyed his wedding and picked me, but would I be okay if I never knew?

My makeup was already done, and the dress looked good on me, I must admit. It was a black satin evening dress that stopped above my knees; it was sleeveless with a deep V-neck showing small cleavage since I hadn't been blessed in the boob department. I grabbed my purse and left the room. I ran into Morris on my way downstairs.

"Mr. Sanchester is—"

"I'm ready," I cut him off with a smile.

"He is in the living room."

"Thanks."

Tristan was staring at a new painting on the wall. He was wearing black sweatpants and a white T-shirt with black Nike shoes.

"Sorry for keeping you waiting."

He turned around to face me; his eyes scanned what I was wearing. His eyes lingered longer on my chest before he met my eyes.

"Do you have somewhere else to be after dinner?"

What a way to compliment someone.

"No."

He stared at my strappy heels and then looked away. He was making me feel like I had done too much. I mean, it was a dinner in a fancy place. Why wasn't he more dressed up?

"Is that what you're wearing?" I asked.

177

"Yeah, we are going to eat and chat, not have tea with the Queen of England."

He is really going to wear sweats and a T-shirt?

"Shall we?"

I nodded.

I wasn't surprised at the number of exotic cars parked in his large garage. He grabbed one key and opened a sleek red Ferrari.

I kept my eyes on the road to make sure we arrived safely since Tristan kept texting on his phone with one hand while the other controlled the wheel. Relief rolled over me when he parked the car in front of the restaurant.

It was a French restaurant, and we made our way in. Adrian and Karen waved at us when we entered. I put on a smile as we approached them. We took our seats in front of them. It was cold in here. I glanced around the bright room, which harbored expensive chandeliers and beautiful paintings of Paris.

"I love your hair, Chloe." Karen's voice drew my attention away from a couple grinning at each other.

"Thanks. It took forever for me to get it to look this good."

"Tell me about it, and men have the guts to complain we take an eternity to get ready," she said, and I laughed softly.

We could be friends, right?

"You look stunning," I told her, and she smiled, mumbling, "Thanks."

She was wearing a silk beige dress. Adrian was dressed in a two-piece suit. Everyone here was dressed in something stylish, except Tristan. Even the waiters and waitresses looked chic. He looked like someone had dragged him out of bed here. I was embarrassed for him.

"Hey." Adrian beamed at me.

"Hey," I whispered.

A waiter arrived and took our orders. It was hard to pronounce some of the dishes on the menu. The only foreign language I'd studied in high school was Spanish, and with Vina always mumbling curses and insults in Spanish, I was proud to say I knew every curse word and insult in Spanish.

"How are you feeling? Adrian told me what happened," Karen asked.

He told her? My entire mental self facepalmed. Of course he had.

"I'm okay. Sorry about that day," I apologized.

"It's fine. Your health comes first." She waved it off with a nice smile. I felt my body relax after I realized Adrian had lied to her about what really happened.

Adrian ordered an expensive red wine. Tristan made me drink water since we were in public because to everyone I was pregnant. I sipped it while we waited for our food to arrive. Karen was talking about her trip to Paris and the places she'd visited.

My phone vibrated, indicating a text. I took it out of my purse and checked it. It was a text from Vina, sharing a meme that had reminded her of me. We used to tag each other in funny posts on social media, but I had deactivated all my socials after the incident.

Adrian stood up from his seat with a nervous smile. *What is he so nervous about?* I watched as he moved to the other side, where Karen was sitting. He brought out a small black box and went on one knee. I gripped my phone tightly. Karen looked like she was having a hard time breathing, as she knew what was about to happen. He opened the box, and the diamond ring in the box caught everyone's attention. She gasped and put a hand over her mouth.

"Will you make me the happiest man in the world and marry me?" he said sweetly.

She nodded her head frantically.

She gave him her hand, and he put the ring on. She had tears in her eyes. People in the room applauded.

He just proposed in front of me? I gulped my water, wishing it were poison. *Someone, just end me from my suffering.* He'd invited me here to come and witness him propose to his girlfriend.

I forced a grin as I watched them kiss. *Control yourself, Chloe.*

It felt like someone was running a sword in and out of my heart. I reached for the wine bottle and got frustrated when I found it empty. I turned to look at Tristan. He was beaming at them. I grabbed his wine and finished it. He glanced at me, and I faked a smile.

"Help me take a picture." Karen forced her phone into my hand.

I tried to look happy as I took the pictures. She made many poses with the ring.

I looked for an excuse to leave as she showed Adrian the pictures. I texted Vina and told her to call me—that way, I could give an excuse of leaving to answer the call and never return. Our food arrived, and my stomach craved the tasty food, but I had to leave. I wasn't sure I could sit through the whole dinner without losing control.

Vina finally called. I flashed them a smile as I stood up.

"Sorry, I have to answer this." I walked quickly out of the restaurant.

"Okay, tell me what's going on," she demanded immediately after I picked up the call.

"Adrian just proposed to Karen."

"*Oh mierda*, that was the reason for the dinner?"

"I guess so."

"That's cruel. He shouldn't have invited you, knowing how you feel about him. Do you want me to come over and keep you company?"

"No. I will just go to the house and drink myself to sleep."

"Be careful, okay? I'm worried about you."

"Yeah, I will call you tomorrow."

"Don't do anything stupid," she said before hanging up.

I called Morris and waited for him to come and pick me up.

"Is the dinner over, Miss Simpson?"

"No, I had to leave because my, um … I'm not feeling too well." I wanted to lie and tell him my uncle's goat had a miscarriage.

"Should I take you to the hospital?"

"No, just take me to the house."

"Okay, miss."

I took off my heels immediately after I entered the house. I headed to the wine cellar, grabbed one bottle of brandy, and went to the kitchen.

I grabbed a wineglass and poured some brandy into the glass. I took my hair from the bun and allowed it to fall to my back.

I took a seat at the island and sipped the brandy with different thoughts in my head. Alcohol was kinda my comfort drink. I took it to avoid overthinking. With the situation I was in, it seemed really helpful. It would have been much better if I'd heard the news about the proposal than witnessed it.

Someone walked into the kitchen. I was expecting to see Morris, but it was Tristan.

"You left because you wanted more wine?" He leaned on the seat far from me.

"No, you left too anyway."

"Adrian kept bugging me to go check on you since you were taking an eternity to return. I had to call Morris, and he told me you were sick.

Care to explain?"

"It wasn't a lie. I was nauseous, and alcohol helps sometimes." I knew that didn't make any sense.

"Aren't you too young to be consuming this amount of alcohol?"

I shrugged.

I was twenty. Maybe it was illegal.

I stood up, got another glass, and poured some brandy for him. He collected it.

"How was the food?" I asked.

"Great. It tasted like paradise. We should go there some other time."

I gave him an eye roll. Maybe I should get him drunk and get the truth out of him. I had never seen him drunk. He was always watchful of the amount of alcohol he consumed.

"You're the first female I have ever come across who drinks like this."

"I'm honored," I said with a bow.

His lips pulled into an amused grin as he sipped his drink. I stared at his lips on the glass; they looked so soft. *What will it feel like to kiss Tristan?* I shook the thought out of my head. Must be the alcohol talking, but I was a slave to my curiosity, and it needed to be quenched.

I had this crazy idea in my head, and I knew I would regret it. I took one gulp of my drink and stood up. I stopped in front of him, and he cocked an eyebrow as he stared down at me, his blue eyes holding countless secrets I wanted to know.

I gripped the front of his shirt and pushed myself up on my tiptoes, my eyes drifting to his full, tempting lips. I was still contemplating what I was about to do until I stopped thinking and took his lower lip in a slow kiss. I felt him tense and suck in a breath.

Is this what it means to have butterflies in my stomach?

I waited for him to kiss me back, but he didn't. I withdrew and stared at his eyes that were now a darker shade of blue. They held raw desire.

"Are you drunk already?" he asked, observing me.

"No."

The word was barely out of my mouth before he pushed my back against the island and claimed my lips in a heated kiss. In rapid reflex, my lips mustered a moan. I responded to every movement of his soft lips. His tongue slipped in, determined and curious as it met mine. Every brush of his lips felt enticing. His one hand gripped my hip, fingers brushing my thigh with tremors of electrifying waves, while the other hand was around my throat, drowning me in a den of death and desire.

I had never been kissed like this. The feeling was beyond my imagination. I didn't know it was possible to feel like this from a kiss—like I wasn't part of my body. It was as if he had been waiting for me to give the signal. His lips moved in sync with mine, intense and hungry.

He sucked on my lower lip and slowly pulled it between his teeth until he broke the kiss. We were breathing hoarsely as we stared at each other. Hesitation lingered in his eyes, but the lust in his eyes loomed larger.

I wanted more, and my body begged for his touch. I wanted to kiss him again.

Like he'd read my mind, he hoisted me up onto the countertop. I ran my fingers through his hair as he moved closer between my legs. I felt my thighs squeezing, a magnetic attraction to meet his crotch.

The heat from our bodies increased the temperature around us. He used one finger to raise my chin as he looked into my eyes like he was searching for something. He swiped his thumb over my moistened lips and caressed my cheek softly. The gesture made me question what I was doing. My heart raced, drumming against my chest.

His eyes were glued to my lips as he leaned down and kissed me slowly. Like he was pumping in a type of oxygen I had never inhaled before. I didn't know if it was the alcohol, but I was enjoying this. I hadn't planned for it to go this far, but I didn't have a care in the world.

My one hand gripped the edge of the counter as his lips left mine and nibbled on my neck, pulling my skin between his teeth and sucking softly on the mark he'd left behind. A soft growl slipped from his lips as he kissed a spot on my throat. He trailed kisses up my chin and took my lips in a deep kiss. His fingers fisted my hair as he pressed closer against me. I could feel the hardness between his legs.

His palm ran up my thigh, through my dress, leaving a trail of goose bumps on my skin. He gripped my skin, digging his fingers, and I could feel the mark he was leaving on me. I stifled another moan when he bit on my lip and sucked on my tongue. His hand trailed higher to the pulsing between my legs.

"Chloe?"

I pulled away, and we both turned to look at Adrian at the doorway, staring at us.

CHAPTER **EIGHTEEN**
DANGEROUS

Adrian's eyes moved from my face to my thigh, where Tristan's hand lay. We were both quiet and didn't pull away from each other.

Why did I keep feeling like an awful person?

"I will be waiting for you in the living room," Adrian said and walked away. There was a hint of anger in his voice.

I turned to look at Tristan. He pulled away, giving me some space. The warmth around me left with him, but my body was still hot from our make-out session.

He grabbed his drink and took a sip. He sat down and watched me as I jumped down from the island. I adjusted my dress and brushed my fingers through my hair. I glanced at Tristan. He stared back at me not saying anything. I just couldn't tell what he was about to say. I turned away and left the kitchen.

I met Adrian pacing in the living room. He stared at my face as if he didn't recognize me. I crinkled my face with my right brow elevated.

"Tristan told me you were sick," he said, pressing his lips in.

I knew he wanted an explanation.

"Yeah, I was feeling nauseous," I said, cheeks itching to twitch.

Why the hell was he here?

He stepped closer and sniffed the air around me.

"Are you drunk?" He looked angry, and I opened my mouth to answer, but he cut me off, "I swear if he was taking advantage of you, I won't let him off easily."

He wanted to go to the kitchen, but I got in the way. *What is he planning to do? Walk in there and beat him up?*

"Leave Tristan out of this. I was the one who initiated the kiss, and I'm not drunk! I don't even owe you an explanation," I yelled. "Why are you here? Shouldn't you be with your fiancée?"

"Yeah, I should be with her, but I decided to come here because I was worried about you."

I tried not to laugh. *Is he expecting me to be fine after inviting me to watch him propose to his girlfriend?* He knew how I felt about him. A warning would have been nice.

"I'm fine," I said, crossing my arms and putting on a bold face.

"I can see that." He glanced at the kitchen and then at me. "Good night." He walked away.

I closed my eyes, inhaling. *What an awful night.* Tristan stepped out of the kitchen when I turned around.

"I'm sorry. I shouldn't have done that. I wasn't thinking clearly," I said with a frustrated sigh.

"That makes two of us," he said and walked away.

I watched him, guilt weighing all over me. I returned to the kitchen and grabbed my stuff and the bottle of brandy. I cursed at myself as I sauntered to my room, pausing at Tristan's door. I leaned closer to pick up any sound.

I didn't know how he was feeling, and I never took him as a rebound. I didn't want him to think that. I turned away and entered my room with my heart beating harder with every step.

I staggered to the bathroom. I stared at my reflection in the mirror; my hair was a mess. Memories of Tristan gripping my hair flooded my brain, the thought of it alone sending sweet chills through me.

I raised my hand and touched the hickeys on my neck, replaying his lips on me and his teeth sinking into my skin. *What am I turning into?*

I shook my head and left the bathroom. I grabbed the bottle of brandy and took a swig.

It was as if I was becoming my past again.

IT'D BEEN A week since the night Adrian had proposed to Karen and Tristan and I had kissed. We both acted like it had never happened and never spoke about it. But I noticed the atmosphere between us had changed. I couldn't look at him for more than three seconds anymore. Tristan now spoke to me like a normal person and tried to have conversations during dinner.

Adrian came to the house often, but we didn't speak much. Tristan didn't seem to care about anything going on. No matter how clueless he acted about the whole situation between me and Adrian, I knew he understood the underlying scenario. He had heard our conversations and seen the way Adrian and I interacted.

I told Vina what had happened that night, and she was like, "You badass! You weren't drunk, were you?"

"I was very sober."

"Good thing he showed up. Now, it's fair. I'm trying to imagine the look on his face when he walked in on you both kissing." She laughed.

"He was just worried about me."

"Keep telling yourself that," she scoffed.

"How is school?" I changed the topic quickly.

"Frustrating."

"What about Grey?"

"He's been distant. I haven't spoken to him since the wedding."

I smiled. I wasn't sure about how I felt about Grey anymore, but I still cared about him. We had been close friends before we thought of dating. He had shown me that a broken heart could beat again.

"So, did he tell you anything? It's been a month, Chlo."

"I know," I whispered.

"What's going on?" she asked in a serious tone.

"It's complicated."

"Oh my God, please don't tell me that kiss turned your brain upside down." She sighed.

"No, it's not that."

"Then, what? Is it Adrian?"

"No," I snapped.

Anything I'd felt toward Adrian was now replaced with rage. It was as if someone had broken me from a love spell after I witnessed the proposal. I had been an idiot to take his sweet gestures as affection. With Tristan, it was like a never-ending maze, and he was still a box of mystery I wanted to unwrap.

There was a long silence as Belvina waited for me to explain. I didn't even know what to tell her. I looked on the bright side. I had a roof over my head. I also had Morris, and Tristan took care of my tuition. It wasn't like my family gave a shit if I was alive or dead.

"You deserve an explanation after all he did to you. Ask him for the truth and get your ass out of there before you get tangled in something you won't be able to escape from," she said and hung up before I could say anything.

Why is she mad at me?

I sighed and stared outside at the darkness. It was Saturday night, and I had been working on a few school projects. I thought of what Belvina had said.

Why am I scared of asking him? I wanted to know his reason and if he would keep his promise about telling my family the truth.

I went to the bathroom and filled the bathtub with warm water and threw in a bath bomb. I undressed and submerged myself inside the water; the strawberry scent engulfed me. I closed my eyes and tried to remember what it'd felt like to be me, but I realized I'd lost that sense of who I was a long time ago. When I had been growing up, it had been hard to find myself, especially in a household where I had to pretend all the time to avoid my mom's judgment and wrath.

Is it wrong of me to be enjoying my stay here? The comfort and freedom?

Vina had had a point. I should get out before things got messy.

I stayed a few more minutes in the tub before stepping out and drying myself. It was almost midnight, and it looked like it was about to rain from the sound of thunder and the occasional lightning that made me jump.

I turned off the lights and went under the covers. Sleeping while it was raining hit different. The sound of the rain was like a peaceful lullaby that put me to sleep. I left the drapes open, watching the trees close by sway to the rhythm of the wind. There was a knock on my door. I sat up as I told the person to open the door.

"Did I wake you?" Tristan asked from the doorway.

"No, I just got in bed."

"Do you mind if I sleep here?"

I hesitated, knowing it would be different, sleeping next to him tonight. I hadn't gotten that kiss out of my head, and every time I entered the kitchen, the counter replayed the scene in front of me. Maybe it had been different for him; maybe he had forgotten we'd ever kissed. I didn't know what he battled within, but if sleeping next to me helped him get some sleep, then I was cool with it.

"Sure," I said, creating some room on the bed for him.

He stepped in and shut the door. The room was dim from the light outside, so he could make his way to the bed.

"Thank you," he whispered next to me, keeping distance between our bodies.

I didn't know why I felt nervous. I hadn't felt like this last time we shared a bed.

"You can hold me if you want," I said, sensing his hesitation from behind me.

I sucked in a breath as soon as his arms wrapped around my bare stomach. I should have considered that. His callous fingers brushed my skin as he moved closer. I blamed the cold outside for the goose bumps on my skin. It was now raining heavily. The pitter-patter sound drowned the noise around us.

I had been still for a minute now, scared to move a muscle. My hips were starting to hurt from the weight resting on it. I shifted slowly to make myself comfortable. My legs brushed Tristan's, and my movement made his hands move lower.

He stayed quiet. I could feel the steady movement of his chest behind me. I adjusted again to find a cold spot on the pillow, and I heard him groan. Was he frustrated with my stirring? Well, he should get used to it because I would be moving a lot.

I closed my eyes and listened to the rain outside. The warmth from his skin engulfed me like a quilt, and I embraced it. I was starting to drift slowly to sleep when he spoke. His voice was so smooth and warm against my skin; I could feel it flow through my body like honey.

"I'm sorry."

"For what?" I asked, my voice coming out low.

"I couldn't get your parents to listen to me. Your mom kept threatening to call the cops if I stepped on her yard again. She won't let me anywhere close to the house."

I remained quiet. I didn't know how I felt about that. Maybe disappointed at my family and relieved he'd at least tried but angry he couldn't fix the damage he'd done. Many people thought the worst of me—that I was a homewrecker.

"I couldn't tell you because I promised to clear up the mess I'd made. I was only able to get the videos down. I'm sorry. I will keep trying."

I didn't say anything. I couldn't pinpoint exactly what I was feeling.

"Chloe?" he called when I said nothing.

I closed my eyes and pretended to be asleep when he moved to check if I was awake. I heard him sigh and mumble a curse.

THE MELODIC CHIRPING of birds and brightness flooding the room woke me up. The intense sunlight burned my eyes as I tried to keep them open. I felt too lazy to stand up and pull the drapes to block the sunlight. *What time is it?* My brain was always slow in the morning.

I felt strong arms around me when I moved. Last night came flashing back. I was surprised he was still here. I looked up at his face that was now a few inches away. Somehow, we had changed positions from last night; he was now cradling me in his arms, my face buried in his neck and his stubble brushing my forehead. One of his arms stayed around my waist and the other around my shoulders. Our legs were intertwined.

Should I wake him up? It was Sunday. Maybe he had nothing to do. It was clearly a late morning, but I didn't feel like pulling away. I snuggled closer and closed my eyes. It wasn't every day you got a human teddy bear.

I WOKE UP alone on the bed, no sign of my teddy bear. It was almost one p.m. I walked to the bathroom and sat on the toilet. I needed tampons; my period was due anytime soon. From the fever and acne appearing on my cheeks, I could tell she was on her way to make a visit. I was one of the unlucky ones who had the worst menstrual cramps.

I took a shower and threw on sweat shorts and a loose T-shirt. Morris smiled at me as I entered the kitchen. I settled for a full meal to make up for breakfast and lunch.

"Where is Tristan?" I asked as he served me some lemon tea.

"He left the house an hour ago."

Did he know I'd heard everything he said last night? I wanted to text him to get me some tampons on his way back. I didn't want to be out in public. I realized I could just order it online and save myself the embarrassment of explaining the brand and type of tampon I used to Tristan.

I went for a walk in the garden after eating. I spent hours on the phone with Belvina after and went to check my school emails for any announcement.

In the evening, I wanted to do something to keep myself occupied. I went to the kitchen and decided to make dinner, which might have been a bad idea because I didn't know how to cook. My mom hadn't done so well in that department. We had a private chef that came over every day to cook because Mom couldn't do anything right in the kitchen. She had given up after she made the lasagna explode in the oven.

"Are you sure you don't need my help?" Morris asked for the third time.

"Yes, Morris. It's not my first time cooking pasta." I smiled at him. It was actually my first time, but I was sure cooking pasta was as easy as boiling water, right?

"You can leave now."

He was reluctant, but he still left.

"What are you doing?" Tristan asked, entering the kitchen with his laptop.

"Cooking?" I smiled.

"Are you sure you can cook?"

I was offended that he'd asked. What if I was a good cook?

"You're about to find out." I smirked as I put the spaghetti in the boiling water. I read the next instruction on the pasta pack—*prepare the sauce.*

"If you need help, call me." He grabbed one bottle of water and sat at the kitchen island.

"I won't need your help," I said, looking over my shoulder at him.

I played my favorite songs from my phone and hummed as I cooked. I moved my body to the beat when it got to my favorite song.

I had stayed with him for a month now. I knew Tristan had a lot going on, and he wasn't worth my kindness or patience. I only hoped he had a good reason for what he had done. But to be honest, I kind of liked it here. I could be myself and do stuff without worrying about my mom's wrath, but I needed to find a way to leave soon.

I screamed the lyrics to *"Dancing with a Stranger"*, using the spoon as my mic.

I heard Tristan laugh, but when I turned around, he was so engrossed in his laptop.

I picked one knife and chopped the onion. The knife slipped from my hand when I tried to dance to the ending of the song.

"Ouch!" I groaned when it hit my right thigh. The cut left me cursing.

"Shit!" I stared at the blood that slid down my skin.

Thank God it wasn't a deep cut. Shallow, but the pain preyed upon my sensitive skin, whipping me with tyrannical thorns.

"What the hell were you doing?" Tristan asked, standing up from his seat.

"It was an accident."

He searched the cabinet and brought out the first aid kit.

"Let me take a look at it."

He took my hand and led me to the living room. I sat on the sofa as he knelt between my legs, bringing out the cotton balls and a small bottle.

"This is what you get for being clumsy."

"I'm not clumsy," I defended myself.

"You don't dance with knives," he whispered, leaning in.

"I couldn't resist. It was my favorite song."

"You're a horrible dancer," he said.

"I caught you watching," I whispered with a bit of sultriness.

"Have you seen the way your ass looks in those shorts? Especially when you started swaying your hips, I couldn't get any work done on my laptop." He groaned, as if it'd tortured him.

"Hmm," I hummed with a small smile. I hadn't known he was that engrossed in my awful dancing.

I closed my legs when he brought the soaked cotton ball closer to the gash on my skin.

"Stay still." He gripped my thigh with his free hand and pushed my legs apart. His warmth rubbed against my thigh.

I held my breath and closed my eyes, ready to welcome the pain. I winced immediately after it touched the cut; the pain shot through every part of my body. I tried to close my legs, but he held tighter.

I threw my head back in pain, biting on my lower lip. I groaned while biting my lip harder, like it would stop the pain.

The pain subsided as I felt the warm air on my skin. I opened my eyes and saw him blowing some air on the cut. The way his lips formed a circle and how dangerously close his lips were to my skin sent my mind swirling with dirty thoughts.

The only thing I could think about was his hand on my thigh and his lips close to my skin. The kiss from last time replayed in my head. I shouldn't be thinking about this. He was the reason for everything wrong in my life.

But I couldn't help the urge to feel his lips and hands on me again. I looked away when he withdrew. He applied an ointment that made the wound hurt more. I looked at him, only to find him staring at my lip still between my teeth. His Adam's apple bobbed, and he had the same look in his eyes from our last kiss.

"Are you done?" I asked almost breathlessly. The thickness in the air was killing me.

"Yeah, let me put on the Band-Aid."

I nodded. He gently placed it and remained on his knees. His eyes lingered on my flushed face and then raked down to my lips and to my neck, kindling my blood with warmth. His slippery fingers slid along my thighs until they reached the hem of my shorts.

My heart was thumping against my chest as he drew closer. He wrapped his hands around the backs of my knees and pulled me closer until I was at the end of the seat and pressed against him.

My body had a mind of its own, making me anticipate his next move. He looked into my eyes, waiting for my reaction to see if I wanted this. I placed my hand over his and traced the prominent veins on his fingers.

I waited for him to close the small space between us, but he only stared at my lips. Time seemed to stop, and everything around us disappeared. His intense gaze held mine, hesitating. Just when I thought he'd pull away, his head dipped down, and his lips met mine in an aching kiss. I gasped immediately after our lips touched. It started softly but got heated as his tongue brushed mine. I gripped the seat tightly, returning every kiss as he ran his fingers through my hair. My legs curled on the floor from the dreamy dance.

No one had ever made me crave something so bad. Kissing Tristan was like fireworks going off in my cells. Could a kiss make someone lose their mind? Funny how a stranger could suddenly make everything feel amazing with just one kiss, knocking your heart off-balance and making you want to kiss them forever.

His large hand gripped my hip, trailing to my ass and grabbing me so hard that I pressed against him and felt the hardness between his legs. I moaned as his hand slipped into my T-shirt, skimming up my skin and cupping my small, sensitive breast.

Suddenly, he pulled away, as if I had burned him. Fear floated in his eyes, like that of a child witnessing a ghost among the darkness. He stepped away from me like he didn't recognize me, and he frantically shook his head as he sat on the floor.

"Tristan?" I called, crawling slowly to where he was.

He gripped his hair, burying his face in his palms.

"Tristan, what's wrong?"

"I'm sorry, Fiona. I'm so sorry," he mumbled.

"What?"

Who is he calling Fiona?

"Tristan, it's me, Chloe," I said, trying to touch him.

"Call Adrian," he said, moving away from my touch.

"Can I help?" I inquired.

"I said, call Adrian!"

I flinched at his tone but ran to get my phone.

Adrian picked up on the second ring.

"Hey, Chloe."

"Adrian, you need to come here quickly. Something is wrong with Tristan."

"Okay, stay calm and keep an eye on him. I will be there in five minutes."

"Hurry," I said and ended the call.

I turned off the electric cooktop and returned to the living room. I sat next to him on the floor. He was quiet, but his hands shook. I didn't know how to help.

"I'm sorry," he mumbled again.

"It's okay. You'll be fine," I whispered, drawing closer.

I hesitated as I tried to put my arm around him. He didn't push me away; instead, he snuggled closer and wrapped his arms around me like a scared kid.

"I'm right here," I said softly as I stroke his hair.

He tightened his grip around me like he didn't want me to let go. It was almost painful.

Adrian arrived with an older man. They both walked to where he was and helped him up, and then they took him upstairs to his room. Adrian stopped me when I tried to enter the room.

"Stay in your room. The doctor will make sure he is okay."

"No, I want to know what's wrong with him!"

I tried to force my way in, but he held me back.

"He will be fine, Chloe."

"I want to know what's going on!" I yelled.

"You're not helping the situation right now. Fucking wait in your room!" Adrian yelled back.

"I'm sick of you guys keeping things from me."

"Please, Chloe."

I glared at him before walking away.

I waited for hours, but I didn't see Adrian. I left my room and paced in front of Tristan's room.

I got tired and sat on the stairs, and I yawned as sleep called to me. I never got to cook my pasta. I stood up immediately after the door opened, and Adrian walked out alone.

"How is he?" I asked.

"He is sleeping, and he is okay."

"What about the doctor?"

"He left an hour ago."

"Are you going to tell me what's going on now or wait until I throw a tantrum?"

"I'm not sure I'm supposed to tell you this, but Tristan had a flashback of something that had happened some years ago. Something must have triggered it, but he will be fine."

I was still taking in what he said. I wondered what traumatic event

Tristan had gone through. *Was it the kiss that triggered it?*

"You should go to bed. It's almost two a.m. Call me if anything comes up," he said with a small smile. He looked like he had something else to say, but he turned away to leave.

"Okay, good night," I mumbled.

No more forehead kisses. I missed that.

"Good night."

I was tempted to open Tristan's room and take a peek, but I fought it and went to my room. It took me a while to get some sleep.

I woke up a bit late. I went straight to check on Tristan. I tried to open the door, but it was locked from inside.

"Tristan?" I called, knocking.

I waited, but no one answered. I knocked again, but he didn't answer. I raised my knuckle to knock again, but the door suddenly opened, making my heart fly to my throat.

Tristan stood in front of me, only in his black boxer briefs, his bedhead making him look so sexy. He dragged me into the room when I opened my mouth to speak.

He seated me on the bed and then sat on the gray sofa in front.

"You wanna know why you're here and why I did what I did in the church?" He sounded tired.

"Um …"

Was this the right time? Were we going to have a conversation with him half-naked?

"Well, if—"

"I will tell you," he cut in.

I felt so uneasy. Why all of a sudden? I tried not to get too distracted, but how was that possible when I had a hot specimen who was half-naked in front of me?

"You're here to help me create a dream," he said after releasing a deep breath.

"Huh?"

CHAPTER **NINETEEN**
PRESSURE

"That doesn't make any sense," I told him, trying not to laugh.

Was he trying to be funny?

"It's simple," he said, leaning back on the seat.

"Oh, is it? If it's simple, you wouldn't need me."

"Your job right now is to listen. I will do all the talking."

"What if I need to ask a question?"

"No questions."

"That's not fair. What if I don't understand—"

"I will explain everything to you."

"Okay, I'm listening." I sat back, using my hands to support my weight.

He sat up, rubbing his chin with his thumb, like he was still contemplating telling me. I looked around the room as I waited for him to say something. I was surprised he had no paintings in his room since he was obsessed with them.

"First of all, I'm sorry I dragged you into this mess. You've been patient with me, and you deserve to know the truth." He paused and looked down at the floor.

"I went through a rough patch a few years ago. I lost everything good in my life, and it made me shut everyone out. My mom believed getting married was the solution to bring light into my life and to help me move on. I wasn't interested, but she wouldn't stop pressuring me to go on with her plans for a better future. I agreed, desperate to escape her whining. I thought getting married to Sofia would help, maybe take away the worries and make her happy. I would do anything for my mom if it made her happy, so I was willing to enter a loveless marriage." He stopped and sighed.

He still hadn't looked at me.

"I felt nothing for Sofia. My mom had chosen her because she was a longtime family friend. She made us go on a few dates, even a romantic getaway, but all I wanted was to be far away from her. I convinced myself I could endure a union with her and not give her any attention, and then maybe she'd get tired and ask for a divorce.

"The morning of the wedding, I wanted to call it off, but I convinced myself again that I could do it. It was at the altar I realized I could never do it, and I had to stop it."

He paused and stood up, running his hands up his face to the back of his neck, as if he was having an internal conflict with himself. He didn't say anything for a minute and kept his back to me. He turned to look at me. He sat back in the seat.

"I know how crazy this might sound, and I want you to know, it was never my intention for things to turn out the way it did. I'm doing this for my mom," he said with a pause.

There was an eerie feeling in the room. He didn't look comfortable with telling me, and I was tired of waiting for an answer, so I didn't stop him.

"With everything going on, you know the...the um...hospital and what happened at the wedding," He scratched the back of his neck, looking anywhere else but at me.

I smiled at how he looked like a teenage boy trying to ask his crush out.

"I want to create a dream for my mom. She is very sick, and ... and she's dying."

Dying? Mrs. Sanchester is dying? I wouldn't have expected anything was wrong.

"She got too busy taking care of me because of what I was going through, making sure I was sane every day at rehab—"

"Rehab?" I cut in immediately.

"No questions," he said, not looking at me.

I held back from rolling my eyes and listened.

"Well, my mom spent each day with me. None of us saw it coming. She was diagnosed with stage four cancer. When we found out, it was too late. It has already spread through many parts of her body." His voice was losing strength.

Cancer? She looked healthy, young, and her hair was still intact. *Or is it a wig?*

"Chemo didn't work for her. She doesn't have much time left, and I want to make her happy." He looked down, rubbing his palms together like it could ease whatever pain he felt inside.

I was tempted to go to him and wrap my arms around him, but I restrained myself. I did not understand his pain. There was just something gut-wrenching about losing someone, knowing he wouldn't ever see her again. All he had left were memories and tears. The hole in his heart could never be filled, no matter how hard he tried to be happy.

It made me want to burst into tears.

"I want to give her something, make her happy before she goes. I don't want her dying and worrying about me. Things didn't end well with the first woman in my life." He paused and didn't say anything for a while.

He met my eyes and then looked away quickly.

"I told myself many times on that altar to just go on with it—maybe married life would change Sofia—but I couldn't for some reason. It was a last-minute decision."

"Adrian knew it was going to happen," I pointed out.

"I told him I couldn't get married to Sofia right from the beginning. He didn't know that was going to happen in the church."

"Then, why did you pick me? Did I look old to you that day?" I'd suspected he could have gone for someone closer to his age.

He fought a laugh at my question.

"After I announced to everyone about my lover and the pregnancy, my plan was to walk out of the church and find a way to convince my mom I wasn't ready to move on yet. I don't know what came over me, but I saw you there at the back, and I had the urge to make everyone believe me, so I said she was in the church."

Yeah, and that I happened to be his lover.

"Why make up such an excuse? You could have just walked out of the church," I asked, my anger getting the best of me as I recalled that day.

"It just slipped out. I guess I needed a reason," he mumbled.

"Why me?"

He paused for a moment and stared at me, his expression softening and hopeful. I wished I could read what was going on inside his head.

"I don't know. Trust me, I was about to walk out of the church before

I saw you."

I scoffed and shook my head at how delusional he sounded.

"I'm sorry for what happened, Chloe. I really am."

"Your apology doesn't change anything," I said quietly.

"I know," he continued. "Right now, to my family, we are very in love, and you're carrying my baby. My grandma is very excited about the baby."

"And you think this is right?" I asked. "How will you explain no baby to her in nine months?"

His eyes spiraled with stupefaction. He had no real answer for me.

"You think your mom will be happy when she is finally gone? When God shows her the truth? Was that really necessary? Why did you wait till the wedding day to pick a new bride when you would have saved the Novas from humiliation and not ruined my life? This is so stupid."

"I only need you to play along."

"I can't. It's not right."

He groaned, thrusting his face into his palms.

"It's totally up to you if you wanna help me or not. If you choose to leave, then it's fine."

"You know what, Mr. Sanchester?"

"Don't call me that," he growled.

"I know you wanna help your mom, but I lost everything, Tristan." I paused and gave it thought. I didn't like the idea, but I wanted to help. I could feel the guilt already, deceiving everyone and going along with his stupid plan to help make his mom happy. Was it worth it?

I turned to look at him, and he was staring at me, eyes begging me to nod with silence. A simple gesture of approval, and he would burst into joy.

"Once this is over, I promise to tell everyone the truth. It's okay if you want it on every news channel in the state, just do me this favor. If you want more money, I will give it to you."

He looked so vulnerable right now.

"I will do it on one condition," I said, raising one finger, emphasizing my sole condition.

He groaned with a hum drumming down his throat.

"Fine, what is it?" He crossed his arms and sat back.

"I need you to promise me you won't hurt yourself again. You know, like punching the mirror with bare hands and whatever you do … you know what I mean."

"It's not something I can control, but I will try, I promise." His face was engulfed in a sorrowful sea.

"What triggers it?" I asked.

"I don't want to talk about it," he said, avoiding my eyes.

I'd figured he wouldn't wanna talk about it. There was definitely more to this situation, and I was going to find out.

"Okay, my dumbass has agreed to help," I said and stood up to leave. There was nothing left for me at home anyway.

He stood up, too, and took a step closer.

Tristan opened his arms, and I just stared at him, confused. He gestured for me to come into his open arms. I chuckled when I realized he wanted to give me a hug. I'd be stupid to turn it down. I moved closer, and he wrapped his arms around me in a warm hug, his skin rubbed against my cheek like a marshmallow.

"Thank you, Cassandra," he whispered with his chin on my head.

I wanted to argue. How did he know the name I hated so much?

"Or do you prefer Cassie?" he asked when I didn't say anything.

"Just call me Chloe. I prefer Chloe," I whispered, closing my eyes.

"I prefer Cassandra."

I ignored him and listened to his heartbeat. I remembered that night I'd thought he was dead.

There was a knock on the door. I groaned mentally and pulled away.

"Open," he said, letting go.

Morris opened the door with a firm smile. "Good morning, Mr. Sanchester. Good morning, Miss Simpson. I hope you slept well."

"Yeah. What about you?" I asked.

"Good, as always. I came to inform you, breakfast is ready."

"Good. I'm starving," I said, rubbing my stomach.

"Go on. I will be down in a minute," Tristan said, walking to the bathroom.

I left with Morris to the dining room.

Tristan was dressed in a dark tailored suit when he joined me at the table. He had this commanding presence about him. He gave me a small smile and took the seat next to me. I leaned closer and brushed my fingers through his hair to tame the wild edges. I didn't know what had come over me. It felt like a reflex.

"Thanks," he mumbled as I nodded.

I caught Morris's smile. He put on a straight face immediately after he met my gaze.

"How are your classes going?" Tristan suddenly asked.

"Awful. I might end up with a B in two of my courses. My finals are around the corner, and I'm scared." I sighed, playing with the scrambled eggs on my plate.

"I can get you a home tutor," he said.

"No, I just need to focus more," I told him. I felt dumb, to be honest.

"Let me know if you need anything, Chloe," he said and glanced at his wristwatch. "I'm late for a meeting, I will see you when I get back," he said, standing up.

He looked down at me, as if he was contemplating giving me a kiss or walking away. He did the latter.

"I wanted a kiss," I mumbled with a frown as he walked away with Morris.

GUESS WHO CAME to visit today. That's right, my period, and it brought some friends—cramps, gigantic appetite, restlessness, acne, and fever. My final exams were next week, and I was relieved it would be over by then.

I had asked Morris to get ice cream and lots of snacks, which I kept in my room. It was currently Tuesday. The first day was always the worst. I grabbed a blanket and a few snacks and went under the bed—that was my comfort zone during moments like this.

I went to sleep after finishing two bags of Cheetos. I woke up when I heard the door to my room open, and I heard footsteps approaching the bed.

"Chloe?" Tristan called.

I didn't answer him because that sharp pain I felt every once in a while hit me, and I groaned.

"Chloe?" he called again, and I could feel him moving around the room, searching for me.

"She is under the bed, sir," I heard Morris's voice.

"What? Why?"

I heard his footsteps getting closer, and soon, he was on the floor, looking under the bed at me.

"Are you okay?" he asked, looking worried.

His hand reached out, touching mine. I held on to his hand like a comforter.

"Period cramps."

"We should go to the hospital if it's that bad," he said, stroking the back of my palm with his thumb.

"I go through it every month; I'll be fine," I said, feeling a little awkward, telling him about my period cramps.

"Sorry," he mumbled.

When I'd first complained to my mom about my period pain, she'd told me to suck it up. That I was a woman and I should get used to it. I never complained again, but sometimes, I just had to smile through the pain.

"Do you want to come out?" Tristan asked, still stroking my hand.

"Not yet."

"Have you eaten?"

"Every hour, but I'm still hungry," I said, and he smiled.

"What would you like to eat?"

"Chicken sandwich with fries, some chicken nuggets, and a vanilla milkshake."

"Is that all?"

"That's all I can think about."

"Okay, I will see you later."

"You're leaving?" I grumbled, increasing my grip on his hand.

"I will be back soon. Let me drive downtown and get you something to eat. My butt has been in the air for five minutes now," he said, and I laughed.

"Fine." I frowned.

I refused to let go of his hand as he tried to pull away. He laughed softly while I smiled and let go slowly. I loved the sound of his laugh. It was boyish and soothing to the ears.

I listened to his retreating footsteps with a smile still plastered on my face. I had never felt like this with anyone—ever. Knowing all his flaws and still accepting them. The content and security I felt, even when I had seen him at his worst was knew to me. I didn't understand what was going on between us, and we both hadn't talked about it.

I remained under the bed until Tristan returned with two takeout bags. I crawled out from under the bed. I hadn't noticed before that he was in his suit.

What time is it?

"I wasn't sure what dip you liked, so I got all four," he said, placing them on the floor, where I sat with my legs folded and a blanket wrapped around me.

I smirked and reached for the milkshake. He sat on the floor in front of me. He took off his suit jacket, and untucked his white button-up shirt from his pants. I stared shamelessly as he removed his cufflinks and rolled up his sleeves to his elbows. My hormones couldn't handle the sexiness right now.

"I'm not eating this alone," I said, dividing the chicken sandwich into two and giving him the other half.

"How are you feeling?" he asked.

"Tortured."

"Maybe there are medications out there that can help."

"Doesn't work for me."

"Um ... I spoke to a friend about it. Sorry if that seems weird. She suggested you use hot water. I got this bottle that holds hot water, and you can place it on your stomach. I gave it to Morris to put the hot water in it and bring it up later. Sorry if I'm overstepping. You just look awful."

"It's fine." I laughed.

I was happy he cared but also wanted to ask about his female friend.

Do I know her? Why would he ask her if I'm supposed to be pregnant? Maybe she knows the truth, but who is she?

"Trust me, you don't want to know my search history right now," he added, and I couldn't help but laugh again. He leaned back and rested his head on the wall.

"Tell your friend I said thank you."

"Only if it helps," he said, reaching for the fries.

I had so many questions. There were so many things I wanted to know about him, but Tristan always had his guard up.

"How long have you known Morris?"

"Seven years. He applied for a cleaning job at the company. Every time I walked past him in the morning, he greeted me and asked me how I was doing. I admired his dedication and offered him a job here."

"What exactly is his job? He pretty much does everything."

"I don't even know." He laughed softly.

"Do you miss your family?" he asked, shifting the topic to me.

"No," I said, staring at the empty cup in my hand. I wanted another milkshake.

There was thick silence as neither of us said a thing. I wanted to go back under the bed and hide there.

"Do you want to go for a walk? You've been inside the whole day."

"That would be nice," I said, packing some fries into my mouth.

"Let me change into something else. I'll be right back." He pushed away from the wall and stood up.

I cleaned up after he left but didn't change my pajama pants and hoodie. I took my blanket with me when he came to get me. He had changed into jogger pants and a dark blue T-shirt. We stepped out of the house, walking side-by-side.

We walked down the sidewalk in serene silence. It was slowly getting dark outside.

"If you could change one thing in your life, what would that be?" I asked, and he stayed quiet for a while.

"June 9 and 27," he said in a soft whisper. He sounded sad.

Should I ask him what happened those days or just wait to see if he will explain?

"What about you?" he asked, looking at me.

"Being born into a better family," I whispered, kicking at a small object in my way.

"How long have you lived here?" I asked quickly, trying to change the sad atmosphere settling between us.

"I got the house when I was twenty, so around eight years."

"Must be nice, having all this at a young age."

"Having what?"

"Money and freedom."

"There is more to life than money. I never got the chance to grow up like my peers. I started at the company at nineteen with little basic knowledge. I had my own dreams, but they didn't really matter."

"Do you regret it?"

"Not anymore. I have grown to love what I do. I cook during my free time, so I'm cool with it."

"There was this time I was cooking with my sister, and I didn't know I'd turned on the wrong burner. Thirty minutes went by, and I was wondering why the chicken wasn't boiling."

"You shouldn't be allowed into a kitchen," he said, laughing.

"I plan to live on takeout when I have my own place."

My waist was hurting so bad when we made it back to the house. I collected the flat bottle, clothed in wool, and went upstairs while Tristan stayed back for dinner. I took a shower and swallowed a pain reliever.

I knew it was still early, but I needed sleep. I turned off the lights and lay on the bed. I placed the bottle on my stomach and closed my eyes.

I didn't know what time it was when someone entered the room. I could tell it was Tristan when he whispered my name. He climbed into the bed and drew closer.

"Hey," he whispered, wrapping his arms around me and pulling me to his chest.

"Hey," I mumbled.

"Are you okay?"

"Just tired from the walk," I whispered, breathing in his scent.

"Can I keep you company?"

"You're gonna regret asking that," I said, smiling in the dark.

"Never," he said, kissing my neck.

I snuggled closer and went back to sleep.

So far, things had been going well, though I'd had a dream where Mrs. Sanchester was chasing me around the house with a baseball bat for lying to her. I was glad I never had it again.

On Thursday, Morris was away to see his family, so Tristan took over the kitchen. He didn't allow me to help with anything because of what had happened with the knife last time.

I sat at the island, watching him spice some chicken tenderloin. He looked like a chef, the way his hands moved seamlessly and how focused he was. I didn't get why he was wearing disposable gloves.

"I'm tired of sitting here and watching you. Please let me help. Last time was an accident. Please allow me. I'm dying here," I begged.

"You can wash the dishes."

That was my least favorite task in the kitchen. I'd rather watch a plant grow or mow the lawn. I should have just sat back and enjoyed the show. Tristan cooking was a turn-on. I wished I were those chicken tenders.

I stood up and walked to the sink; only three dishes were in the sink. It was better than nothing. I went to work. Tristan came to rinse his hands. He stood behind me and caged me in his arms as he washed his hands. He placed his chin on my head. I didn't know why he enjoyed doing that.

I stared at his hands. That was when I saw the fresh bruises. Anger bubbled inside of me. I turned around immediately, making his chin leave my head. He grabbed a paper towel and dried his hands. My eyes didn't miss the bloodstain.

"You promised," I said.

He looked down at his knuckles and ignored me. Oh, there was no way I was letting this go.

"You told me you—"

"I told you, I can't control it!" he snapped, looking at me.

"Of course you can. You just have to try."

"Don't act like you know what I'm going through."

"Well, maybe if you tell me, I could help!"

"I don't need your help!"

"Are you going to live your whole life like this? Torturing yourself for whatever happened?"

"It's none of your damn business how I live my life!" His jaw clenched.

"Why should I even help you with your lie when you won't stop? We had a deal, and if you do not keep to your end of the deal, then I won't help you!" I yelled.

"You don't understand, and you won't understand."

"Try me."

"There are boundaries, Chloe. Don't cross them."

I clenched my hands tightly. "Then, I should leave."

"The last time I checked, you're broke, and no one will give you a place to stay; it's just me. Why don't you do what you're here for and stay out of my business? 'Cause I never asked you about the hideous mark on your back."

My lips faltered. My voice vanished as my body turned pale, like chalk.

CHAPTER **TWENTY**
SILENCE

Tristan's eyes were impassive as I stared into them. I couldn't believe what he'd just said. He had seen it, and he'd called it hideous. Did it look that horrifying?

I gave him the meanest look I could muster up and turned away. I ran out of the kitchen with tears blinding my vision as I ran up the stairs to get to my room.

I shut the door and leaned on it, and then I slid slowly to the ground. I tried to stop the sound escaping my lips, but I couldn't.

Hideous mark?

I pulled my knees to my chest and hugged them tightly as the tears kept falling. I sat there, crying for a long time. I stood up and walked to my closet. I brought my clothes out and pushed them inside my suitcase. Why had I even agreed to help him?

All I could think about right now was proving him wrong. I stopped and slumped on the bed with frustrated tears. I felt so helpless. I zipped up the suitcase. I still had three more suitcases left. I was too angry and couldn't spend one more minute here.

I dragged the suitcase to the door and stepped out of my room. I rolled it all the way downstairs with tears falling down my cheeks.

"Go to hell!" I yelled as I opened the front door and walked out, pulling hard at my suitcase that didn't want to move. I let go of the suitcase and kicked it, only to be rewarded with a harsh pain on my toes.

I dragged the suitcase with me, all the way to the gate and down the street. It was dark and quiet outside, a cool breeze dancing in the air. I looked back at Tristan's mansion as I put a great distance between us. I stopped and let go of the suitcase.

I sat on the suitcase and cried. *Where am I even going?* I didn't have a dollar to be proud of. I buried my face in my palms and sobbed.

Ten minutes went by before a black Lamborghini pulled closer and parked on the side of the road. I watched as Tristan stepped out in haste, a worried expression plastered on his face.

I shot him a glare and ignored him. I wiped my tears away and tried to put on a tough face. I played with the strap on my sandals as I waited for an apology and an explanation. From my peripheral vision, I saw him sit on the sidewalk. He said nothing for a while as the snaps of crickets chirping chewed at my ears.

"I'm sorry. I didn't mean any of that. I shouldn't have said that," he said, and I stayed silent.

"You have every right to be mad at me. I shouldn't have come at you like that or said anything about your scar. I have no idea what you went through or how you got it. You don't have to accept my apology or forgive me right away. I just want you to know I'm sorry for what I said."

Wasn't planning on it.

"I didn't even get a good look at it that day. Ignore everything I said. I was an asshole, trying to avoid conversations about my problems.

I don't like people telling me to control what's happening, like it's that easy. Chloe," he said, pulling closer.

I looked away, trying to hide the tears wetting my cheeks.

"Here," he said, bringing his hand closer for me to see. There were tiny scars spread on his wrists and on the back of his palm. "Go ahead. Say whatever you want about them. Call them whatever you want if it will make you feel better," he said, and I gave him an incredulous look.

"Seriously, Tristan?" I asked and pushed his hand away. "I'm not gonna stoop to your level. I can't believe you would even consider asking me to say bad things about your scars. Is that how you make yourself feel better? By preying on people's insecurities?"

He said nothing but looked away. He bit down on his lips and looked ahead like he was fighting his emotions.

"I'm sorry," he said in a voice I could barely hear.

I shook my head and stood up. I grabbed my suitcase and headed back to the house. Tristan stayed back, not returning to the house. I tossed my suitcase aside and slumped on the bed, ready to cry out all the pain.

I felt more insecure about the mark on my back now. He'd called it hideous. I closed my eyes and sobbed.

MY CLOTHES WERE all over the floor when I woke up. I groaned and stayed back in bed, arguing with myself if I should leave the room. My stomach grumbled. I'd skipped dinner last night. Maybe he had eaten it all alone while I cried my eyes out. I stared at the ceiling, like it could tell me what to do.

I remained in bed and ignored Morris when he came to knock

on my door. Tristan came next a few hours later, begging me to eat something. I didn't answer anyone. I stayed locked up in the room the whole day.

Tristan showed up later in the night, apologizing again. I didn't know how long he stood behind the door, talking, because I dozed off.

THE NEXT MORNING, Morris begged me to eat something he left at the door, but I was afraid it was a trap, set by Tristan. I got tired of crying, so I lay in bed, moping. His words had really cut through me. I had hidden the scar from everyone, except Vina and Grey. They'd never called it hideous. At least, not to my face. I had been scared to look at it, scared it would be as hideous as Tristan had called it.

I hated that I didn't hate him as much as I wanted, but I planned on ignoring him for as long as I could.

I covered my head with the pillow when I heard Tristan's voice again but removed the pillow when I heard another voice.

"Are you still alive? I swear I'm going to have his head on a spike and use it to decorate your grave."

Vina!

I stood up and rushed to the door, unlocked it, and opened it.

"Jesus, Chlo, you scared me," she said as I threw my arms around her.

I looked back at Tristan, who looked relieved to see me. He was still dressed for work. I glared at him and pulled Belvina into the room.

"Wow, you are living like a queen in here. This view is like the gate to paradise," she said, looking outside the glass wall.

"What are you doing here?" I asked, sitting at the edge of the bed.

"His butler came to pick me up from campus. Morris, I think. He said you'd locked yourself in the room for two days and refused to let anyone in. Is that true?" She looked over her shoulder at me.

"Yeah."

"What did that *el cabrón* do? I knew he had done something from how desperate he sounded. Like you'd died."

I was tempted to tell her everything about our deal and his mom but felt it wasn't mine to share.

"We had a fight."

"Did he hit you?" She looked pissed, as if her tiny size could take him down.

"No, it was an argument."

"About what?" she asked, sitting next to me on the bed.

I didn't want to talk about it. There was just too much personal stuff to share. Even if I shared every detail of my life with her, it wouldn't feel right, telling her what had led to the fight.

"I forgot. So, how are you preparing for the finals?"

"What did he do, Chloe?"

"It's nothing serious, Vee."

"You locked yourself in here for two days, and the room looks like you wrestled with your clothes. Did he hit you? Be honest with me."

"He didn't, I swear."

"Then, what did he do?"

"We'll talk about it later. Now, tell me how you're preparing for the finals. I have been procrastinating."

"I bribe myself with two episodes for every chapter I read. I want a tour," she said, standing up.

I sighed and pushed myself off the bed.

We hung out on the patio for a few hours before she left. I'd tried my best to keep her busy, so she wouldn't ask about the fight again, and it'd worked.

My stomach grumbled as I picked up the empty wineglasses we'd used. I found Tristan cooking when I entered the kitchen. I ignored him, putting the dirty wineglasses in the sink. I was starving, and the tasty aroma lingering in the air wasn't helping. I opened the fridge and searched for any leftovers to eat.

I was sad Morris was not back. I wanted him to fix me something to eat. I rubbed my stomach as I grabbed a pack of strawberries. Tristan was standing behind me when I turned around. I shot him a glare and tried to walk away, but he got in the way.

"I'm sorry," he said softly. "I'm really sorry for what I said that night. I know my apologies aren't enough, and I can't forgive myself for saying that about your scar," he whispered, stepping closer.

I pressed my back to the fridge. My face still maintained a murderous stare.

"Please say something," he begged, raising his hand and cupping my cheek.

Push his hand away and walk out. How hard can it be? Extremely hard because I was hooked and slowly giving in.

"I hope you'll forgive me someday," he whispered, tracing my eyebrow with his fingertip.

My body warmed to his touch and tempted me into accepting his apology.

"I love your dress," he said with a small smile and pulled away. "I'm making your favorite," he said, returning to the food on the electric cooker.

I wanted to tell him I didn't want to eat, but that would break my vow of not talking to him. I also wanted to tell him he looked sexy in the apron but held back the words.

I sat at the island with the strawberries. I stared at him every so often, unable to control myself, and every time I looked up, he was already staring at me. I should leave, but I was hungry, so hungry that I could eat grass right now.

Tristan walked to the island and placed a plate of spaghetti in front of me.

I shall not fall into temptation.

"Please eat," he said and walked out of the kitchen after tossing the apron to the counter.

I stared at the food, the smell already making my mouth water with those damn meatballs. I picked up the fork and started eating the food. He peeked into the kitchen and stared at me. I wanted to pretend I hadn't touched anything, but the food was midair, close to my mouth.

Tristan smirked and walked away.

I T'D BEEN A few days since the incident with Tristan. He apologized every chance he got, but I shut him out and refused to say a word to him. He tried desperately to make conversations at the dining table but ended up talking to himself.

My finals were drawing closer. Vina and I studied sometimes through FaceTime, asking each other questions. From the number of questions I failed, I knew I wasn't close to being ready. Every time I tried to study math, I got headaches.

I slammed the book closed in front of me and finished the bag of Cheetos and bottle of juice keeping me company. I texted Vina a meme of my dilemma and undressed for a bath since I had Cheetos dust all over me.

Tristan was lying on my bed when I came out of the bathroom and turned to look at me. My eyes tried to remain on his face and not his bare torso.

"Can I sleep here?"

He was testing me. I would keep my vow of silence for as long as I could. I didn't give an answer. I grabbed my pajama set and went back to the bathroom. I cursed him as I slipped on the silk shorts and cami top. I held my hair back with a rubber band and came out of the bathroom. He was still on the bed, his eyes on me.

"You have a cute belly button," he said, and I glared at him.

I reached for the light switch and flipped it off. I climbed into bed and lay next to him, not uttering a word. I kept a safe distance between us, pushing myself to the edge of the bed.

"Can I hold you?" he asked, his voice soft and almost lost in the air.

He was making it hard for me to keep to my vow of silence. I could let out every word I had been dying to say to him. I moved closer to him. My gesture gave him his reply.

I could feel him smiling against my neck as his hands snaked around my waist. I tried to block out the feel of his hands on my bare skin. His scent wrapped around me, and suddenly, he was all I could breathe.

"I regret everything I said. The silence is driving me crazy. I can't concentrate on anything. You make it so fucking hard," he whispered, his voice caressing my ear like silk. "Say something, please. I miss the sound of your voice," he groaned, pulling me closer to his body, as if that would make it easier to get a reply out of me.

My backside was pressed to his crotch, and his hand slowly moved to my stomach.

I was counting on my self-control right now.

There was a long silence as neither of us spoke. I stared into the darkness, waiting to hear his voice again.

"Good night, Chloe." He kissed my neck, his action sending currents through my body.

We lay in silence. I closed my eyes and tried to force sleep upon me, but Tristan's fingers remained busy on my waistline, slowly drawing circles on the same spot; it was all I could think about. I wondered how something so little left me hot and bothered.

I imagined his hand somewhere else, his rough fingers skimming all over my skin, and his sinful lips everywhere. A soft moan escaped my lips, and I felt him stiffen behind me. I tried to cover it up with a cough.

"What's on your mind, *hmm*?" he whispered, his finger now trailing up my stomach and down to my waistline. "Is it my finger? You like this?" He repeated the motion of his fingers on the same spot.

The soft brush of his fingers, plus the smoothness of his voice, was a delicious combo my body couldn't resist. I was suddenly a slave to his voice. Was it my three-year celibacy that was making me so sensitive?

"Tell me what you want, Chloe."

I wanted his hands everywhere.

"How does this make you feel?" he whispered into my ear, moving his fingers up the space between my breasts.

I knew he could tell how my body was responding to his action. He could feel my pulse rising and the change in my breathing.

"Don't fight it." He nibbled on my ear, his hands not quite where I wanted them. "I won't do anything until you tell me to," he rasped.

I pressed into him, and his thick erection jabbed my backside. He moaned at my action, and it was the sexiest sound I'd ever heard.

"There are so many things I want to do to you right now," he said against my neck. "I just need your words."

He was trying to trick me into talking to him. Nope, not falling for it.

My body wanted it, his touch, his lips, but a voice at the back of my head was screaming at me to pull away and walk out, reminding me of his words.

"I want to feel you, listen to the sounds you make when I fuck you with my fingers, taste you, and watch you come apart."

That was it. His filthy words, and I was doomed. It happened so quickly, like I wasn't in control of my body. My desires held me captive and compliant. My head tilted a little to meet his face in the dark. I could make out his silhouette, and I could feel his eyes on me.

"Say it," he whispered mere inches from my lips.

I moved to kiss him, but my lips ended up on the corner of his mouth. I felt his smile.

"Your lips are the softest I've ever felt," he said.

I drew closer and took his lips in a deep kiss. He responded almost immediately, his hand slipping slowly into my cami top and his fingers coming up and wrapping around my throat in a sinful bliss that made me moan into his mouth.

His other hand roamed my hip and backside, his big palm kneading my ass. He broke the kiss and whispered, "How far do you want to go? Stop me if you feel uncomfortable with anything."

He waited for me to say something, but I remained silent.

"Are you seriously not going to say anything? How do I know you want this?" he asked.

I kissed him again. He laughed into the kiss and bit my lips. His hand left my neck and traced the valley between my breasts. I pulled away from the kiss and closed my eyes as his hand dived lower and into my shorts.

He kissed my neck as his fingers found their way between my legs. I squeezed my thighs, unable to control the pleasure it brought.

"So wet. I could drown between your legs," he groaned.

He found my sensitive spot and circled it with his thumb. My legs parted for him, and the moans kept slipping out of my lips as I squirmed from the pleasure. I gasped in delight when he slipped in a finger.

"So tight. Fuck, you feel good," he growled against my lips. "I wish you would say something. Tell me what you're feeling. How do you like it?"

He trailed kisses up my neck to my chin and took my lips in a hungry kiss. I melted into him as he added another finger; my hips followed the movement of his fingers. Tristan released a throaty groan at the rocking of my hips against his erection.

"I love how your pussy swallows my fingers," he groaned, adding another finger.

I moaned so loud, gasping at how his fingers filled me.

"I could listen to that sound forever."

I leaned into him as the waves of pleasure swept through me. My toes curled as I felt my soul leaving my body. He increased his pace, his other hand crawling up my stomach and cupping my tit. I gripped on to the sheet with uncontrollable moans as his head dipped down and took my nipple in his mouth through my shirt.

My back arched as he sucked on the sensitive bud while his fingers worked wonders between my legs. I couldn't take it anymore. It was too much pleasure and hard for me to breathe. I brushed my fingers through his hair as he flicked my nipple with his tongue.

"Come for me, baby. Give it to me. I want it all," he whispered against my nipple and drew it between his lips.

My climax hit me. My body shook and muscles tensed. Tristan kissed my shoulder as my body relaxed.

The guilt and shame came next. I felt like slapping myself for having no control over my desires and giving in to him. I pulled away and crawled off the bed.

"Chloe?"

I rushed to the door, trying to get away. I ignored his voice and ran downstairs to the guest room. I locked the door and slumped on the bed, feeling like an idiot.

I STAYED IN the guest room the next morning until I was sure Tristan was gone for work. He had followed me last night and asked me what he did wrong and if he went too far. He'd left when I gave him no reply.

I returned to my room and took a shower, and then I went down to eat. I grabbed a few books after eating and went to the garden to read. Nothing felt better than the sun on my face and the cool breeze disturbing the pages of my book. The butterflies in the garden were so pretty that I wanted to hold one captive in a jar, so I could stare at it every day.

I forced myself to read a book recommended by my professor for my final exams. I was surprised to see Adrian walking to the garden. He waved at me as he got closer.

"Hey," he greeted with that gorgeous smile.

"Hi." I closed the book and sat like a lady. "Shouldn't you be at work?" I asked, noticing his casual outfit.

"I'm taking some time off."

"Nice."

"How have you been?" he asked, taking the seat in front of me.

Miserable, was what my mouth craved to say.

"Good."

Things had changed between us; we hadn't talked or laughed together anymore since that night.

"What happened to your neck?" he asked, leaning closer to take a look.

I touched my neck, trying to make sense of his question, and it dawned on me that the marks were from last night. That explained why Morris had kept staring at me with concern.

"Oh, it's an allergy," I said and pushed my hair to the front to cover it.

Adrian only nodded and said nothing, the expression on his face neutral.

"How's Karen?" I asked, trying to keep the conversation going.

"She is good. She says hi."

He leaned closer to the table and took my hands.

"I have missed you," he said softly, drawing small circles on the back of my hands with his thumbs.

I waited for the butterflies in my stomach and the sparks, but I didn't feel anything. I guessed my feelings for him had died the night he proposed to Karen in front of me.

I had had my fair share of love. I wasn't lucky in that department. All my relationships had been disastrous. I always fell for the wrong guys, guys I thought I could be happy with. No matter how awful they were, I kept going back because I thought I was going to meet the perfect guy. Grey was kinda it. He was the type of guy I wanted to get married to and hopefully start a family with, but our relationship had ended because of Tristan's lies and somehow what I had done in the past.

Adrian was never meant for me. I was the type of person who fell easily. Sometimes, I wanted to rip my heart out for doing that. I wasn't so sure about what was going on between Tristan and me, so maybe we were just two messed up people, confused about our feelings.

"Yeah," I said, pulling my hands away.

"I'm sorry about that night. I thought you were already over your feelings for me."

"I am now, so you have nothing to worry about."

He nodded slowly, as if he understood why.

"How are things with Tristan?"

"Good."

"I don't want things to remain like this. I miss talking and laughing with you about everything. I'm sorry for the space I created in our friendship."

"Seriously, Adrian, it's all in the past, and I'm over it."

"So, we are cool, and you promise you won't run off again every time I come to visit?"

"I promise." I laughed.

"Thank you." He beamed, a genuine smile that made me feel better.

"When is the wedding?"

He laughed softly before answering. "Next year. Are you coming?"

"Weddings are now my worst nightmare, but I will think about it."

We talked more before he left.

I watched the new episode of my favorite show, *Good Girls*. It was almost nine p.m., and Tristan was not back.

I told Morris I wasn't hungry before I went up to my room. I had my bath and wore my pajama set. I tried to go to sleep but stayed awake for an hour, tossing from one edge of the bed to the other. I got down from the bed with a frustrated sigh. I walked around my room, stretching.

I was feeling hot and sweaty when I finished my little exercise, so I decided to go for a swim. I wore my black bikini and grabbed a towel. I stopped and looked at the mark on my back in the mirror.

Hideous mark. My mind looped the phrase again, striking me with stark sorrow.

I looked for a light top. I wore it over the bikini and left the room. The lights in the kitchen and living room were off. I went to the wine cellar and took one bottle of white wine and a wineglass.

I removed the top and entered the pool. The water was warm and soothing. I swam for a few minutes before pouring myself some wine. I sat at the edge of the pool, using my legs to play with the water.

I reached for my top when I saw Tristan walking toward the pool. He wore lounge pants that hung low around his waist and nothing above. I wanted to feel confident about my body and my scar, but I couldn't. I slipped on the shirt and looked at the sky's horizon. The moonlight reflected on the pool like a mirror. I admired the moon as it stood proudly in the sky between the darkness. Like the moon, I had my own dark side too.

He came to sit next to me. My eyes drifted to his legs that were now inside the pool. He had rolled up the legs of his pants to avoid wetting them. We sat in silence, only the sound of my legs dancing in the water.

"I know you're still mad at me. I take full responsibility for everything I said that night and whatever I did last night to make you run away from your room."

I opened my mouth to say something but closed it. I wasn't ready to talk to him yet. He sighed at my silence.

"I want to make things right. How can I make it up to you?"

I stood up with the wine left in my glass and took my towel and left.

I went to my room, battling the urge to go and give him all the answers he wanted. I walked to the tall glass panel facing the pool and the garden. He stared at me from where he sat. He waved, and I stabbed him with my gaze and pulled the drapes together.

MORRIS MADE MY favorite breakfast. Tristan was already off at work. I studied for the rest of the day and took a long nap in preparation for tomorrow's exam. Tristan was back early from work, but he stayed in his room and didn't come down for dinner.

"Miss Simpson?" Morris called after dishing out my food.

"Yeah?"

"Mr. Sanchester needs your help. He said it's urgent."

"When did he tell you that?"

"He just called."

I stood up and left for his room. *What is so urgent? Should I call Adrian?* I ran up the steps, trying not to miss a step.

Don't panic.

Not again! Don't tell me he …

I couldn't watch him hurt himself. *What am I even doing?*

He made me so angry, yet every time he was in danger, I couldn't help but run to him.

CHAPTER **TWENTY-ONE**

TRUST

I pushed his door open without knocking. I looked around the room for him but didn't find him.

"Tristan?" I stepped in and shut the door.

I heard the shower running. I crinkled my face in confusion as I walked to the big bathroom. He was under the shower. The steam from the water made the glass blurry, so I didn't see him completely nude.

"What was so urgent?" I asked, crossing my arms.

"Oh, you're here." He turned off the shower. "Could you pass me a towel?"

"Is that why I'm here?"

He didn't answer.

"Tristan, is this the urgent thing you called me for?"

"Just pass the towel. I will tell you when I come out," he grunted.

I walked to the towel rack hanging on the wall, stacked with black, white, and gray towels. I grabbed the white towel and walked to the shower.

"Here." I knocked on the glass.

He opened the door and collected it. His wet hand brushed against mine, which seemed to be on purpose from the smile pulling at his lips. I turned my face away immediately.

"You're still mad at me?"

"Why did you ask for me?"

"Just tell me what to do to make up for what I did," he said, stepping closer. He had the towel tied around his waist, and his wet hair was still dripping water.

I was pissed. I hadn't planned on breaking my vow of silence so soon.

"I miss the sound of your voice," he said, stepping closer, his hand sliding slowly to my waist and his other hand reaching up to cup my neck. "I miss you," he whispered, brushing the drop of water from his hair that touched my nose.

"Let me take you on a date," he suggested, and I rolled my eyes with a scoff. "What's your ideal date?" he asked, and I was tempted to reply.

My eyes caught a small word inked on his triceps. I was lucky to see the word. I hadn't even known he had a tattoo. It was almost hidden.

"Who is Nadia?"

Something flickered in his eyes, but he covered it up quickly.

"My wife," he said, pulling away.

My breath ceased.

"You have a wife? And you are asking me out on a date?"

He walked past me and left the shower, and here I'd thought, we were making up. I followed behind him, not ready to drop the topic.

Was he lying? I had never heard about his marriage.

"You have to tell me something, Tristan," I said, my voice at the cusp of yelling.

"I don't want to talk about it. We can talk about something else," he said, brushing his wet hair back.

"Talk about something else? You want me to say yes to a date after the bomb you just dropped on me?" I laughed.

"You don't have to know everything, Chloe."

"Seriously?" I said, annoyed at the way he was shutting me out.

He walked to the towel rack, changing the towel around his waist. He grabbed a smaller towel and dried his hair without saying a word. I turned to walk away, but he held me back.

"I'm sorry," he whispered and pulled me closer. "I'm not ready to talk about my past," he whispered, holding my gaze in the mirror and grasping my hand like he didn't want to let go. "It's not an easy topic for me," he told me and brushed my hair back as our eyes met in the mirror.

I gave him a slight nod.

"So, what was so urgent?" I asked.

"Nothing. I just wanted to hear your voice and get your attention."

"I thought you didn't like attention?" I asked, tilting my head to the side to look at him.

He was quiet, and I saw a small smile.

"Can I see it?" he asked, gesturing to my back. "Your scar?" he added, waiting for a reply.

Different thoughts were going through my head right now, and I was terrified of what he would say next about the scar. I turned around to look at him. I didn't see myself ever trusting him.

"If you don't trust me, why should I trust you?" I said and left the bathroom quickly.

I WAS UP early the next day, though I had difficulty getting some sleep because of what had happened in the bathroom. After I'd left his room last night, I had gone to the dining room, and ate without him.

I was still thinking about the date that might never happen.

I forced myself out of bed and walked to the wall; I pulled the drapes apart to allow some light into the room. I turned away with a groan when the sunrays from outside burned my eyes. I allowed my eyes to adjust to the light before pulling the drapes properly.

I found a note on my nightstand. It said, *Good luck on your finals*, with a *T* at the bottom. I knew it was from Tristan.

I went to the bathroom and brushed my teeth before sitting down to take my exams. It lasted for three and a half hours.

I was starving by the time I finished. I smiled at Morris as he served me my breakfast. My phone rang when I was about to take a bite of my French toast.

I looked at my screen. Adrian was calling on FaceTime. I dropped the bread and picked up the call. He greeted me with his trademark smile, the smile that had once made my heart melt.

"Hey." I waved.

"Hey, Chloe." He brushed his full hair back.

I noticed the dark circles beneath his eyes.

"Are you okay? You look exhausted," I asked.

"We were up all night, packing for our vacation."

"You're going on vacation?"

"Yeah. Bali."

"Nice."

"Who is it?" I heard Karen's voice from the other end.

"It's Chloe," he told her and turned to look at me.

Karen appeared; he kissed her on the lips, and she sat on his lap. I must admit, they looked cute together.

"Hey, Chloe." Karen smiled.

"Hi, Karen. How long are you guys staying?"

"A month, right?" She looked at him, not sure about her answer.

"Yeah." He nodded.

"Well, have fun and don't forget to bring me something."

"Sure," Karen said, sounding more excited about the vacation.

"I will fix us something to eat. Bye, Chloe," Karen said.

"Okay, bye!"

She kissed him on the lips and left.

I decided to ask Adrian about Nadia. I wanted to know if Tristan had told me the truth because I was so sure he wasn't married.

"Can I ask you something?" I asked when I heard the bedroom door close.

"Sure." He nodded.

"Uh, do you know—"

"Hey, man," Adrian cut me off, staring at something behind me.

I looked back and saw Tristan standing behind me. I'd thought he already left for work.

"Hey," Tristan replied with the smooth curve of his lips upward.

He stared down at me with that look I couldn't read. He was so good at that.

"Morning." He beamed at me and walked to the seat in front of me.

"Sorry about that. You wanted to ask me something," Adrian said.

"Oh yeah." I glanced at Tristan.

He stared at me like he wanted to hear the question too.

"Can you take pictures of the places you visit in Bali?"

"Sure, I'll do that, but I'm not a good photographer."

"It's fine. Bye." I ended the call, not waiting for him to say anything.

I gave Tristan a firm smile and began eating.

His two-piece black suit brought out his beauty. He looked smart and powerful. His silver Cartier wristwatch matched the cuff links on his crisp suit.

"How was your exam?"

"Not bad."

"Do you have any plans today?" he asked as Morris served him his coffee, a toasted bagel, and cream cheese.

"Yeah, I'm hanging out with my best friend."

"Do you need anything?"

"A car to drive around and maybe an ATM card."

He brought out his wallet and dropped a credit card and debit card in front of me.

"Morris will take you to the garage. Pick any car you like."

"Okay."

He smiled at me again, a smile that held a secret. He only drank his coffee and left for work while I sat there, thinking about what had just happened.

I PICKED A blue Lamborghini convertible. It looked brand-new and had the stench that riddled a new car. It'd been a long time since I'd driven a car. I played my favorite song as I drove to my old school to pick up Vina. The wind was in my hair, and my sunglasses shielded my eyes from the sun. I couldn't remember the last time I'd felt so at peace and free. I thought of running away, far from here. I had a car and two ATM cards, so I had everything. I pushed the thought away. I couldn't leave Vina behind, and it wouldn't feel right, taking off like that.

I turned down the volume when I got to the school. I texted Vina, telling her I was outside. I looked at the tall college buildings and students around the campus. I missed this place. Freshman year had been fun.

"Chloe!" Vina screamed from afar, which got a lot of people's attention.

I watched her petite figure hastily walk toward me. She hugged me before I could get down from the car.

"Gosh, I missed you," she chimed.

"I missed you too."

"I have been looking forward to this day all week." She got into the car, giggling. "*Gaua*, is this your car?" she asked, looking around and touching the plush leather seats.

"No, I borrowed it only for today."

She smiled mischievously at me.

"What?"

"Nothing. Where are we going first?"

"Let's get some smoothies first, and I have a lot to tell you."

"I can't wait. Start spilling. I have been deprived of every juicy story." She leaned back.

"We are going shopping!" I squealed.

"I thought you were broke. Wait, did you steal his money?" She looked impressed.

"No?" I waved the cards in her face.

"I see you're doing great," she said, and I rolled my eyes.

"So, any updates on Tristan?" she asked, relaxing on the seat with her knees propped up.

I was annoyed with her habit of placing her feet on the seat, but it wouldn't be my first time complaining. Her usual reply was, "My shoe is clean," or, "Relax. It's a new shoe."

I filled her in on what had been going on with Tristan.

"Wait, he asked you on a date?" she asked immediately after I brought it up.

"Yeah, but then I found out he has a wife."

"That makes no sense. Maybe she is dead."

"I don't know. Everything with him is complicated."

"You're not falling for him, are you? It was just one kiss, right?"

"Um ... well ... we might have ... sorta ... made out again and some other stuff."

"Wait, you like him?"

"I don't know." I shrugged.

"Just be careful. I still don't trust him or his family."

"*Trust* is such a foreign word to me right now," I mumbled with a sigh.

"Go for it if you want; I mean, why not make the most of your time with the Greek god before you leave? Just try not to catch feelings," she said.

It's too late for that.

He was like a serpent, always deadly, but he'd already stung his fangs into my heart.

"So, you have free access to his property now, huh?" she asked, connecting her playlist to the car's stereo player.

"It's the least he could do after making me homeless and an orphan." I sighed, making a turn to the smoothie parlor.

"When you say other stuff, you mean, you went past kissing?"

I sighed, knowing she wouldn't drop the topic until I gave her every detail. I didn't tell her how ashamed I'd felt after it happened.

WHEN I GOT to the house, I put on the two-piece swimsuit I'd bought today from the Chanel store and left the room to go for a quick swim. The water was warm. I lay back, staring at the stars as I moved my legs in the water.

The silence filled my head with questions about my life. I thought about my parents and my sister. *Do they miss me? Am I dead to them?*

I went back under the water and swam for a while before coming up for some air. I was surprised to see Tristan sitting at the edge of the pool with his legs in the water.

How long has he been here? I was sure he saw the scar.

He gave me a smile as I stared at him, trying to get answers to my own questions. He'd already seen it. I didn't want to hide it anymore. I wanted to be confident about my scar.

He wore red swim shorts, the moonlight glimmering on his skin, and I suddenly wanted to lick wine off his six-packs abs. He gestured for me to come closer to where he was. I brushed my wet hair back with my hands and swam to him. I remained inside the pool but next to his long and toned legs. There was a bottle of wine beside him with two wineglasses.

"I don't plan on drinking tonight," I told him as he opened it.

"Actually, this is a new wine that is going to be released next week. I told the person I had someone who was very in love with wine, and promised him I'd bring him feedback after you tasted it."

"New wine?"

He smirked at my question.

"Only a sip and tell me what you think," he said, pouring the white wine into the wineglass.

"Okay."

I collected the wine, using my other hand to support myself. I took a gulp instead and another and another. Perhaps I was only gulping down my regrets, both past and future. Tristan laughed and poured himself some.

"Wow, this is good." I smiled.

"You like it?"

"I love it!" I moaned. I finished the one in my glass and held out my glass for more.

"You should come out of the pool." He gave me a hand and helped me out.

I sat next to him and sipped my wine.

"What age did you start drinking?" he asked.

"Fifteen. The first alcohol I tasted was tequila."

"Nice for a start, I guess," he said with an amused grin.

There was a soothing silence around us, and I liked it.

"Does this count as a date?" he asked.

"Just because we are drinking wine and staring at the stars doesn't mean we are on a date," I said, and he laughed softly.

"So, will you go on a date with me?"

"I don't know," I said and took a sip from my drink, trying to hide the smile forming on my face.

He nodded. I stared at his face as he looked up at the dark sky that stretched across with an infinity of stars and the moon emitting the softest glow of light. My hands itched to touch his strong jawline and the delicate features of his face. He looked down at me, meeting my eyes.

"Stop staring at me like that," he said with his eyes lingering on my lips before flickering to my eyes.

"Like what?" I pretended to be confused.

"Like that," he said, pointing at my face, an adorable smile plastered on his face.

"Like what?" I shrugged, keeping up my act.

He laughed softly, shaking his head. His laughter was like music to my ears. He had an adorable laugh, and I loved it.

"Like what?" I pressed, leaning closer.

"Like you want me to kiss you," he said, turning away from me.

Maybe I wanted him to.

"Do you want me to kiss you, Chloe?" he whispered, his voice caressing my ears.

"I'm still mad at you," I said, and he smiled, leaning closer to me.

"Please don't go back to ignoring me," he groaned, and I smiled.

"You can kiss me," I whispered.

"It's not the alcohol talking, right?" he asked as he cupped my cheek, his thumb brushing my skin like a feather.

"I have barely finished my glass, Tristan," I said, and he glanced at my glass to confirm.

"You're not going to regret this later, are you?" he asked, guiding my lips closer to his. His nose brushed against mine, our lips mere inches from touching.

"Are you?" I asked back, my eyes flickering between his lips and crystal-blue eyes.

"No," he said before bringing his lips to mine in a slow kiss.

I closed my eyes and responded to his kiss. His tongue met mine in a union. A throaty groan escaped his lips as I drew his lower lip between my teeth and went in for a deep kiss. The sound only increased my yearning for his touch.

His full lips were so soft and moved smoothly with mine. His hand moved to my right arm; he ran his thumb gingerly down my arm, sending sparks through my body.

I loved this feeling. I loved his touch. I loved the way he kissed me with relentless need. So what if all this was a lie? What if I was doing the wrong thing? I didn't know where my life was headed, and nothing felt right anymore. I would just go with anything I could get at this moment. Go with the flow and see where it took me. Maybe we didn't know what we were doing, but we enjoyed doing it.

I moved closer, putting my hand around his neck. I deepened the kiss, and he followed every movement of my lips. He pulled away but not completely. His forehead rested on mine. He ran his thumb over my swollen lips, pulling my lower lip down with his eyes glued to my mouth. I was out of breath from the heat spreading through me like fireworks.

His head dipped down and kissed before I could catch my breath. His hand roamed up my hip, his fingers pressing into my hip as he swallowed the moans leaving my lips. The sweet tingles spreading through my body dissolved every ounce of resistance away. Forgiveness set you free, and I couldn't stay mad at him forever. He'd already made up for his mistake, and I just wanted to move on from it.

I found myself moving to his lap and straddling him. My legs wrapped around his waist as I found a comfortable position. He smiled against my lips and kissed me softly, like his lips were writing poetry on mine.

I gasped softly when Tristan's hand glided to my backside, grabbed me, and ran smoothly down the length of my thigh. His fingers trailed up and played with the rope of my bikini bottom. He smiled against my lips and pulled away. My arms remained around his shoulders as his fingers kept playing with the rope holding my bikini together. He pressed a kiss to my nose, and I giggled.

"I'm slowly getting addicted to you," he said tracing my collarbone and skimming down my chest.

He leaned closer and kissed my shoulder. He kissed the corner of my lips and buried his face in my neck. I giggled when he bit on my neck a little harshly, and I was certain he'd left a mark.

"I don't care how complicated this gets," he said, kissing a spot below my ear.

He pulled away and stared at me with a softness I had never seen on him. I felt something shift in my chest, and it terrified me. I withdrew from his lap and sat next to him. We stayed in silence with our legs shivering in the water but far from cold. His arm stayed around my shoulders, and I rested my head on his shoulder.

I wanted to ask about Nadia. I wanted to know everything about him. But I loved the serene atmosphere and didn't want to ruin it.

I put my glass down and entered the pool with one intention in my head. *Show him the scar and let go of the fear.*

"That's not safe," he said before I went under.

I sprang up with a smile.

I removed my top and threw it outside the pool. Tristan's eyes feasted like a king as he stared at me, like his voice had vanished. As the wind whipped them, I covered my breasts.

I can do this.

I took a deep breath before turning around, showing him my

exposed back. I could feel his eyes; they were drilling into my skin. I wanted him to stare at it for as long as he wanted. Boldness shielded my fear. He entered the water, and soon, he was behind me. He touched my shoulders, which made me flinch.

"You didn't have to," he whispered, turning me around.

I allowed my hands to fall off from around my chest. I had not just stripped my shame, but my insecurities as well. I looked into his eyes, searching for something—perhaps the truth—but more so, I searched for a place I hoped to belong.

"It doesn't change anything about you; you're still you, and I admire the person you are."

My eyes burned, tears threatening to come out.

"I'm sorry if I made you feel bad about yourself. You're beautiful, Chloe," he said, caressing my cheeks softly with his thumbs.

"They say the strongest people are the ones with scars. I don't want you to feel ashamed about your scar because of what my dumbass said. You're a survivor, and you should be proud," he said, lips curling into a sacred smile. "I might not know your story, but just know you're extraordinary."

"Didn't know you had that in you," I said as he brushed my wet hair back and cupped my cheeks.

"There are a lot of things you don't know about me," he whispered while I laughed.

His eyes crinkled at the edges as the corners of his lips turned upward. He leaned down and kissed me softly. I pressed my body to his, kissing him back.

"What the hell is that on your back?"

The delicate drumming of my heart morphed into disaster. We pulled away to look at who'd just spoken.

What is she doing here? At this time of the night?

CHAPTER **TWENTY-TWO**
EXES

"Sofia?" I mumbled immediately after I saw her.

Bright red lipstick laced her lips. I quickly moved behind Tristan, staying where I could see her, keeping myself covered.

"Hey, Tristy," she said with a bit of sultriness in her voice. Her black heels had gold chains around the ankles, and her short hair looked glossy from here. Her burgundy dress was too revealing, fitting her careless nature.

"You didn't tell me you were coming," Tristan said, putting one arm around my waist and pulling me to his back.

Sofia glanced at me before talking. "Since you dumped me at the altar for a little girl and decided I didn't exist anymore, I came to say hi."

I rolled my eyes and stared at her red nails that weirdly stole my attention.

"I can't believe you almost put my brother in a coma because of her. He had to get a nose job done, you know."

"Next time he tries to hurt her again, he won't get so lucky."

Are they talking about Ralph? What did Tristan do to him?

"I hope she's worth it, Tristan," Sofia said, looking at me with thick resentment clouding her eyes.

She smiled and turned to Tristan.

"We were friends before we started dating. I don't hate you for your stupid decision. I wasn't planning on getting pregnant anyway. I'm becoming a full-time model next year, and I need this body. Who has time to nurse a crying baby?" She said.

Tristan just stared at her, not saying anything.

"Thanks for caring, but you should've called." Tristan sounded annoyed.

"Sorry for ruining the 'moment.' " She added air quotes with her long nails to the last word.

"Anyway, what was that scary thing on your back?" She crossed her arms with a pose, shooting out her right hip.

I was about to tell her it was none of her concern, but Tristan beat me to it.

"It's none of your business," Tristan said.

"Whatever," she scoffed.

"Why are you here, Sofia?" he asked like he knew she was lying.

"To talk." She looked serious now. "In private," she added, looking at me.

"Okay, I will meet you in the living room."

Tristan waited for her to leave before turning around to look at me. He brushed the wet baby hair that stuck to my face and looked at me with concern.

"Are you okay?" he asked, as if he expected me to be in tears.

"Yeah. Why not?"

"Stay here. I will be right back." He gave me a soft smile and came out of the pool.

I sighed and put on my bikini and shirt. I stayed in the water for a while. I got tired of waiting for him and got out of the pool. I drank more wine and dried my body. I squeezed the water out of my hair and dried it more with the towel. I took the remaining wine and left. I didn't see them in the living room. I looked around but didn't find them.

I frowned and went to drop what I had in my hands in the kitchen.

I took a shower when I got to my room. I put on my favorite flannel pajamas shorts and a hoodie that covered the pajamas shorts.

I decided to do some reading. I threw a few magazines on the bed and made myself comfortable. My mind drifted to Tristan and Sofia. *Where are they? I thought they wanted to have their talk in the living room. Are they …*

I shook the thought out of my head. Tristan didn't like Sofia, but I still had a feeling she was here to seduce him.

"Focus. Focus. Focus." I hit my forehead with the book. I flipped through the pages.

I was about to open the next magazine when someone knocked on my door.

"Chloe? Are you awake?"

An unknown fluttering sensation coursed through my stomach at the sound of his voice.

"Yeah." I tried to sound normal, but I could hear the excitement in my voice.

He opened the door and walked in, dressed only in his gray sweats that hung low around his waist. His sculpted chest and abdomen snatched my eyes.

"Sorry for taking so long." He sat close to where my books lay. His torso was directly in front of me.

I bit on my inner lip and tried to distract myself. I really wanted to lick wine off his chest.

"I didn't see you guys in the living room," I said, sitting up and keeping a safe distance between me and his solid torso.

"She said she wasn't comfortable with us inside, so we went to the garden."

I nodded a bit, relieved, but I wanted to know what they'd talked about.

"She came to talk about what had happened in the church. She wouldn't stop crying. It took an hour to calm her down," he said like he could read my mind.

I didn't know what to say, but I noticed the atmosphere around us had changed. I returned to my magazine, humming a response.

"What are you doing?" he asked, leaning closer to the magazine in front of me.

"Studying." I joked.

"You can do that tomorrow since you're free—unless it's urgent." He packed everything and dropped them on my nightstand.

"What a bad influence." I frowned, and he laughed.

"It's late. You spent the day with your best friend and went swimming. You should rest," he said.

"Yes, Daddy," I said mockingly, but the look on Tristan's face told me he had taken it the wrong way.

"You just reminded me of my dad—that's all." I laughed, trying to ease the tension settling in the air.

He nodded with a tight smile, biting on his lip.

He walked to the other side of the bed and climbed in. I folded my legs and faced him.

He rested his back on the headboard, propping one leg up.

I didn't know if it was the alcohol, but I was feeling confident right now, and I wanted to open up about my horrible exes and who had left the scar on my back. I didn't trust him, but I wanted him to open up to me about Nadia and Fiona. Baby steps.

"Wanna hear tales of my horrible exes?"

"If you're willing to share, I'm all ears."

"Before I begin, don't judge me. I was desperate, and I did dumb stuff."

"I won't judge," he said and crossed his heart.

I beamed and began my story. "I grew up in a family where almost everything we did had rules. My mom was a sucker for rules, and I was a sucker for breaking them. I hated it, but I couldn't say that to my parents. I wanted more. I wanted to experience more. I wanted to grow up fast and be free."

I glanced at him; he was staring at me with keen interest. His eyes dilated, and his arms folded.

"I had popular friends in high school. I envied them so much 'cause they got to do whatever they wanted. I always felt left out during some discussions because I didn't know what they were talking about. We were rich, but we never went on vacations. There were so many places I wanted to see, especially Paris and the Bahamas." I paused and laughed softly at myself.

"It got worse when they started talking about boys and parties, their first kiss and sex. I wanted that." I played with the hem of my hoodie.

"I heard a senior was throwing a party, so that was my opportunity. I snuck out that night to go to the party. I met Marco, who offered me a drink, my first taste of alcohol."

I chuckled, and Tristan smiled. "He was cute, kind eyes, and all that. He was the first senior I dated, but he dumped me for a transfer student.

My second boyfriend …" I stopped and took a deep breath; this was where it got terrifying.

"You don't have to tell me," Tristan said, taking my left leg and placing it on his thigh.

My senses focused on the movement of his palm up and down my thigh in a soothing gesture.

"I'm fine." I smiled. "His name was Luke, and he was a junkie. He taught me how to smoke and do other drugs I can't really remember. I lost my virginity to him; most of the sex we had, we were high on drugs. It was fun at first. We went clubbing, did a lot of crazy shit. We broke into wealthy people's estates and went through their stuff. I enjoyed getting high and the thrill it brought, but he started acting strange, getting into fights with people that didn't supply his drugs on time. The day I tried to confront him, he pushed me on the floor and tried to strangle me. He became so aggressive." I paused and gave him a sad smile to show him I was strong. "I got a beating when I tried to talk to him again, and that was when I ended it.

"My third boyfriend, Milo, was nice and really sweet at first." I stopped and laughed, a laugh that brought tears to my eyes.

"He used to tie me to a seat and make me watch him have sex with different girls."

"What? Why?" Tristan's face creased into anger and disgust as his jaw hardened and nose wrinkled.

"It was like a fetish to him; he got off on it."

"And you still stayed with him?"

"He threatened to tell my parents about my wild life outside if I tried to leave him because he knew everything about me, and we were kind of family friends. He broke it off after we fucked at a party. Three days later, he told me he couldn't remember if he had used a condom.

I had been too wasted to remember either. I freaked out and asked my sister for help. She got me a pregnancy test, and we checked; it came out negative. But we forgot to get rid of the test, and my mom found it in my room a week later. She demanded an explanation, and I only told her about hooking up at a party. Mom sent me to a summer camp for delinquents, but it only got bad there because I got mixed with people worse than me. We used to sneak into the woods and get drunk and do drugs." I paused and felt like throwing up at the memory.

"When I returned from the camp, I had to put up this pretense that I was a better person, but I could tell whatever faith my parents had in me was hanging on a thin thread. I had become the black sheep of the family and tried my best to keep up the facade that I'd changed. I kept sneaking out, going to parties, and drinking.

"My fourth ex, Dominiano," I said with a frown, his warm gray eyes appearing in my head. "He was the perfect definition of *bad*. His beauty turned heads. His smile could light up—"

"Just get straight to the point. You're boring me with that fangirl talk."

"Ooh, someone is jealous," I teased, kicking his leg.

He scoffed and said nothing.

"Dominiano was nice, but everyone found him terrifying and mean. He treated me differently though; he made me feel special and made everyone treat me like his queen."

"Seriously?" Tristan groaned, getting frustrated at the praise.

"I just wanted you to know he was a nice guy at first, and jealousy doesn't look cute on you." I smirked, and he glared at me. "Well, Dominiano had a secret, and it didn't take me long to find out—"

" 'Cause you're very nosy," Tristan cut in.

"It's part of me. I found out he was the son of a drug lord, and he was also working for his dad."

"So, you dumped him?"

"No, I loved him, so I stayed. He allowed me to hang out with his gang, who happened to work for his dad too; they were all nice, except Grey."

"Your ex?"

"Yeah, he was friends with someone in Dominiano's gang, but he wasn't involved in the business. He only hung out with us. He didn't like me. He was always glaring at me. The feeling was mutual anyway."

"Why?" he asked with a laugh.

"He was always telling me how I didn't belong with them. He once called me a desperate bitch. Dominiano broke his nose that day and beat the shit out of him, so he stopped coming. I got used to the gunfights, and I happened to meet his dad once, but he didn't like me. I snuck out every night to their hideout. There was a bloody fight with another gang one night I got there. I didn't know what had happened, but I was scared for my life and for the other guys, so I called the cops."

"Wait, what?" His eyes widened in surprise. He gestured for me to keep talking.

"I was trying to help. I didn't stop to think of the consequences. I was scared! I was only seventeen and too young to die." I tried to defend myself.

"Yeah, that was stupid."

I shot him a glare. "I know. You don't have to remind me, and you said you wouldn't judge," I said, grabbing a pillow and hitting him on the arm.

"Sorry." He laughed. "What happened after that?"

"Some of them got arrested, but Dominiano and four others got away. He took me with them to a small apartment to hide until the search was over. He suspected someone from the other gang had called the cops, but I ratted myself out."

"Oh God," he groaned with a facepalm.

"I had to. If he'd found out later, he'd have killed me. Dominiano had anger issues, and it got very scary. Betrayal equaled death."

"Go on."

"Well, Dominiano went crazy when I told him. He threw harsh words at me in front of the guys. He grabbed a fistful of my hair and dragged me to the only bedroom in the apartment. He said he wanted to give me a punishment I would never forget, a punishment that would make me miserable." I stopped as I recalled that day.

"What did he do?" Tristan asked in a soft tone, his hand moving again on my thigh.

"He … he forced himself on me. He told me he wasn't going to use any protection. He wanted to get me pregnant with the next heir to his father's business. That was his punishment. I cried and tried to fight him off, but he was too strong. I begged him to stop, and he surprisingly did. I don't know why he stopped, but thank God he did." I blinked the tears in my eyes away.

"You can stop now," Tristan said, but I insisted on finishing my story.

"He was hell-bent on punishing me. He dragged me back to the living room and asked one of the guys for his knife. He put the knife over the gas cooker and let it burn for some minutes. I tried to run away when I saw what was coming, but he told the guys to hold me down." I paused and tried to hold my tears back.

"He zipped down the back of my dress and tried to draw a *D* with the hot knife. I screamed. I made it worse when I tried to fight them. It only made the cut ugly. I passed out and woke up in a dark alley with a note in my hand. He told me it was over between us, and if I ratted him out to the cops, he'd come back for me. I was too weak to find my way home, but Grey came. His friend had called him and told him where I was. He took me to the hospital and stayed with me."

I sighed softly, the memories starting to overwhelm me.

"But I had to go home that night. The doctor was against it. I didn't want my family to get worried and call the cops."

"No one in your family knew?"

"My sister. She once caught me smoking weed in the bathroom after I returned from camp, and she warned me to stop, but she never told my parents. I told her about all my boyfriends. She never liked Dominiano. She wanted to tell my parents about the attempted rape, but I begged her not to. To my parents, I had changed."

"You didn't tell her about the mark on your back?"

"I only told Vina 'cause she saw it and now you. Grey also knows about the scar."

"How did you end up dating Grey?"

"After he saved my ass, I never saw him again until I got to college, and we were taking the same course. We pretended not to know each other for some time, but later, we became friends. He finally asked me out. It was hard at first 'cause I thought he was going to be like the rest, but he changed a lot in my life."

"Can I ask you something?" Tristan asked.

"Sure."

"That day in the church Grey mentioned something about you having an affair with a married man. Is that true?"

I swallowed the dryness in my throat. I looked away from Tristan and stared at my hands.

"We don't have to talk about it," Tristan said rubbing my thigh smoothly.

"His name was Jeremy. I met him at a bar where I'd managed to get in with a fake ID. We talked the whole night and he bought me a drink. I told him I was twenty-one but I was sixteen then, and he told me he was twenty-six. He was so nice and bought me gifts every time we hung out. Two weeks later, I found out he was married and had a kid. I wouldn't say we dated but the attraction was there. I never saw him again after that."

"I'm sorry you went through all that. You're stronger than I give you credit for," Tristan said, and pinched my thigh.

I smiled.

"You attract the worst men."

"Yeah, and you're one of them."

"Yeah, I am," he whispered.

"The fact that you didn't shed a tear after telling those stories shows how strong you are. It's a rare superpower," he said with a genuine smile.

Thank God he didn't see the ones trying to come out.

"I'm glad I met Grey," I whispered after some time.

"I'm glad I met you," he said more to himself, but I was able to pick up the words.

My cheeks turned warm even if I tried not to overthink it. I glanced at the wall clock and yawned.

"Come here." He tapped on a spot next to him.

I moved to where he was and lay down, turning my back to him.

"Good night," I said with a yawn.

"Good night, Chloe," he whispered close to my ear.

I could feel the warm air from his nose. I closed my eyes and tried to sleep, but he put one arm around my waist and pulled me closer to his naked chest.

I switched off the lamp and stared into the darkness. I turned around and faced him. I felt his eyes on me.

"There were moments I wanted to go to my parents and talk to them about what had happened, but I was terrified because I didn't want to lose their trust or taint the picture of me they had in their head. I struggled with the pain and nightmares in silence, in the comfort of my room and with no one to talk to, no one to help me get on the right path," I whispered.

"You're so brave to fight all that alone. I have never met someone like you. I admire your strength. I want to hold you like a baby right now," he said, pressing a kiss to my forehead.

"Hold me like a baby then," I said, snuggling closer, and he laughed.

"I also really want to kiss you."

"I can't hear you. I'm sleeping."

"Heartbreaker," he groaned.

"Oh my God, you have a heart? I never realized."

I gasped in fake surprise, and he burst out laughing. His chest vibrated with his soft laughter.

"Real funny, Chloe," he said and pinched my hip.

I laughed and smacked his hand away.

"I still want to kiss you," he whispered into my ear, his voice sizzling against my skin.

I smiled and found his lips in the dark. I molded into him as he pulled closer. My leg draped over his waist as his fingers skimmed my hips, slipping into the hem of my shorts and continuing to my back. His fingers brushed the scar.

He groaned when I bit on his lower lip and pulled it between my teeth before trying to pull away, but he pulled me back, his tongue sliding in and his fingers fisting my hair. His kiss was raw and enticing. I returned every kiss, running my hand up his chest.

"We should go to sleep," he said breathlessly but kissed me again.

"Yeah," I rasped between kisses.

It took a while before we broke apart and decided to catch some sleep. I was glad I'd told him about my horrible exes; it felt like a weight had been lifted off my body.

Maybe he'd tell me about Nadia soon. I wanted to know who she was.

CHAPTER **TWENTY-THREE**
NADIA

I woke up alone on the bed. I'd told Tristan about my wild past, and I was glad I'd gotten that off my chest. I hadn't spoken about it for a long time, and honestly, it was good, telling someone.

I felt so lazy today. I just wanted to stay in bed and do nothing, but I needed food. I forced myself out of bed and went to wash my face and my mouth.

Adrian and Karen had already gone on their vacation. I wished I could go on one too.

I walked down the stairs, holding the railing to support my lazy bones.

"Good morning, Miss Simpson. How was your night?" Morris asked, placing some toasted bread on the dining table.

"Awesome. Did you have a great night?"

"Yes, Miss Simpson."

I smiled at him and took a seat.

My phone rang before I could reach for the toasted bread. Tristan's name appeared on the screen. I couldn't remember saving Tristan's name on my phone. I hadn't even known I had his contact info.

"Tristan?" I said to be sure it was him.

"Hey, Chloe. Did I wake you up?" His deep voice, almost raspy, graced my ear.

"No, I'm actually in the dining room."

"Okay, um …" He paused and hesitated with whatever he wanted to tell me.

"Is something wrong?"

"My mom called."

"Is she okay?" I panicked.

"Yeah, she told me she was sending her chauffeur to pick you up."

"What for?"

"She only told me she wanted to spend the day with you and get to know more about you."

"Is that safe? I mean, she might want to know about us and maybe force me to the hospital to check if the baby is okay."

"My mom hates hospitals. I already told her you're not comfortable with talking about how our relationship started or the pregnancy."

"Okay," I mumbled.

"Be ready before twelve."

"I will try."

"It's fine if you don't want to go."

"I want to." It'd be rude not to show up.

"Are you sure? I can tell her something came up and you couldn't come."

"It's okay. I wanna go out a little more," I said.

"Okay, try to have fun," he said before hanging up.

"Sorry, Morris, something has come up," I told him with a frown.

I grabbed the toasted bread and ate it on my way to my room. It was almost eleven a.m. I searched my wardrobe for something simple to wear.

I spent an hour getting ready. I went for a green floral sundress that stopped above my knees and matched it with a pair of sandals. I left my hair down and wore my charm bracelet and a golden chain that had my name on it.

Morris knocked on my door when the chauffeur arrived. I grabbed my small black bag and left my room. The ride was short, and my stomach flipped when the car stopped. To be honest, I was nervous about spending a whole day with Tristan's family.

I gave Eduardo, the chauffeur, a smile before walking up the steps to the majestic three-story estate. I inhaled before pressing the doorbell. Large pillars supported the top, and long sofas with round designer pillows decorated the porch.

I looked around at the lawn that was so neat that one could sleep there. I stared at the peach Jeep wrangler parked outside the garage as I waited for someone to open the door. My heart jumped when the door opened.

A lady in a maid dress smiled at me, her neat bun above her head fitting her oval face. I wished I could pull up a cute bun like her and not look like someone that had gotten electrocuted.

"Hi," I said, gripping the strap on my bag.

"You must be Miss Chloe Simpson. Welcome to the Sanchester estate. Mrs. Sanchester is expecting you in the living room upstairs."

"Give me your voice already," I said immediately after she was done talking. Her voice was adorable, too adorable.

"Hi, I'm Sarah."

"Hi, Sarah." I grinned.

"Mrs. Sanchester is waiting." She stepped away for me to move in.

I followed her as she led the way. I kept looking around. The interior was breathtaking. Each furniture had a unique design. The artifacts were beautiful and looked original. Large paintings hung on the tall walls. I wondered how much the one that looked like someone had thrown up on it cost. *What really went through these painters' heads?*

"Did Mrs. Sanchester announce to everyone I was coming?" I asked after I noticed the way some of the maids were smiling at me.

"Not really. Everyone who works here knows you. Nana talks about you all the time. Nora made a bet with everyone that you're going to have a boy, and Mrs. Sanchester adores you so much," she said as we climbed the grand stairs with red Italian carpet running down the steps.

I felt a sudden tightness in my chest. It consumed me slowly. I was deceiving each one of them, and the guilt made me more nervous to be around them.

"Here." She stopped in front of a door.

She knocked, and I heard Mrs. Sanchester's voice.

"Come in."

I took a glance at Sarah and let myself in.

"Chloe!" Nana screamed, standing up from her recliner.

"Hi, Nana."

She wrapped me in a tight hug.

"You smell so good," she whispered and pulled away.

"Thank you."

"Hello, Chloe." Mrs. Sanchester gave me a side hug and a kiss on the cheek.

She looked so delicate. I was scared to hug her back. Staring into those blue eyes, I felt sad.

"Welcome, sweetie," she added with a broad grin.

I turned to look at an older lady who was sipping tea like she was in the presence of the queen. Her lips curled into a kind smile. She stood up and approached me. My eyes caught her platinum hair that looked too glossy for her age.

"This is my elder sister, Lilian," Mrs. Sanchester introduced.

"Hi."

"Come here, you doll." She took me by surprise, giving me a warm hug and stroking my back.

"She is so beautiful," she said with a scrutinizing gaze. "Now, I know why my naughty nephew couldn't resist you," she said, and they all laughed.

"How many months?" she asked, looking at my stomach that was too flat to convince anyone I was carrying a baby.

I tried to shoot it out, but I was scared they might notice since they all had their eyes on me.

"Three months."

"Wow, and the baby bump is still hidden," Lilian said, and I smiled with a shrug.

"It might show itself soon," Nana said, coming to stand beside me.

I loved her so much.

At eighty-seven, she was still lively and strong. Both my grandparents were in home care, and every time we visited them, they only spoke to my parents 'cause they forgot we were their grandkids. My mom reminded them every time, but they still forgot.

"Do you take one of those yoga classes for pregnant women?" Lilian asked.

"No."

"I heard it helps a lot. I know someone who owns a yoga studio; it's not far from here. I can call her and sign you up. If you want," she added when I didn't say anything.

"Um … yeah, I would love to go," I stuttered.

It didn't take her long to speak to her friend. After she ended the call, she informed me I was starting Saturday.

The rest of the day went better than I'd expected. Lilian wasn't so bad. She made jokes about her kids that got me laughing until my stomach hurt. Nana and Lilian held a chess tournament, and I was team Nana all the way. Mrs. Sanchester tried to teach me how to play, but I was too slow to comprehend what she was saying.

Nana shared her tea recipe with me.

Spending the day with them just showed me how stuck-up my family was. My mom was always concerned about manners, and there was hardly room for fun. Jokes around my mom were a sign of disrespect.

I didn't regret leaving the house to hang out with them.

"How DID IT GO?" Tristan asked me during dinner.

"It was fun. Your aunt Lilian is very funny."

"Please tell me she didn't make any jokes about me." He frowned, his lips pouted and eyes pinned to his food.

He looked cute, and I fought the urge to grab my phone and take a picture.

"Sadly, no. She only spoke about her kids, but I'm sure she'd tell me next time," I said and smirked at the end.

"What else did she do?"

"She signed me up for yoga class."

"Yoga class?" His lips quirked in amusement.

"Yeah, yoga class for pregnant women."

"And you agreed?" He seemed surprised.

"There's no harm in joining a yoga class for pregnant women. They will go easy on us since we're pregnant."

"We?" he emphasized with a laugh.

I glared at him and ate my food.

"Look, if you don't want to go, I will speak to—"

"It's fine. I'm tired of staying here all day anyway."

"Okay, but if you're not comfortable, let me know."

"It's just yoga." I shrugged.

"You don't look like an athletic person."

"Ouch. Are you saying I'm fat?"

"No." He laughed. "You're perfect. Fat or not, it wouldn't change how I feel about you."

I laughed at how he was trying not to stutter. He looked confused as he stared at me.

"I was messing with you," I said.

"You're a rare kind."

I didn't question him.

We left the dining room when we were done eating. We walked side by side upstairs, to our rooms. I was trying to get Tristan's attention as he typed away with one hand on his phone while the other hid in the pocket on his black joggers.

I thought of putting one leg out and watching him fall since he wasn't looking anywhere else but his screen. He put his phone away like he knew what was coming. I groaned internally as we got off the flight of stairs.

"Good night," I said with a short wave and turned to go to my room, but he was following me. "Did you forget the way to your room? It's right there." I pointed to his room.

He walked past me and entered my room.

"Tristan?" I rushed after him.

He was already on my bed when I entered the room. He tapped the space next to him with a small smile on his lips.

SATURDAY, I FOUND myself sitting on a purple yoga mat with ten women around me, each with a baby bump. I was the only one with no baby bump. A few people had already given me that *are you supposed to be here* look.

I was in the middle of two women, who kept glancing at my stomach as we did what our yoga trainer instructed. I was enjoying it. Maybe it was because I wasn't pregnant like the rest.

"Sorry, what trimester are you?" the lady to my left whispered.

"Um … first."

"Oh," they both said in unison, nodding their heads slowly.

"You're so lucky. You should have seen me in my first trimester," the one at my right said.

"Me too. Even at two months, the bump was already visible," the lady behind me said.

I hadn't even known she was listening.

MY WAIST WAS aching by the time I got home. I went straight to bed, not bothering to shower—not like any of the exercises had made me sweat. I woke up to someone whispering my name and tickling me. I frowned at Tristan when I opened my eyes.

"What time is it?" I asked, looking outside. It was already dark.

"Almost nine. Are you okay?" he asked, running his fingers through my hair in a gentle and slow manner, like it was fragile.

"Yeah, just a minor waist pain."

He pulled away, giving me the *I told you so* look.

"You slept with your shoes on," he said as he untied the shoelace.

He removed the shoe and massaged my toes soothingly. I really needed that.

"I enjoyed it. Everyone was curious about my flat stomach," I said with a wide smile. I'd felt like a celebrity today.

He scoffed and massaged my legs. I sighed in content. His large hands trailed up my thighs in a gentle massage and went up to the globe of my ass. I giggled and smirked at him.

"That feels good," I moaned as he massaged my shoulders and down my arms.

His long fingers interlocked with mine.

"Were you a masseur in your past life? Because your hands are gold," I said as his fingers trailed up to my neck and caressed every angle delicately.

He laughed and said nothing.

He gripped my legs and pushed them apart, standing between my thighs.

"Uh … what are you doing?" I felt heat crawling up my skin at the view.

"Giving you a waist massage," he said, holding both sides of my waist.

Sweet currents flowed through my veins when he ran his thumb down the birthmark at my waistline. I watched him as his long fingers roamed my skin in circles.

The massage started nicely, but it got sensual, and I had to bite my lip hard to stop the moan trying to escape my lips. He stared at my face with a smirk.

What a devil! He knew what he was doing.

Like that wasn't enough torture already, he leaned down and trailed wet kisses from my belly button up. I arched my back, trying not to make any sound but failed. He moved my shirt up as his lips got higher. He traced my ribs as he glided his hand up, almost slipping into my sports bra.

My stomach grumbled, making him stop. I covered my face with my hands, feeling embarrassed. I heard Tristan laugh.

"Someone is hungry." He kissed my belly button and dragged my shirt down. "Let's get you something to eat." He stepped away and got off the bed. He took my hand and pulled me out of bed.

Wrong timing, stomach. Of all the times to grumble. I never told you I was hungry. I argued with my stomach, and it made the stupid sound again.

"Hang in there, buddy," Tristan said, tapping my stomach.

We both laughed as we left the room.

IT HAD BEEN a week since I'd started the yoga class, and honestly, I felt better from the little exercises. I made friends, and I avoided conversations about pregnancy.

Karen and Adrian were back early from their vacation. They said it got boring, staying at the hotel, and many tourist centers were closed. Adrian called three days later and invited me to their engagement party.

"Wow, things are really moving fast," I said to myself as I shopped for a nice gown.

I went for a mermaid red gown that had too many laces, but it looked decent. It arrived the next day with a small purse I'd bought to go with it. I made sure the gown wasn't too tight because to everyone, I was pregnant.

I started getting ready two hours before the time we were supposed to leave. I didn't want us to be late because of me.

I wore my black strappy heels and packed my hair in a sleek ponytail. My forehead was making me second-guess my hairstyle. I spent thirty minutes on my makeup, which came out glamorous. I applied my nude lipstick and wore my jewelry.

Tristan knocked on my door immediately after I was done. I opened the door quickly.

Thank God he wasn't wearing those sweats. He looked handsome in his dark classic-fit tuxedo. I grabbed my phone and took a picture of him, unable to stop myself. I opened my mouth to say something, but he covered my lips with his. The kiss was short but sent sparks to every part of my body.

"I just had to," he whispered softly when he pulled away. His hand didn't leave my waist. He stared at me in a way I had never seen before, like I was a rare gem he was seeing for the first time.

"You look too beautiful to be real."

"That sounded like an insult." I frowned.

"Oh, um … you look stunning. Is that better?"

I smiled at how unsure he looked.

"And you look like a prince from those Disney stories I read when I was little," I whispered, running my palm up his chest.

I didn't know what we were or what was happening between us, but it felt too good to deny.

"What?" He looked confused and disappointed.

"They're too handsome to be real," I said, and he laughed lightheartedly. "You look good," I whispered, adjusting his black bow tie.

His crystal-blue eyes stared at me like he had something to say but didn't want to say it.

"Thank you for cleaning my lipstick," I joked.

"You want it back?" He leaned down to kiss me, but I held him back.

"We are running late," I said, and he groaned.

We left the house with his hand securing my waist until we got to the car. The ride lasted for twenty-five minutes. It was a grand hotel. I knew this place, but I had never been inside.

Tristan helped me up the steps, holding my hand to guide me so I wouldn't miss a step. I gave him a soft smile, and we went inside the luxurious building.

The ballroom was big. There were many guests here already even though we were five minutes early. The decorations were beautiful and very lovely; all I could see was glitter. The bouquet of flowers on each table matched the rose-gold silk material covering the tables.

"There they are." I heard Adrian's voice.

He was rocking a fancy, dark suit. Karen trailed behind him in a short dress that had glitter everywhere; she looked like a disco ball but stunning.

"You look amazing," Adrian told me with a broad smile.

"You too." I grabbed a drink from the waiter passing, and they all laughed at me.

"It's nonalcoholic," I defended myself.

"You guys stick around while we welcome the others," Adrian told us before leaving with Karen.

I had one mission tonight—to ask Adrian who Nadia was. I was waiting to have some time alone with him, and it didn't take long for my wish to be granted.

Tristan was busy speaking with some business ally when Adrian came and offered me another glass of apple cider.

"Red looks better on you than any other color."

"Now, I feel like I will look ugly in other colors." I frowned.

"No, you look beautiful, no matter what color you wear," he said after a brief laugh.

"Aww, thanks," I said, placing a hand on my chest. It was time to ask him about Nadia. "Can I ask you something?" I asked, glancing at Tristan.

He was too engrossed in whatever he was discussing with the man in front of him.

"Sure."

"Do you happen to know who Nadia is?"

He glanced at Tristan immediately after I asked.

"Is she Tristan's wife?"

"What?" He looked confused.

"Is Nadia Tristan's wife?" I asked again.

"No," he said with soft laughter.

Had Tristan lied?

"Then, who is she?"

"Um ... she is ..."

"Me."

A voice came from behind.

CHAPTER **TWENTY-FOUR**
JAIL

"Me."

I turned around, only to meet Tristan. He was smiling, but at the same time, he was glaring at me.

Karen came and took Adrian away, saying she wanted him to meet someone.

Wrong timing, girl.

I was left with Tristan, who looked very furious. He left his remaining wine on a nearby table and grabbed my arm, pulling me to the exit with him.

I didn't want to create a scene, so I decided not to struggle, but I stood my ground when we got to the parking lot. I pulled away from his hold, making him stop.

He loosened his tie and faced me. "Why are you so stubborn?"

"It's my hobby." I shrugged coolly.

"Get in the car," he said with an icy stare.

"But we just got here. It's your best friend's engagement party. We can't just leave. You didn't even inform him we're leaving."

He walked to the car and entered, ignoring everything I'd said.

"Seriously?" I grunted. "I'm not leaving," I said, crossing my arms.

"I will tell you what you need to know," he said calmly.

"Okay," I said and entered the car.

The ride was quiet. I noticed how he was clenching and unclenching his hands around the wheel. He hadn't said a word since we'd left.

I glanced at him; his face hardened and then softened, like he was fighting his emotions.

"I don't even know why you're upset. I didn't get the answer I wanted."

"I warned you to stop. You don't have to know who she is, goddamn it! You don't have to know everything, Chloe!"

"Why can't you tell me? I opened up to you about my past."

"I never asked you to!" he snapped, turning to look at me with cold eyes. The softness in his gaze a few minutes ago was gone. "For once, why can't you do as you're told? I only ask you to be patient with me. I will tell you what you need to know but not now. Stop going behind my back, asking questions that will only hurt!" he yelled.

"You know what keeps hurting me? The fact that you won't tell me anything or let me in. I care about you, and I wanna help with—"

"The only help I need from you is to convince my family that we're in love and you're carrying my baby," he cut in.

"How were you expecting me to react, Tristan? You told me Nadia was your wife, and then you asked me out. You avoid the question every time I bring it up. Excuse me for trying to clear my confusion. I thought since we have something going on between us, you'd open up a bit to me!"

"Something? Between us?" He said it like those words sounded strange to him. He glanced at me; his oceanic eyes were mocking me. "Are you still that dumb and desperate kid who doesn't know the difference between lust and love? We have nothing between us, Chloe. I thought after your ugly experience with your exes, you'd be more sensible on that topic."

That had to be the first thing someone had said to me that left me completely speechless and numb. All those words struck me like I was death personified. How could he be someone else all of a sudden? I tried to find my breath. My emotions were complicated and not readily verifiable. I squeezed my knees and tried to get myself together. How could someone break me with just words?

It hurt. It really hurt.

"Chloe?" His voice was soft, but I knew the monster behind that softness.

"Stop the car," I said, not looking his way. I unfastened my seat belt and waited for him to stop.

"Chloe …"

"Stop the car, or I will break the window and jump out!"

That made him stop. I opened the door.

"You're an asshole!" I spat and slammed the door, not caring if I damaged the car.

"Chloe!"

I kept walking, not looking back. I didn't know where I was going. I wanted to be anywhere but around Tristan.

"Chloe!" he kept calling, but I ignored him.

I hated him. I hated how he could be so sweet one moment and be something else entirely the next moment. Everything with him was like chasing the moon to find its origin but ending up going in circles.

"Chloe," I heard him call, his footsteps echoing behind me.

"Go away, Tristan," I sighed.

"I'm sorry," he said, grabbing my arm.

I turned to look at him with a deadly look. His face softened, and his eyes looked empty, not giving anything away.

"Get the hell away from me." I snatched my arm away, glaring at him with tears gathering in my eyes. I didn't want him to see me cry. I didn't want him to see how much his words had destroyed me. Just words.

My heels clicked on the ground as I kept walking straight. I didn't hear his voice again. I looked back and saw that he was gone. Wow. I had expected him to follow me around, apologizing, until I agreed to come home with him. I really sucked at this relationship thing.

The cold air made me aware of what I was wearing. I tried to think of anything else but what he'd said in the car. It still broke my heart that he had driven off without even trying to beg me. I'd expected more.

I winced as my feet throbbed from the short walk in these heels. I looked around me and only saw four people. I reached down and removed my heels. I exhaled in relief as my feet relaxed on the cold floor. I walked down the sidewalk with my heels in one hand. I knew this place. It wasn't far from my house.

I wondered if my parents would let me in if I knocked on the door. I didn't want to go back to Tristan's place. I'd just feel furious the whole night. I found myself heading to the place I'd once considered home. My feet kept prompting me to go farther. I took a glance at my neighbor's house as I walked past the tall building. I missed babysitting Hanna, but her parents probably hated me now, like everyone else.

I had been walking for almost ten minutes, enough time to reflect on my miserable life. My footsteps slowed as I got closer to the house that held so many memories. I paused and remained on the sidewalk.

What am I doing here?

I wanted to turn away and walk far away from here, but I also wanted to walk to the door and knock. I imagined what their reaction would be when they saw me.

I was about to walk to the door when I saw my mom from the large glass window. I saw the rest of my family. They were in the dining room, and they looked happy. Happy without me. Mom was smiling so wide as she served Dad, who had a small grin on his face, and Ciara was laughing. It was as if I had been erased from their life.

Did they still have my pictures, or had they burned every picture of me they could find?

The pain in my chest became almost unbearable. I crumbled to the dirty floor and broke down.

I stood up as someone rode past me on a bike. I wiped my tears away and walked away. I found a bus stop after walking for twelve minutes. My feet hurt like I'd been walking on thorns. I groaned and took a seat on the bench at the bus stop. I didn't know where to go from here. Tristan couldn't care less about where I was or what happened to me. I tried to hold the tears back.

I hated life. Why was living so exhausting?

I could sleep here. I didn't like that my life was a mess. I leaned back on the metal bench and groaned in frustration. I wanted to be three again. The age when I'd had nothing to worry about. The age when I had been very happy.

Tears gathered at the edge of my eyes. I closed my eyes and tried to keep my mind calm.

"Chloe?"

I knew that voice.

"Grey?" I sat up on the seat as he kept staring at me with worry evident in his eyes. I looked pitiful right now. "Hey," I mumbled, putting my arms around myself and avoiding his eyes.

"What are you doing here?" he asked, eyes fixated on my bare feet.

I didn't say anything. I stared at my toes, relieved they were attractive.

"Wanna talk?" he asked and came to sit beside me. That familiar scent I had once been in love with hit my nose.

My eyes stared at his black Nikes. They looked good.

"Chlo?" he called, sounding more worried.

I finally looked at him. Those brown eyes I'd loved staring into and those curls I'd enjoyed running my fingers through.

"I was taking a walk." It wasn't a lie, and it wasn't the truth either, but the look on his face told me he didn't believe me.

He stood up, making my heart drop. He was going to leave me too. No one wanted to be around me.

I was confused when he picked up my heels and took my hand.

"Come on," he urged, gently pulling me up.

I followed, not arguing. We walked quietly down the sidewalk.

"If your feet are hurting, I can give you mine, though they'd be big for you," he said, staring at my feet.

"It's fine. It feels good," I said with a light laughter. I wanted to ask him where we were going, but I kept quiet and followed.

"Have you eaten?" he asked, swinging my hand to and fro with our fingers interlocked, like old times. I'd forgotten how much he loved doing that.

"Yes," I admitted.

Tristan and I left the party without eating anything, and food could ease my mood right now. Food made everything better.

"There is a diner down the road. I wish I had brought my car."

"It's fine. The weather is nice tonight," I said and inhaled, pretending to enjoy the cool wind on my face.

"You look great. What's the occasion?" he said, staring down at the red gown.

"Thanks. An engagement party."

He looked like he had more to say to me but was holding back. We walked quietly to the diner. He held the door open for me, and I made my way in. We took a booth at the back and made our order.

"So, what happened?" he asked, glancing at me as he leaned closer to the table between us.

I noticed he still had the silly bracelet I had given him on our first anniversary.

The guy I thought liked me just told me I'm stupid for mistaking lust with love, I wanted to say but settled for, "I fought with the person I live with."

"You mean, Tristan Sanchester, your ... lover?" he said with an inexplicable edge to his voice.

I wanted to explain everything to him, but I couldn't, so I allowed him to think the worst of me.

"How bad was the fight that he left you at the bus stop, looking like it was the end of the world?"

"I don't wanna talk about it." I dismissed it, playing with the napkins on the table.

"Were you planning to sleep at the bus stop?" he asked when our food arrived.

I quickly grabbed my fried shrimp and dip.

"To be honest, I was. I don't plan on going back tonight."

"You can spend the night at my place if you want," he offered, his voice soft, like it was a harmless request.

"Um ... thanks," I mumbled, and he smiled.

"So, are you excited about being a mother?"

My hand stopped midair at his question. I avoided his eyes as I swirled the shrimp in the dip, like a child.

"Don't answer. Let's eat." He laughed it off.

Why does everyone still believe I'm pregnant? I still look the same. Aren't there visible symptoms for pregnancy? And I'm supposed to be, what, three, or is it four months pregnant? I'm losing track of the lies. My clothes are not that loose to hide a baby bump. Why is everyone acting so clueless?

"I will be done with my prerequisites at the end of this year," Grey said, smiling.

"Really? That's cool."

"Vee told me you take online classes now."

"Yeah." That was all I could say. I didn't want to talk about myself. I only wanted to eat and sleep the night off. Maybe wake up with amnesia. I wouldn't mind forgetting who Chloe Simpson was because I hated her.

We left the diner once we were done eating. I had to wear my heels for the short walk to Grey's place. He tried to make conversation every chance he got, but I kept shifting the topic to him or something completely random, like asking stupid questions about where the sun always disappeared to in the night.

We rode the elevator with a family to his penthouse. I turned away when he punched in the password to unlock the door.

"It's still the same password," he told me as he opened the door.

I hid my smile as I walked in. The memory of us he kept still didn't change how much he'd hurt me in the church when he walked out without fighting for me.

"You know where the guest room is," he said behind me.

I looked around the room with its expensive furnishings. I had helped him pick out some of the furniture and home decor. Suddenly, I felt uncomfortable, coming here; memories of us were etched in every corner of the penthouse. I wondered if he still had the Polaroids of us hanging on his wall.

I turned around to thank him, but my phone started ringing. Grey and I caught the caller ID before I rejected the call.

"Tristan," Grey mumbled.

"Thanks for letting me—" My ringtone cut me off. I sighed and rejected Tristan's call again.

"You know how to help yourself around. If you need anything, you know where to find me," he said and walked away, his tone cold and angry.

What was with everyone changing personalities tonight?

I sighed in frustration as the phone started to ring again. I blocked Tristan's number and went to the guest room. I undressed and went for a shower. When I came out, sweatpants and a T-shirt were lying on the bed for me. I put them on and went under the covers, contemplating leaving the room to talk to Grey about his sudden attitude.

I turned off the lights and grabbed my phone. There were ten missed calls from Adrian and three from Morris. I switched off the phone and forced myself to sleep.

"Dumb and desperate kid ..."

"Lust and love ..."

"We have nothing between us, Chloe."

His words echoed in my head, and I found myself crying to sleep.

I didn't see Grey when I woke up. I washed my face and brushed my teeth. I planned to leave here and go and see my best friend. I didn't want to return to Tristan's place anytime soon.

I searched for my phone when I reentered the room, but I didn't see it. I sat down and tried to trace it back to last night, and I remembered leaving it on the nightstand. I sighed and left the room.

I walked to the door and tried to open it, but it was locked from the outside.

I was about to panic when the door unlocked. Grey smiled at me as he stepped in with takeout bags.

"You're up."

"Yeah, I wanted to leave, but I was locked in."

"Oh, sorry. I didn't want my friends walking in here since they have access to the password."

I didn't say anything, but I studied him as he walked to the dining table and placed the takeout bags on the table.

"I went out to get us breakfast."

"I'm not hungry. Have you seen my phone?"

"Here," he said, bringing it out from his pocket.

"What are you doing with my phone?" I asked, collecting it quickly.

"It wouldn't stop ringing, and I knew you needed sleep."

"But I switched it off."

"No, you didn't."

"I did."

"Whatever. Come, let's eat."

"No, I'm leaving."

"You're going back to him?" he asked, approaching me. His facial muscles hardened into something deadly.

I was scared for my life. I ran to the door, desperate to escape from whatever he was planning to do.

"I won't hurt you, Chlo," he said, looking hurt at my reaction.

"Open the door, Grey," I said, unlocking my phone.

I pressed my back to the wall as he walked to the door. He opened the door and let me out.

I walked away quickly, unable to get over the fear I'd felt inside his apartment. I dialed Belvina's number as I rode the elevator to the lobby, but she didn't answer. I groaned and slid slowly to the elevator floor. Thank God I was the only one in here. My phone started ringing. I was annoyed it was from Morris.

I picked it up and cleared my throat to sound okay. "Hello, Morris."

"Hi, Miss Simpson."

"Is everything okay?"

"Mr. Sanchester is at the hospital. His mom passed out."

I covered the speaker and mouthed a scream, making no sound. "Okay, send me the address."

"I will do that right away."

"Thanks." I buried my face in my hands and groaned.

I hoped Mrs. Sanchester was okay.

CHAPTER **TWENTY-FIVE**
BLANK

I came out of the cab and made my way to the hospital building. I walked to the receptionist in the lobby hastily.

"Hi," I said in a quiet voice.

"Hello. How can I help you today?" the nurse asked with a soft smile that showed off her one-sided dimple.

"I'm here to see Mrs. Carmen Sanchester."

"When was she brought here?"

"This morning."

She typed loudly on the keyboard with her long fingers.

"And who are you to her?" she asked.

"A family friend."

"Fourth floor, room 25."

"Okay, thanks," I said.

"Here." She gave me a visitor's card.

I went straight to the elevator, filled with two nurses and a small kid. I searched for room 25 when I got to the fourth floor. It was down the hallway at the left. I adjusted the big T-shirt and sweatpants and took a deep breath. I knocked on the door and gripped the cold metal door handle. I opened the door, and every head turned in my direction.

"Hi," I said with a small wave, faking my best smile. I walked in and shut the door behind me.

Nana came to hug me. Nora waved at me from where she sat, reading a *J-14* gossip magazine. Tristan was sitting next to his mom's bed, holding her hand like if he let go, she would disappear. He turned to look at me. He had a red eye, as if someone had punched him in the eye. I wished I were the one. I would have given him a bloody nose too. He stood up from his seat. His eyes scanned what I was wearing.

"Hey," Tristan said.

I could see the questions written on his face as he stared at the clothes I had on me, but he didn't voice them. He reached to hug me, but I walked away, pretending not to notice. I glared at him, taking the seat next to Nora.

I could feel his eyes on me, but I didn't look his way. I turned to look at Mrs. Sanchester. She was still asleep.

"How is she?" I asked Nana, who kept a brown blanket around herself like it was freezing inside the room.

"She is better. The doctor said she will be discharged tomorrow. Don't worry; it was nothing serious," Nana said with a warm smile.

I took a glance at Tristan. He was staring at me. I wanted to ask how he had gotten the red eye and if it hurt, but I turned away and picked up my phone. I hated how much I cared. I want to hate him for everything he said last night.

"Everything okay, honey?" Nana asked, drawing my attention away from my phone.

"Huh?" I mumbled, a bit confused at her question.

She gestured toward Tristan, who was sitting next to where his mom lay. I looked away, not sure of what to say.

"You should take him out for a little air. I'm sure he'd listen to you," Nana said, giving my hand a warm squeeze.

"Everything is okay, Nana," I assured her.

"I have spent eighty-seven years on this earth, so I can sense when something is not right," she said.

Maybe it still was all pretense for him and nothing more. Vina had warned me about getting myself tangled in his mess, and I had fallen into his webs of lies.

We stayed until Mrs. Sanchester woke up. We spoke to her for an hour before a nurse came and informed us to leave, so she could rest.

"You guys head home. I will drop Mom off tomorrow before I leave for work," Tristan said to Nana and Nora after we stepped out of the room.

"Good night, Chloe," Nora said.

"Take good care of yourself and the baby." Nana hugged me and gave me a kiss. She did the same to Tristan before leaving.

I sat down on the nearest seat and ran my palms down my thighs to my knees. My limbs felt numb, and my back ached from today's events. I leaned back on the seat and allowed my shoulders to relax.

Tristan took the seat next to me. I felt his eyes on me. I turned my face away and stared down the large hallway where a nurse play with a small boy who looked like he was three. *What a cute sight.* My stomach growled, reminding me I hadn't eaten the whole day. I hugged it with one arm, hoping it would block the unpleasant sound.

Tristan stood up and came to stand in front of me. I looked anywhere else but at him.

"There's a restaurant close by. Let's go and get something to eat."

His voice was calm.

"I'm fine," I muttered, not looking at him.

"Please," he asked and tried to touch me.

I snapped, "If you touch me, I'm going to scream."

He dropped his hand. He looked around before resting his eyes on me. I eyed him warily and clenched my fists. My stubborn stomach growled again.

"Excuse me." I heard him say to a young nurse that was passing by.

"Yes?" She smiled sweetly at him.

"My girlfriend here has not eaten anything the whole day, and she's being stubborn. I'm worried about her health and that of the baby."

Her eyes first moved to my stomach and then my face. I rolled my eyes and stared at the busy hallway.

"It's very wrong to starve yourself while you're pregnant. I suggest you go with your boyfriend and get something to eat. We have a place where you can get food here. I could take you there."

They both waited for me to say something.

"She is very stubborn. Maybe you should get a doctor to convince her."

"Or maybe you could get a doctor to check if there is really a baby in here," I said daringly and pointed at my stomach.

He asked the nurse to leave and sat back on his seat. We sat in silence for a while, neither of us saying anything.

"I'm sorry," he said, facing me.

I didn't say anything but instead stared at the white wall in front of me. Apologies wouldn't heal the pain and anger inside of me. He had gone too far last night, and I wasn't sure if I could forgive him.

"I'm sorry for everything I said last night. I didn't like you going behind my back. I wish you'd be more patient with me, Chloe," he said in a quiet tone that carried regret. "I understand if you're finding it hard to forgive me, but don't starve yourself," he added and waited for me to say something, but I remained mute.

"You can go home. I will stay," he said after a few seconds.

"Your car keys?" I asked, extending my hand.

He gave them to me without any question.

I stood up and left, not saying a word. I drove to Belvina's place and parked on the street a few feet from her house. I picked up my phone and called her. She answered the call on the second ring.

"I'm outside your house. The white car on the street," I said, leaning back on the seat.

"What? Is everything okay?"

"Yes, meet me outside and bring me something to eat 'cause I'm starving," I said and groaned.

"Okay," she said and ended the call.

My mind drifted to last night. It was like one moment, everything had been perfect, and the next minute had been total chaos. I snapped out of my thoughts when someone tapped on my window. I unlocked the door for Vina, who was wrapped in a fluffy hoodie and short shorts. She entered inside the car and shut the door.

"Here you go. I will just have to tell my mom the remaining tacos and burritos mysteriously disappeared," she said as she gave me the plastic pan.

"Thank you," I said with a smile.

"Aren't you going to give me a hug first?" Vina frowned as I opened the pan.

"Sorry. I'm just so hungry," I said and leaned closer to hug her.

"Is everything okay?" she asked me after I pulled away.

"Yes," I replied, bringing out the burrito.

"You just drove to my house at eleven p.m., asking for food. How is that okay?" she asked.

I didn't say anything but ate the food.

"Is it Tristan? What did that *hijo de puta* do?" She looked furious.

"I'm fine. I just wanted to see you," I said with a smile.

"*Mentirosa*, come here," she said and pulled me in a hug. "Whatever it is, I'm always here to listen and kick ass," she whispered, and I smiled.

"Something happened last night at the engagement party," I began.

"Ohh, tea," she squealed, leaning back on the seat.

I ate as I told her everything that had happened last night and this morning with Grey.

"I don't blame you for freaking out. That was creepy as hell. I would have reached for the knife and dice him," she said after I told her about Grey. "But can't you be patient with Tristan? I mean, it might be a hard topic for him, and you're digging for info, which makes him feel like you don't trust him."

"I don't trust him," I said.

"Yeah, I get it, but if you care, try to be patient with him or just leave if it's too much for you."

"What if he is really married to this Nadia? I hardly know anything about him. I'm not even sure he feels a thing for me. He made it clear it was all lust to him."

"I'm having migraines from all the drama with Tristan. I don't know what to say anymore."

"Let's talk about something else." I laughed.

We talked about school and celebrities as I ate the burrito and tacos. I forgot about my problems, just hanging out with her. We lost track of time as we spoke and laughed in the car. I almost broke into tears as we said good-bye to each other.

It was almost two a.m. as I pulled into the driveway in front of Tristan's house. I sighed before getting out of the car. I walked into the house, feeling distressed. Morris had already set the table with different food and was waiting for me.

"Welcome, Miss Simpson," he greeted.

"Hi, Morris," I said and headed for the stairs.

"Mr. Sanchester told me you haven't eaten since morning. I made you enough food to eat," he said, halting my movement.

I felt awful that he had gone through all that for nothing.

"I have eaten. I'm sorry you had to go through the stress." I gave him an apologetic smile and walked to my room.

I undressed and went for a shower. I stayed under the water with different thoughts running through my head. I stared at the water that went down the drain.

Was I supposed to get used to this? I wondered what my life would have been like if I'd never followed my sister to that wedding.

I brushed my wet hair back and washed my body as my hands started to look like prunes. I walked out of the shower when I was done. I stared at my reflection in the mirror as I brushed my teeth. I was starting to hate it. My blue eyes didn't look bright anymore, and it was hard to recognize the person staring at me.

I looked away and brushed quickly. I dried my body and left the bathroom. I paused when I saw Tristan in my room. He stood next to the door like a bodyguard, his tall structure filling the doorway.

"Morris told me you refused to eat. I brought you something to eat," he said and gestured to the bedside table with his chin.

"I have eaten," I said and walked to the closet.

"Can we please talk?" he asked.

"There is nothing to talk about!" I snapped.

"I know I messed up, and no matter what I say to you right now, it's not going to ease the pain I caused you," he whispered.

"I have a request," I cut in, stepping closer to him.

"Sure, anything."

"If you want me to help you to keep deceiving your family, that's fine by me, but from now on, you stay the hell away from me."

His face fell at my request, but I wasn't done yet.

"Go back to ignoring me, like you were doing when I first got here. Pretend I'm invisible. I don't care. You've made your point clear. I was an idiot for thinking we had something going on and for trying to help. I'll keep my distance. You won't even notice my shadow from now on. All I ask of you is to keep to your end of this deal, or I will leave. I have an uncle willing to take me in," I said.

Rest in peace, Uncle Phil.

"I will play the fake pregnant lover, but that's all. Don't expect anything else. Stay away from me. I'm sure you can figure how to make that work, Mr. Sanchester," I said and walked away.

"I'm trying. I really am, Chloe, but a minute away from you is torture. Everything I said that night was—"

"Don't," I cut in. "I don't wanna talk about it. Just leave," I added.

He turned to leave but paused and turned around. His eyes drifted to the clothes on the bed. "Did you sleep with him?" he asked, staring at Grey's clothes I had worn to the hospital.

"Does it matter? There is nothing between us anyway. I can fuck whoever I want."

His facial muscles pulled together. His lips pursed, and his eyes stretched into slits. He looked angry as he held my intense gaze that didn't waver. He turned away and walked out of the room, slamming the door. He could think whatever he wanted. I didn't care.

I dressed up for bed and went to sleep.

TRISTAN KNEW HOW to stay invisible. I hadn't seen any sign of him in the house for the past three days. The house felt empty, and the silence was becoming deafening, so much that I had to force Morris to watch TV with me.

I went for a walk in the garden after I was done eating breakfast all by myself again. It was Saturday. I knew Tristan was home, but I had not seen him. I spent hours on FaceTime with Belvina as she talked about the flowers in the garden, calling out the names and what they stood for. I wasn't surprised. She'd told me her mom was a florist before they moved here. I went back inside the house, as the scorching heat from the sun had made me sweat.

I grabbed my laptop and did a job search, randomly looking up affordable apartments. I might have dozed off because it was dark outside when I woke up. I left my room to get something to eat. There was a nice scent in the air mixed with a mouthwatering smell that made my stomach churn. I paused at the dining room when I saw the white scented candles and red wine on the dining table.

"Hey." I heard Tristan's voice. He walked to the dining table with a set of dinner plates.

I looked around for Morris, but I didn't see him. I couldn't deny that a part of me was happy to hear his voice, which suddenly sounded foreign to my ears.

"Wait, please," he said when I turned to leave. "Please sit," he said, pulling out the seat for me.

I hesitated for a while, battling with the thoughts in my head. I sat down and watched him as he took the seat in front of me. The dining room lights were off, only the candles lit up the room.

Tristan gave me a small smile from across the table. He bit his lip, as if he was nervous about something. I fought hard not to admire the way the lights from the candle made his beauty unreal.

"Where is Morris?" I asked in a cold tone.

"I told him to spend the night with his family," he said, leaning closer and resting both hands on the table.

His tousled blond hair was begging to be touched. My eyes lingered at the stray hair that had fallen to his forehead.

This is not the time to look sexy, Tristan.

I moved my eyes back to his that held different emotions I couldn't pinpoint.

"This is for you," he said, picking up something from the floor.

He outstretched the box of red roses to me, and I only stared, not taking it. Did he think it was going to be this easy?

"Please," he said.

I hesitated before taking it. I picked up the card inside. *Sorry for all the shit I said.*

I took a glance at him, and he was staring at me like a nervous kid. I put the flowers away and said nothing. He reached for a wineglass and opened the bottle of wine. He poured me some. I eyed him suspiciously as I took the wine and put the glass down.

"What's all this about?" I asked.

"I know you want me to keep my distance, but I can't. It's been hard without you. I feel like I'm suffocating every night, and just the sound of your footsteps from across the room takes away the pain. Even if you're so close, I still miss you, and it's killing me."

He looked tormented as he stared at me, waiting for me to say something but I remained silent.

"I want us to start over, which includes being patient with each other. I promise I will tell you everything you need to know—not all at once, but baby steps," he said. He sounded desperate.

"Why does it matter? It was lust all along."

"No," he said sharply. He exhaled and buried his face in his palms and then brushed his hands back to his neck. "That's not true, Chloe."

"Then, prove it to me. Show me," I said, looking into his eyes.

He looked shattered and seemed to be in battle with his emotions.

Just let me in, please, I wanted to say.

"I don't get it. What is so important about this Nadia?" I asked, throwing my hands in the air.

I waited for him to say something, but he didn't.

Please say something.

"Why is her name tattooed on your skin? Is she somehow connected to whatever you have going on?" I inquired, but he was still quiet.

His eyes looked at anywhere but my face.

"Tell me something, anything!" I asked, leaning closer to the table.

He shook his head, as if the questions were too much for him. I wanted to pull away and let go of it.

"She doesn't exist! She is not real!" he yelled.

CHAPTER **TWENTY-SIX**

8 LETTERS

"What?" I mumbled. "But you … she … how?"

I was so confused; it didn't make any sense. Why would he snap every time I asked if she wasn't real?

"She doesn't exist. Not anymore," he said again, sounding frustrated.

"What do you mean, not anymore?"

"It's just a random tattoo, okay?" he said, trying to dismiss the topic.

"What happened to her? I know it's not just a random tattoo." I leaned closer to the table.

He looked away, finding it hard to tell me.

"You can talk to me, Tristan. I can't do this if you're gonna keep me in the dark."

"I can't," he said without looking at me.

For some reason, he sounded like he was about to break . He finally met my gaze. He moved closer and took my hands in his; his warm and rough hands gave mine a soft squeeze while his thumbs drew little patterns on the back of my palms.

"Am I not enough for you?" he whispered softly.

"I don't know. Each day with you feels like a mystery. I'm just picking up any crumbs I find, and I want the whole thing."

"Even if it hurts?"

I didn't know how to answer that. I wanted to know more about him, about Nadia, and whatever it was that had happened. It might come back and bite me in the ass later if we kept avoiding the topic.

"Hey," he whispered. "I hate myself for hurting you. I know I have been an asshole, but I want to be more for you, Chloe. Ask me anything about me. I will answer, but I'm not ready to talk about my tattoo or my past."

He brought my hand to his lips and kissed my knuckle. I expected him to let go after, but he held it to his cheek. I was tempted to touch the bruise beneath his eye. Who had done it to him?

"I don't want to be that guy who makes you cry. I want to be the guy who puts a smile on your face every day. I have become so attached to you, more than I ever imagined, and I don't want to ruin that, Cassandra."

He gave me a soft smile and kissed the back of my palm again. I tried to fight the smile tugging at my lips.

"Chloe is fine," I said and frowned at the mention of my middle name even if it sounded so eloquent and poised from his lips.

"I like Cassandra. It's a beautiful name," he muttered, his eyes sparkling with the flames from the candles around us. I scoffed and fought the smile trying to form on my face. "My middle name is Nolan," he told me, and my eyes widened in surprise.

"Doesn't fit you," I said, and he laughed softly.

I looked into his beautiful eyes, wondering if I should give him another chance. I pulled my hands away from his grasp. I needed to concentrate without his touch distracting me. I took another sip from my wine as I tried to control my emotions. I wanted to believe him, but he made it so hard, using my insecurities against me every time he got angry.

"Can we please start over?" he asked softly, extending his hand for me to take.

I stared at his solid arm, like he was offering me a sword to use and kill myself.

"I will prove my feelings to you if you give me the chance."

"I don't know, Tristan. I wanna be patient with you, but I don't know how long. I wanna know what I'm getting myself into if we advance with whatever we have between us. I also wanna know if whatever happened in your past is beyond me. I'm not sure I can do this," I said and stood up.

His smile fell, and he dropped his arm, as if my words had sucked the life out of him. I returned to my room with different thoughts spinning in my head like a tornado.

I opened the door leading to the balcony. I sighed softly and gripped the railing. I stared at the skyline that lit up the city. I closed my eyes and relished the soft caresses of the cool breeze on my face. Tristan had made me question everything in my life. I wanted to forgive him. I wanted to look past everything he had done and try to be happy, but I wasn't ready.

I forgot what it felt like to be normal. No family, a fucked up life, and stuck with the person who had taken it all from me. Sometimes, I saw him as the hero, but I got reminded that he was the villain, and he showed me that every time he flipped.

What was I still doing here? Why was I helping him live a lie? He'd said one month, and it had been more than that. His mom didn't look like someone who was critically ill and dying, and it made me a little suspicious. The fact that he wouldn't tell me anything made me angry.

Some days, I wanted to leave, but I cared too much about him, and I hated myself for that. I opened my eyes and laughed at myself; it eased the pain.

I stayed outside for a while, watching the stars and allowing the memories of me and my sister counting the stars to torment me. I missed that bitch.

It'd been a week since Tristan had asked for us to start over. I'd rarely seen him since, but balloons with *I'm sorry* kept appearing in my room every day. I popped each one with my hair pin and threw them away.

I only ran into Tristan once on the staircase, and he walked past me like I was invisible. I knew I shouldn't feel hurt by his action because it was what I'd wanted. It was hard to deny that I missed hearing his voice and annoying him. It was lonely and quiet here. I didn't do well with those two terms, which explained why I was always hanging out with Morris. The temptation to ask about Tristan was hard to control.

It was Friday night, and Morris served me some Italian chicken skillet. I twirled my fork around the chicken as I stared into space. I missed Tristan. I fucking missed him, and I wanted to see him.

"Miss Simpson?" Morris called, taking the seat in front of me.

I put my fork down and sighed softly as I met his worried eyes.

"Sorry, my mind is all over the place," I groaned.

"I can make you something else if you don't like the chicken skillet," he said.

"No, I love it," I said and picked up the fork to start eating.

"Mr. Sanchester is a good man. He is just going through a rocky path right now. I'm sorry he hurt you, and I can see how sorry he is too," he said and gave me a warm smile.

"Thank you," I mumbled.

"He hasn't left the house in a week, and every time I bring food to his room, he is either still sleeping or in the bathroom. Some days, he doesn't even eat the food, and yesterday …" He paused and contemplated telling me.

"What happened?" I inquired.

"The mirror. I think he is doing it again," he finished.

"Thank you for telling me," I said, and he nodded.

"I will get you your favorite drink," he said, and I smiled.

I WENT UP to my room for a shower and dressed up for bed in silk pajama shorts and a small top. I grabbed a fantasy book to read, desperate to escape to another world. It was almost midnight by the time I was halfway through. I could hear the rivulets of rain outside and the thunder roaring from a distance.

I put my stuff away and left the room to get some late-night snacks. I paused in front of Tristan's room. His light was still on, so I assumed he was still awake. I knocked and got no response. Tristan hardly answered anyway. I wanted to turn away and run back to my room, but I stayed back. Why was it hard to stay away?

"It's Chloe. Can I come in?" I asked.

I waited a few seconds for him to answer. I took a deep breath and opened the door. He wasn't in his bed or anywhere in the room. I stepped in and closed the door behind me. I could hear the sound of the keyboard from a corner; he should be in his home office. I walked to his study and found him in front of his computer. A cup of coffee kept him company.

"Go to bed, Morris. I told you to only come here when I call for you," he said, not looking my way.

"Hey," I said, resting one shoulder on the doorframe.

His head whipped in my direction, and he stared at me like he didn't recognize me. He looked exhausted. The dark circles beneath his eyes and his tousled hair made him look like a walking corpse.

"Chloe?" he called in a quiet tone I could hardly recognize. "Do you need anything?" he asked and looked away, returning to whatever he was doing on his computer.

"I'm bored."

"It's midnight. You should be in bed."

"I can't sleep."

"You can watch a movie or do something you enjoy."

"I don't feel like it," I said and stepped into the room. It looked fancy for a home office. "What are you doing?" I asked, slumping on the cozy leather couch.

"Working," he replied. "Any specific reason why you're here?" he asked, turning in his seat to observe me.

I bit back a smile and looked away from his face.

"I told you, I'm bored, and you're the only person awake."

"So, you need company?"

"Something like that." I shrugged.

"I have some magazines on the table," he said and returned to work.

I stood up and looked around. I stopped at the wine bar and grabbed one bottle of scotch and a glass. Someone snatched the bottle from me before I could open it.

"Not tonight," Tristan said, putting the bottle of scotch at the top of the bar, far from my reach.

His towering height stood an inch away from mine as he put the drink away. My hands itched to touch his chest that was so close to my face. I could make out the outline of his pecs and abs from his black T-shirt. The wave of heat from his body made me miss our night cuddles. I missed the brush of his stubble against my cheek and the way he always drew small circles on my hip. He pulled away and returned to his seat.

"Buzzkill," I sighed and sat down again. I leaned closer to the large chessboard on the table. "Can we play chess?" I asked.

"I need to work, Chloe," he sighed.

"Just one game." I pouted.

"Can you play?" he asked.

"You're about to find out." I smirked.

I moved to the floor and sat down, placing the chessboard between us. I took the white side of the board and left the black side for Tristan. He brought his coffee with him and took the space in front of me. His long legs folded.

I stared at the chessboard, trying to recall everything Nana had taught me, but I could only remember moving the pawn. It didn't take two minutes before Tristan kicked my king out. We played another round, and I was still clueless. I could see Tristan holding back his laughter anytime I moved.

"Come on, Chloe. I'm giving you all the chances to win here," he said, and I rolled my eyes in defeat.

"Okay, you got me. I suck at chess," I admitted.

"I can teach you," he offered.

"Don't bother; it's a waste of time."

"Do you have anything else you want to do?" he asked and took a sip from his coffee.

"I brought my Uno cards with me. You can't beat me at that one."

I wasn't surprised Ciara had packed it. She'd been hell-bent on getting rid of the cards because I always beat her at it.

"Okay, bring the cards."

I stood up and rushed to my room, bubbling in excitement. I got the cards and went down to grab a bottle of apple cider wine. Tristan frowned at me when I entered the room with the bottle.

"It's nonalcoholic," I said, sitting down on the polished wood floor.

I shuffled the cards and shared them between us. I smiled at my wild cards.

"Loser gets to stand under the rain for fifteen minutes," I said, and he agreed, barely paying attention as he organized his cards.

Tristan went first, and he didn't have the right card. I took a swig from my drink and played my wild card. I giggled when he didn't have the card I'd requested.

"Uno," I chirped after a few minutes of dropping and picking cards.

Tristan smiled and gave me a high five. I picked up my drink to take a sip, and that was when I noticed the number of cards Tristan had. He was deliberately letting me win. I reached closer and took his cards. He'd had every opportunity to win, but he hadn't.

"I'm going under the rain," I said and stood up.

"You won, Chloe."

"Because you let me."

"You don't have to go in the rain. It's not necessary. We can do something else or play again."

"I'm still going," I said and walked away. I could feel myself shivering as I ran down the stairs.

"Chloe," Tristan called, trailing behind me.

I increased my pace and walked to the back door, leading to the backyard. I looked back at Tristan before stepping outside. I gasped at the shower of rain that soaked me. I laughed and looked up at the sky.

"Time's up. Let's go," Tristan said, extending his hand for me to take but I refused.

I remembered he didn't like the cold.

"You're going to catch a cold. Come back inside," he said, stepping into the rain to get to me.

"This is relaxing," I said and put my face up to feel the raindrops on my skin.

"Let's go," he said, taking my hand.

"Just try it. It's calming," I said, pulling him back. "Close your eyes and look up," I whispered.

He hesitated at first and stared at me like I wasn't making any sense. He sighed and gave in to my request. He closed his eyes and put his face up.

I watched the raindrops fall on him like glitter dust. His hair stuck to his forehead, and his lips parted slowly at the droplets that touched his lips. He sighed in relief and smiled. I stared at the water that rolled down his lower lip, and I stepped closer like I wasn't in control of my body. Tristan opened his eyes and looked down at me when he felt my movement.

"That felt nice," he said in a rough tone.

"Yeah," I mumbled.

We stayed quiet for a while, fighting the thoughts in our heads as we held each other's gaze.

"I missed you," Tristan whispered, cupping my left cheek. "It was fucking hard, pretending you weren't there. Do you know how many nights I stood in front of your door, dying to talk to you and have my arms around you? I'm not perfect, Chloe; I know that. I know some days, I fuck up and make mistakes, and I regret it every day. I'm sorry for that night. Sorry I always mess up and give you reasons to doubt my feelings for you, but I do like you a lot, and it hurts so bad to pretend you're not next door," he said.

I looked away, not expecting his words to affect me so deeply.

"Every time I open up to you, I only get hurt in return," I said.

"I know," he let out, putting his hand down and pulling away from me. "I don't want to talk about what happened. I don't want to go down that memory lane. I wish you could understand how it hurts, just trying to think about it. I'm sorry I get defensive when it comes to my past. I just want you to know, it was never lust. It was much more."

I didn't know what to say. I bit on my quivering lip and watched the water drip down his gorgeous face.

"I'm sorry," he said again and turned away to leave.

I walked in front of him and blocked the way.

"Good night, Chloe," he said and tried to take the other way, but I got in his way again. He gave me a questioning look, but I said nothing.

Boy, I was starting to feel the cold. I tried to stop myself from shivering. I could feel the goose bumps crawling on my skin. I stepped closer to him, not sure of what I was doing.

How long can I be patient with him? How long can I pretend it doesn't hurt for him to keep me in the dark? We can work it out. Let's focus on what we have now, and maybe he'll eventually trust me enough to tell me what happened.

"What do you want?" he asked as I closed the space between our bodies.

"You, us," I whispered.

"I'm not going to have sex with you because you're bored."

"I'm not bored," I admitted, almost increasing my tone. My life was a mess already. Nothing was going the way I wanted it. So, yes, I wanted this. I didn't care what we were. I felt something for him I couldn't explain to myself. I couldn't escape from this, no matter how much I tried.

"No," he said, stepping back.

"What?"

"I want you so bad but not like this."

"What do you mean?" I asked, already feeling like an idiot for offering myself to him.

"It's not lust, Chloe. I don't know how else to prove that to you, and if I go on with this, it will prove your point."

He thought I was testing him?

"I want this," I assured him, stepping closer, but he took a step back, as if battling with his self-control.

Maybe that apple cider had had alcohol in it because my brain only wanted Tristan's lips on mine more than anything right now.

"Don't tempt me. I won't be able to resist," he said hoarsely with his eyes on my lips.

"I missed you too, asshole." I pouted.

He remained three feet away, his eyes flickering from my lips to my eyes every so often in the stillness between us. A thousand million raindrops fell around us, the sound drowning the silence between us. It was getting colder as I waited for him to come to me.

"It's killing me," he rasped.

Before I could ask him what he meant, he was in front of me, and his lips were against mine. Cold and soft, hungry and gentle. I pressed against him, responding to his kiss instantly.

He pulled away and stared at my face. I waited for him to kiss me again, but he didn't. He rubbed his nose against mine, and his lips brushed delicately on mine, barely touching. His action only made me want more. I pushed myself closer, giving him the green light, but he held back.

"Are you real?" he asked, running his thumb over my cold lips.

"No, I'm a hologram," I said.

He laughed softly, pulling me into his arms and hugging me with so much need. I didn't want him to let go. The warmth from his body sank into my skin as his hug swallowed me. He kissed my neck softly, a gesture that made my heart swell. It was painful and excruciating because I knew I couldn't resist him any longer.

It was hard, fighting for something you knew was bad for you. My emotions dominated my reasoning, knowing he might prey on my insecurities again, but I was willing to give us a chance. This time, we'd be patient with each other. The heart wanted what it wanted, I guessed.

He leaned in and took my lips in a slow kiss. As if starving, he deepened the kiss, almost knocking the air out of my lungs. His hand moved slowly to my neck. His grip was gentle yet firm. I returned every kiss, following every pace of his lips as ecstasy sprang around my body, my legs shivering. It felt like it'd been years since we'd last kissed.

He drew me closer, like he couldn't get enough. His tongue found its way into my mouth. I ran my hand up his hard chest, tracing the thick ridges through his wet shirt. When I got a throaty groan from him, I did it again. I felt hot all over. All thoughts about the rain and cold disappeared from my head.

Tristan guided me to the door, and soon, we were back inside the house. He kicked the door closed without breaking the kiss. His firm grip around my throat was a new feeling that increased the hotness between my legs.

Tristan swiftly had my back to the wall. His kiss became rough, and I liked it. It felt like I was floating in another universe. I could get lost in this feeling forever. The delicious current made me moan in anticipation.

He gripped my hips and picked me up. I wrapped my legs around his waist and traced his stubble with my finger as our lips moved in sync. I loved the roughness of it on my cheek. He carried me upstairs to my room, his palms gripping my ass.

He had my back against the door as soon as we stepped into my room. I wanted to touch him, but he wouldn't let go of my hands, which he had pinned above my head with his left hand. I pressed my body on him, wanting more. He withdrew and stared at me, as if he was second-guessing doing this. He let go of my hands. I pushed myself on my tiptoes and kissed him, running my fingers through his hair. The deep groan that escaped his throat sent a wave of desire from my heart to my chest and down toward my inner thighs.

I tugged at his shirt. He pulled away and took it off in a flash. His prominent V-line caught my eyes first.

Finally. My perverted brain sighed in relief.

My eyes shone as they drilled into his skin, devouring him. I ran my hands up the curves on his torso, feeling the texture of his skin. He looked down at me, watching me with hazy eyes, his breathing quick. I pulled my hands away to take off my shirt, but he stopped me.

I could feel his thick length knocking against my thighs, warmth welcoming me. He opened his mouth as if he had something to say but stopped himself.

"I want this," I assured him.

"Let me," he said in that voice that had my whole body itching for his touch.

I sucked a breath as he went on his knees. His large hands trailed up my thighs into the hem of my pajama shorts. I forgot how to breathe as his lips touched my skin. I looked down at him, hoping my knees wouldn't buckle from the intense pleasure soaring through me as I watched his lips trail up my thigh to the center of my legs. He inhaled the wetness between my legs and moaned.

He pulled away and stood up. He leaned in with a small smile on his lips as he took my lips in a slow kiss. His hands swept up my stomach through my wet shirt that did little to hide my puckered nipples. His thumbs flicked at my sensitive buds, and I moaned into his mouth.

He withdrew and pulled the top over my head, leaving me bare to him in only my pajama shorts. The way he stared at me made my insides jump with joy. I was vulnerable physically, yet the way he viewed my body as a temple made me feel safe.

He nibbled on my neck, leaving marks behind. I moaned when he dug his nails into my hips and brushed his fingers into my shorts. I gasped softly when he gripped my hair and trailed wet kisses from my jaw to my neck. The heat between my legs intensified, and I stifled another moan. He pulled away, and I whimpered at the loss of contact.

"Touch me. Don't hold back," he ordered, staring at my hands, which I kept by my sides.

Our lips met in a frenzied kiss. I felt his hand going up my back, touching the scar. I tensed, but I relaxed when he kept touching it like it meant nothing. I found the courage to move my hands. My hand slipped into his pants and grabbed his ass, fingers pressing into the solid skin. He smiled against my lips and took my lower lip between his teeth. He moved to my neck, leaving marks behind every bite. He nibbled on my earlobe and drew it slowly with his lips. I closed my eyes, relishing the pleasure it brought to my body.

He pulled down his jogger pants. My heart pumped faster, and I stared with wide eyes at his thick erection and how big he was. I would need a wheelchair after this. That wouldn't even fit down my throat.

He smirked and picked me up, playfully tossing me over his shoulder. I laughed and recalled the night he had taken me to my room in this same position. He placed me on the bed and crawled delicately to my body. He ran his fingers through my hair and kissed me deeply. I moaned when he grabbed a handful of my hair and pulled it as his lips moved against mine, so carnal and volcanic.

I pushed my hips up to feel him. I groaned in pleasure when he moved his hips brazenly on mine, rubbing himself against me. His hand slid smoothly up my hip to my ass, gripping me. I moaned against his lips and interlocked my fingers through his hair. He hooked his fingers through my shorts, the silk material wrapping around his finger. He took off my shorts, leaving me in my underwear.

He flipped me around, taking me by surprise. Goose bumps formed on my skin, running wild and free, as he began to place wet kisses on the back of my thighs and slowly up to my ass. I gasped when he bit my ass cheek. I buried my face in the pillow as my core cried for attention. His finger brushed teasingly against my slit through my underwear. I wanted him to add more pressure, but he kissed my clit instead. He could rip off my panties. I didn't care.

His next action knocked the air out of me. He kissed my scar and touched it delicately. I was a bit nervous, but he kept trailing kisses on the mark until he reached my shoulders.

"You're beautiful. So damn beautiful," he whispered into my ear and kissed my temple.

I turned around and stared into his eyes. They seemed to promise safety and patience.

"You owe me a date," I said, caressing his cheek. I traced the fading scar beneath his eye. "Who did it?" I asked.

"Adrian. It was a misunderstanding, but we are cool now," he said with a small smile.

I brought his lips to mine and kissed him softly. It started out gently but intensified as need surged through our veins. Tristan groaned against my lips when I wrapped my fingers around his pulsing erection.

"Do you wanna come in my mouth?" I whispered, increasing the pace of my hand. I felt him twitch around my fingers. I'd be disappointed if he didn't last thirty seconds.

"Next time. I'm craving something else right now," he said and removed my hand.

He kissed my neck and ventured down to my chest. I arched my back when he took my nipple in his mouth while fiddling with the other with his rough palm. He sucked on the sensitive bud and flicked it with his tongue. His lips journeyed down my chest to my stomach and to my waistline.

I thought my brain shut down when he buried his face between my thighs, his tongue and fingers showing no mercy. I gripped the sheets. Uncontrollable moans escaped my lips as he gripped my thighs and held them apart, placing my legs on his shoulders. The sensation almost drove me crazy as I tried to breathe. I had never experienced such pleasure, and it shook me as I reached my peak and screamed his name, my whole body shaking.

I hope Morris is a deep sleeper.

"Wow," I mumbled breathlessly, still trying to come off my high as Tristan crawled closer.

His lips glistened with my pleasure as he smirked at me. He swiped his tongue over his lips, licking it off, and I was turned on all over again at the sight.

"I think I'm addicted already," he said, moving his hand to the apex of my legs and sliding one finger into me.

I gasped at the contact. He added another finger as he held my gaze, watching me like a masterpiece. I closed my eyes and arched my back with each stroke of his long fingers.

"Look at me," he growled.

I obeyed, locking my eyes with his. There was just something surreal and deep about it, as if our souls were communicating. He leaned closer and kissed me. I laced my fingers in his hair and moaned into the kiss as another wave of pleasure hit me like a tsunami.

"I'm not done with you yet," he said, licking his finger.

I might just pass out from all this sexiness.

"I want you on my face," he said, touching my lips.

Breathe, Chloe. Breathe.

"You don't have to if you are—"

"No, I want to," I cut in, cupping his cheeks.

I had never done it, but something about his voice made me want to do anything he asked. He gave me a wicked smile and lay back on the bed.

"Don't hold back. Ride me," he said, running his hand smoothly up my thigh as I straddled his face, my most intimate part exposed to him.

He trailed feathery kisses up my thighs to my dripping core. I grabbed on to the headboard immediately after his tongue brushed over me. The rain did little to block the sound of my moans as my hips moved of their own accord. I guessed the night was far from over.

I threw my head back, brazenly rocking my hips against his mouth that sucked and bit on my sensitivity. His hands gripped my backside and slowly skimmed up my stomach to my flushed breasts. I came apart as he pinched my nipples. That was hands down the most epic orgasm I'd ever experienced.

By the time it was over, I felt dizzy from all the pleasure. Tristan cradled me in his arms, kissing my head and stroking my hair as my body tried to recover from the best feeling ever. I snuggled closer to him, panting. My soul had not returned to my body.

"Sleep. We can do it another time," he whispered.

I wanted to argue, but I was exhausted, and I found myself nodding.

I could feel his thick erection hitting my stomach, and I felt bad that he hadn't gotten to feel all the pleasure he had given me. We lay naked in the bed. Tristan kept tracing my scar with his fingertips, and it made me fall asleep quickly.

I WOKE UP to the sound of someone humming. I tried to block out the sound and return to sleep, but it was hard to ignore. Did I wake up in a Snow White fairy tale? She was the one who hummed to animals, right? Or was it Cinderella? Shit, I was growing old.

I opened my eyes with a frown and stared at the entrance to the bathroom, where Tristan was humming. Someone had apparently woken up on the right side of the bed.

He walked out of the bathroom with a towel tied around his waist. He smiled at me as he walked to the bed. I realized I was still naked, and the sheets stayed around my waist.

"I want to paint you right now, but I can't even draw a circle," he groaned, sitting next to me.

I blushed and closed my eyes as he kissed my shoulder, his fingers skimming up my back. The smell of his aftershave made me want to lean closer to him.

"Are we still on for the date?" he whispered close to my ear.

I opened my eyes and tilted my head to the side to look at him.

"For real this time, how about tonight I take you out to dinner?" he asked, brushing my hair out of my face.

"Dinner sounds great, but what about, um ... the baby bump and being out there in the open?"

"I don't care what anyone thinks anymore, but if you're uncomfortable, I can pay to get everyone out of the restaurant, or we could have it here in the house. I'll cook."

"It's fine." I grinned.

"Perfect. Do you need anything for the date? Maybe to go shopping or visit the spa?"

"Are you insulting my wardrobe?" I gasped, playfully hitting him.

"No." He laughed. "I was wondering if you might need something new."

"I don't."

"Well, if you do, bill it to my account." He gave me a quick kiss and stood up to get ready for work.

"How is your mom?" I asked, staring at his ass as he walked to the closet.

"She is doing okay," he answered from the closet.

I snuggled under the covers and drifted to sleep. As much as I wanted to watch him put on his suit, my eyes wouldn't stay open.

The potato chips made a satisfying crunch as I chewed on the salty snack. My eyes remained glued on my laptop as I watched a psychological thriller that had made me stay in the room since morning. I felt annoyed when my ringtone interrupted me. It was Tristan.

"Hey," I said sweetly.

"I just left the office. Be ready before I get there."

Ready? For what?

"I can't wait to spend the evening with you," he said.

Oh shit. The date!

"You're gonna bail when you see the dress I have on me," I teased, looking down at my big T-shirt, covered in crumbs from the potato chips.

"Chloe," he groaned.

"Bye!" I said quickly and hung up.

I rushed down from the bed and ran to my wardrobe. I never took the time to pick out what to wear. I undressed and ran around the room, only in my underwear and bra as I changed clothes after clothes.

I got frustrated and called Belvina on FaceTime. She was in the bathtub.

"Any reason you want to see me naked?" she said, finding a place to balance her phone, her breast on the screen.

I looked away, cursing at her while she laughed.

"What? You're also naked," she said, smirking.

"What are those marks on your body?" she asked, leaning closer to her phone.

I looked down at the fingernail and bite marks Tristan had left all over my body from last night. He'd just loved branding me every chance he got. For some weird reason, I'd liked it.

"Oh, don't tell me," she said, shaking her head in realization.

I explained my situation to her, and her eyes lit up like stars in the sky.

"I was born for this. Show me what you have," she ordered.

I placed my phone on the bed, using my pillow to hold it up. I showed her my whole wardrobe, and it only took her five minutes to match an outfit. I didn't bother with a shower as I put on a draped, ruched black silk dress, my scar safely hidden. I walked to the dresser and straightened my hair as Vina told me about her new coworker who made her want to jump off a cliff. With her help, I was able to get my makeup done quicker than when I did it on my own.

"Guess how many screenshots I have taken of you. They will make premium memes." Vina laughed.

I rolled my eyes as I put on my accessories in haste.

I smiled at myself in the mirror as I applied the lip gloss; even I couldn't stop admiring how good I looked.

I heard footsteps approaching my room, and I knew it was Tristan.

"I will talk to you later. Bye," I said quickly and hung up.

I stood up and grabbed my strappy heels. There was a knock on the door as I tried to force my leg into the first heel. The door opened, and Tristan appeared, looking drop-dead gorgeous. I could stare at him forever—that was how good he looked.

"Almost done." I grinned.

He walked into the room in his expensive suit. His long legs approached me, and it was hard to breathe as he went on one knee in front of me. His callous fingers gripped my leg and helped me to put on the shoe. I did the straps while he helped with the other shoe.

I mumbled, "Thank you," as I did the last straps that stopped at my knee.

He stood up and leaned closer to me, his hands on each side of the bed, holding me hostage.

"You weren't kidding about the damn dress," he said, biting his bottom lip.

"At least you're not wearing sweats and a tee," I said, adjusting his

315

collar.

He laughed in the small space between us. I expected him to lean in for a kiss, but he pulled away.

"Let's go," he said, taking my hand.

"One minute," I said and ran to my wardrobe to look for a purse. Vina had forgotten I needed one. I picked a black leather purse and forced my phone inside, not sure of what other valuables I needed to take inside the purse.

"Ready," I said, hooking my arm with Tristan's.

Morris gave me a bouquet of flowers when we got downstairs. Tristan looked away when I took a glance at him. I shook my head and smiled at the pretty flowers. The note in the middle said, *You make every day worth living. Mine.*

I took a glance at Tristan with my cheeks on fire. He gave me a genuine smile, one I rarely saw.

We got to the car and took the backseat as Morris sat behind the wheel. Tristan's hand remained on my thigh the whole ride as he asked Morris a few questions about his family and something about a room in the house.

"When is your birthday, Morris?" I asked.

"April 21," Tristan replied.

"Mine is August 12," I said to Morris.

"One week after my second granddaughter's birthday," Morris said, beaming.

"Aww, how old is she?"

"Nine. She is a very smart kid and is the captain of her softball team."

He seemed so proud. I wished my parents looked that proud when they talked about me.

"When is yours?" I asked, looking at Tristan, who looked lost.

"It's not important," he said.

"Why?"

"I don't like birthdays," he said with a smile that didn't reach his eyes.

"Why?"

He sighed and looked away. He had that same look on his face that he had every time I asked about his past. The one where he avoided my eyes and tightened his jaw.

"What was your favorite sport in high school, Miss Simpson?" Morris asked, drawing my attention away from Tristan.

I told Morris about how I'd sucked at every sport I joined in high school and that they always kicked me off the team.

"What would you like me to bring for you, Morris?" I asked as the car came to a stop in front of the restaurant.

"Nothing, thank you."

"I'm still bringing something," I said as I stepped out of the door Tristan held open.

His hand stayed on the small of my back as the doorman opened the door for us.

The cool air pricked my skin as soon as we stepped inside. I should have brought a jacket. The interior was breathtaking, spacious, and well lit with expensive chandeliers.

"I will be right back. Let me get our table," Tristan whispered close to my ear and walked away with his warmth I needed.

I looked around as I waited. My breath ceased when my eyes met my mother's. I thought she'd be surprised, seeing me, as I was to see her, but she looked irritated and enraged.

CHAPTER **TWENTY-SEVEN**
EUPHORIA

My mom looked away first, unable to stand the sight of me. She was with her group of friends, the ones she met up with once in a while. She faked smiles and laughter, as if she enjoyed their company. I had seen the way she rolled her eyes and hissed when their names appeared on her phone screen.

"Let's go. Our table is ready," Tristan said, placing his hand around my waist. The gesture pulled me out of the darkness slowly consuming me.

I turned to him with a forced smile. I took one last look at my mom and found her friends staring at me with contempt and eyeing me with mischief. Tristan must have noticed my hesitation to move because he followed my gaze and saw my mom.

"Oh shit," he mumbled, increasing his grip around me. "I didn't know she'd be here. I can make another reservation for—"

"No, I'm fine. I will pretend she is not here," I said, placing my hand on his chest.

"Are you sure?"

"Yes, lead the way. I'm starving."

He nodded and led me to the table at the far end. He helped me to my seat before taking the seat in front of me. He had purposely made me sit on the seat facing away from my mom and her friends. I didn't mind.

I ran my palm down my arm to ease the cold away. I hadn't expected it to be this cold inside.

"Here." Tristan took off his jacket and gave it to me.

I put it on, whispering my thanks. The jacket swallowed me, covering the beauty of my dress, but I would rather stay warm than drown in the cold.

A waiter arrived, and I turned to Tristan for help with the menu. We were served some champagne before the waiter left. I took a glance at Tristan, not sure about drinking in public.

"You can drink if you want. I doubt you ever turn down alcohol," he said.

I rolled my eyes with a glare as I took a sip. He smiled, his eyes scanning the menu.

"Has it always been this bad?" he asked.

"What?"

"You and alcohol."

"It's just something to take the edge off. I'm not an alcoholic. I know how to control it."

"Okay, if you say so. Then, I will make you a deal," he said, leaning closer to the table.

Why did I find his hands sexy?

"I don't like where this is going," I admitted.

"No alcohol from now on till your birthday," he said, and I laughed, finding his deal funny.

"Are you serious?" My laughter ceased. "But there are moments I really need it."

"Deal?" he said without waiting for me to concede.

"What do I get in return?"

"Anything you want," he said, leaning back in his seat.

I wondered if that included asking about his past.

"Deal." I put my hand out for a shake, and he took it. His thumb coming out to trace my skin gingerly.

"Does my drinking irritate you?" I asked, holding his gaze.

"I'm just worried about how much you drink. My wine cellar hasn't been that empty in years."

"At least someone is making use of it." I shrugged, and he laughed softly.

"I know how bad it can get. It separates you from reality and messes with your thinking. I have been there, Chloe, and I would hate to see you go down that path, especially at a young age."

"Okay, Dad," I sighed, and he didn't look impressed at my answer.

He let go of my hand as a waiter served us our appetizer. I eyed the tiny dish that looked like a snail clothed in lettuce and salmon.

"It's cute," I commented.

I was tempted to look back at my mom. I wondered what she was thinking. She probably thought it was all true. She would never believe me. I was about to look back when a hand touched mine.

"Don't," Tristan said. "I can make another reservation if it bothers you to be in the same room with her."

"No." I shook my head and began to eat my appetizer. I could still feel Tristan staring at me. "Seriously, I'm fine." I forced a smile.

Honestly, I was uneasy, being on a date with him in the same room with my mom, who probably thought the worst of me right now.

"I will be right back. I need to use the restroom," I said, standing up.

I took off his suit jacket and left it on my seat. He watched me as I walked away, and I felt bad for ruining the moment.

A lady stepped out of the restroom when I entered. I walked to the sink and gripped the edge. I heard the clicking of heels from outside. Soon, the door opened. I stared at my mom through the mirror. She looked angry. I wished she'd give me a hug and ask me how I had been. She looked around the room to be sure we were alone.

"It's all true then, and you tried to deny it. You could have picked anywhere. Why did you have to make me look bad in front of my friends? Do you always have to ruin everything?"

I wanted to stand my ground, but I still respected her as my mother. Every word remained stuck in my throat, and I tried to hold the tears back. I wasn't going to let her see me cry.

"I regret giving birth to a child like you. Why didn't you just die in my womb? My life would be so much better."

"Mom!" I gasped at her words.

"I'm not your mother," she snapped. "This new life you've built for yourself, it won't last long, honey," she said and left.

The tears came down quicker than I'd expected. I didn't want anyone to walk in here and see me like this, but I couldn't stop it. Her words had made me want to disappear from existence. It was the worst feeling ever when the person who had given me life wanted to take it away from me.

"Chloe," Tristan called, knocking on the door.

I wanted to ignore him and cry out the pain, but at the same time, I wanted to blame him for my pain.

"Chloe, are you in there?" he asked, knocking harder.

I could tell he was getting impatient with my silence.

I didn't want him to see me like this or to feel bad about bringing me here. I grabbed a paper towel and dabbed the tears away. The waterproof mascara and eyeliner were still intact. I fixed myself and smiled.

"Yeah, just give me a minute."

I adjusted my dress and walked to the door. I opened it and found him waiting.

"Hey," I said sweetly.

"You got me worried," he said, taking my hand. He pulled me to his body and put his arms around my waist.

"You're making me want to skip dinner," he said, staring at my lips.

"We probably should not be doing this here," I said and tried to walk away, but he pulled me back.

He stared into my eyes. His expression changed into something else.

"You were crying," he said in a tone that carried anger and sadness.

His thumb reached out and brushed the corner of my eyes. I hoped he hadn't cleaned the wing I'd created; it had taken three tries to get it right.

"I saw your mom—"

"She is not my mother," I said quickly.

"What did she say to you?"

"The worst thing you could possibly say to someone you gave birth to. It only got to me for a moment. I'm fine now." I smiled.

"Let's go. I will take you somewhere else."

I didn't argue. I was tired of lying that her presence here wasn't affecting me, especially after what she said to me. I took his hand, and we returned to the table to get our stuff. Tristan paid the bill, and we left.

"Can we go to a museum or an art gallery? I have no appetite to eat again," I said when we entered the car.

"Let me see if any museum is open right now," he said, bringing out his phone.

"You're so sweet," I said, poking him, and he rolled his eyes while I laughed.

He found one and gave Morris the address. I held on to Tristan's arm and refused to pull away from him.

"Who was your celebrity crush when you were a teenager?" I asked, my fingers tracing his cuff link absentmindedly.

"What?" He laughed at my question.

"Just curious." I shrugged. I was curious about a lot of things.

"Um … I can't remember."

"You're lying." I nudged him. "Tell me, who was it?"

He laughed briefly, trying to avoid the question.

"Jennifer Aniston," he finally admitted.

"Hmm, teenage you had taste."

"I still have taste," he whispered close to my ear. His hand sliding to my hip in a possessive grip.

"Who was your celebrity crush, Morris?" I asked, looking for something to distract me from Tristan's grasp on my hip.

Morris couldn't remember the name of his celebrity crush, but the whole ride, he talked about how much he'd enjoyed watching her on TV. It was probably a celebrity from the '80s.

The car came to a stop in front of a tall, massive building. We stepped out of the car and strolled down the cast-iron street with lamps lined on each side, their white light illuminating the streets. A few people hung around, taking pictures, while others just sat down, engrossed in a conversation. Tristan and I made our way into the building, his hand securing the small of my back.

"This is my first time in a museum," I told him as we approached an art gallery.

"Really?" He looked down at me in surprise.

"Yeah. I have never been on an airplane either."

"No, you're lying," he said in disbelief.

"My mom isn't a big fan of traveling, so I have never left California."

"We're going to fix that," he assured me with a smile as we stopped in front of an artwork made with straws.

I wondered how people come up with these ideas.

We did a lot of walking. The museum was like an unending maze, and it was hard to stop exploring the art pieces and unique creations on display. At some point, I wanted to take off my heels and hold them in my hand but stopped myself.

Someone grabbed my hand from behind. I was ready to fight off the creep, but when I looked down at the tiny hand and dove eyes staring at me, I was bewitched. She was the cutest little girl I had ever seen, and she was crying.

"Oh, hey, sweetie. What happened?" I asked.

"I can't find Mommy," she cried.

"It's okay. We'll find your mommy for you," Tristan said, squatting in front of her and taking her small hands in his large ones.

The little girl was crying so hard that she started gasping for air. She must be terrified. It was a colossal museum. It was going to take forever to find her mother.

"What's your name?" Tristan asked, brushing her tears away with one swipe of his thumb.

"June," she mumbled.

"Okay, June, let's take a deep breath."

She obeyed. They did it five times together. I suddenly wanted to become pregnant as I watched them. June was calm now. Her tears ceased.

"Good job. Now, let's go find your mom," Tristan said, scooping her up in his arms. He took a glance at me and gestured for us to go.

"Is this your wife?" June asked, looking at me.

As little as she was, I couldn't guess her age from the way she spoke.

"Soon, she will be," Tristan said, and I fought away the redness growing on my cheeks.

"Okay, June. Can you look around the room for me and let me know if you see your mom?" he asked, and she nodded.

We walked around for a while. Tristan kept chatting with June as if they hadn't just met ten minutes ago. It amazed me how well he interacted with her. The chirpy tone. How he knew certain cartoons and Disney princesses.

"Mommy!" June screamed.

A young lady turned back and rushed toward us, looking relieved. It seemed she'd been searching for her daughter too.

"Oh my God, June." She took her from Tristan's arms and wrapped her arms around her. "God, you scared me."

"I made new friends. Can I invite them to my tea party? Please, Mommy." June pouted.

"We found her crying. She was looking for you," I said.

"Thank you so much. She was beside me one minute, and the next minute, she was gone," the lady said.

"Glad we could help," Tristan said.

"Okay, let's go. Daddy is looking for you," she said to her daughter.

"Bye." June waved at us as they walked away.

I smiled and looked at Tristan; he was still staring at them. He looked disconnected from this world. His expression was sad and angry as his smile vanished and his eyes seemed tense.

"My feet are killing me. I think we've seen enough," I said, holding his hand, hoping to break him out of his thoughts.

He turned to look at me with an absent grin.

"Can we leave now?" I asked, almost losing my balance on my heels from my sore feet.

"Sure."

He called Morris when we made it outside. The car arrived. We entered and left. I took off my heels and placed my feet on Tristan's lap, begging for one of his magical massages. I leaned back on the seat and sighed in content as his callous fingers wrapped around my left foot.

"Sorry I forgot to get you something to eat, Morris. We can stop by a diner, and you can—"

"Thank you, Miss Simpson, but I'm not hungry," Morris cut in.

I leaned into Tristan, resting my head on his shoulder. I was exhausted.

"Thanks for tonight. I had fun," I whispered. I closed my eyes and slowly drifted to sleep.

I woke up when I felt someone lift me up. I opened my eyes and found Tristan carrying me in his arms into the house. I snuggled into his chest and closed my eyes. I opened them again when he placed me on the bed.

I stared at him as he pulled the duvet to cover me.

"Do you need anything?" he asked, keeping his distance from me.

I blamed him for looking so hot, standing there in that suit with four buttons undone, his tie loosened, and his sleeve rolled up. I wanted this image of him to be engraved in my brain forever.

That's all I'm wishing for, Godmother.

"A kiss," I said in a soft tone.

He smiled and moved to the bed. He leaned down and gave me a quick kiss. I pulled him back when he tried to pull away. His lips met mine in an intense kiss. I dragged him to the bed, not breaking the kiss.

"I have been dying to kiss you all night," he whispered against my lips, coming down for more.

His tongue slipped in, and his fingers were in my hair, gripping and pulling. My leg draped over his waist, and his other hand wandered up my thigh to my hip.

I didn't know how long we lay there, just making out and our hands roaming every inch of skin we could find, but it was the best feeling after a long night.

"It's late. You need sleep," he said breathlessly as he withdrew, his thumb caressing a spot in my neck.

"Okay," I rasped, leaning closer, and like a magnet, our lips joined again in an aching kiss.

I brushed my fingers through his hair and skimmed them down to his chest. My fingers relishing every pec and taut muscle beneath his shirt I had managed to unbutton.

"Chloe," he groaned.

"Hmm?" I smiled against his lips.

"I could do this all night, but you look tired," he whispered, tracing my bottom lip.

"Don't leave yet," I said, snuggling closer, burying my face in his neck. My body relaxed, and I searched for sleep in the pool of darkness that engulfed me.

"Good night," he whispered, stroking my hair, his arm cradling me to his body.

THE NEXT FEW days felt like everything was back to normal. Tristan was suddenly everywhere. He didn't stay in his room as much as before. He used every opportunity he found to hang around me. He watched movies with me even if he hated it; he played Uno cards with me, even when he was tired; and he had not given up on teaching me how to play chess even if it drove him crazy that I kept getting it wrong.

He was everywhere, not only physically, but also in my dreams, in my head. My mind kept gravitating toward him. There were moments I still recalled what my mom had said to me that night, and I wanted to hate him for it, but I couldn't.

Wednesday evening, I was craving ramen, and it was almost midnight. I didn't want to disturb Morris, so I went down to the kitchen, tiptoeing to avoid waking anyone. I grabbed a pot and a pack of ramen noodles. I tried to follow the steps on the pack. I poured the seasoning and added some powdered bouillon and threw some vegetables inside.

I took a seat at the island and used my phone as I waited for the ramen to cook.

"Are you cooking?" Tristan asked, entering the kitchen. He didn't look like someone waking up from sleep.

"Yeah, I'm hungry," I said, staring at him longer than I'd intended.

He walked to the cooktop with both hands in the pockets of his sweatpants and peeked into the pot. He looked back at me with an amused grin. He grabbed a spoon and took a taste.

I waited for his feedback, but his face twisted in distaste. He shook his head and burst out in laughter.

"How is it?" I asked, standing up.

"What did you put inside?" He laughed, and I frowned.

"I'm sure it doesn't taste that bad. I followed the steps correctly," I said, picking up the spoon and taking a taste. I spat it out immediately. It tasted very salty.

Tristan laughed while I glared at him.

He grabbed the pot and poured everything in the sink. He grabbed a new pack and started making another one.

"Do you want me to put some shrimp in it?" he asked, looking over his shoulder at me as he grabbed some stuff from the freezer.

"Yes, please."

He returned with some vegetables and a bag of shrimp. I stood back and tried to memorize everything he was doing, but after the fourth step, I'd forgotten the first step. My mouth watered as he stirred the noodles with different mixtures.

He grabbed a bowl and poured the hot ramen inside. He placed it in front of me with chopsticks.

"Has anyone told you how sexy you look when you're cooking?" I asked as I picked up the chopsticks.

He only smiled and walked to the sink. I moaned in content after the first taste. I thought I had a new favorite food.

"Do you want some? We can share," I asked.

He took the seat beside me and joined me to eat the ramen. He told me about his childhood experiment with food, how his mom always kicked him out of the kitchen and warned the maids not to allow him close to the kitchen.

We didn't feel like sleeping by the time we were done, so I suggested we play Jenga. I grabbed a bottle of red wine. I promised Tristan I'd only drink one glass, and he grudgingly agreed. We spent an hour sipping wine, laughing about our favorite childhood memory as we played the game.

Three a.m., we were still up, talking, and Jenga blocks had fallen. I brought up another game that Tristan found ridiculous but agreed to play. The game was to find the fastest person to retrieve three items from the kitchen while blindfolded. Yeah, it was stupid.

"I'm right behind you, so don't think about cheating," I whispered into his ear as I tied my scarf around his eyes. My fingers skimmed up his toned chest through his shirt. I kissed his cheek and pulled away.

"This is making me horny," he groaned with a frown. "How about we play this in the bedroom?"

He smirked, and I elbowed him playfully.

"I'm hitting the timer. Ready. Set. Go," I sang.

I trailed behind him as he walked slowly toward the kitchen. He extended his hand forward to avoid bumping into a wall.

"Watch where you're going," I teased even if he was going the right way. I laughed as he paused and moved his right leg forward, trying to feel any barrier.

"This is stupid," Tristan hissed as he walked cautiously to the dining room.

I laughed so hard when his crotch met the edge of the table. He grunted and hunched as he took in the pain.

"Chloe," he groaned while I kept laughing.

"You are doing good, baby. Keep going; you're almost there," I cheered for him, and he scoffed.

He made it into the kitchen, one hand shielding his crotch from any danger. He found the cabinet easily and grabbed three mugs. He held them in one hand and started making his way out of the kitchen.

I couldn't help but laugh as he crept around the dining room to avoid another accident. He walked to the living room and tried to locate the center table, but he tipped over the edge of the couch and fell. He knocked down the bottle of red wine, and it spilled all over his chest.

"That wasn't supposed to happen. Are you okay?" I approached him and went on my knees next to him.

He sat up on the floor and took off the blindfold. He looked down at his stained shirt and frowned. I knew it was a serious situation, but I couldn't stop myself from laughing like a maniac.

I lay on the floor, writhing as laughter overwhelmed me. I looked over at him, and he was fighting off the smile tugging at the corner of his lips as he watched me.

"Are you done now?" he asked, and I giggled.

"Don't make me shut you up," he warned and crawled toward me.

He stared at me as he hovered over me, his hands at the sides of my head. I pulled my lip between my teeth, trying not to lose it. I burst out laughing again as I replayed the scene of his epic fall.

Tristan's lips were against mine in an instant. His kiss was raw, hungry, intense, but smooth. It took a split second for me to return every stroke of his lips. He supported his weight with his elbow as he pressed against my body. His tongue claimed the depth of my mouth, and I moaned. My legs curled on the floor as his taste invaded my senses and silenced every thought.

His fingers fisted in my hair. My hand roamed every taut muscle beneath his shirt. I gasped when he brushed his knee against my pulsing core. My hips rocked with his movement. He pulled away with a wicked grin, leaving me aching.

"I'm never playing that again," he said, and I fought off a fit of giggles. "Seriously, I slammed my dick against the table. It's not a nice feeling," he said with a pout, looking over at the dining table.

I wanted to cradle him.

"Sorry, it was so funny to watch," I whispered.

I sat up and pulled closer to him, where he was kneeling.

"Does it still hurt?" I asked, placing my palm on his crotch.

He sucked in a breath as I started moving my hand slowly, stroking him through his sweatpants.

"Yes, it hurts so bad," he rasped.

I pushed myself up onto my knees and brought my lips to his neck. His length thickened, and I could feel the pre-cum as I ran my finger over the crown. I trailed kisses up his neck to his strong jawline. His head dipped, and he met my lips in a heated kiss. I swallowed his throaty moans and increased the pace of my hand. I opened my eyes and watched him. I could stare at him forever; seeing him so vulnerable and close to losing himself was a piece of art.

I removed my hand and pulled away as I felt him jerk in my fingers. He gave me a dark look, and his eyebrows creased in confusion. With a devious smile, I bent over and pulled his dick out. He gasped immediately when my lips wrapped around him.

"Oh fuck, that feels so good," he groaned, fisting my hair and fucking my mouth.

I fought to take him all, but it was impossible with his size. I gagged but kept going as I felt him getting close to his climax. I wrapped my fingers at the base as I kept sucking, biting, and licking.

His thighs shook, and his grip tightened around my hair. I swallowed every drop of his pleasure until there was no more. I pulled back, my thumb swiping the cum on my cheek. I licked it off my finger and met his eyes. He looked dazed as he stared at me, as if he couldn't recognize me.

"If this is the prize for the game, then it's my favorite game."

"I wanted to make up for making you slam your dick into the edge of the table."

His eyes lingered on my mouth. I looked down at the bulge in his pants and smiled triumphantly.

"Bedroom?" he asked.

"Yes, I'm feeling so sleepy." I faked a yawn and stood up.

The room was a mess, and I felt awful for Morris. I forced Tristan to clean up with me before we went upstairs.

I turned around after Tristan closed the door. He had followed me to my room and still had hunger in his eyes that matched the longing taking over my body.

He took a step closer, filling the space between us. "You have a gorgeous mouth," he said, tracing my lips with his fingertips.

He slipped a finger into my mouth, and I sucked it while he watched.

He removed his finger and leaned closer to my face, his eyes searching mine for any indication I wanted this. I pressed my body against his as our lips met in a slow kiss, kindled with passion and need. His hand came up to my neck as our lips molded together; his other hand trailed up my thigh and into my shirt.

I tug at his stained shirt, and he withdrew to take it off. He cupped my head, pulling me back to his mouth. I melted into him, euphoric sparks flowing through my veins. He pulled away and slowly went down on his knees. I tried to find my breath.

His long fingers skimmed up my inner thighs. The only barrier between us was my underwear and the large T-shirt I had on me. I tried to stay still as his lips followed the trail of his fingers. I gasped when he ripped my panties off.

"Ouch," I groaned.

"Sorry, I will get you another one," he said, looking up at me with a small smile. "Take off your shirt," he ordered in that voice that made me obey everything he said.

He kept his eyes on me as I pulled the material above my head and tossed it to the side.

"Damn, baby," he whispered, his eyes raking my body.

I swallowed nervously at his deep stare.

"Hold on tight," he warned before his head disappeared between my legs.

His fingers and tongue drove me to euphoria. He gripped my right thigh and draped it over his shoulder, his fingers digging into my skin in a firm grip as his tongue pulled me to the edge. The wave of pleasure shooting through me was maddening.

I brushed my fingers through his hair. The moans slipped out of my lips. I felt it, a feeling of ecstasy. It shook my whole body as I came apart, screaming his name. He pulled away and stood up. His lips found mine again in a deep kiss. He led me back to the bed, not breaking from the kiss.

"Lie back and spread your legs," he said, and I obeyed.

He stood at the foot of the bed, staring at me as he took off his sweatpants. I stared at the thickness between his legs. How bad was it gonna hurt? It'd been three years since I'd slept with anyone.

"We can stop now if you're not sure about this," he said, stepping closer. "I want you to be sure this is what you want. I also want you to enjoy it and cherish this moment."

"I'm sure," I said, sitting up.

"Lie back," he ordered.

I lay back. He stepped closer and spread my legs wider; he released a throaty groan as he looked at me.

"I could stare at you forever. I don't even know where to begin," he said, skimming his fingers down my legs and up my thighs. His little action left a pool of wetness between my legs.

"I can't wait to feel your tight walls around me, watch you as you come over my cock and listen to the little sounds you make when I hit that spot that makes you gasp," he said softly.

He reached down and kissed my legs, his lips trailing up to my thigh, and soon, he was at the apex of my thighs, teasing me with his fingers and tongue. His rough stubble brushed my skin, leaving goose bumps.

Another orgasm shot through me, and I writhed on the bed, trying to squeeze my legs shut at the intense sensations ripping me apart. Tristan withdrew and kissed my stomach up to my chest. His lips wrapped around my nipple, sucking and biting. My back arched as uncontrollable moans filled the room.

"I will be gentle, but that's not a promise," he said kneading my breast.

A small laugh slipped out of my lips.

"Stop me if it hurts too much," he said, and I nodded.

"Are you on the pill?"

"No," I rasped. I would die if he stopped now.

"I will be right back."

He got down from the bed and went back to the bathroom, searching frantically for something. He returned with a condom. I watched nervously as he ripped it open.

"Let me." I stopped him.

He gave me the condom, and I sheathed his pulsing cock.

He teased my clit a little with the tip of his cock before sliding in slowly while I tried to adjust to his size.

"Fuck! You feel so good and so fucking tight," he rasped, leaning down to kiss me.

He thrust deep into me with no warning. I arched my back and yelped in pain. My breathing ceased. I hadn't been prepared for that. Tristan paused his movement and swallowed the sound of my pain with kisses.

His hand reached between my legs and tried to ease the pain away. It was working because all I could focus on were the electrifying currents spreading through me. I kissed him, trying to urge him to move.

He thrust slowly into me. The pain was still there, but the pleasure was building up slowly, and I wanted him to go faster, so I could reach my peak. I could tell he was struggling to keep a slow pace because he didn't want to hurt me.

"More," I moaned, brushing my fingers through his hair.

"I don't want it to hurt," he said, still holding back.

I was close but not close enough because he wasn't going deeper and faster to get me there. I pushed him aside and switched our position. He looked surprised as he watched me straddle him.

"Just seeing you on top gets me so hard," he grunted, gripping my hips.

I guided him into my entrance and groaned at the sore-sweet feeling that filled me. I started moving my hips, going slow, and soon, I picked up the pace.

Tristan moaned, gripping my backside in his palms. Our moans and the sound of our bodies slapping against each other filled the room. My hips moved faster. I threw my head back at the sweet currents taking over my senses, the pleasure almost making me dizzy.

"Look at me," he growled.

I opened my eyes and met his oceanic gaze on me.

I was about to hit my climax when Tristan switched our position in a flash. I was lying halfway on the edge of the bed; my head was almost touching the floor, but I didn't care because I could feel him deep inside me. I wrapped my legs around his waist as he thrust into me, his one hand holding my waist tightly while the other hand trailed up my stomach and his fingers wrapped around my throat. I gasped at the intensity of pleasure drowning my senses. I flicked my nipples as he kept pumping into me with urgency.

"Oh fuck," I moaned.

He pulled me back to his body when we were both so close to our peak, and our lips locked in a slow kiss. As my hips moved fast against him, he held on to me, pressing our bodies together. Sweat glistened our bodies like gold as we both found our release—one moan, one breath, and one body.

He held me in an embrace for a while as we tried to catch our breath. I felt him growing inside me again, but the soreness between my legs made it hard to move now. I winced as he pulled out of me. He got down from the bed and went to discard the condom.

I lay back on the bed, spent and panting softly. I closed my eyes, feeling too exhausted to stay awake.

My PILLOW FELT so hard. I ran my hand up the solid object, trying to figure out what had happened, but I heard a groan.

I opened my eyes and found my pillow to be Tristan's chest.

"Morning," he whispered with a soft smile. He brushed my hair back and caressed my cheek with his thumb.

I realized I had slept halfway on him the entire night. I tried to move my legs that were entwined with his under the sheets. The sudden soreness between my legs stopped me. I might need that wheelchair. I could hardly move without feeling the pain between my legs.

"Are you okay?"

I gave him a smile and lay back on his chest.

"Don't you have work today?" I asked instead.

"I already told my secretary I would be coming in late." His thumb drew lazy circles on my skin.

There was a knock on the door, making my heart jump. Tristan pulled the sheet up to cover my back. The door opened, and Morris walked in.

"Good morning, Mr. Sanchester," Morris greeted.

I kept my eyes shut, pretending to be asleep.

"Drop it right here."

I felt something on the bed. I opened my eyes when I heard the door close. I smelled freshly baked bread. I turned to the other side and saw breakfast on a wooden tray.

"Hungry?" Tristan asked.

"Hell yes!" I ignored the soreness between my legs and sat up.

I groaned as I walked to his closet and grabbed one shirt. He was smirking at me as I walked back to the room, almost staggering. He was resting his back on the headboard with one arm behind to support his head. The sheet stayed around his waist.

"I want to wake up to this every morning," he said as I walked to the bed.

I took a seat in front of the tray, hungry and tired.

"I want to wake up to this every morning," I said, pointing at the tray.

A scowl appeared on his face.

I giggled and moved closer to his face. "I want to wake up to this beautiful face every morning," I whispered, giving him a kiss on the cheek.

"You missed this spot," he said, pointing to his lips.

I shook my head and leaned closer, kissing him softly but he wanted more. He gripped my waist and deepened the kiss.

He pulled me closer, making me straddle him. He ran his hand smoothly up my thigh to my waist. I pulled away when he began to trace my spine with his fingertips. I was too sore for another round.

"Sorry, but I need food." I pulled away and returned to the waiting treat.

"I'm going to get ready for work." He walked to the bathroom, completely nude, while I just stared, chewing the strawberry in my mouth. "Are you coming?" he asked, looking over his shoulder at me.

"Food first."

He chuckled, disappearing into the bathroom.

He didn't take long in the shower. He came out with a white towel tied around his waist.

"Won't you eat something?" I asked with a mouthful of toasted bread.

He walked to where I was with water dripping down his hair. I fed him the toasted bread in my hand.

"That's okay," he told me after the second bite. "I have a meeting at eleven." He placed a kiss on my cheek and pulled away.

I ate the bread and drank the orange juice. I had never felt this hungry.

"HEY," TRISTAN WHISPERED, trying to wake me, but I blocked his voice.

We had been sleeping in the same room since we'd started having sex.

He bit my earlobe and rubbed his stubble against my cheek.

"Chloe." He kissed my nose.

"Okay, I'm going to get ready for work."

I hummed in response.

He smacked my ass and came down from the bed. I refrained myself from attacking him. I snuggled under the covers, already missing his warmth. There was a crash from the next room.

"Tristan?" I called, sitting up. I looked around, but he wasn't in the room.

Another loud crash from his room, and it made my heart jump. I got down from the bed as another crash followed. I ran out of the room. Morris was already running up the stairs.

I opened the door and saw him smashing a painting on the floor. He looked very angry. My jaw dropped when I saw, like, a dozen of the paintings hanging on his wall. They were all identical. It was a cute painting of tiny infant feet in a heart shape. His room hadn't had any paintings. How had these gotten here?

"Tristan?"

He was a completely different person as he broke the painting. Morris entered the room and looked horrified.

"Oh my, who ... I will get rid of them right away, sir." Morris looked confused as he ran around.

"Take it all away!" he screamed, throwing the one in his hand across the room.

I stood close to the bed, not knowing what to say. Why was he scared of the paintings? He was obsessed with them.

"Take them away. Get them out of here!" He covered his eyes with his shaky hands, breathing heavily.

I walked to him and wrapped my arms around him. He stilled at first.

"Chloe?" He sounded like he hadn't known I was in the room. He pulled me closer and wrapped his arms around me, almost squeezing me.

I could hear his heartbeat. It was beating so fast, but it didn't take long for it to return to normal.

CHAPTER **TWENTY-EIGHT**

DARKNESS

I sipped the bottle of water in my hand, wishing the bottle wouldn't go empty.

It felt so awkward, sitting here and not knowing anything Adrian and Tristan were talking about.

Morris walked into the living room; he looked a bit nervous. I wanted to give him a hug. He'd been busy taking care of the paintings and the mess Tristan made in his room.

"The CCTV was tampered with. There's no recording of last night or this morning," he said calmly, like someone would hit him if he rushed his words.

"Whoever put those paintings in my room has to be familiar with this house," Tristan said.

"Or you have a stalker," Adrian said, leaning back on his seat.

"For Christ's sake, it's been five years." Tristan groaned, running a hand through his hair.

He was clearly agitated, and I wished they would fill me in on what was happening. I hated when people kept me guessing. My curious mind just wanted to be satisfied.

"Don't tell my mom about this," Tristan warned Morris before dismissing him.

I waited for them to explain it to me, but they just glanced at me and carried on with their conversation.

"I think you should increase the security around here," Adrian suggested.

"The last thing I need right now is to return to rehab," Tristan mumbled, sounding scared.

Adrian's phone vibrated on the table; he took a glance at his screen and smiled.

"Sorry, I have to leave. Call me if anything comes up. Bye, Chloe." He stood up and headed for the front door.

"Bye." I waved.

I took a glance at Tristan. He had his head in his palms. I stood up from my seat and walked to where he was. I placed my hands on his shoulders. He flinched and turned to look at me. His eyes looked haunted and tired.

"It's me," I said with a soft smile.

He'd been jumpy since this morning.

He pulled me to his lap and wrapped his arms around me. He was quiet and squeezed me into his arms.

"I promise to explain everything to you soon," he whispered.

I nodded and hugged him back, stroking his hair.

Later in the evening, we lay in silence on the bed. Tristan was fast asleep, his head resting on my chest and one arm draped over me. I continuously brushed my fingers through his hair as I stared at the wall like it had every answer to the questions in my head.

My eyes trailed over Tristan's face, and my fingertips traced his eyebrows and every feature of his face, like a paintbrush caressing a canvas. This man in my arms, who I'd grown so attached to, had unlocked a part of me I hadn't discovered. I felt myself smiling at how peaceful he looked in his sleep. It was nice to see him relax after watching him panic the whole day since he had seen those paintings.

What was it about the paintings that had terrified him? Was it Nadia?

I sighed and closed my eyes.

It was Saturday, and I was home alone. I dropped my phone on the counter and searched for a snack in the kitchen cabinet. My hand fiddled for the bag of Cheetos as my short legs pushed up to increase my height.

My ringtone stopped me from grabbing the bag of Cheetos. I groaned and picked up the phone. It was Adrian. Tristan was too busy to call anyway. He'd told me he had a board meeting today with important people.

"Hey, Adrian."

"Are you busy?"

"No," I replied and jumped, grabbing the bag of Cheetos.

"Meet me outside the Chinese restaurant; it's just a few minutes' drive from where you are."

"Everything okay?"

"Yeah."

"Okay, I will be there."

I ate the Cheetos as I drove to the restaurant. I wiped my mouth and combed my hair with my fingers.

Adrian waved at me when I entered the restaurant, decorated with red Chinese lanterns. The interior had bright shades of red, and the place looked very inviting. I took the seat in front of him with a smile.

"Did something happen?" I asked, a bit worried. It had been a long time since we'd hung out.

"No," he said and laughed. "Just wanted to hang out like old times. I hate how things are between us," he said.

A waiter arrived to take our order. Since the incident with Karen, the hollowness in our friendship was still there.

"So, how has it been going with Tristan?" he asked after the waiter left with our order.

"Good. He finally told me about Nadia," I lied, hoping to get something out of him.

"Really? It's not something he likes talking about," he said, looking too surprised.

"It's nothing big anyway." I scoffed.

"He would have been a good father."

"Good father?" I lost my character for a moment at his words.

"A good father to his daughter, Nadia," he said like he expected me to know.

"Daughter?" I mumbled. "Tristan has a daughter?" I sat up in my seat, still trying to digest what he'd just said.

"I thought he told … oh, he never did," he muttered in realization and looked outside the window.

"Nadia is his daughter?" I asked, like I needed more convincing. I hadn't expected it to be this. I'd expected a crazy ex or his first love.

"I'm sure he is not ready to talk about it," Adrian said.

"What happened to her?"

"I'm sorry. I can't tell you anything. You have to wait for Tristan to tell you himself."

The whole waiting thing was starting to get annoying.

"Okay," I mumbled, staring at my hands.

I didn't know how long Tristan expected me to wait. I wanted to know what I was getting involved with.

"He cares about you, Chloe."

"I know, but he won't tell me anything. It makes me feel like a stranger."

"You should know, this is a painful topic for him. You're only going to push him away if you keep trying to force it out of him."

I said nothing. He opened his mouth, as if he had more to say, but shut it and stared at me.

It was starting to make sense now—the way he'd interacted with little June and the sadness in his eyes when her mom had taken her away. I had so many questions, but I knew I couldn't get the answers.

"How is Karen?" I asked, trying to keep the conversation going.

He told me about their plans for the wedding and how Karen was a minimalist. I pretended to enjoy the food even if the new revelation clawed at me, destroying me from inside while I faked a smile at Adrian.

We parted ways after eating and talking for hours. I took a deep breath when I entered the car.

"He has a daughter?" I whispered to myself, still allowing the information to sink in.

I felt a part of me falling apart. I began to question all our moments together.

I wished I'd never asked. Maybe it would have been better to stay in the dark. Now, I couldn't stop thinking about it. Was he still seeing his daughter or the mother of his child? Oh shit! This was too much to take in.

I decided to call Vina. I didn't want to be close to Tristan with the different emotions I was feeling right now. I grabbed my phone and called her. She picked up on the first ring.

"*Holà!*"

"Are you home?" I asked.

"*Sí*, are you coming? Please say yes."

"Yes."

"Really?"

"Yes, Vina," I said, and she screamed in excitement.

"Wait. You don't sound excited. Is everything okay?"

"I will tell you everything when I get there," I mumbled and ended the call.

It was a twenty-minute drive from where I was. I parked the car and put some Cheetos in my mouth before coming out of the car. I adjusted the orange floral dress I wore. The warm breeze was not doing me any good. I dragged the dress down and walked to the large doors.

Belvina hugged me immediately after she opened the door. I hugged her back and refused to pull away. I really needed it.

"Are your parents home?" I asked.

"No."

She smiled at me when we separated. She dragged me into the house and shut the door.

"I think I messed up. I feel so awful, but at the same time, I feel so angry," I said as we both slumped on the sofa. "I really suck at this," I groaned, placing my head on her lap.

"So, I'm going to be your therapist today," Vina said.

"And my best friend," I told her.

We always shared everything with each other, especially when one of us needed the other person's help. I needed a little pep talk right now from her. As much as the topic felt too personal, I could trust her with anything, even my passwords.

"Okay, so tell me what happened."

"I tricked Adrian into telling me about Nadia," I confessed.

"Oh shit. Let me guess. You didn't like what you discovered?"

"Yes, I wish I'd never asked. Now, I just feel like I invaded his personal space," I said and groaned.

"He's going to be so mad when he finds out you went behind his back and did some digging."

"Wow, what a therapist you are," I said, and she shrugged. "I wish he'd trust me enough to tell me," I whispered.

"Girl, it's not that easy. We all have different ways of coping with stuff. Maybe he went through shit and thinks it's better to keep it to himself. He'll open up eventually if you stop being a detective."

"Tristan is going to be so mad," I said and groaned again, as if I could feel his wrath already.

"It's going to be fine," she whispered, stroking my hair. It made me sleepy. "It's all about patience," she said, sounding like the therapist I wanted.

"Too bad I wasn't born with that."

"You love him, and he loves you. Wait for him."

"Let's not jump to conclusions here."

My phone started ringing.

"Who is it?" Vina asked when she saw the look on my face.

"Tristan," I mumbled. "Do you think Adrian told him?" I asked.

"He wouldn't have. He's better than that," Vina defended him with a smile.

"I can't." I dropped the phone on the couch, watching it ring.

Vina picked up the phone and answered the call. I groaned and buried my face in my palms.

"Hey, Tristan."

"Where is Chloe?"

"How rude. You can't even say hello."

"Is Chloe okay?"

"She is sleeping. She is not feeling too well."

"I will send Morris to come over and take her to the hospital."

"It's just a headache. She is lying here, snoring. Don't worry about her."

"I don't snore," I said in a low tone.

"I have never heard her snore."

I smiled when I heard him say that.

"You still owe me a hello."

"Hello, Belvina."

"Better. Bye, Tristan." She ended the call. "He's so sweet," she said, throwing my phone at me.

"Did he sound angry?" I asked, picking up my phone.

"No," she said, walking to the kitchen.

I closed my eyes and allowed the sleep to take me.

I woke up later on the sofa. I looked around for Vina but didn't find her.

"Vina?" I called, standing up and stretching my arms.

"Yes, in the kitchen!"

I shuffled to the kitchen, yawning.

"I heard you snore. I'm not lying," she said as I took a seat at the island.

I grabbed two cookies from the jar in the middle and ate noisily.

"Tristan called, like, multiple times."

"Did you answer it?"

"No."

"Good," I said, taking more cookies.

"Hungry?" she asked, placing a bowl of salsa sauce in front of me. She brought out a bag of Paqui tortilla chips.

"Yes," I moaned.

"What time is it?" I asked.

"Almost seven p.m."

"Do you think Tristan is still seeing the mother of his child? I wonder what happened between them. I didn't even know he was married before," I rambled.

"Give me your phone," Vina demanded.

I pushed it toward her, and she picked it up.

"What are you doing?"

"A Google search on Tristan Sanchester," she replied, tapping swiftly on my phone. "It doesn't say anything about his previous relationships or daughter," she said, looking at me.

"You think Adrian lied?" I asked.

"I don't know." She shrugged. "No way," she gasped after looking at the phone again.

"What?" I asked, standing up.

"Did you know today is your *novio*'s birthday?"

"No. No one said anything about it."

"Well, it's today, and you're seventeen hours late."

"Are you sure it's today? Adrian would have said something or his family," I said, and she gave me the phone.

"It could be wrong. You know what they say; don't believe everything you see on the internet."

"Should I call him and ask?"

"No, dumbass. Surprise him. After going behind his back for information about his past, you owe him a great night. It might even ease the suspicion."

"So, what kind of surprise should I give him? You know I'm a disaster in the kitchen," I asked, and she smirked.

"Birthday sex hits different, you know," she said with a sly smile.

I laughed and shook my head at her suggestion.

"Okay," I said, taking the bag of chips and the salsa sauce to eat in the car.

"Call me tomorrow and give me all the details," she said as we walked to the front door.

"Pray I don't mess this up," I said.

"I won't be surprised if you do," she said, and I glared at her.

"Love you. *Adiós*," she said after we shared a hug.

I blew her a kiss as I walked to my car.

I STOPPED BY the pastry store on my way and bought a small cake. The ride back to the house was just me arguing with myself. I looked beside me at the red velvet cake I'd bought. I smiled at the bodyguards outside. They had been lingering around since someone had broken into the house and hung those paintings in Tristan's room. I didn't see Morris when I entered the house. Maybe he had gone to visit his family.

I went upstairs to check if Tristan was home. I opened the door and found the room empty. I went back downstairs and got a bottle of red wine and two wineglasses. I got everything set and sat on the bed, waiting. My heart skipped when I heard the front door open.

Why was I nervous, like I was about to give a speech in front of a large crowd?

I'm scared I might not do it right or he might not like it. Maybe it's too cliché. What if he hates red velvet cake? What if he is allergic to the scent of the candles? All thoughts flew out of my head when the door to his room opened.

"Happy birthday!" I screamed as soon as I saw Tristan.

He looked surprised at first. It changed to anger when I started singing; it must have been my voice. He wouldn't be the first to hate it. I picked up the cake and continued singing as I walked to where he stood like a statue.

Why wasn't he smiling?

"Stop," he said with a tight jaw. "Who told you? My mom?"

"No."

"Adrian?"

"No."

"Go to bed, Chloe. It's late," he said and walked away to the closet.

"Come on. It's your birthday," I groaned, and he said nothing.

"What about the cake? It cost me sixty dollars," I said with a frown. He pretended not to hear me.

"What a waste," I sighed and walked out of the room.

I went downstairs and got a bottle of brandy from the wine cellar. I downed one glass of the alcohol and poured more.

I felt like I was dating a stranger. There was more to Tristan's story. I wanted him to trust me enough to tell me. I had tried to remain patient with him, but each day felt like a mystery, and it terrified me that he might be keeping something big from me.

The doorbell echoed in the building. I was feeling too angry to face anyone. I took one more gulp and walked to the front door.

I opened the door without checking the door camera. My eyes widened in surprise at the person in front of me.

"Grey?"

"I know it's all a lie. I know you are not pregnant," he said breathlessly, like he had run a marathon to get here.

I stared at him, not sure what to say.

"Sorry it took me so long to figure it out," he rasped. "Chlo." He moved closer and held my face in his hands. "I messed up big time. What I did was very stupid. I can't imagine how hurt you felt that day. I should have stayed and fought for you. I should have proven to everyone that the bastard was lying. I'm so sorry, Chloe."

I pulled away, putting some space between us. He looked hurt, and I could see the guilt in his eyes.

"It's fine, Grey. It's in the past now," I said, avoiding his eyes. I could still remember how he'd freaked me out last time I was in his apartment.

"I'm probably the worst boyfriend on earth."

"Was," I corrected him.

"Right," he mumbled and stared at his feet and then back at me.

"It's all my fault. I should have done something. I was so stupid." He groaned and punched the air. "That bastard—"

"Don't call him that," I cut in.

He looked surprised.

"Chloe, he ruined your life. He took everything away from you. Are you happy here? Why did he do it? Did he tell you? Why is he keeping you here?!" he screamed the last sentence.

"I don't know, but I'm glad to be far away from the people who broke my trust. The people I thought would fight for me and have my back through good and bad," I said with my arms folded.

"You can move in with me. Stop playing along with his lies. I will speak to your family. I will try and convince them."

"Good luck with that." I heard Tristan's deep voice from behind. It almost made me jump. I'd thought he was angry.

I saw Grey's jaw clench, and his hands fisted. He looked like he wouldn't mind killing Tristan right now.

"How did you get past the bodyguards at the gate?" Tristan asked.

"I told them I was family and showed them a picture of me and Chloe." Grey shrugged.

"You think you're smart, huh?" Tristan snickered.

"Lying fucking bastard!" Grey spat.

"Grey, calm down," I said, too scared to witness a fight.

"Yeah, calm down," Tristan said, wrapping his arms around my waist from behind. "You have ten seconds to leave before I call the cops and charge you for trespassing," he added, leaning closer to my cheek and pressing his lips to my temple.

I took a glance at Grey; his eyes were drilling into where Tristan held me.

"Drop the act. There's no audience for you to entertain with your filthy lies!"

"Act?" Tristan laughed softly. I could feel the vibration from his body.

I pushed his hands away and shot him a glare. He wasn't helping.

"You should head home. It's getting late," I told Grey.

"What has he done to you, Chlo?" he asked, stepping closer but Tristan got in the way.

"I have stolen her heart," Tristan said, and Grey clenched his fists, fighting the urge to knock the grin off Tristan's face.

"I don't know what you're up to, but if I find out, I won't hesitate to tell the whole world the truth, and if you ever hurt Chloe—"

"I will never hurt her," Tristan cut in, taking my hand. He gave it a light squeeze.

"You've hurt her already, you moron. Your lies and—"

"Grey, please go home," I begged.

"I will be back," he said more to Tristan than to me.

I watched him walk back to his car.

I pulled my hand away from Tristan's grasp and entered the house. I went back to my drink. I sat on one of the sofas and gulped the alcohol. I was starting to feel the effect drill through my body.

Tristan stood behind the sofa with his arms folded. There was a long silence between us.

"Look, I'm sorry for earlier," he said.

"So, how old is Nadia now? Are you still seeing her mother? Why were you kicked out of their lives?" The questions kept flying out of my mouth without control.

I waited for him to say something, but he was quiet.

I looked behind me and found him walking away.

"There goes the typical Tristan, always running away like a chicken," I sneered.

He stopped and turned around. "You know, I was starting to think this thing between us was real, but you won't even give me a chance."

"You left me with no choice! I'm sick of the secrets," I yelled.

"So, you had to go behind my back? You do that every time and expect me to be cool with it. Well, I hope you're satisfied now."

"No, I'm not. I wanna know if you're still seeing her mother."

"Why don't you figure that one out yourself, just like you found out about Nadia?" he said, walking closer. "And to think, I made up my mind to apologize for ruining the birthday surprise," he mumbled, sounding disappointed.

"Why won't you just tell me?!"

"You don't have to know about my past. You know how I feel about you. You don't have to go around digging for secrets that will tear us apart."

"I want to!" I stood up and moved closer. "I hate that you're keeping things from me. It's been four freaking months!" I said, breaking down in tears.

"Don't you think I deserve the truth after what you did to me? After everything you put me through?" I asked, stepping closer.

He said nothing but stared at me, his eyes like steel, masking the truth.

"I can't be in a relationship where I feel left out, Tristan. A relationship is about trust, sharing your pain and struggles with each other. I want to know. Stop making me feel like a kid who can't handle anything that comes her way."

"I can't with you right now," he said and began to walk away.

"I'm sure they left you because of the beast you are!" I screamed as his figure disappeared up the stairs.

I heard the door slam upstairs, the collision echoing through the building.

I slumped on the floor in tears. I didn't even know why I was crying, but I was frustrated. I was angry with myself. I gulped more alcohol as I cried. I grabbed my phone and called Vina.

"Hello? So, how did it go? From the time you're calling, I'm guessing it didn't go well."

"Vina," I sobbed.

"Chlo? Are you okay?" She sounded alarmed.

"No, I'm a big mess," I cried.

"Are you drunk?"

I wanted to deny it, but she knew the answer already.

"Kinda," I slurred.

"What did you do?" she groaned.

I told her everything that had happened since I had left her place.

"Oh God, you shouldn't have."

"I was upset."

"You don't know what he is going through. It must be hard for him. Stop pressuring him."

"I couldn't control it." I sniffled.

"Now, you listen to me." Her voice boomed with authority. "Drop that alcohol, go to your room, take a bath, and go to bed. Tomorrow, take your stupid ass and go apologize to him."

"Apologize? How is this my fault?"

"For Christ's sake, it's his birthday. Did you really have to? You are in love with him, and I'm sure he feels the same. Why don't you stop being a nosy bitch and wait for him to tell you? Good night." She ended the call before I could open my mouth to object.

"Great," I mumbled and dropped the alcohol in my hand. I brushed my hair back and stared at the huge chandelier above me. My three-years sobriety badge would be laughing at me right now. I was a huge mess.

My hangover made me stay in bed the whole day. Vina had been avoiding my calls and texts. She was angry with me. My outburst from last night was still replaying in my head. It felt like torture.

I avoided Tristan for one more day, pretending to be asleep or locking myself in the shower until I was sure he had gone to bed.

The next day, I summoned the courage to go and apologize to him. I walked up to his room after dinner. I had hoped he would come down for dinner, but he'd told Morris he was busy with work and only asked for a cup of coffee. I knocked, but he didn't answer. He never answered anyway.

I opened the door and found him in his home office that looked larger than my closet. He was busy on his computer with a few files next to him.

"Can I come in?" I asked, knocking on the wall.

"Yeah," he replied, not looking back.

I walked in with slow steps, like it could stop the thumping in my chest. I rehearsed my apology speech in my head again as I stopped one foot from where he sat. He closed the file in front of him and turned around in his seat. I tried to keep my eyes on his face and not his shirtless torso.

His eyes scanned what I was wearing. *Great.* Today, I'd decided to wear my big pajamas set. He was checking me out? I probably looked like a stick wrapped in a blanket.

"Did you discover one of my skeletons?" he asked, folding his arms.

"I'm … um … I'm sorry for that night. I was a little drunk." Well, that was not how the apology speech was supposed to start. "I shouldn't have done that," I said, trying not to stutter.

He didn't say anything. He stared at me like he was waiting for me to say more.

"I … I was angry and … um … I … I said stuff that …"

"I have never seen you lost for words. I'm not mad at you, Chloe, but I accept your apology since it was the hardest thing you've ever done," he said with a playful smile.

358

"So, we are cool?" I asked.

"Yes, if you help me type this," he said, raising a paper.

"Really? You're not mad about what I said?"

"I was, but I'm over it."

"Okay, but quick warning: my fingers are not that fast," I said, walking to his large desk.

I leaned closer and tried to type a sentence, but Tristan gripped my hips and pulled me to sit on his lap.

"Make yourself comfortable," he said, moving his hands to my waist.

I tried to focus on what I was typing as his fingers played with the waistband of my pajamas.

"How have you been?" he asked, giving me a soft squeeze on the waist.

"Good." I tried to keep my composure.

"You smell nice. New shampoo?" He leaned closer to my hair.

"Yeah," I replied.

I adjusted on his lap to find a comfortable position. Tristan's sharp intake of air made me smirk. I moved again, and he groaned. I tried to move again, but he gripped my hips, halting my movement.

"If you do that again, I won't hold back," he said, running his palm down my thigh and up to my waist.

My mind didn't care about the typing anymore. I wanted him to touch me everywhere. One day away from him, and I was starved.

"You owe me, Chloe, so keep typing," he said close to my ear.

I tried to ignore the heat that spread to every part of my body, and the bulge in his pants wasn't helping. I kept my eyes on the keyboard and continued typing.

"We had a deal, and you've been drinking," he said, sounding disappointed.

"I'm sorry."

"We can work something out to help," he said against my neck as his lips trailed up to my ear.

I gasped when he slipped his rough palm up my stomach, his finger brushing against the space between my breasts. His other hand dipped into my pajama pants, his fingers circling my most sensitive spot. I gasped as his hand slipped into my underwear and touched me where I wanted.

"Already so wet," he rasped.

My fingers paused on the keyboard, and I closed my eyes when he put three fingers into me.

"Keep typing," he whispered, nibbling on my earlobe as his fingers thrust into me.

"Can't I continue later?" I asked, out of breath.

He laughed lightheartedly against my neck. His hands left my body, and he sat back. I grumbled at the loss of contact.

"No, that's an important paper I need to prepare for tomorrow," he said, and I rolled my eyes.

I decided to tease him a little. I leaned closer to the table, shooting my backside out. I smiled at the sound that escaped his lips.

"Come here," he said, pulling me closer to him.

He angled my head from behind and met my lips in a hungry kiss. I withdrew and stood up. I climbed on his lap and straddled him. Our lips found each other again like the north and south poles of a magnet. Tristan ran his palms down my ass and gripped me. I moved my hand up his chest to his neck as our tongues found each other. I'd missed him so much. It was as if we'd been away from each other for years. He slid his hand up my back, touching my scar and brushing his fingers smoothly against it.

"I could flip you around and fuck you against my desk, but I need to work," he said kissing my neck.

I rocked my hips against him as we became a bit aggressive, my core brushing brazenly on his hardness. Tristan broke the kiss, and we both tried to catch our breath.

"Damn, I missed you," he said, brushing my hair back with his fingers.

"I'm sorry for being such an ass," I said.

"That is not something someone like you admits."

"Way to turn me off," I said, playfully hitting him on the chest.

"If you want us to work, you need to wait for me to tell you and stop going behind my back, digging for my past," he whispered.

"Okay," I whispered.

I leaned down and nibbled on his lower lip. He grunted and pulled me closer for a deep kiss. He withdrew, making me groan in aggravation.

"Sorry, but this is going to be quick," he said and stood up with my legs wrapped around his waist.

"Sounds like someone won't last ten seconds," I said as we walked to the bedroom.

"With you, it's almost impossible." He said, putting me on the bed, and he was quick to come for a kiss.

His tongue grazed my teeth, and he sucked on my upper lip, making me groan in pleasure. I leaned back and took my shirt off. He trailed kisses up my stomach to my chest. He moved to my neck and pulled at my skin with his teeth.

I arched my back, intimately running my fingers through his hair as he sucked on my nipple and fiddled with my other breast. I couldn't hold the moan back as I closed my eyes. Getting lost in the wave of pleasure. He reached for the waistband of my pajama pants and slowly pulled it down.

"I want you on all fours," he rasped, digging his fingers into my hips. I did as he'd asked.

I sucked in a breath when he entered me from behind. His fingers in my hair as he thrust into me hard and fast. He grabbed my hands and pinned them behind with one hand while the other hand gripped my hair, his thrusts harder and carnal.

Soon, every thrust was accompanied with anger. I took it all, allowing him to let it all out. I buried my face in the pillow as I moaned like a wanton.

This was definitely not how I'd expected the apology to turn out.

Make-up sex really hits different.

I WOKE UP to someone tugging at my hair.

"What are you doing?" I groaned at Tristan, who was busy doing God knew what on my hair.

"Braiding."

"Ouch!" I winced at the sharp pain from his braiding.

"Almost done. Relax," he said with a soft laugh.

I touched my hair when he was done and glared at him.

"The word is, *thanks.*"

"For causing me pain?"

He smiled and raised my chin, so he could kiss me. It was slow and laced with passion.

"You look sexy. I feel like a stylist right now," he said, staring at the hideous hair that made me look like one of those dolls from a horror movie.

I rolled my eyes.

"What time is it?" I looked around the dim room.

"Almost six a.m. I will be leaving for work soon," he said, caressing my cheek with his thumb.

I turned to look at him.

"Is something wrong?" he asked, pausing the movement of his thumb on my cheek.

"No, I missed you." I beamed, resting my chin on his chest. I placed a kiss on the center of his chest and touched his stubble.

How had this happened? How had I ended up falling for the person I'd once wanted dead for ruining my life?

"I promise to explain everything to you."

"It's fine. Take all the time you need."

He cocked his brows in surprise.

"I will wait, Mr. Sanchester." I moved closer and kissed his lips.

He grabbed my hand and placed my palm on his chest. I could feel his heartbeat and the warmth from his body. He was quiet and just stared at me with his lips curved upward.

"Do you feel that?" he whispered, and I nodded.

"All for you," he said, and I cocked my eyebrows in utter bewilderment.

"For a long time, I thought my heart had stopped beating, and it was just my body existing. That night you kissed me, I felt alive for the first time in years, and now, I believe I'm not just existing." He interlocked his fingers with mine against his toned chest.

The next words that left his mouth left me paralyzed.

"I love you, Chloe."

I was quiet and just stared at him, not saying the words back.

"It's fine if you don't feel the same. I just wanted you to know. I know I have given you reasons to doubt my feelings, but I'm not giving up on winning your heart."

I couldn't say it back for some reason. I kissed him again, not liking the silence I'd created. I moved slowly on top of him. He broke the kiss and looked me in the eye as he sat up.

"Promise you won't leave after knowing everything?" he asked, cupping my cheeks.

"I saw you at your worst, and I stayed. I won't." Partly because I was broke, but now, it was because of him.

He looked relieved as his face relaxed. He took my face and kissed me passionately. He switched our position, hovering over me. I smirked at him. He pushed my legs apart and ventured down to the throbbing between my legs. He was gentle this time. He made love to me, memorizing every inch of my body.

He ended up going late to work.

LATELY, A LOT had changed between us. I promised Tristan and Vina that I'd lock Detective Chloe away and wait for him until he was ready. I saw a new Tristan. The Tristan I wanted to spend my whole life with. He took me on dates every weekend and forced me to visit the spa every Friday.

I quit the yoga class since I was starting to get suspicious stares from everyone. I'd suggested one of those fake-pregnant thingies, but Tristan had told me to stop attending the class.

The four bodyguards guarding the house seemed useless. Whoever was messing with him still found a way in and didn't plan on stopping. The person still succeeded in torturing him with whatever had happened.

He started having nightmares, where he kept muttering, "Forgive me, Fiona."

I didn't question him, but I was there to help. I was always around to provide some comfort and to assure him he was safe. He would hold on to me tightly in sleep, like a scared child, and apologize for waking me up.

Tristan went crazy after he found a blue dress on his bed. He ripped the dress apart and refused to say a word to me that day, but he held onto me the whole night while he slept.

The other day, he'd found some baby onesies in his room. He'd broken down that day—the first time I'd ever seen him cry. He kept spacing out, and I almost gave up on talking to him. It made me sad to see him so wrecked and detached from reality. I was still clueless on the situation, and I wished I could help.

I made it my mission to catch the monster torturing him. More guards were hired, but it still didn't help.

Who the hell was this person? And what did he or she want? The person had to be someone he knew. It wasn't just anyone.

WEDNESDAY, TRISTAN DECIDED to sleep in his room. He told me he wanted to be alone and needed some space. I was worried about leaving him alone. I stayed awake in bed, staring at the ceiling. Was he okay? What about his nightmares?

I sat up in my bed when I heard a crash from his room.

"Tristan?" I ran out of my room to him.

I opened the door and found him throwing things around and cursing loudly.

"Tristan, stop!" I screamed, but he continued. I ducked when his laptop came my way.

"Tristan." I moved closer.

I tried to touch him, but he threw his bedside lamp away. I was too slow to dodge it. The lamp made contact with my head before I could save myself. I welcomed the darkness that surrounded me. A grueling and ghastly wave of nausea tangled itself all over my numb vessel.

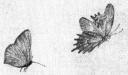

CHAPTER **TWENTY-NINE**
REHAB

"She is waking up." I heard from beside me as I tried to open my eyes.

"Chloe?" someone called, taking my hand. It felt rough and cold.

I tried to follow the voice, to escape the darkness around me. My vision was still blurry as my eyes fluttered open. The back of my head was pounding.

"Chloe?"

I closed my eyes and opened them again. Adrian's gray eyes stared at me with relief.

"Adrian?" I mumbled, still a little dazed.

"Oh, thank God, Chloe." Karen's voice came from behind him. She moved closer and hugged me.

"I'm glad you're okay," she said, pulling away.

"How do you feel?" Adrian asked, staring at my face as if he didn't recognize me.

"Funny."

"I will call the doctor." He gave my hand a gentle squeeze and left.

I took in my surroundings. The room was wide. There was a table by the corner with fresh flowers on top. The long couch was pushed to the wall, and a TV was mounted in front of the bed. I looked down at the hospital gown. I shut my eyes and took a deep breath as I recalled what had happened.

"Where is Tristan?" I asked with my eyes still closed. I waited for an answer but got none.

I opened my eyes, looking at Karen with my right brow raised. She looked uncomfortable. The door opened when I was about to speak, and I could almost swear I saw relief wash over her face. Adrian walked in with a short doctor. The doctor smiled at me as he got closer.

"Hi, I'm Dr. Michael."

"Hi," I mumbled.

"How are you feeling?" the doctor asked.

"My head hurts."

"Anything else?"

"No."

"Okay, miss. I need you to cooperate with me."

"Okay." I nodded.

"How many fingers do you see?"

"Three."

"Are you sure?"

"Yes." I almost rolled my eyes at him.

"How many do you see now?"

"Two," I replied dryly.

He glanced at Adrian and Karen. Their faces were masked with confusion. He stepped closer and used a penlight to check my eyes, and then he pulled away.

"What?" I asked, feeling left out.

"We are going to keep you here for a few days to make sure there's no brain injury."

"How many days?" I mumbled.

"Three to five. Have a nice day, miss." He left, smiling widely.

"Is it that bad?" I asked, looking at them with a frown.

"I'm sure you'll be out of here at the end of this week," Karen said.

"I hope so," I whispered. "Where is Tri—"

"We'll be right back. Let's get you something to eat," Adrian cut me off.

He took Karen's hand, and I watched them leave. They were avoiding the question.

I felt a strong urge to pee. I got down from the bed. I rolled the pole where the IV was hanging as I walked to the bathroom. I did my business and decided to rinse my face. I walked to the small mirror hanging above the sink.

I gasped when I saw the person staring at me in the mirror. The left side of my face was covered in bruises and small cuts, which had Band-Aids over it. Had the lamp broken on my face?

I shook my head, inhaling deeply. It wasn't his fault.

I rinsed my mouth and returned to the room. I wanted to make a call, but I didn't have my phone.

Adrian and Karen arrived with takeout. I sat up in bed and watched them set everything in front of me.

"*Bon appetit.*" Karen grinned and stepped back.

I stared at the food in front of me and looked back at them.

"What's wrong? You don't like it?" Adrian asked.

"Or do you want me to feed you?" Karen asked.

They both looked confused.

"Where is Tristan? And don't lie to me," I demanded.

"He is okay. He's somewhere safe."

"Somewhere safe? Where?"

He glanced at Karen, as if he needed her permission before he could tell me.

"He was taken to the rehab."

"What? Are you sure he—"

"We can talk about this later. Now, eat," he cut in with a serious tone.

I ate the food with no real appetite. Karen packed everything when I was done. I turned my attention to Adrian when she was done.

"He is receiving treatment. He will be fine," he told me. "He didn't mean to hurt you; when he realized what he had done, he went crazy. He called for help. He is really sorry for what happened."

"Well, I hope he gets better," I said.

"He will." Adrian smiled.

"Can I speak to him? I want him to know I don't blame him for what happened."

"I will tell him," he said instead.

"Is he far away?"

"He is receiving help. That's all that matters. Focus on getting better," he said, trying to avoid more questions.

"How long have I been out?"

"A few hours," Karen replied.

"Thanks for coming," I told them.

"We'll always be here for you, Chloe," Karen said sweetly.

"Sorry we have to leave, but we'll be back in the evening," Adrian said.

"It's okay."

They each gave me a hug and left. I sighed and sank into the bed. I found myself touching my face. I recalled that day, the look on his face. What had driven him mad? What had he seen?

Mrs. Sanchester and Nana came to see me the next day. I felt sad when she broke down, apologizing for what had happened. Nana made me watch a comedy show with her. It was nice to have a good laugh in the midst of the darkness. They stayed the whole day and left when it was starting to get late.

The next three days in the hospital were boring. I was tired of watching the news, but I got a little addicted to the soap opera that made me so emotional that I cried.

I asked Mrs. Sanchester if I could speak to Tristan, but I was told he didn't want to talk to me. Adrian agreed it was better for him not to contact me since he was still being treated.

I was so happy when I was informed I was getting discharged the next day. Vina visited me on my last day in the hospital. She arrived with my favorite milkshake and a bag of Cheetos.

"You look like Frankenstein," she said, looking at my face.

"Come on. It's not that bad." I frowned, touching my face.

"Just kidding. So, have you heard from Tristan?" she asked, lying next to me.

"No, he doesn't wanna speak to me. I have tried, but everyone thinks it's better not to keep in contact with him."

"But do you blame him for what happened?"

"Not at all. Something pissed him off, and he lost control. He wasn't himself when I entered the room. It was like I was staring at a possessed Tristan. I tried to reach out to him, but this happened," I said and sighed.

"I hope he receives enough help and gets better," she whispered, stroking my hair as I rested my head on her shoulder.

"Me too. I wish I could speak to him." I blinked my tears away.

"Are you drinking that milkshake or not? I won't hesitate to take it back," Vina said, and I put a protective hand around my drink.

She joined me to watch my favorite soap opera, and we drooled over the hot main lead.

MORRIS TOOK ME home after I got discharged. He kept looking at me with pity, and I had to smile at him to convince him I was okay.

"If you need anything, Miss Simpson, I'm here," he told me when we entered the house.

The house felt so empty as I climbed the stairs. I wondered how long Tristan was going to be at rehab. I entered my room and took a proper bath. After, I wore yoga pants and a white hoodie. I sat on the floor in front of the glass wall. I stared at the pool, recalling the night I had shown him the scar on my back. What I had with him was different, and I didn't want that with anybody else. I wished he'd speak to me. Had he listened to any of my voice mails?

Maybe we brought out the worst in each other. We were perfectly imperfect, but what was beautiful about what we had was that when it got difficult between us, we found our way back to each other. No matter how many times I messed up, he still accepted me. I didn't care how broken he was. I was willing to fight through this with him. If only he'd let me.

I missed him.

I left my room after a few hours and found myself in his room. His furniture had been replaced, and the room looked new. I lay on his bed and closed my eyes.

"It's not your fault," I whispered, pulling the pillow to my chest.

There was a knock on the door.

"What?" I sighed, wanting to be alone.

The door opened, and Adrian walked in with a small smile. I sat up as he approached the bed.

"How are you?"

"Good," I mumbled.

"Can I sit?" he asked, gesturing to the space next to me.

"Sure."

He sat down and brought out something from his pocket. "This is for you." He extended it for me to take.

I took a glance at the check for five million dollars.

"What's this?"

"Tristan asked me to give it to you and ask you to leave. You can take any car you want, and if you need more money—"

"What?"

"He thinks he doesn't deserve you and is scared he might hurt you again. He is concerned about your safety."

"I wanna speak to him."

"You know you can't. There is a lot going on. We don't know his attacker's next move. He is scared, Chloe. Anything could happen to you."

"I'm not leaving," I said, tearing the check into pieces.

"He is not coming back."

"You're lying." I shook my head in denial.

"He needs to be away, Chloe."

"I wanna be there for him and fight this with him," I whimpered.

"I'm sorry," he said, which was his way of telling me I couldn't see Tristan. He stood up to leave. "If you change your mind, call me."

I wouldn't.

It'd been three months without Tristan in the house. Words could never explain how much I missed him. A text from him would make me the happiest right now, but all I got from Adrian and his family was that he is getting better.

I stayed in my room, keeping myself busy with schoolwork most of the day. I would have been miserable and died from the pain of his absence, but Vina had been coming around a lot and trying to keep me sane.

"Just a word, please," I said to my phone as I waited for Tristan to reply to my hundredth text.

Did he even miss me? Was I the only one going crazy from being away from each other? I was willing to go through the whole process with him, to be there to provide some support, but here I was, alone with Morris in this big house that was starting to feel haunted.

My phone rang. I picked it up quickly, hoping it was him, but it was my dad. I answered the call with tentative fingers.

"Chloe."

My heartbeat paused.

"Dad?"

"Can we meet?"

Meet? All of a sudden? Is Mom dead?

"Meet? Um ... yes. When and where?"

"I will text you the address."

"Okay," I said, and he ended the call.

I tried not to panic. It'd been almost a year, and he was reaching out now. I hoped something terrible hadn't happened.

I stood up and changed into a pair of blue denim jeans and a black halter top. I slipped on my sneakers and held my hair back with a white ribbon.

I ARRIVED BEFORE my dad at his favorite restaurant. I took a seat at the outdoor space overlooking a cinema. I relished the feeling of the sun on my skin as I waited for him to come. I had not been in a public space for a long time, and I was sure by now, everyone that knew about what had happened in the church was expecting a baby. Though it felt like it was already forgotten since I wasn't getting the usual stare I got from a few people when the event had first happened.

I felt nervous all of a sudden. Was he coming with everyone? Maybe they'd realized it was all a lie and wanted to ask for my forgiveness. I didn't know his reason for the sudden meeting. Was I supposed to be excited or angry?

I should be mad at him. I should have ended the call immediately after I heard his voice, but I had been too scared that there might be an emergency, and also, I missed my dad.

"Chloe?" I heard my dad's voice from behind.

I stood up to face him. It felt like forever since I'd last seen him.

"Hi, Dad." My lips broke into a big smile.

"You look taller," he said, staring at me from my head down to my feet.

"It's been, like, seven months," I said.

He took the seat across from me, and we ordered different drinks. He went for a beer, and I went for a tropical juice. I was disappointed my mom and sister hadn't come, not like I'd expected them to.

"How are you?" he asked.

"How do I look?" I grinned.

"Better than I expected."

"I'm happy, Dad. I really am."

"I'm glad to hear that."

"How is Ciara?" I asked.

"She was offered a job in Seattle, so she left."

"Wow. How long?" I guessed I was really not part of the family since Ciara hadn't cared to tell me.

"Last month."

"What about Mom?" The word *Mom* tasted bitter on my tongue.

"She is doing okay; she misses you."

I knew that was a lie.

"Sure," I scoffed.

"How is ... um ... the baby? Is it a boy or a girl?" He looked happy.

"Isn't it obvious already?" I tried to keep my voice down as anger gripped my every word.

No one would buy the lie anymore. There was no baby.

"There is no baby. There never was. It's been almost a year, and look at me."

He was tongue-tied for a few seconds. I fought the urge to stand up and leave. I could feel all the rage now, I remembered the look on their faces that day and how they threw me out. The night I had seen them laughing and dining like I never existed.

"I'm sorry," was all he said, not even looking at me.

My hand balled into a fist under the table. What was I expecting from this meeting?

"I tried to talk to your mom, but she was so adamant. I could tell something didn't seem right, but I—"

"You never cared," I cut in bitterly.

"There was not one day you were not on my mind."

"Then, why didn't you reach out? It's been freaking seven months. I needed you, Dad."

He didn't say anything. He looked down at his hands, avoiding my eyes. I didn't want to blame him. He tended to listen to whatever Mom told him. He was someone with a soft heart, and Mom had a big influence on him.

"He tried to tell us," he mumbled.

"Who?"

"Tristan Sanchester. He came over to the house after we kicked you out. He had blood on his shirt, and I was scared something had happened to you. Your mom wouldn't even give him a chance to talk. She threatened to call the cops, and he had to leave."

I was lost for words. I remembered that day at the hospital when he'd disappeared and left me with Adrian.

"What … what did he say?"

"He said something about a lie, and he apologized. I didn't hear much 'cause your mom slammed the door on his face."

I stood up, not sure I could spend another minute with him.

"I'm sorry for what happened. I will explain everything to—"

"Don't. It doesn't matter anymore."

"Let me know if you need anything," he told me.

"I won't. Tell Mom I'm still alive." I turned away and walked to the car I'd parked at the side of the road. I buried my face in my palms and inhaled deeply. My emotions were all over the place. I took one last glance at him and drove off.

I WAS EXHAUSTED WHEN I got home. I stretched my arms after taking off my sneakers. I heard a noise from the kitchen. Morris must have been making dinner. I felt dehydrated from today's sun. I dropped my bag and walked to the kitchen.

"Hey, Morris," I said, opening the fridge.

I took one bottle of water and faced him with a wide smile, but my smile fell when I saw Tristan staring at me. I let go of the bottle and approached him with quick steps.

His stubble was now replaced with a beard. His lips curled upward slowly, guilt glaring right at me as his eyes monitored my moves.

"I know you hate me now for—"

"Shut up," I cut in, running toward him and jumping on him in pure excitement.

He stumbled back, unable to keep up with my force, and tumbled to the ground. I wrapped my arms around him, welcoming the familiar scent that filled my nose.

"I'm glad you're back, and I don't hate you," I told him, increasing my grip around him.

"I'm so sorry, Chloe," he whispered and kissed my head.

He wrapped his arms around me, I melted into him.

"I'm sorry," he said again, kissing my neck.

We stayed quiet on the cold marble floor, not pulling away.

"It was fucking hard. It's been torture without you here," I murmured into his neck.

"I missed you." He brushed his fingers through my hair. "I was starting to get jealous of Morris," he said and laughed softly at himself.

"Morris? Why?" I asked, pulling away to look at him.

I'd almost forgotten how handsome he was. As much as I was irritated by the beard, I had to admit, he rocked the look.

"Because he got to see you every day while I listened to everyone's complaints at group therapy."

I laughed, and he just stared at me like he was waking up from a dream.

"Are you hungry?" I asked, trying to pull away but he held me back.

"Let me be greedy for one more minute," he mumbled, engulfing me in a warm embrace.

We lay in silence, holding each other like it was our last time seeing each other.

"I'm a horrible person. I shouldn't have … I—" he began.

"Tristan, it's okay," I interrupted.

"No, none of this is okay. I fucking hit you with a lamp. How is that okay?"

"Yes, you did, but you were not yourself," I said, pulling away and cupping his face.

"This is going to haunt me for the rest of my life. I should have avoided it somehow and …"

"Listen to me," I chipped in. "I don't even remember it. Let's move on and leave it behind."

"I hurt you. I put you in a hospital bed and—"

"I can cook pasta now. Morris taught me," I said chirpily.

"We need to talk, Chloe."

"I'm sick of the guilt speech. I feel awful too, Tristan, for not doing enough to help. None of what happened is your fault. I never blamed you."

"You have no idea how much your presence in this house means to me," he said with a sad smile, tracing my face with his fingers.

I had faith that he was going to get better, and I wanted to be here to help. He was human, and he had flaws, like everyone else.

"I could teach you how to make my Nana's favorite food," he offered.

"Okay, I'm in," I said with a clap.

We got off the floor, and I grabbed the bottle of water I'd abandoned. I realized he was staring at me as I gulped down the water. I turned to him with a questioning look. He looked as if he couldn't believe this was real. He took my arm and pulled me closer. He kissed me softly, not rushed or aggressive, but slow, as if he wanted to cherish this moment.

"Thanks for staying," he whispered against my lips.

"Thanks for not killing me," I said jokingly.

"I'm really sorry," he said, and I laughed, realizing it was too early for such a joke.

"When did you get here?" I asked.

"Last night?"

"Wait, what?"

"You were already sleeping, and you looked so tired. You were gone before I left my room this morning."

"My dad called; he wanted to see me."

He looked tense.

"I told him the truth. I can't believe he still thought there was a baby."

"We should make that official," he said.

"What? The baby?" My blood froze.

"I meant, the truth about no baby." He laughed.

"What about your mom?"

He stiffened for a moment before replying. "I will tell her the truth."

Cooking with Tristan was annoying and fun at the same time. He was bossy most of the time, and I almost gave up on learning his Nana's recipe. The food was great, and to be honest, I forgot how it had been made after an hour.

I wanted to ask about his treatment, but a part of me knew he wouldn't tell me. Today had to be the best day I had had since the incident.

The bodyguards were fired. Tristan believed it was over. I wasn't sure if the person was satisfied.

Whoever it was, I hoped he or she was happy now.

LATER THAT NIGHT, we both stayed awake in bed. I snuggled closer to him in the dark. I knew he was still awake. His beard grazed my cheek.

"Are you still having nightmares?" I asked quietly.

"Yeah, but not every day," he whispered.

"Were you badly hurt?" he asked after a while.

I could feel his eyes on me in the darkness.

"No."

"I'm sorry for hurting you. I will say that every day if I have to," he mumbled.

"I'm not holding anything against you," I told him.

"Thank you for staying. I thought I'd lost you." He increased his grip around me.

"I'm here. I won't let go or walk away. You're stuck with me. No refunds," I whispered, and I felt his smile against my cheek.

"Where have you been all my life?" he asked and kissed me before I could think of an answer. I didn't even have one.

I WOKE UP when I heard a noise outside. I untangled myself from Tristan's arms and checked the time. It was past two in the morning. I glanced at Tristan and quietly got down from the bed to avoid waking him up.

I left the room to check if it was Morris. I saw a silhouette from where I stood at the stairs.

"Morris?" I asked, going down with steady steps. I found the switch at the staircase and turned the lights on.

It wasn't Morris. I was sure of that. The tall form and long legs convinced me it was someone else. The person took off before I could take a good look.

"Hey!" I ran down the stairs and followed the figure.

The intruder had a black hoodie on and looked too lean to be Morris. It had to be the monster tormenting Tristan with those memories from his past. I ran faster. Thank God for those laps my PE coach had forced me to finish back in high school.

I was gaining on the form. We ran past the pool to the other side of the yard.

"Stop!"

I increased my speed and knocked the body down with my whole weight. I pulled the hood down, and my eyes couldn't believe who I was staring at.

"*No way*," I mumbled.

CHAPTER **THIRTY**
ENEMIES

"No *way*," I mumbled in utter shock. "Karen?"

"Hi, Chloe," she said with a sinister smile, not bothered about being caught.

"You have been the one all along? Why?"

"I wish I had time for chitchat, but I don't. Sorry I have to do this." She stabbed my neck with a syringe before I could process her last sentence.

I collapsed on the ground like a lifeless being. I was numb all over. I tried to move, but it was impossible. I got frightened as I imagined the worst-case scenario, but I didn't show it. I felt paralyzed from my head down. I could only move my eyes.

"What did you do?" I asked her as she stood up with a malicious grin plastered on her face.

"Don't worry; it will wear off in three hours," she said, squatting beside me.

She stroked my hair like she wanted to put me to sleep.

"You shouldn't have come after me." She pulled my hair, almost ripping it off my scalp. She stood up, glaring at me with evil intent.

"Why are you doing this?"

She cackled at my question. "Isn't it obvious? To make him suffer for what he did to Fiona."

Fiona? Who the hell is Fiona? Tristan had said her name that night we made out and again in his sleep.

"What did he do to her?"

"I don't have time to talk. I need to get back to my real boyfriend before he wakes up and finds me gone. Foolish Adrian thinks I'm in Miami. Fiancé, my ass. I have not seen my boyfriend for a month because of him. I can't wait for this to be over." She sighed and rolled her eyes.

"But first, I need to make sure my secret is safe." She walked away and returned with the net used for cleaning the pool.

What was she going to do with that? I hoped it wasn't what I was thinking. I tried to move, but every part of me felt stiff and heavy.

I still had my voice. *Scream.*

"Somebody, help!" I screamed as loud as my vocal cords could sustain.

"Stupid bitch!" Karen smacked me on the head with the pole. "I never liked you anyway. Your death won't bother me," she said maliciously. Her eyes looked wicked.

"Hel—"

She hit me in the face, shutting me up. I coughed out blood, and I could feel the blood dripping from my nose.

"You think he gives a shit about you? You're so dumb. No one will even notice when you're gone. I'm doing the world a favor."

"Go to hell," I coughed.

"I will meet you there. We might be roomies." She laughed.

She held the metal handle up. She smiled at me before hitting my head. Like that wasn't enough, she hit me harder again until I blacked out completely.

I GROANED AS I tried to open my eyes. My head was hurting like hell. It was like a carnival was going on in there. I allowed my eyes to adjust to the white ceiling. Was this heaven? Was I dead already? I never got to expose Karen, and I never got to tell Tristan I loved him.

I felt movement beside me. I turned my head and saw Tristan sleeping. He was sitting on a wooden seat with his head resting on the bed.

I'm still alive! I can expose Karen!

I smiled and touched his face. Thank God I could move my body and feel things again. I ignored the pounding in my head as I turned to face him. His thick eyelashes fluttered, and then his eyes opened.

"Hey, sleeping beauty," I whispered. I could barely recognize my own voice.

"Chloe?" He stood up, staring at me like I wasn't real. He leaned closer and placed a kiss on my head. "You woke up," he whispered, caressing my cheeks. He kissed every part of my face before kissing my lips. "I'm so sorry." He looked so drained.

I smiled weakly at him, brushing my thumb against his face. *He shaved his beard? Why? I wanted to do it.*

"I'm so sorry, Chloe." He looked like he was about to break down.

The door opened. Adrian walked in, holding Karen's hand. My hand dropped from Tristan's face.

"You!" I glared at her. I hated how weak my voice sounded. "It's her,"

I said hoarsely. I wished my throat didn't feel so dry.

"What?" Tristan asked, looking behind him.

"It was Karen. She did this to me. She has been the one all along."

They all shared a confused look and stared at me like I was crazy.

"It's okay. The doctor said you'll have difficulty recalling what happened."

"I'm fine, Tristan. I swear she was there yesterday."

"Chloe, it's been three weeks."

"What?" I mumbled.

"I would never hurt you, Chloe. You're like a sister to me," Karen said sweetly.

"Shut up!" The pounding in my head increased.

"Hey, calm down," Tristan whispered, holding me down as I tried to sit up.

"You guys have to believe me. I caught her that night. She injected me with something and hit me on the head. I'm not lying!" I screamed, getting frustrated.

The heart monitor began to beep, and the pounding in my head worsened.

"I will get a doctor." Tristan ran out of the room.

"Chloe, relax. You're hurting yourself," Adrian said while Karen smirked wickedly beside him.

I wished he would turn and see the look on her face.

"Don't worry; you're going to be okay," Karen said softly with a smile that seemed to be mocking me.

"You're despicable. You won't get away with this," I said, shaking my head at her in pure disgust. The heart monitor was not helping the pounding in my head. I felt weak, and my heart beat uncontrollably.

"Chloe, breathe. You're going to be fine. It's just a panic attack,"

Adrian said, staring at me and at the heart monitor.

The door burst open. A doctor walked in with a nurse. His round glasses made him look younger. He approached the bed with long strides.

I tried to even my breathing, but I couldn't. The doctor glanced at the heart monitor and extended his hand to the nurse. She gave him the syringe lying on the steel tray. His lips stretched into a thin line as he checked the IV connected to my hand.

I turned my gaze to Tristan. He gave me a soft smile, a smile that hid the deep worry within. The bags in his eyes were visible from here I saw the doctor inject something into the IV.

My body relaxed, and my eyes closed slowly. I allowed the sleep to drown me.

WHEN I WOKE up, no one was in the room. I stared blankly at the ceiling. How could they not believe me? No one ever believed me. It was like a curse.

Tristan had said it'd been three weeks. *Does Vina know? What about my family?*

The door opened. Tristan walked in with a takeout bag. He gave me a warm smile as he walked to the bed.

"You're awake. I brought you something to eat."

"I'm not hungry," I said plainly and looked away.

"Okay, what's wrong?" he said, taking the seat next to the bed.

"What's wrong?" I turned to look at him. "I told you the person behind my attack and the person responsible for the stuff you found in your room, and you thought I was crazy."

"I don't think you're crazy. I have only known Karen for, like, six months. She is not the one, and the doctor said—"

"To hell with what the doctor said! I am fine. I remember everything from that night. She's the one, Tristan. She mentioned Fiona that night. She said she was doing this for her. Remember Fiona? The one you always call when you're having a nightmare," I said in desperate need for him to believe me.

Something flickered in his eyes. He looked away from me and stayed mute for some seconds.

"Tristan?"

"That's impossible, Chloe. Karen wasn't even in town that night. I'm sure it was someone else." He groaned and ran both hands down his face.

"I am not making this up!" I almost screamed. Frustration flowing through my blood cells.

"You have an internal injury in your brain, and the doctors—"

"Why won't you believe me?" I cut in with tears in my eyes.

"Chloe, I'm not calling you a liar. You just got out of a coma. You need to focus on getting better. I'm working on it. I will catch whoever this person is. If I had known this wasn't over, I wouldn't have fired the bodyguards. The security footage from that night was all blank, but don't worry; we'll find the person responsible. I promise."

"It's Karen. You have to believe me," I whimpered.

"I'm sorry you got involved in this. It's my fault. Karen didn't even know until she got back from her trip last week," he said, taking my other hand.

I gave up and said nothing. Karen had had this planned out. She'd lied about her trip. He wouldn't believe me if I told him it was a lie. I tried to hold back my tears. *Why wouldn't anyone believe me?*

"You were almost dead when I found you. I'd thought you were in the bathroom when I didn't find you in bed. I called your name, but you didn't answer, so I stood up and went to check, but it was empty." He paused and released a breath. "I checked your room but didn't find you. I went downstairs and found the back door open. I saw your body floating in the pool when I came out. You were almost dead." Tears glistened in his eyes.

I couldn't believe that witch had dumped my body in the pool.

"Do you know how it felt, watching the doctors trying to revive you, trying to bring you back? I thought I had lost you." A tear escaped from his left eye and rolled down to his chin.

I was in tears too. He leaned closer to my face. He wiped my tears away with his thumbs and kissed my eyelids.

"I'm so sorry, Chloe," he whispered.

I moved my IV-connected hand and wiped the tear that had escaped from his eye.

"We'll catch whoever this monster is, I promise."

It's Karen! I wanted to scream.

"Now, will you eat something?" he asked, sitting back on his seat.

I wished he'd believe his enemy was closer to him than he thought. I had to figure out another way to expose her.

"Yeah." I nodded.

"I was going to force you anyway," he said, emptying the contents of the bag.

Three weeks? I was unconscious for three weeks? Had Karen done anything to him? He looked very tired. Had he been spending the night here with his head on the bed?

"Why are you staring at me like that?" he asked, cocking a brow.

I'd forgotten how good-looking he was with those blue eyes that reminded me of the ocean.

"So, I was almost dead?" I said, avoiding his question.

"You could say that."

"Wow," I mumbled, shaking my head in disbelief.

"Eat up."

"Did my best friend call?"

"Yeah, she was here two days ago. I already informed her you're awake, but she has a test today. She said she'd come in the evening."

How was I going to catch up on three weeks schoolwork? I was better off dropping the class.

"I can't wait." I sighed in relief.

VINA WAS ALREADY in tears when she entered the room. She cried for half an hour before saying a word.

"You smudged your eyeliner," I told her immediately after she stopped crying.

"Seriously? I just emptied my tear sac because of you, and that's all you can say?" She frowned.

I laughed and hugged her with my free arm.

"I love you," I told her with a pout.

"I love you too. I'm glad you're okay."

"How was your test?"

"I don't want to talk about it," she grunted. "Do you remember anything from that night?"

"Yes!" I adjusted myself on the bed, ready to tell her. Vina would believe me.

"Really?" She sounded surprised.

"What? You also think I'm crazy?"

"No, it is just that the doctor said—"

"I remember everything. Why won't anyone believe me?" I cut in.

"I believe you. Fuck the doctor's words. Tell me what you remember," she said with a soft smile.

"It was Karen."

Her jaw slightly dropped. "Adrian Parker's fiancée?"

I nodded. I went on and told her everything that had happened that night.

"*Puta de mierda*! I will have her head on a spike the next time I see her. She'd better prepare her obituary picture. That *perra* tried to kill you. Does she have any idea that I can't live in a world without you?"

"Shave her head while you're at it," I said in anger. It was not like she was going to do it—but knowing Vina, she might.

"Noted. They don't believe you at all? Even your *novio*?"

"No one ever believes me. Well, except you."

"The doctor told us you will have a hard time recalling what happened and you might make up something."

"That's stupid."

"I'm so happy to see you. When the doctor confirmed you were almost dead and he couldn't save you, I almost passed out. It was as if I'd lost my other half. Your boyfriend went crazy and tried to beat up the doctor. He had to keep trying till they got a response. It was chaotic that night. But *gracias a Dios* he did," She sighed in relief. She squeezed my hand softly as she whispered, "We'll expose that wretch. We'll find a way."

"We will," I agreed with a smile.

Tristan's family came to see me the next day. They brought doughnuts and cupcakes. They stayed the whole afternoon. I was so exhausted after they left. Tristan left with them to get some clothes from the house.

I closed my eyes and tried to sleep. I groaned internally when the door opened. I knew it wasn't Tristan 'cause he'd just left. I pretended to be asleep.

"Oh, our little princess is having a nap."

My eyes opened at the voice.

"What do you want?" I asked, glaring at Karen's evil form. I couldn't believe I had once been jealous of her.

She took slow steps toward me. Her black stiletto heels made spooky sounds that reminded me of a horror movie. The sly smile on her red lips widened as she stopped in front of me.

"Lucky you, you got another chance to live."

"I know, right? Your plan failed," I said with a triumphant smile.

"Not really. As long as everyone thinks you're crazy, no one is going to believe you. Stop trying."

"We'll see about that," I said boldly.

She laughed briefly, shaking her head. Her large waves bounced over her shoulders. I wished I'd had my phone with me, but it was in the house. Suddenly, the look on her face changed. Her laughter ceased, and she gave me a dangerous look as she stopped next to the bed.

"If you get in my way"—she gripped my hair, pulling it, and I yelped in pain—"I will destroy you. You won't be alive to see your boyfriend suffer to the point of taking his own life."

"Stop," I groaned. I searched for the emergency button with my hand.

"Nuh-uh. I wouldn't do that if I were you," she snarled, stopping my hand.

She pressed the IV cannula connected to the back of my palm. I was scared it would break inside my skin.

I screamed in pain. It was unbearable. Every cell in my body wanted me to rip off her head, but I had to be smarter. I had to be patient.

"Last warning, Chloe: stay out of my way." She let go of me and pulled away.

"What did he do?" I asked, tears blurring my eyes.

"He killed my best friend. He killed both of them." *Killed both of them? Is she talking about Nadia and Fiona?*

Her tears spoke far louder than her words. "Stop trying to save him. He is not worth it," she said, wiping the tears away and smiling. "You don't know the monster you're living with," she added and left the room.

I arched my back in pain. Tears brimmed my eyes as I stared at the back of my palm. Two nurses rushed in, looking alarmed as they approached me to ask questions. I showed them my hand and said nothing.

I HAD BEEN given a sedative last night, so I could sleep. I didn't say anything about Karen's visit. I tried to act normal in front of Tristan. Karen's words kept replaying in my head. I didn't want to believe anything she'd said about Tristan killing her best friend.

Tristan had left to get breakfast while I waited for the doctor to show up and do his rounds. The back of my palm was swollen from yesterday. They'd had to move the IV to my other hand. The door opened.

My head whipped to the doorway. My breathing ceased.

This is not real. It can't be.

"Dominiano?"

"Surprise."

CHAPTER **THIRTY-ONE**
MEMORIES

My throat went dry, and my heart raced as I stared at my worst nightmare. I was frozen for a moment. I noticed his blue scrubs. *He works here? Dominiano is a doctor?*

He smiled broadly as he walked in. The stethoscope around his neck didn't go with the tattoos covering his skin.

How on earth did he become a doctor?

He looked taller and broader. His face was still the same. He still wore big rings on his fingers. His raven hair was long and curly. He reminded me of a young Avan Jogia, Vina's childhood crush.

"Great meeting you here, Chloe." His accent had not changed.

He stopped next to the bed. I searched skillfully for the emergency button with my hand.

Memories of that night flashed in front of me. My heart was beating so fast, telling to get away. This was the right time for Tristan to return.

"Hi." That was all my voice could manage.

"How are you feeling?" he asked, reading the heart monitor. He looked like he knew what he was doing. He turned to look at me when I didn't answer.

"Fine," I replied as he chuckled softly, the sound sending chills through me.

"I get it. You are in shock. Strange for us to meet like this, huh?"

I nodded.

"I know, right? Who would have thought someone like me would want to be a nurse?"

Nurse?

"You ... you work here?"

For a moment, I thought he had come for me. He had threatened to kill me and my entire family if I told anyone his secret. How did he know I'd told Tristan about him?

"Yeah. When I found out you were here, I wanted to see you."

That scared me. Why?

He went on, checking my vitals while I kept my hand on the emergency button in case anything happened. He asked me a few questions about my health, and I replied, trying to stay calm. I always knew he was smart, but I never in a million years would have thought of him becoming a health care worker.

He finished scribbling something down and took the seat beside the bed. He sat back and crossed his legs. I cocked my eyebrows at him, wondering why he was still here.

"I'm glad I found you again. This is my chance to take good care of you after what I did to you."

I was surprised to hear that. "Why?"

"After my dad passed away, a lot changed. I couldn't continue his business. He left me millions, and I didn't know what to do with it." He laughed.

Dirty money.

"I met someone. We just got married, and she is pregnant with triplets."

His face seemed to shine behind his smile.

"Rose was an angel sent to me. She helped me after I lost my dad. She made me see the world differently and inspired me to save lives."

I saw his wedding ring. He wasn't lying, but I still had my doubts, so I kept my hand on the emergency button.

"I am not the same person, Chloe, and I'm very sorry for hurting you. I wish I could go back in time and change things."

"It's fine. I don't even remember it." I waved it off with a laugh.

I wished he would just leave; his presence terrified me and made me uneasy.

"What about the scar?"

"I just tell myself I once had wings."

He nodded with his lips dipped down in sadness. I could see the guilt written on his face. He looked like he had so much to say to me but didn't know where to begin.

"So, you and Tristan Sanchester. How did you get involved in such a scandal? And the baby?"

"It's a long story."

"Okay, maybe you will tell me another time." He stood up.

Another time? You wish. I hope I never see you again.

"If you need anything, let me know and stay out of trouble. It seems that part of you is still there."

I faked a toothy grin.

"Take care, Chloe. I will see you before I leave."

Please, no.

"See you later, Chloe."

He waved, and I reciprocated.

The door opened when he turned to leave. Tristan smiled at me before looking at Dominiano.

"Hi," he said, bringing his hand up for a handshake. Dominiano accepted. "I hope she's better."

"Yeah. Take good care of my Chloe," he said and looked over his shoulder at me.

Tristan looked a bit confused at his request, but he nodded. Dominiano left as Tristan walked in with two bags in one hand.

"What did I miss?" he asked.

"You won't believe what I'm about to tell you."

"Try me," he said, folding his arms.

"That was Dominiano, and he works here. Can you believe that?"

"Dominiano? Your ex?" His smile vanished and he appeared enraged as his facial muscles clenched.

"Yeah, but—"

He was already running out of the room before I could explain.

"Tristan, wait."

He didn't look back.

"Oh God," I groaned.

I LOOKED AROUND at my new hospital room. I couldn't believe Tristan had attacked Dominiano and moved me to another hospital. I glared at him. He smiled at me and switched on the TV.

"You shouldn't have done that."

He ignored me.

"He is married and will soon become a father. He said he is not the same person."

"I don't care," he sighed. "He's lucky I didn't draw a *C* on his face with a scalpel," he added before stepping out of the room.

I sighed and watched *The Wendy Williams Show* on the TV. The door opened. Adrian and Karen walked in, holding hands.

"Hey, how are you doing?" Adrian asked with a small smile.

"Still breathing," I said to Karen instead.

"Good to know," she said.

"How do you think Adrian will feel after the truth comes out?" I questioned calmly. I saw her jaw clench.

"I know she is unwell, but I can't keep coming here if she only sees me as the person responsible for what happened to her," she said, faking a cry.

Adrian sent a pissed look my way as his expression hardened.

"It's okay. You can go home. I will meet you later," he whispered to her.

"Okay." She kissed his lips and turned to look at me. "Take care, Chloe." The look on her face said the opposite.

Adrian moved closer to the bed after she left. "I know it's not your fault, but you are hurting Karen for no reason."

"No reason? She doesn't care about you. She doesn't even love you, Adrian. She has a boyfriend. She is only using you to—"

"That's enough!" he snapped. "You've taken this too far. I know you're unwell, but this is getting on my nerves. Stop it already. You don't get to be jealous, Chloe."

"What?" I cut in immediately and laughed. "Jealous? I. Am. Over. You. Adrian. Parker," I said each word in rage.

"Then, leave her alone," he said and left the room.

Karen was a great actress. She had him wrapped around her fingers.

She was good—poor Adrian. I exhaled and tried to keep my mind calm. So much was going on in my head.

Tristan returned, not looking upset anymore.

"I brought you your favorite," he said, showing me the bag of Cheetos.

I rolled my eyes and ignored him.

"I'm sorry. I wasn't comfortable with you staying there after everything he did to you."

"Whatever," I murmured and closed my eyes.

"Okay, that was not the answer I was expecting. Are you okay?"

"Yes."

"Wanna go for a walk? The doctor said you should walk around for a bit."

"I'm tired."

"Come on, Chloe."

"I don't feel like taking a walk right now," I snapped.

"Okay. Everything all right? You can talk to me," he whispered, taking my hand.

I didn't answer. I stayed quiet, and soon, the tears were falling. I wasn't sure of the reason I was crying, but the tears kept coming. Tristan sat beside me and put his arms around me. No words, just his embrace was enough.

WE WENT FOR a walk the next day. My legs wobbled as I felt a noose around my stomach, but soon, I got used to the feeling.

I stared at the other patients in the building as we walked outside. Tristan held my hand, drawing circles on the back of my palm. It was warm outside today. The warm breeze felt nice on my face. I smiled at the sun and held on to Tristan's arm.

"I bought us a penthouse. We can stay there until all this is over and the person is behind bars."

"Does anyone know about it?" I asked.

"My family and Adrian."

"Then, I guess Karen already knows."

"Chloe, please," he groaned, and I rolled my eyes.

"You shouldn't have told anyone. You can't trust anyone right now, not even Adrian or your family." My voice almost escaped me as I uttered the final word.

"We both need a place to hide, just you and me," he said, interlocking our fingers.

"Then, book a suite in a fancy hotel. No one has to know, just the two of us."

"Just the two of us?" He beamed, the corners of his eyes crinkling.

"Yeah, no one else should know we're staying there," I said, looking him in the eye.

"Okay," he agreed.

I sighed in relief while he smirked.

We succeeded in booking a nice suite in a hotel downtown. I'd gotten discharged yesterday, and we had everything planned. Tristan gave Morris a month off, and we left immediately after Morris was gone.

The suite was big. It had a spacious living room and a large bedroom that had the best view of the city with a small balcony. No one knew we were here. We'd told everyone we were going on vacation.

The doctor had given me some pills and informed me I'd be having migraines in the future due to the damage Karen had caused.

"This feels so good," I moaned, rubbing my back on the black leather couch.

"You know what else feels so good?" Tristan asked huskily. He drew closer to my body, running his hand up my thigh under my dress. "You." He approached my lips and placed kisses down my jaw to my neck while my chest shook in laughter.

He reached for the silk belt holding the dress together and loosened it. I closed my eyes and arched my back as his hands explored my body. I ran my fingers through his hair, stifling a moan as he kissed my thighs and threw my legs over his shoulders.

"We haven't unpacked. You know that, right?" I rasped as his lips drew closer to my core.

"We can do it tomorrow, or I can stop," he said, pulling away.

"No!" I protested.

He laughed and met my lips in a slow kiss.

A little break never hurt nobody. I might as well enjoy this.

We stayed two weeks in the suite with no cell phones to communicate with anyone.

It was spectacular. We got to know more about each other. We played silly games. He taught me how to cook, I forced him to watch chick flicks with me, and we made love every night.

I didn't want it to end. We were away from Karen, from gossip, and there wasn't much to worry about here.

We were sitting on the floor in the bedroom after making love. I had his black T-shirt on while he wore only his boxer briefs. We sat in silence, our eyes gazing at the city's surreal view from the glass wall. I'd always been so distracted that I never realized what it truly looked like until now.

I took a sip of my drink and placed my head on his shoulder. The TV played a soft song I could not recognize, but I found myself vibing with it.

"Fiona was my fiancée."

I was surprised when he suddenly spoke.

"We dated for almost ten years, and we were planning on getting married. I had known her since I was ten, and she was my first everything." He paused and took a sip of his drink.

"We loved each other so much. Our connection was intense. She was my best friend and so much more. We knew every detail about each other. She understood me like no one else, as if our minds were linked together. I just knew I wanted to spend the rest of my life with her. We got engaged when I was twenty-one. It was a drunk joke at first, but when we got sober, we made it official." He paused and laughed briefly.

"We wanted to take things slow. We stayed engaged and lived together. It felt like we were already a married couple, and we didn't care how long it'd take to get married. She got pregnant a year later. We wanted to call her Nadia. I had everything set in the nursery and couldn't wait to welcome her. Nadia was the most beautiful baby girl ever." His tone lost strength.

I'd never known he held so much pain.

He was quiet for a minute. To me, it felt more than just that. My brain wanted to know so bad, yet my heart was preparing for the setback.

"We were so happy. Everything was perfect, and our little girl was like a glue to our relationship, but I ruined everything. It was all my fault." His hand clenched.

I entwined our hands to provide some comfort.

"I was such an idiot." I could hear the pain in his voice.

"She was only three months old when it happened. I ... I was home alone with her while Fiona was out, shopping. I was coming down the stairs with her in my arms. I ... I ... I missed a step ... and everything happened so quick. I just remember holding her tight against my chest, trying to protect her from the fall as we crashed down the flight of stairs." He paused and broke down.

I drew closer and put my arms around him.

"It's okay," I whispered. My voice wrapped around him like a veil, and his shivering seemed to stop.

"I had hit my head and blacked out. I didn't know how long, but when I woke up ..." Tears streamed down his quivering face.

"She was beneath me in a pool of blood. She wasn't moving. No sound, and she wasn't breathing. She was bleeding from her nose, ear, and her head. I had done that to my daughter. I killed her, Chloe. There's no one else to blame."

"Tristan, it's not your fault. It was an accident."

He shook his head at my words, blaming himself for what had happened.

"Fiona crumbled. Nadia's death destroyed us, but it hit her harder. She stopped talking to me. We became strangers in our home, and three weeks later, I found her body in the bathtub." He sniffled and ran his palm down his face.

"She was so young. She wanted to travel around the world, but she never got the chance to. The baby didn't even grow to..." He gulped, choking on his tears.

"Fiona is dead, Chloe. I would've avoided her death. I should have been careful. I should have paid attention to Fiona and not given her some space," he sobbed.

"Shh, it's okay," I whispered, stroking his hair.

I moved closer and pulled him into my arms. He cried like a baby, heavy sobs and tears, blaming himself over and over for their deaths.

"It's okay," I whispered, kissing his head.

"That's why I don't celebrate my birthday. It was the day I found Fiona's body in the bathtub," he told me.

I couldn't bring myself to imagine what he had gone through, losing the love of his life and his daughter. The guilt was still in him.

"It was hard to heal from the pain. Knowing I was responsible for what happened to them, I couldn't live with myself. The image of my baby girl bleeding beneath me and my lovely Fiona, lifeless in the bathtub, drove me crazy. I couldn't escape it. That was how it all started—the nightmares, anger, depression, suicidal thoughts, and guilt. I wanted to end it all. I hated myself for everything that I did. I keep thinking of how Nadia would have been—her first steps, first words, and the woman she would have grown up to be. Fiona would have been ..." He choked on his tears, unable to finish his sentence.

He squeezed into me as the sound of his crying increased.

"Maybe I deserve worse," he cried.

"You'll be okay," I whispered, still stroking his hair.

So much pain for one person.

CHAPTER **THIRTY-TWO**
EXPOSED

We returned home after spending two weeks at the suite. Morris still had some time off, so we had the house to ourselves. The little time we had been away from psycho Karen was the best. It was like the whole world had disappeared for those two weeks, and it had just been us, getting lost in our feelings and learning new stuff about each other.

We had only been back for three hours, and I was already worried about Karen. Tristan had texted Adrian, informing him we were back from our mini vacation. I should have taken some time to plot a move against Karen. The only ones who would be greatly affected when the truth was out would be Adrian and Tristan.

I promised to make dinner tonight. Well, it was a dare from Tristan to see if his *hard work* had paid off.

We went for a swim first. Goose bumps appeared on my skin as I entered the pool. The cool splash splintered my body like bullets. I missed the night we'd spent at the suite, talking in the bathtub while Tristan washed my hair. It had been warm and safe. Now, everything felt cold and unsafe.

We swam for a while and played around in the water before we decided to move to the Jacuzzi beside the pool for some warmth.

The heat from the Jacuzzi made me groan in content. We relaxed inside, drinking champagne and sharing stupid jokes we found funny.

"Okay, I got one." I raised a finger after laughing at his joke.

"Hit me." He smirked.

"So, there was this lady who was cheating on her husband every time he went to work. Here is what the husband did when he started noticing it."

"What?"

"He would call her every day and ask her to turn on the blender to know if she was home."

"What?" He laughed briefly.

"Stupid, right? Well, he decided to call their son one day, and he asked the boy, 'Where is your mom?' And he was like, 'She left the house with the blender.' "

We both laughed out loud.

We stayed in the Jacuzzi for too long. Our fingers had begun to resemble prunes, and the heat was beginning to wear us out. The sun was starting to disappear below the earth's horizon, leaving the sky with an array of oranges, pinks, and reds that scattered above us like a watercolor painting.

I crawled toward Tristan and climbed on him, straddling his thighs. He released a throaty groan as I moved my hips in circles. He wasted no time, pulling my bikini bottom aside and thrusting into me. My hips met every thrust with urgency as I held his soft gaze. He brushed his fingers against my hard nipples and nibbled on my neck. His other hand fisted in my hair.

Our bodies shook as we cried out in pleasure. His lips found mine, and I responded to his kiss. I smiled against his lips and withdrew from his face. My arms wrapped around his shoulders as I stared at the beautiful sky.

"You're the best thing that's ever happened to me, Chloe Simpson," he whispered, tucking my wet hair behind my ear.

"Well, you're the opposite," I said and pressed a kiss to the tip of his nose.

"Ouch, Chloe." He winced, touching his chest, as if I'd just stabbed his heart with a dagger.

I laughed lightheartedly, and he smiled.

"Can I ask you something?" I said, holding his gaze.

"Sure," he replied, resting one hand on my hip.

"Did you hate me the first few weeks I was here? I didn't get why you were always so mad at me."

He sighed softly and stared at a spot on my throat. He was quiet for a few seconds before he met my eyes.

"I never hated you, Chloe. I was mad at myself, not you. I took everything away from you, and I couldn't give it back to you, so I tried to stay away from you till I came up with a plan to fix the damage I had done, but you were everywhere. It was impossible to avoid you—to not notice the way you glared at me from across the table, how your eyes shone and your eyebrows elevated after you liked the taste of your wine, or how you would sing karaoke in your room while I was trying to sleep."

My cheeks reddened in embarrassment, and I stifled a laugh. I hadn't known he could hear me singing under my blanket while doing karaoke from my laptop.

"You annoyed the shit out of me. You were everything I hadn't expected, and I only wanted to scare you away because you were starting to terrify me."

"Really? You were scared of me?"

He traced my jawline. "Yes."

"Was it because I ran after you with a knife?"

"No." He laughed. "It was because I couldn't stop paying attention to everything about you."

I smiled and leaned down to kiss him softly on the lips.

"Neither could I," I whispered against his lips.

TRISTAN SAT AT the island, watching me with an amused grin as I tried to make sushi.

"Call me if you need help," he said as I struggled to mold the rice into the correct shape but kept failing miserably.

"I got this. You should be rooting for me," I told him as he tried to suppress his laughter.

"You are doing great." He clapped. "Is that what you want to hear?" he said and looked back at the laptop in front of him.

I glared at him and concentrated on the sushi in my hand.

A crash in the living room stole our attention. I abruptly dropped the rice to the floor and turned to see if Tristan had been hurt. Tristan was fine, but he, too, stared curiously behind him.

I assumed Karen had come to pay a visit. How generous. I hoped she'd brought a first aid kit.

"What was that?" I asked, dropping the spatula in my hand and replacing it with a frying pan.

"Wait here." He gave me that *don't you dare go against me* look.

I rolled my eyes and trailed behind him with the frying pan in my hand. One of the expensive ceramic vases in the living room was shattered on the floor.

"She is here," I whispered behind him.

His head snapped back like he hadn't noticed I was following him.

"I told you to stay in the kitchen," he said.

"She won't get away tonight." My jaw clenched with determination. I tried to walk past him, but he gripped my arm and pulled me back.

"Chloe," he groaned.

"Like I will listen to you. We might as well do this together. Use your muscles. I got this to hit her big head." I raised my weapon to demonstrate.

He chuckled and shook his head at me. "How are you sure it's Karen? Maybe the vase just fell on its own."

"Yeah, or a ghost is in the house, huh?" I said sarcastically.

"No one is here. Go back to the kitchen while I clean this up."

"Really, Tristan? You're just going to let her go?"

"There is no—"

A noise from behind us cut him off.

We both looked back and saw a figure running through the back door.

"Told ya." I winked at him and went after her.

"Hey!" Tristan yelled after me.

"Just call the cops!" I screamed over my shoulder at him.

She didn't waste any time, coming for a visit. She'd probably gotten tired of waiting.

"This is going to be fun." I sped up.

Her hood fell off her head, revealing her long hair that kept lashing at her neck as she ran.

There was no way I was letting her go. I increased my grip on the frying pan as I got closer. I raised the frying pan as I got very close to grabbing her hair. I swung it, hitting her hard on the head. She fell with a *thump* on the grass.

"Man, that felt good!" I said, staring at her unconscious form.

"The cops are on the way. Did you get the person?" Tristan asked, running to where I was. He scrutinized my body, searching for any hint of injury.

"Have a look."

He moved closer, and the expression on his face was priceless. I couldn't wait to see Adrian's face.

"Karen?" He squatted next to her body.

He stared at her face for a few seconds before standing up. He turned to look at me. His lips were slightly parted, like he didn't know what to say. He ran his palms down his face and wrapped his arms around me tightly.

"I'm so sorry for not believing you. I'm really sorry," he said, running his hand up and down my back in a soothing way. "I feel so awful right now. I'm sorry, Chloe."

"I will only accept your apology if you promise to give me a foot massage every day." I withdrew and smiled at him.

"I promise."

"And teach me Nana's recipe."

"I already taught you that yesterday, and it was the fifth time," he groaned.

Playfully, I shrugged and stuck my tongue out at him.

"Fine," he said, wrapping his arms around my waist.

"Thank you," I whispered.

He turned to look at Karen again. He stared at her like he was trying to remember something.

"Do you know her from somewhere?"

"No, Adrian introduced her to me. I had never met her before that."

"Well, she knows Fiona. Maybe she is related to her. She told me she was here to make you pay for whatever happened."

There was a darkness in his eyes that made him look like a frightened kid, but he hid it with a smile. I hated seeing him like this.

"She's not related to her," he said, still staring at her. His tone was different. "Let's take her inside. It's getting cold outside," he said quickly and tried to carry her, but I stopped him.

"I will do it." I grabbed her leg and dragged her body with me to the house.

Tristan texted Adrian and his mom as we waited for the cops. I sat on one of the sofas and kept my eyes on her. I hated that I was right. For some reason, Tristan looked bothered by her presence. I couldn't wait for the cops to come and take her away. Hopefully, things would get better.

I stood up when she started moving. She groaned, sitting up on the floor. She rubbed the back of her head, wincing at the pain.

I raised the frying pan to hit her again, but Tristan stopped me.

"Relax. The cops will take care of her."

I dropped the frying pan and glared at her. She smiled smugly and made herself comfortable on the floor.

"What do you feel like? A hero?" Her voice rattled with rage.

I reached forward and punched her across the face. My fist made contact with a satisfying crack. I pulled my hand away and shook it out.

"Now, I do." I grimaced when my knuckles began to hurt.

Karen raised her hand to her nose. When she pulled her hand away from her nose, fresh blood poured.

"Chloe." Tristan grabbed my wrist.

He pulled me away from her. It was a good thing he had; otherwise,

I would be tempted to punch her again.

"Is that all you got?" she said, laughing.

I yanked my wrist out of Tristan's grasp. I reached out and grabbed a fistful of her ebony hair. I pulled it harder than she had mine, ripping some out in the process.

"Chloe, stop." Tristan put his hands around my waist and pulled me away from her.

I glared at her, held back by Tristan's arms.

"Now, you know how that feels," I spat the words at her with a satisfied smirk. Damn, revenge was really sweet.

Adrian burst through the front door. He looked worried. He slowed down when he saw Karen. His eyes widened at the sight of his fiancée sitting on the ground, looking like she had just been dumpster diving.

"Karen?"

"Hi," she said dryly and rolled her eyes. She tried to wipe the blood oozing out of her left nostril.

"Aren't you supposed to be in Texas to see your brother?" He frowned, looking from Karen to Tristan and back again.

My heart dropped for him. He had no idea.

"Grow up. All those things were lies. I don't have a brother." Karen rolled her eyes at the bewildered expression that formed on Adrian's face.

"So, Chloe was right?" He slowly approached her. "Do you even feel anything for me?" he asked. His heart shattered to oblivion.

I could see the sorrow swirling in his enigmatic eyes. Even his posture had drooped down.

She removed the engagement ring and threw it at him. "Oh, before I forget, I sold the real one and got that fake one to replace it." She smiled.

"You …" He clenched his fists, not knowing what to say.

I immediately felt sorry for him. The woman he'd thought loved him never did. I watched him sadly as he tried to make sense of this situation.

"Yes, Adrian, I was using you to get close to Tristan, so I could carry out my plans."

"Wow, and you were just going to get married to me?" he yelled, but she just rolled her eyes, like he was acting childish.

The police sirens filled our ears with hope. Mrs. Sanchester arrived with Nana. Three officers walked in with their guns pulled out.

"I don't care about going to jail, Tristan. At least Fiona would be happy you got to relive those memories."

Tristan clenched his hands. His jaw hardened as he stared at her.

"Don't listen to her," I whispered.

"You killed her, Tristan. You killed her and the baby!"

"Shut up!" Tristan growled.

"What? Did you lie about it to her?" she asked, looking at me.

"He didn't lie," I defended him and shot her a glare.

"How would you know? He has done nothing but lie to you since you got here."

I tried to block out her voice as a flicker of doubt entered my mind.

"Officers, take her away!" Tristan said.

"I know everything, Tristan. I know why you brought her here."

That got my attention.

"Take her away!" Tristan yelled.

"You're never going to be anything but a murderer!" she screamed as one of the officers pulled her up. "Fiona would be here if it wasn't for you!" she said, crying. The tears had come so suddenly. Not there one moment and then there the next.

"I know," Tristan mumbled in a pained voice.

She pulled away from the cop holding her and moved closer to him. She leaned into his face and glared into his eyes. The tears ran down her cheeks, making her look miserable.

"I called you that day, three fucking hours before she took her life. Why didn't you answer?! I knew something was wrong. She left a weird message, and I called you multiple times, so you could keep an eye on her, but you never answered."

"I'm sorry," he mumbled.

"It's too late! She's dead, and you're the one who killed her!" She turned to me, laughing out loud humorlessly. "Aww, poor Chloe. Did he tell you why he did all that in the church?"

"Yeah, he did it for his mom."

She scoffed at my answer. "Lies, lies, lies," she said and laughed. "When are you all going to tell this little girl the truth?" she asked and stared at Mrs. Sanchester.

"Get her out of here," Tristan said to the cops.

"What are you guys not telling me? You told me your mom has cancer, and she doesn't have much time to live."

"Really? Cancer?" Karen laughed.

Everyone in the room stared at her.

"Why should I believe a psychopath like you? You tried to kill me," I said, crossing my arms.

"You got in the way. Sorry, not sorry. Besides, you think I would waste my time, making that up?"

"Do you really believe you were seeing him for the first time at the wedding? According to my research and also Adrian's help"—she gave Adrian a smile—"you ran into each other at a restaurant. You stepped on him, and instead of apologizing, you asked him to apologize for standing in your way. He refused, and you were adamant about it. Adrian had to come between you two and apologize on his behalf."

I did recall that day. It was two years ago, and I'd totally forgotten about it. Tristan had no stubble back then from what I remembered, and Adrian had long hair. That was why he'd looked so familiar that day at the wedding. I'd convinced myself that I had seen him in a magazine.

"Please tell me you didn't lie?" I turned to look at him.

"I'm sorry." His eyes avoided me. Tristan's face filled with regret

"Why am I here?!" I screamed, my emotions getting the best of me. *Why did he lie to me? Do I mean nothing to him?* My heart began to race as pain pierced beating organ—at least, what was left of it. My thoughts clogged my brain, trying to find an explanation.

"Maybe you should ask his mom. She knows."

I took a deep breath, trying to soothe my nerves. When I felt calmer, I turned to her. "Mrs. Sanchester?"

Tristan's mom studied her hands to avoid the question.

"Even the old hag too." Karen laughed.

"You all knew?" I turned to each of them.

It was becoming harder to keep myself under in check. I needed to break something. I angrily brushed my hand through my hair.

"You made me put so much effort into proving to you that I was pregnant!"

"I'm so sorry," Mrs. Sanchester cried.

I laughed humorlessly. *Do they think this is a joke? Who am I supposed to believe?*

"Oh, and that whole hospital thing with his mom was an act, so you could return to Tristan after you left. I can't believe you fell for it." Karen only added fuel to the overflowing fire, and she knew it. Her amused and proud look made me want to slap her across the face.

I didn't know what to say. Different emotions ran through my body. I began to shake, losing control of the way this was affecting me.

"Everything was a lie?" I turned to Tristan. I couldn't hold the tears back anymore. "Why am I here? Tell me!"

"Interesting question. You see, after he killed my best friend and her precious baby, he began to suffer the consequences, but then he tried to move on—or should I say, his family thought that would help him?" She laughed, pausing when no one found what she'd said funny.

"Well, at first, they thought Sofia was a good choice for him to start over, but I guess you have already met the spoiled brat. So, by the time they got to the church, he knew it was a bad idea and couldn't carry on with it. From what Adrian told me, he recognized you and picked you from the crowd because ever since that day he'd met you, he never forgot you. You reminded him of a part of himself that—"

"Stop," Tristan warned her.

"You made him see the world differently that day, Chloe. I guess it became more than that, and I had to step in since he wanted to move on as if nothing had ever happened with Fiona. You became the perfect candidate for his family," Karen said.

"Perfect candidate?" I mumbled.

"Yeah. His family wanted to let you go at first, but your presence in the house started changing him. You made him happy again. They thought having you here would serve as a distraction for his internal turmoil and demons. You are just a diversion from the pain, someone to suck away the nightmares. Too bad I could not watch him smile or laugh. I wanted him to keep suffering. I didn't want him to move on. I wanted him to remember how he had taken them away." Every bit of her voice dripped with venom.

I turned to look at Tristan. I tried to find my voice as I opened my mouth to speak.

"You destroyed my life for nothing? You all did!" I screamed at them, completely vexed.

"Wow, I was brought here as a distraction?" I said and laughed at myself.

I laughed at how stupid I had been to believe him. How stupid I had been to fall for him. It had all just been one big game to them. I was nothing but a distraction. The memory of Tristan calling me a distraction when I was in the car sank in. He had really meant it. The damn bastard had fooled me. They all had.

"A distraction," I whispered to myself and laughed again.

One more to add to my list of crazy exes, I guessed. At least, Dominiano had been straight about what he would do to me, but Tristan … he was truly a snake, sucking me dry every time I felt refreshed.

CHAPTER **THIRTY-THREE**
NUMB

"Wow, I was brought here as a distraction?" I said and laughed, moving closer to Tristan.

I ignored his intimidating height and looked him in the eye. I saw the pain in his eyes as he met my gaze, but it didn't change the pure hatred surging through me.

"I wanted to tell you. I was scared you would leave," he said and tried to avoid my eyes.

"You wanted to tell me? That I was distraction? When, Tristan? When?!"

I pushed at his chest, harder with each subsequent question. He didn't budge. I pulled away and broke down. I had never felt so worthless and heartbroken in my life. The feeling was worse than being disowned by my family. I had given my heart to him, and all he had done was spit it into the sewers.

Had he thought of Fiona when he was inside me? I wanted to throw up.

"Why?" I sobbed, grabbing my hair in my fists.

I felt like I was going crazy. Nothing was making sense. I felt used. I felt like an idiot.

My cry filled the house. I didn't care if they were all watching me. My life meant nothing to them. They probably saw me as an experiment to help Tristan.

"Chloe …"

I raised a finger, stopping him. I didn't want to hear more of his lies. All he'd ever done was lie to me. Did he even love me? Or was that another lie to keep me here?

"I hate you! I hate all of you!" Tears rolled down my cheeks.

"That was the reason you never asked about the baby, even when I was not showing," I said, looking at Mrs. Sanchester and Nana.

They were good actresses, pretending to be worried about my health and that of the baby's.

"Seems like my job here is done. Let's see how you overcome losing another important person in your life, Tristan," Karen said with a satisfied grin. She didn't struggle with the cops anymore. She glanced at Adrian and winked at him.

There was a long silence in the room after the sound of the sirens faded into the night.

"I wanna hear you say it. Did you ever see me as a distraction?"

"I only—"

"Yes, or no?" I cut in.

"Chloe, I—"

"Answer the damn question!" I snapped.

"Yes, but it—"

"I don't wanna hear anything else." I sniffled.

"I never wanted this. I didn't want you to leave. That was why I lied.

I know what we did was very selfish," Tristan said with a pained tone.

"But you chose me, Tristan. You picked me yourself! You made my life hell!" I screamed at his face. "My family, my boyfriend, my friends—you took everything away! Does my life mean anything to you at all?"

I turned to look at Nana. "Even you, Nana?"

She kept her face down. I'd admired her so much. They'd all known about this. They'd planned this.

"You guys never cared. His life was far more important to you. You didn't care about how your lies were going to affect my life. It was all for him. You all disgust me. I can't even look at you without seeing you all as monsters."

"We are so sorry. We didn't know how to tell you." Mrs. Sanchester said, stepping forward but I moved back.

"We are really sorry, Chloe." Nana's voice irked me. She could even kill someone yet remain this sweet.

"Sorry is not going to change anything! It won't change what people think about me. It won't heal anything. I lost everything because of his lies, and it was all for this—a distraction?" I sobbed, almost choking on my tears. My head was starting to hurt. I didn't know which to pay attention to—my head pounding or my heart aching.

I turned to look at Tristan. After everything I had gone through for him, I had forgiven him. I cared so much about him. I loved him, even after seeing the kind of person he was, but what was it to him? A distraction.

He ran both hands through his hair with a groan. He kept his eyes tightly shut. He opened them and stared at my wet face and puffy eyes.

"I didn't want you to find out this way. I wanted to explain everything to you myself. I know I—"

My hand connected with his cheek, shutting him up. I regretted believing him.

"Hit me all you want. I deserve worse. You're not a distraction to me anymore!"

I wondered at what point he'd stopped seeing me as a distraction.

"You're not worth loving and not worth any happiness, Tristan Sanchester. I hope you are well now 'cause I'm done." I gave each of them a dirty look and headed for the front door.

"Chloe, please wait." Tristan grabbed my forearm from behind, stopping me.

"Don't touch me!" I pulled my hand away. "Find another distraction. I'm done, and I hope I never see your face or that of your family again. Don't even think of coming after me. I can be a psycho too, you know. Stay. Away. From. Me, all of you!" I shot him a glare and walked out of the house. The house that held so many memories, both good and bad.

I'd lost everything to him, just to be his distraction. He had been using me all along. I shook my head as I walked out of the gates.

It was cold outside. My flimsy silk nightgown and flip-flops didn't help, but I supposed it was a true wake-up call at how cold the world was. I walked down the sidewalk with my arms around myself, not sure of where I was going. No one was outside here. I heard Tristan had bought this part of the town to avoid clingy neighbors and to keep to himself.

I shook his name out of my head and continued my walk. I didn't know where to go. Should I return to my family? On second thought, I didn't want to be near my family. They had thrown me out when I needed them. I hadn't heard from my dad since the day we'd hung out.

I sneezed as the cold entered my body. The cool breeze scattered my hair. I was too busy comforting myself with my hands to arrange it.

I wished someone would drive by and give me a ride. I didn't care if it was a serial killer or a kidnapper. I wanted to be far away from this part of the town, away from these heartless people who called themselves humans.

Tears welled up in my eyes as I remembered what had just happened. I found myself in crying again. I was glad no one was outside here to hear me cry my heart out. I kept walking with wet and puffy eyes that made my vision blurry.

I got tired and stopped. My limbs felt numb from the cold. I slumped on the ground in heavy sobs. I had never experienced any pain like this. It wasn't physical. It was the type of pain that ripped me into pieces inside. The type that burned every cell in my body until I wanted to end it. My body and feelings were a canvas for men to scribble on with delight but actually ruin.

I didn't have a family. I couldn't return to school because everyone kept staring at me with disgust like I was trash. Maybe I was trash. All my exes had treated me like garbage.

Lies! Lies over and over!

"Ahhhh!" I screamed at the dark sky.

Was God seeing this? I'd heard he didn't leave the wicked unpunished.

I felt someone sit beside me on the ground. I ignored the familiar scent and kept screaming at the sky.

Adrian sighed heavily next to me. He must be heartbroken after seeing the real Karen.

How does it feel to be used, huh? Not good, right? I wanted to say that to him, but I decided to ignore him.

I looked up at the sky and screamed again, as if some kind of miracle would suddenly happen or that I'd at least feel better but it only made my throat dry.

I stopped and coughed from the tears.

"I'm sorry," he apologized after a long silence. "For not believing you and not telling you the truth about why he kept you around. I didn't know Tristan had lied. I'm so sorry."

I didn't say anything. He had known it was going to happen, but I still didn't find him at fault. He had been a sweet person until Karen showed up. We had gone from friends to strangers.

"I know my apologies are useless right now. I don't know the right words to say to you …"

"Just stop talking," I grunted, and he nodded slowly.

There was a sudden craving for alcohol. I pinched my arms to control myself, but it was fruitless.

I couldn't go to a bar like this, nor did I have any cash. My craving became stronger. This was the right time for some alcohol. I had gone months without it with Tristan's help, but now, I needed it.

"Can you take me to your place?"

He probably had some alcohol in his house.

"Sure. Wait here. I will get my car."

I nodded as he stood up.

"Adrian."

He stopped and turned to look at me.

"Don't tell anyone I'm going to your place. Pretend you never saw me."

"Okay." He smiled.

It didn't take long for his white Range Rover to arrive with him behind the wheel. I stood up and rushed to the other side, desperate to get away from the cold.

Seeing the way I was rubbing my arms for warmth, he reached behind the seat and grabbed a big jacket, giving it to me. I wrapped it around myself, resting my head on the window as the car moved. The whole ride was silent, and I was glad for that. His house was just a fifteen-minute drive from where he'd picked me up.

I held the large jacket around me as we walked to the front door. His house was like a breath of fresh air and very inviting. It had a plain structure but looked expensive. The interior gave a minimalist style, spacious but had simple furnishing. It looked like an aesthetic with the monochrome color blending so beautifully with the house.

I went to the fancy bar at the corner and grabbed a bottle of brandy and a brandy glass. Adrian watched me as I downed the liquid, which burned my throat. I was waiting for him to start defending Tristan, like he always did, but he picked another brandy glass and joined me.

We sat in silence, just drinking the brandy.

I decided to say something. "Sorry about Karen."

I saw his jaw clench.

"It still feels like a dream to me," he said, laughing. "She has to be the best actress I have ever seen." Sadness filled his voice. He took a long sip.

"Oh God, I'm so sorry. I shouldn't be talking about that. You're going through a lot already," Adrian apologized quickly.

"It's fine."

I poured more brandy into my glass. I wouldn't mind drowning in alcohol until I felt nothing. It always took away the pain. I wanted to be numb to everything. I couldn't bear the heartbreak. I had never felt this worthless, like no one cared or loved me.

"Where is the bathroom?" I asked, standing up from the stool.

He showed me the direction, and I left with my drink and the jacket around me.

I needed some time alone to figure things out. I was broke and homeless, and I didn't want to stay here. I shut the door and sat on the sparkling marble floor. I buried my face in my palms and took a deep breath.

My head wouldn't stop pounding. I downed more alcohol to get my mind off what had happened. I didn't want to think about it. It only hurt even more. I felt tears in my eyes. I blinked them away and pulled my knees up to my chest.

Have I just been a distraction to Tristan all this time? I believed him. I started to trust him.

The knock on the door broke me out of my thoughts.

"Hey, is everything okay in there?"

I cleared my throat to answer. "Yeah."

"If you need anything, let me know, Chloe."

"Sure."

I heard him leave.

I didn't want to stay here. I wanted to be far away from anyone related to Tristan. Adrian had promised not to tell anyone he saw me. I didn't want anyone to know I was here. I could spend the night here and figure out the next step tomorrow morning.

I finished my drink and stood up. The aching in my head worsened. It made me dizzy. My eyes were starting to hurt, like someone was punching me nonstop in the eye.

I stumbled to the door with one hand at the right side of my head. I paused at the doorway and leaned on the doorframe for support.

"Adrian," I called when the pain got unbearable.

I groaned, letting go of the brandy glass in my hand. It shattered on the floor, echoing a crash in the house.

I slumped on the floor and clutched both sides of my head. I curled into a ball on the cold floor, trying to fight the pain tearing my head apart. It was as if my heart were drumming away the pain, but my head received every shock wave.

I had never felt such pain. It must be the migraine. I screamed. A tornado of turmoil twitched against every fiber of my body.

I gripped my hair like it would stop the pain. I kept screaming, praying Adrian would show up soon.

Where did he go?!

CHAPTER **THIRTY-FOUR**
DROWNING

I gripped Adrian's arm as he carried me to the long sofa in the living room. He placed me gently on the sofa, like he was holding an egg.

"Hey, you're going to be fine," he whispered, stroking my hair.

I nodded frantically, wanting his words to be true. *Am I ever going to be fine?*

"I will be right back."

He left me alone. I whimpered, gripping the sides of the sofa. He returned with a glass of water. Maybe it was the migraine. I'd left the pills at Tristan's place. All my belongings were there. I had to get them back.

Adrian pulled the table in the middle of the living room, closer to where I lay. He sat down without resting all his weight on it.

"Maybe we should go to the hospital."

"No, it's okay. The pain is subsiding."

He didn't look convinced. "Is this the first time?" he asked, concern coating his face.

"Yes," I lied. Anything to avoid going to the hospital. I was sick of staring at the white walls and the nauseous smell of disinfectants and medicines.

He moved his hand closer and placed his palm on my forehead. "Shit! You're burning up." He stood up in a flash and left.

He returned with his car keys and a small blanket. "I'm taking you to the hospital."

"No, I'm fine. It's nothing serious, I swear," I said, sitting up, but my body didn't feel the same anymore. My strength was wearing out, and I was aware of the goose bumps on my skin. "I will be okay once I have some rest."

I grabbed the blanket, wrapping it around myself, and lay back.

"I will make you some soup. It's not going to be as good as you expect," he said, laughing at himself.

I nodded with a lazy smile as he left to make the soup. He returned a few minutes later with a hot soup.

The soup was awful. It was tasteless and looked like he'd just boiled some garlic, cloves, and mushrooms. I forced myself to finish it even if it burned my tongue. I returned the empty plate and thanked him.

"I will take you to your room," he told me after he returned from the kitchen.

He held my arm as we climbed the stairs. The pain in my head wasn't as bad as before. He pulled the comforter up to my neck after I lay on the queen bed. He touched my forehead again. I flinched due to his terrifyingly cool touch.

"You are still hot." His voice was wrapped in sorrow.

He left and returned with a small towel soaked in cold water. He gently rubbed my face and my arms and placed the towel on my forehead.

"He never wanted this. That's all I want you to know," Adrian whispered.

"He destroyed my life. He ruined everything for me. I don't care if he gets run over by a car."

He just stared at me after I was done talking.

"I will be back to check on you."

I closed my eyes and went to sleep instantly.

THE SOUND OF the door opening woke me up. My eyes squinted at the sunrays from outside. *What time is it?*

"Hey." I heard from behind me.

I turned to look at Adrian. He was holding a tray filled with French toast, blueberry jam, bacon, and my favorite coffee. I could tell they were takeout from the logo on the Styrofoam cup and I knew Adrian couldn't cook anything.

"Hi." I sat up slowly and rested my back on the headboard.

"How are you feeling?"

"Much better than last night," I said and sighed in relief. I moved my messy hair back to see clearly.

He dropped the tray in front of me and placed the back of his palm on my forehead.

"I'm fine now, Adrian," I said when he pulled his hand away.

"What about your head?" he asked with a scrutinizing stare, like he could catch any lie that left my lips.

"I don't feel any pain." Except the pain in my heart that wouldn't stop.

"I will get you some painkillers just in case."

"Okay," I mumbled.

He smiled at me and left.

He returned with a small bottle. He dropped it on the nightstand and sat next to me on the bed. His tousled hair needed some brushing. His black hoodie matched the mood on his face. I saw the bags underneath his eyes. Had he gotten any sleep last night?

He'd stayed up, taking care of me while dealing with the truth behind his relationship with Karen. No matter how many smiles he wore, I knew underneath, he was bleeding and hurting.

"Have you eaten?" I asked, adding jam to the French toast.

"I had coffee."

"Just coffee? Eat this." I forced the French toast with jam into his hand. "I have enough," I said quickly when he opened his mouth to reject it.

He chuckled softly and ate it with a shrug.

"Thanks for last night." I gave him the best smile I could muster up.

"I think I owe you a lot after everything I did to you, so don't thank me."

"Yeah, you definitely do." I nodded my head.

He laughed at me.

"I promise I will leave once I figure things out, but for now, you never saw me, and you don't know where I am."

"Yes, ma'am." He threw two fingers in a salute.

I smiled and ate my bacon. I'd missed the old Adrian. It was nice to have him back.

I TRIED TO figure my life out. I wanted to remain off the radar. I had stayed here for almost a week, and I already felt like a burden to Adrian even if he kept telling me I could stay for as long as I wanted.

I didn't want to return to my family or contact anyone. Maybe I would be forgotten. Nobody cared anyway. If I went missing, it wouldn't mean anything to my family because I was dead to them. Grey had probably moved on, and Vina ... I missed her. She was the only one who believed me. She was the only one I could turn to for advice, but I didn't want to contact her. I knew she'd be worried about me by now.

I needed to sort things out myself, but it was hard. Tristan made it hard. No matter how much alcohol I consumed every night, he was still there. The memories, I wished they would disappear.

I cried every time I was in the shower. I was happy that the water always washed my tears away. I needed a new life—a life without Tristan, a life without any of my exes, a life without my family, and one not surrounded by monsters. I had to create it.

I hid the alcohol in my hand under the bed when I heard Adrian's footsteps. He was back from work. I'd promised him I'd stop drinking for a few days, but it wasn't working. I needed it to stop me from going crazy.

He knocked on the door, calling my name. I let him in with a fake smile.

"How are you doing?"

"I'm good."

"I will freshen up and fix us something to eat."

I wished I could cook for him, but I had forgotten all the cooking lessons I had gotten from He Who Shall Not Be Named.

I joined him downstairs after brushing my mouth to get rid of the alcohol's smell. I decided to help cut the vegetables while he did the rest. Turned out, we were both awful in the kitchen, but we tried to cook something edible.

"Chloe?"

My heartbeat paused. Maybe he knew I'd been drinking.

"Yeah?"

"How long are you planning not to contact anyone? Everyone thinks you've gone missing."

"Good. It should stay that way."

That was all I told him, and I returned to cutting the vegetables.

"They are all looking for you—your friends, your family, your ex. They are searching for you."

I didn't say anything.

"It's hard to pretend I know nothing about your whereabouts when they are all going craz. They want you back. Everyone is searching." He waited for me to say something, but I was quiet. He carried on. "Your best friend created a website for you to come back home. Your mom sued the Sanchesters. They are still handling the case in court."

I was missing out, but it was better that way. I increased my grip on the knife. I was furious. *My family wants me back now? Wow, what a great family.*

"I know Tristan hurt you. I am not trying to defend him or anything, but he—"

"I'm not feeling too well. I will go up and rest my head." I dropped the knife, quickly walking out of the kitchen.

I locked the door to my room and sat at the foot of the bed. *Everyone knows the truth? Then, why am I not happy?* The truth was out, but it still felt like something was missing. I wasn't thrilled with the news. This was what I'd wanted, but it didn't seem like I cared anymore.

I swallowed the dryness in my throat and lay on the bed. Life was so complicated.

I should go and apologize to Adrian; he hadn't meant any harm. I found him in the living room on the phone with someone. He whispered into the phone when he saw me and ended the call.

"I'm sorry I walked away like that. It's all too much to handle," I said.

"It's okay, but how long do you plan on hiding?" he asked me as I walked to the dining room.

"If you want me to leave, I will leave. I'm not ready to face everyone. I want to be alone even if it has to be a year."

"I'm not asking you to leave. I can't keep lying and watching them suffer. Tristan is in deep shit because he is at fault for your disappearance. I'm not trying to save him, but things could get worse if you don't come out."

I sat on the nearest seat and groaned. This was way harder than I'd expected.

"I'm not ready," I told him, almost breaking down in tears again.

"I know how hard it must be for you. Take your time. I will wait, I don't care how long."

I stood up and gave him a hug. We both needed it. He hugged me in return, stroking my back.

"Sorry if I'm giving you a hard time," I said against his chest and inhaled his nice cologne.

"It's fine," he whispered.

The whole drama with Karen must be taking a toll on him. He'd been avoiding the topic, but I knew he was still hurting.

"Chloe?"

We both heard Tristan's voice.

CHAPTER **THIRTY-FIVE**
CHOICES

"Shit!" Adrian mumbled, quickly removing his arms from around me.

We pulled away from each other and turned to look at Tristan. He looked like a dead man walking. His eyes were pale and bloodshot. He wore a peach sweatshirt and black jeans. His hair looked fuller, and his stubble was slowly being replaced with a beard.

His blue eyes stared at me. I clenched my fists, digging my nails into my palms. There was dark anger within me that needed release.

"*Asqueroso pedazo de mierda!*" I said with gritted teeth. It was one of the insults I'd picked up from Vina. It meant *disgusting piece of shit*.

He looked so surprised. He said my name again but in a soft whisper, like he couldn't believe it was me. He took a step toward me. I stepped back, frowning. He stopped and tried to say something, but no words left his lips.

His eyes moved from me to Adrian. He now looked pissed.

"You kept her here? She has been with you all this time?" His voice rose at the end of his sentence. He looked betrayed as he stared at his best friend.

"She didn't want anyone to know."

"You should have at least …" He stopped and groaned, not knowing what to say.

I wanted talk, but I stopped myself. I didn't want to utter a word to Tristan. I got furious, just staring at him. His eyes stayed on me. Our eyes met for a brief moment, but I looked away and headed for my room.

"Chloe," he called, coming after me.

I walked faster, not looking back. I could hear his heavy footsteps as he trailed behind me, trying to talk to me. I opened my door and stepped in hastily. I shot him a glare and slammed the door on his face.

I heard him groan as I walked to the bed and sat down.

"Chloe, please listen to me." He knocked on the door. "Chloe, please."

He stopped knocking. There was a long silence. I waited for him to leave, but he started talking.

"I'm sorry. I didn't mean to hurt you. I know you're never going to forgive my family and me. I wanted to tell you, but I was scared. I was scared to lose you after growing so attached to you." His voice mingled with regret and pain. He paused for a few seconds. "I can't lose you." He whimpered.

Oh my God, he was crying.

The only times I had seen him cry was when he saw those baby clothes and when he told me about Fiona.

"You were right. I don't deserve to be happy. I don't deserve your forgiveness. Shit! I don't even deserve any part of you. I wish I'd treated you better than your exes. You are more than what you think you are to me, Chloe."

Tears tore through my eyes, rattling me to the core with silent sobs. I was an emotional mess. The vegetables I'd cut earlier must have been mixed with onions.

"Your family wants you back. It was my fault you got kicked out. I didn't think of the consequences. Please go back to your family. They need you right—"

I stood up and ran to the bathroom. I didn't want to hear more.

The tears rolled down my cheeks before I could stop them. I turned on the shower and sat under it. I cried as the water sprinkled on my skin. A river of regret, cycling down again and again.

I hated myself for still caring about him, for missing him even a little bit. I wanted my feelings for him to die instantly. I wanted every memory of us to disappear from my brain. I stayed under the shower, just crying my heart out. I decided to take a bath. When I came out, I didn't hear his voice again. He was gone.

I dressed up for bed and buried myself under the covers. I stayed up for a few hours before finally getting some sleep.

I woke up past nine in the morning. I left the room after brushing my teeth and rinsing my face. I was surprised to see Adrian at the dining table, eating. He should have been at work.

"I knocked, but you didn't answer. I assumed you were still sleeping." He smiled at me as I took the seat in front of him.

"Aren't you going to work today?"

"I am, but I'm leaving here by twelve."

"Oh."

He left and brought me something to eat. He had lots of takeout stacked in his fridge. I stared at the pancake and syrup he'd placed in front of me.

"Thanks." I beamed.

"He promised not to tell anyone."

I nodded and continued eating.

After he finished eating, we watched a movie together before he left. I lay back on the couch, searching for something to watch. I paused when I saw my parents on a local news channel. My mom was drenched in full tears. *Fake tears.* They were being interviewed in the house. I knew that from the home decor in the living room.

"We miss her so much. It wasn't our fault. If we had known that bastard was lying then ..."

I turned off the TV and huffed. She was doing this for her reputation. I knew she didn't care one bit about me.

I went back to my room and stayed under the covers. My mind drifted slowly to that night Karen had spilled the truth. I felt like my existence was meaningless to anyone. It was like an old wound had reopened, and I knew this one was going to take a long time to heal—or maybe an eternity.

I couldn't stay here forever. All the plans in my head didn't make any sense, mainly because I was broke.

I closed my eyes and allowed my mind to relax.

At six p.m., I dragged myself to the kitchen to make dinner for Adrian. I played loud music to distract myself from thinking about Tristan in the kitchen with me.

Adrian arrived an hour later. He looked impressed. He laughed as he left to freshen up. I had everything on the dining table before he came down.

"I should be the one doing this." He took a seat.

"No, I have already gone through enough torture with your awful cooking skills."

"Ouch, Chloe," he said, and I laughed.

"I was just being honest." I shrugged.

"It's your birthday. I should be the one to make you dinner."

"My birthday? Sorry, what is today's date?"

"August 12."

I gasped. I'd totally forgotten my birthday.

"You forgot?" His face swam with surprise.

"Yeah," I said, laughing, and he joined in.

He stood up and returned with a cake. When had he bought that? How come I hadn't seen it? He started singing. I laughed so hard that tears gathered in my eyes. I blew the single candle in the middle as he clapped.

This wasn't how I'd planned on celebrating my twenty-first birthday. I had never had a big birthday party. It was always my family, friends, and me. But celebrating it like this with Adrian was memorable.

"How did you know?" I asked.

"Tristan told me."

I rolled my eyes at the mention of his name.

"Here is my gift to you."

He dropped a small box in front of me. I picked it up and opened it. It was a debit card.

"I didn't know what to get you in particular, so do all the shopping you want with the card."

"Thank you." I smiled.

His phone rang when he opened his mouth to say something.

"Excuse me. I will be right back." He picked up the phone and left.

He returned a few minutes later with a weird expression on his face. "It's Tristan. He wants to wish you a happy birthday."

I hesitated. He'd just make the day awful for me. I sighed and nodded.

"He is drunk," he warned me before putting the call on speaker.

"Chloe?"

"I'm here," I said, sounding annoyed.

He exhaled in relief. "Happy birthday, baby. If you were still here, I would have thrown you the biggest party and flown you to Paris to celebrate. It's my fault you didn't get to celebrate it with your family or the way you wanted. I'm so sorry," he slurred.

"I hope you find someone who makes you happy. Someone who won't be an asshole to you. Someone whose goal is to make you the happiest person every day. I love you. I will never stop loving you, Chloe."

He ended the call.

I bit my tears back. Adrian didn't say anything. We sat in silence. I tried not to let my emotions control me.

"Drinks?" Adrian asked.

I nodded. I really needed one right now.

"Since it's your birthday and you're finally legal to consume alcohol, I will let you drink."

I smiled.

We moved to the living room and sat on the floor. We kept drinking and talking until we were too drunk to stand.

I dozed off on him, saying something I myself didn't understand.

I WOKE UP in my bed. I saw some painkillers and a bottle of water on my nightstand. I took it and went for a bath. I missed Morris's hangover soup. I missed him.

It was past one in the afternoon. I spent the rest of the day putting my plans in order and making up my mind. I was twenty-one now. Twenty years had taught me a lot. It was time to make the right choice, time to fix my life, time to start over again. I was the only one who could bring myself up and give myself the life I wanted.

I skipped dinner, telling Adrian I was not hungry.

I made my decision.

I WOKE UP very early the next day and made breakfast. Adrian came down in a dark two-piece suit. He looked surprised to see me awake.

"You are up early."

"Yes!"

I watched him as he ate his scrambled eggs and French toast.

"I'm leaving," I announced.

He almost choked on the coffee he was sipping.

"Sorry," our voices sang simultaneously.

"You are leaving?"

"Yeah, I have made my decision. I think I know what I want now," I said with a soft smile.

"I'm proud of you, Chlo. I will miss you. When do you plan on leaving?"

"Today."

I saw his face fall.

"And you're just telling me?" He leaned back on his seat with a scowl on his face.

"Sorry, I made up my mind last night."

"Are you going back to your family?"

"No."

"Tris—"

"No!"

"Then, where?"

I just smiled.

"Chloe?" He frowned.

"Relax. I will be close by."

"Are you leaving town?"

"Maybe."

He stared at his coffee, almost looking sad at my answer.

"Can you lend me some cash? I will pay you back once I get a job," I asked.

"Yeah, but don't pay it back."

"I want to. I will pay every penny back. I owe you a lot after everything you've done for me."

"It's nothing big, Chloe. We are friends. Friends look out for each other."

"Thanks, but I'm still paying you back."

"Do you need a ride?"

"No, I will take a cab to get my things."

"If you don't want to go there, I can get them for you."

"It's fine."

"Are you sure?" I could sense the fear in his voice. Every word he said seemed to be laced with caution.

"Yes, eat up."

"Okay, Mom."

I kicked him from under the table.

He wrote me a check for a hundred thousand dollars. We spoke for a while before he left.

I TOOK MY bath and got ready to leave. Adrian had picked out some dresses and shoes from the store for me to wear while I stayed hidden in his house. I adjusted the thin straps of the red cami dress that had a slit on the right side of my thigh. I packed the stuff I had inside Adrian's Gucci carry-on duffel bag. I smiled at the room and walked out.

The cab driver kept staring at me from the rearview mirror. I shot him a glare, but he kept stealing glances at me.

"Do you mind? I didn't pay for you to stare at me like a creep."

"Sorry, you look like the missing girl."

"Oh, I get that a lot." I looked outside the window.

My heart raced when the car stopped in front of Tristan's mansion. I told the driver to wait while I got my things.

Morris's face almost turned white when he saw me. His eyes shimmered, as if he had found gold.

"Hi, Morris."

"Miss Simpson? You came back!"

It was the first time I had seen him this happy.

"Actually, I came to … get … um … my stuff."

"Oh." His smile turned upside down.

"Sorry." I gave him a hug.

"Please don't leave him," he begged me when I pulled away.

"I'm sorry," I said again and headed for the stairs.

"I wish you'd met him when he was different. He was a very kind and loving person before he lost them. Do whatever your heart desires,

Miss Simpson."

I took a deep breath and climbed the stairs. Nothing was going to change my mind. I deserved a little happiness, too, and I wouldn't get that happiness around Tristan or my family

I glanced at his room as I walked to my old room. Memories of everything we had done together—every fight, every funny moment, every tear—clouded my brain.

I saw a few of Tristan's belongings in the room.

"He has been sleeping here since you left." I heard Morris's voice from behind me. "He really loves you, Chloe."

Wait, did he just call me Chloe? First time ever!

"Please help me with my boxes and suitcase," I said instead.

He looked disappointed.

I packed everything I owned and allowed Morris to help take them to the car. I stared at the door to Tristan's room.

Is he home? Won't he come out and see me?

I wanted to see him for the last time, just a glance. I shook my head and left. I apologized to Morris again before entering the car.

I needed this break. My heart needed it. One by one, I had to force out the stakes plunged into it, only then would I ever feel even remotely normal again. I was worthy of a life of happiness.

I stared at the glass-layered mansion as the car moved. I saw him. I saw Tristan. He was staring at me from my room, the room I'd just left. His eyes struck me with arrows, not from a deadly archer, but Cupid's. I now knew the man for who he truly was.

He raised his hand and waved. I looked away and leaned back on the seat.

This was it—time for a fresh start, a new beginning.

No toxic family.

No exes.

ACKNOWLEDGMENTS

To my mom, for being there for me and supporting me through the whole process even though she had no idea what type of book I was writing. Your constant words of encouragement made me finish this book. I hope you never get to read it, LOL.

Rebecca Johnpee, you are the friend that everybody needs. I don't even know where to begin because there are a million things I could say about you. There were moments I got frustrated and almost gave up, but you told me to keep going. You were the only one I could vent to about everything, and your support played a big role in making this book. I hope you publish yours soon, so everyone can see what a great writer you are.

To my readers. Thank you for your endless support through the whole process. The transition from writing online to self-publishing was scary, but you guys inspired me to keep writing. Thank you for always being there.

ABOUT THE AUTHOR

Juliet Ever is a college student with a wild imagination, known for taking her readers on an emotional roller coaster and leaving them wanting more. She has been writing stories since elementary school and has developed a passion for writing ever since. She is a lover of reality shows and psychological romance movies. She enjoys cooking and staying indoors.

Connect with her on Instagram for more content and news about her new books.

Printed in Great Britain
by Amazon